GO IT ALONE

SCARLETT FINN

Also by Scarlett Finn

GO NOVELS
GO WITH IT
GO IT ALONE
GO ALL OUT
GO ALL IN
GO FULL CIRCLE

EXILE
HIDE & SEEK
KISS CHASE

WRECK & RUIN
RUIN ME
RUIN HIM

**THE BRANDED
SERIES**
BRANDED
SCARRED
MARKED

**FORBIDDEN
PREQUEL DUET**
ALL. ONLY.
ONLY YOURS

NOTHING TO...
NOTHING TO HIDE
NOTHING TO LOSE
NOTHING TO DECLARE
NOTHING TO US
NOTHING TO SAY
NOTHING TO GAIN
NOTHING TO YOU
NOTHING TO THIS
NOTHING TO DO
NOTHING TO FEAR
NOTHING TO DENY

THE FORBIDDEN NOVELS
FORBIDDEN DESIRE
FORBIDDEN WANT
FORBIDDEN WISH
FORBIDDEN NEED
FORBIDDEN BOND

TO DIE FOR...
TO DIE FOR TRUTH
TO DIE FOR HONOR
TO DIE FOR VIRTUE
TO DIE FOR DUTY
TO DIE FOR LOVE

**LOVE AGAINST THE ODDS
STANDALONE COLLECTION**
SWEET SEAS
HEIR'S AFFAIR
RESCUED
MAESTRO'S MUSE
GETTING TRICKY
THIRTEEN
REMEMBER WHEN...
RELUCTANT SUSPICION
XY FACTOR

KINDRED SERIES
RAVEN
SWALLOW
CUCKOO
SWIFT
FALCON
FINCH

THE EXPLICIT SERIES
EXPLICIT INSTRUCTION
EXPLICIT DETAIL
EXPLICIT MEMORY

MISTAKE DUET
MISTAKE ME NOT
SLEIGHT MISTAKE

**RISQUÉ & HARROW
INTERTWINED**
TAKE A RISK
FIGHTING FATE
RISK IT ALL
FIGHTING BACK
GAME OF RISK

LOST & FOUND
LOST
FOUND

ONE

"HOW ARE YOU feeling about it?" Clyde asked down the phone.

Sitting on the window-seat in her childhood bedroom, staring out at the vast backyard her mother was so proud of, Harlow Sweeting couldn't decide how to answer her former colleague's question.

It wasn't that she didn't know her feelings, but articulating everything going on inside her was impossible. Language couldn't do her emotions justice. The words just didn't exist.

Being adrift wasn't new. It had been her normal for three months.

"I guess I knew it would happen eventually," she said.

There was a smile in Clyde Flaxman's voice when he spoke again. "That wasn't really an answer to what I asked."

She sighed. "I know."

"Ryske died three months ago. You didn't even pause to pack or say goodbye. You left the city and went back to your parents' house the night he died. You've been holed up there ever since."

The night of Ryske's death was a blur. After puking in the ambulance bay outside the hospital, Harlow fled Bale's side and hadn't looked back.

"I called you. I said I was sorry for disappearing like I did," she said, tracing the edge of the glass pane between her and the world.

Being so close to freedom, and yet separated from it, was an apt representation of her life since losing him. She had all the comforts her parents' detached home could offer. With five bedrooms, separate dining and den spaces, the residence was opulent in comparison to many others. In the city, witnessing what some people endured, her living conditions left nothing to complain about. Yet it felt wrong.

"I waited two months for that call," he said and quickly followed up. "I'm not asking for another apology. You apologized already. Not that you had to. I told you that you didn't need to apologize. You went through a trauma, I understand that. But what you're doing isn't healthy. You barely leave your parents' house. You won't see a counsellor… How can you think you're ready to start dating? Have you asked about your old job? Is there a possibility you can get it back?"

Closing her eyes, her head bumped against the wall. "I told you I'm through with social work."

"What about your criminology degree? You were so close to finishing. Have you picked it up again? You mentioned teaching."

Once, when he'd cornered her in a conversation. "What would I have to offer students?"

"A unique perspective," he answered like it was obvious.

Because she'd fallen in love with a crook and lived in his world for a brief flicker of time? Those weren't experiences she was in a hurry to share.

"Teaching would mean moving back to the city," she said. "There's nowhere to teach out here."

"What's wrong with moving back? I told you before that you can stay with me until you get on your feet. You've got to do something. You can't just stay home for the rest of time."

Career seemed like a ridiculous aspiration given what

she'd been through in the last few months. Her perspective on everything had changed. She just hadn't figured out how to focus yet.

"Rupert never moved out of our old place," she said. "He's still there."

Silence followed for a score of seconds. "And you think you should move back in with him?"

"It was what Ryske wanted."

He took a deep breath. "You don't like to talk about him with me, with anyone, I get that. I do. But the guy I knew, the one who decked me for sitting beside you, did not want you moving in with another man. Especially one who didn't make you happy."

"How do you know Rupert didn't make me happy?"

"Maybe because we've been talking on the phone several times a week for a month and I'm getting to know you. In every call, you mention either Rupert asking you out or your mother encouraging you to go out with him. Whenever it comes up, you make a sound as though dating your ex again would be equivalent to getting root canal. You left the guy once. You didn't just leave him, you broke an engagement and moved away; you changed your whole life. People don't do that because they're happy."

"Yeah?" she asked. "And look how that turned out."

Another silence.

"Harlow, I'm not saying your life is a picnic now or that it ever has been. But it's never smart to make life-altering decisions or big changes when you're grieving. You're not at the acceptance stage yet."

She was so sick of everyone telling her what she was or wasn't, and what was best for her.

"You don't know what stage I'm at," she snapped.

He took the outburst in stride. "No, I don't. Sometimes I think you're bargaining, sometimes I think it's depression... other times I'm not sure you've moved past denial."

Sitting up, she clutched the phone tighter. "I won't slot into the cycle for your convenience," she said. "I was trained on the stages, same as you. You know what else I know? He's dead. Ryske is dead and there's nothing bringing him back. How's that for denial?" That single event defined her now. Every thought brought her back to it time after time. "You know what? Maybe you're right. I do have to move on to acceptance. And I can't possibly do that if I'm hanging on to things connected to my life with him."

"Harlow—"

"Goodbye, Clyde. Don't call here again."

Hanging up the phone, she threw it onto the bed. It bounced and clattered to the floor, but she didn't care if it was broken. Grabbing the pillow from her back, she squashed it against her face and screamed out loud; something she'd done a lot since returning home.

Still screaming into the pillow, telling herself the anger was better than the paralyzing tears she'd drowned in the first few weeks, a knock on her bedroom door interrupted.

By the time she lowered the pillow, it was already opening. Her mom peeked around the edge, wearing a familiar meek smile that was a total con. Jean Sweeting didn't care if she was intruding or not.

"Did I hear shouting?"

Something about being home forced a concerted effort not to revert to petulant teenage defiance. "No, Mom," she droned.

"It sounded like I did."

Inhaling, she turned, sliding her feet off the window seat to put them on the floor. "What do you need, Mom?"

The question gave Jean all the invitation she needed to make herself at home. Scurrying into the room, she came over to sit with her on the window seat, Jean cast a quick curious glance at the phone on the floor, but erased her confusion to smile Harlow's way.

"I'm glad you used that turn of phrase," Jean said, stroking the back of her daughter's hand. The excitement shimmering around her made Harlow nervous. Anxiety rose when Jean leaned in. "A little bird told me you have finally come to your senses."

Freeing her hand from her mother's grasp, Harlow curled her fingers around her own wrist. "Let me guess, that bird was called Rupert and he told you I agreed to go out with him."

Her mother's smile was exuberant. "You're making the right decision, sweetheart."

Jean tried to touch her face, but Harlow ducked back and stood up. "I agreed to go out with him. I didn't agree to marry him or move back in or pick up where we left off."

It was crazy. She'd just implied to Clyde that moving back in with Rupert was a possibility. Now, just a few minutes later, she was insisting it was a ludicrous idea.

Breaking up with Rupert after six years together had been an easy decision. She wouldn't say that aloud to anyone, she didn't want to hurt his feelings. Rupert was no monster; he was a decent guy. The truth—that Harlow was only now ready to admit—was that she'd never wanted to accept his proposal in the first place.

The engagement was meant to be a trial, but Jean and Rupert's mom ran with the idea as soon as the ring was on her finger. After being engaged for a year, the prospect of a wedding became too real for her to continue ignoring. Rupert's declaration that he wanted her to leave her job and be a stay-at-home mom, provided the excuse she needed to put an end to their relationship.

Both families had been devastated. She'd tried to stick around for a while to make amends, but the freedom of no longer being with Rupert opened up possibilities. At that point, all she'd known was what she didn't want from life. Until the end of the engagement, she hadn't been free to think about what she *did* want.

In the process of figuring it out, she'd left suburban social work and relocated to a rough inner city district to take up a new post.

After dealing with an emergency call during one particular on-call shift in that new department, her whole life had changed. On her walk home that night, a bleeding man crashed into her, sending both of them to the ground and down the proverbial rabbit hole.

She might have been responsible, in part, for saving his life that night. Not that it mattered. Instead of standing in front of the armed assailant, protecting the stranger, she should've let the perp shoot. Turned out it was the bleeding man's destiny to die anyway.

Two months on from that fateful first meeting, after she'd fallen in love with him, the bleeding man was gunned down in front of her and lost his life.

Ryske.

Her Crash.

Dead.

"I understand that you want to take your time," her mother said as she did frequently.

Right. Her mom. Home.

She didn't believe her mother's patience any more now than she had every other time. Her poor, naïve mother. Once upon a time, Harlow herself had been unaware of what really living could feel like. Ryske had showed her that… before he was cruelly taken away.

Crouching in front of her mother, she gathered their hands together. "Mom, I'm never going to love Rupert like you want me to."

"Sweetie," Jean said, touching her jaw. "You can be content with him. He'll look after you."

Keep her safe. That was what Ryske said too. Content. A safe existence. A safe life. That was all he'd wanted for her.

"I don't know if content is enough."

"What is it that you want?" her mother asked. "Love? Love is rare, sweetheart. Of course your father and I want you to have everything that will make you happy… But you have to be sensible too. You can't wait forever. Do you want to waste your life waiting for a love you might never find?"

Sinking to her ass on the floor, she crossed her legs and slipped her fingers under the leather bracelet on her wrist. She'd had love. She'd found it and squandered it. What had held them back? She couldn't even remember anymore.

Three months ago, she'd been in his bed, in his arms, in his life and now…

Love wasn't what she sought. Not only was she sure she'd never find love again, but she was sure she didn't want to. Ryske was her love. Her great love. Whether they'd consummated that love or not didn't matter.

Most of the time, she was numb. Only things connected to Ryske provoked feeling. Love for him. Grief that he was gone. Anger at those responsible for stealing him from her. Anything else, everything that wasn't him, left her empty.

During their calls, Clyde pushed for answers she couldn't give; her emotions hadn't reordered themselves yet. Though, her friend was probably right about how ready, or rather unready, she was to be dating.

Since her return home, Rupert had asked her out several times. Every time, her answer was no. A tactful no, if she could muster it. The last time he'd asked, her energy, and ability to find an excuse, failed her. It meant nothing. Dating and relationships didn't register on her priority list. On any list. It didn't matter who she was spending time with when she couldn't spend it with Ryske.

Still clinging to her bracelet, the weight of her mother's expectation bared down on her. By now, she was used to it.

Tipping her head back to show a smile, she projected what her mother wanted to see: a settled, compliant daughter.

"I said I would go out with him. Isn't that proof I'm willing to give it a shot?"

"Excellent," Jean said, cupping her face. "This weekend will be the perfect chance."

Dinner conversation around the family table wasn't always easy to follow, mainly because she'd developed a habit of phasing it out. Nothing anyone said meant anything. It was all inconsequential, unimportant, uninteresting… Yet, she had a vague recollection of…

"Daddy's SweSec thing?" she asked, wrinkling her nose in doubt.

Why would her mother want her at a corporate event?

Discussions often went on around her. Bits and pieces filtered through. Something must have gone in because she knew her father's company, Sweeting Securities, was hosting a networking reception at a hotel this Saturday.

"The company's annual event, yes," Jean said. "You should go with Rupert. It will be filled with existing and potential clients. It's a perfect opportunity for you to get to know people."

Her spine curved in a slouch; anxiety bubbled in her gut. "I don't know if I'm ready for all those people, Mom."

The idea of sitting alone in a restaurant with Rupert, surrounded by others, hadn't been appealing. Socializing at a busy event could be beyond her capabilities. Dealing with a crowd, being lost in a mass of people drinking and partying, could rouse flashbacks of the night in Floyd's when Ryske sank to his knees.

He'd never got up again. Never been on his own two feet ever again after that.

A lump dammed her throat. That image was burned into her mind. The blood on his fingers, on his shirt. The realization in his eyes. The moment he knew he'd been felled… They'd all been powerless to stop it.

In her nightmares, she lived through losing him over and over. The weakness in his fingers when she'd put them to her throat. The vulnerability in his voice… The words he'd whispered to her before he faded away.

"Harlow."

The note of urgency in her mother's tone snapped her from a daze. How many times had Jean said her name? It couldn't be a surprise she wasn't paying attention. Disappearing into her own thoughts had become a regular occurrence.

"I'm sorry, Mom," she said. "What were you saying?"

"You'll be safe at the event," Jean said, curiosity in her gaze though she wouldn't dare give it voice, probably fearing it would lead the conversation down a path she wouldn't like. Jean Sweeting was the queen of ignoring what she didn't want to see. "And there will be plenty of distractions."

Something else occurred to her. "Isn't the SweSec event in the city?"

Her mom nodded. A spear of dread pierced her. She hadn't been back to the city since fleeing it on the night of

Ryske's death.

"Your sister will be there, and your father and I, of course," she said. "And if it's too much for you, Rupert will be happy to bring you home... He still lives in your old apartment."

Not so subtle. Nothing would make Jean or Harlow's father, Brysen, happier than if things went back to the way they'd once been.

"I know that, Mom," she said, burying a groan in the back of her throat. "Can you put that out of your head? Please?" The last thing she needed was extra pressure. "I won't be going home with Rupert. I don't want you to think that one date is going to put us back to where we were. It won't."

Clutching the engraved panel on her bracelet, she read its etched words and touched the black star she'd had tattooed on her wrist just days after coming home.

Was she drifting in her own world again?

The concept of time was lost these days.

Her mother's fingertips touched the underside of her chin to lift it up. "Whoever he was, he didn't deserve you."

Jean could be accused of having a blinkered view on life. The woman had her own priorities and knew them well. Often in pursuit of her own goals, Jean lost sight of things like common courtesy.

But, in the times it wasn't directed at her, she often admired her mother's tenacity. It wasn't a bad quality to emulate either.

In Jean's rare moments of consideration, when she looked beyond her typical boundaries, her mom could display remarkable insight.

"He did deserve me, Mom," she whispered, trying not to let her tears overwhelm her again. If they did, she might not win the renewed battle to contain them. "I didn't fight hard enough to make him see that."

Concern creased Jean's brow. "Married?"

A blub of a sob came out, though it was sort of half laugh. "If only it had been that simple."

She'd have put a knife in the ribs of her competition

and taken her man if it had been that straightforward. If given the choice, she'd do anything to have Ryske back. Anything.

In the nights she lay awake whispering to him, Harlow talked out different scenarios. If death hadn't separated them, what could the future have held? Ryske had told her to go back to Rupert, to be safe. If she had, would Ryske have stayed away?

Could her Crash have left her in the bed of another man while he lay in his own imagining Rupert doing things to her? Things her Crash wanted to do to her? He'd said he loved her. Ryske had said it.

Maze's previous declaration that his friend felt that way perplexed her at the time; she couldn't deny it messed with her head. Ryske's misfit crew of Dover, Noon, and Maze knew her love better than anyone, and they'd sensed something between the couple from early on.

But it wasn't until she'd heard the words from Ryske's lips that she could grasp their truth. He was in love with her. He hadn't taken her up on the offer of her body in the closet because he couldn't trust himself to let her go. That was the only sense she could make of it.

If Ryske made love to her, he wouldn't have been able to conceal the truth of what he felt. Maybe he would've said the words. That would've changed things. As long as she resented him, and believed he'd used her, she could walk away. If he'd confessed the truth and depth of his feelings, she would've fought for him.

Ryske had asserted that leaving the city and going back to Rupert was in her best interest. But if they'd crossed that final line with each other and had sex in the closet during their last argument, letting her go may not have been so easy. That's how it played out in her mind anyway. With him gone, she could make up any truth and believe it. The ability to prove or disprove any theory was lost right along with him.

Jean kissed each of her daughter's cheeks while saying she had to go check on dinner.

Being alone didn't bother her. If anything, she was more at peace when she didn't have to put up a front for anyone. Alone seemed right. She wanted to be alone. Alone with thoughts of Ryske.

Crash had once told her he would shield her from anything that could hurt her. It turned out he hadn't been able to shield her from the one thing that would hurt the most: losing him. How would she ever bounce back?

TWO

AFTER AN HOUR at the SweSec function, she wanted to leave. Rupert was doing his job networking and schmoozing. She hadn't meant to abandon him to it, but after the tenth similar conversation, she'd excused herself to go to the restroom and might have accidentally gone to the bar instead.

Life wasn't what it was supposed to be.

The whole event was making her sick. Everyone in their flowing gowns and glitzy jewels got a glare. What did any of this matter? What did any of it mean? How could anyone be happy and laughing? Didn't they know Ryske was gone?

Disgust. That was all she could muster. Who knew that losing the man she was supposed to spend her life with would turn her into such a cynic?

The bartender brought her double Scotch and the bitter liquid hit her throat hard. That was what she needed, what she wanted. The fog of intoxication beckoned. She hadn't touched wine since the night of losing Ryske. Even at dinner she resisted, despite her parents' insistence. Hard liquor, on the other hand, was just fine; no trouble there.

Oblivion was welcome. It was on the nights she got blind drunk alone in her room that her conversations with Ryske were most real. Conversations usually turned to arguments that she'd bury in her pillow just like her screams. How dare he leave her? How dare he abandon her and expect her to deal with this alone? She'd call him selfish and spiteful, but the arguments always ended the same—with her in tears apologizing, begging him to come back to her.

Putting the drink on the bar, the leather bracelet on her wrist got her focus. Her mother had asked her several times not to wear it, right up until the moment Rupert arrived with the limo to pick them up. He'd told her she was beautiful, but cast a frown over her wrist.

Ryske's braided leather band double-wrapped and didn't match the elegance of her cocktail dress. It was much looser on her slender wrist than it had been on her man's thick, capable arm. The stark tattoo didn't scream sophistication either. Still, she was proud of both.

She hadn't explained the tattoo, or the bracelet, to anyone, and had no intention of doing so. Slipping her finger under the warm leather, the ridges of the internal engraving Ryske got done for her, gave strength. *Felix culpa*. His fall hadn't been intentional or happy. It had been caused by momentum, gravity, and blood loss.

Replaying the conversation they'd had the night they met made her smile. It was usually a mistake to think about that night because it led to her thinking about every other encounter they had.

God, she missed him. Her heart ached for him. Her body needed him. She just couldn't stop…

"Never thought I'd see that again."

The voice was more of a feeling than a sound. She had to have heard it, but the way it pricked the hairs on the back of her neck straightened her spine one inch at a time.

She didn't turn and didn't have to. The owner of that voice was no stranger.

"What are you doing here?" she asked, her tone guttural.

Hatred and anger boiled around her heart, hardening it when he loomed closer.

"Well, when I heard the name Sweeting, I couldn't refuse, could I?" he asked. "Who'd have thought your family would be so welcoming?"

Spinning around, she landed her disgust on him. "If I were you, Mr. Hagan, I would walk out of here quietly now… while you still have the chance."

"I was invited, Harlow," he said, moving past her to hold up a finger to summon the bartender. "Let me buy you a drink, we'll reminisce over old times." He ordered and gave her the chance to as well; she didn't flinch. The venom in her glare grew more potent with every second. "What would you like to talk about first? The day I had him stabbed, or the day I had him killed?"

"How about the night he started fucking Anwen… or how many times he fucked your sister?" she spat. "Why don't we talk about how a man of your means is so inadequate when it comes to pleasing women? Just what is it about you that chased them to him?"

His jaw worked. She could hear him grinding his teeth. Oh, satisfaction was sweet.

Leaning in, he growled his words. "I would've thought watching the life slip out of his broken, demented body would've taken your fire. I see it's only increased it."

"You're damn right. Don't ever forget that I saw the man who pulled the trigger. I know exactly who took him from me."

The side of his mouth rose in a depraved smile. "Then why is it that my man is still walking free? I did my job, Miss Sweeting. It was my job to take out the trash… to erase the man who threatened my family. I protected my sister from enduring a lifetime of suffering with him."

"And I'm sure she's so pleased about that." The twitch in his brow betrayed tension in the siblings' relationship. Her smile grew again. "Oh, or perhaps she's displeased with you dictating to her. Imposing your will on a strong woman is never a smart move. It wasn't your place to make decisions for her."

The more she pushed, the higher his irritation level rose. When he'd held her prisoner and controlled her with threats of hurting Ryske, she'd learned how to rile Jarvis Hagan. She wasn't sorry to be getting a reminder of how gratifying it was.

"You should be thanking me," he hissed. "You think I don't know you were in love with him? The proposal was bullshit. Ophelia thinks she knows the world, but she's naïve. Ryske didn't love her. He wanted her for her connection to me and my money. It wouldn't surprise me if the two of you were in on it together."

Ophelia wasn't as dumb as her brother thought. Although Harlow still believed that the female Hagan wanted Ryske to love her, she was also determined in her desire to punish her brother. Ophelia's motives for accepting the proposal weren't as clear cut as Hagan believed them to be.

Harlow gestured to the room. "Look around you, Jarvis. I don't need your money."

He spat out a scoff of amused disgust. "This is nothing. Nothing to what I have. Why do you think your father is so eager to court my fortune?"

Unintimidated, she leaned a little closer to murmur, "Because he doesn't know the truth of who you are and who you consort with."

His brows rose. There was an almost smile on his lips. "Who? Scum? Need I remind you that you were fucking that scum? How would Daddy feel about that? How would your fiancé feel about it? I know what it is to be made a fool of by that man. Would you like me to tell your beloved Rupert Marlowe the truth?"

Now it was her turn to be smug. "Rupert and I are not engaged and we haven't been for some time. He knows nothing about Ryske, and I would be willing to bet that as long as your precious consortium is plotting world domination, you don't want anyone to know about your association with him either." Turning toward the bar, Hagan inadvertently revealed she'd hit another sore point by the way he lifted his glass to his lips in an attempt to hide his reaction, but it was too late. "Or maybe Gil Parratt did see the truth of who you were after Ryske set him on the right path." Leaning in, her lips almost grazed his ear. "Even in death he's winning. God, he's hot, isn't he? Dead for three months and he's still turning me on. Anwen and Ophelia didn't stand a chance."

She picked up her clutch and twisted the seat of her stool, intending to leave. Hagan snatched her wrist. Both of them looked down at the point of contact to see Ryske's bracelet resting along the edge of his hand.

"Tell me, Miss Sweeting," he said, touching the leather, she jerked her hand away. This bastard had no right to touch anything that once belonged to her love. "Why didn't you do your duty?"

"My duty?"

"Yes," he said. His chin jutted up at a proud angle illuminating how sure he was of himself. He sipped his liquor. "My job was to defeat him. I accomplished that. Yours was to avenge him. Instead you tucked tail and ran…" Looking down his nose, Hagan didn't disguise his scrutiny. "I anticipated that killing him would start a war with his crew. Yet all of you faded away. Now who's winning?"

All of them? Believing it would be too difficult, she hadn't contacted Dover, Noon, or Maze since Ryske's death. How could they have disappeared too? She couldn't fathom it.

"Maybe we're biding our time," she said, despite knowing it was a lie.

There was no plan to avenge Ryske. No plan to get payback for his death. Not from her anyway.

The truth smacked her in the face. She'd let Ryske down. All the time she'd been hiding and wallowing, she been failing him.

"The easiest hit I ever planned," he muttered a moment before sidestepping and widening his grin, much as he had when Ophelia happened upon them at a previous party. This time it wasn't Hagan's sister interrupting them, it was Harlow's date. "Mr. Marlowe!"

Rupert came to her side, putting a hand on her shoulder and appearing somewhat bewildered by Hagan's familiarity. "I'm sorry, I don't believe we've met."

"Harlow," Hagan said without disguising his pleasure at her disgust. "Wait, I got it. I just realized, you'll be Harlow Marlowe when you get married." He snapped his fingers. "I love it."

"We're no longer engaged," she said. Against her better judgment, because she was painted into a corner, she cleared her throat and did her duty. "Rupert Marlowe, this is Jarvis Hagan."

"Ah, Mr. Hagan, of course. I'm sorry, so many new faces tonight." The men shook hands. "I didn't know you and Harlow were friends."

"Yes," Hagan said, smiling at her. "We were acquainted while Harlow was living in the city."

Rupert's hand fell from her shoulder. "I see."

"Rupert," she said, taking her clutch from the bar and slipping off her stool. "I'm ready to go home."

"Harlow—"

"I don't need an escort," she said, picking up her glass to toss the rest of the Scotch into her throat.

"No. Of course you don't. You are a woman who knows how to take care of herself, aren't you, Harlow?" Hagan's smirk drove her to the edge of her restraint. Man, she wanted to smack him in the face. "Still, a man can't be too careful. Never know who your woman might run into out there on the city streets."

"Better men than I'll find in here I'm sure," she hissed.

His lips twisted like he struggled to contain a smile. "I can take you home, Harlow," Hagan said and pointed a finger.

Swiping his hand away before it could reach her cheek, she snatched Hagan's glass and tossed the liquid in his face. "Not if you were the last breathing man on Earth."

Spinning around, she stormed through the smiling people with only one goal. To get the hell out of there. She was a fool. A disappointment. She disgusted herself.

"Harlow," Rupert called from behind her. "Harlow, wait."

Catching her arm, he spun her around in the middle of the hotel lobby. "Go back inside, Rupert. I don't need you."

"I'm not going to let you leave alone. We arrived together. We'll leave together. I have a driver outside—"

"I'll get a cab."

"A cab? A cab from here to your parents will cost a fortune." He picked up her hand, pulling himself closer to stroke her face. "I could get us a room, if you're not up to the crowd. We could order room service, drink some wine…"

His effort was sweet. It wasn't fair of her to let him believe there was hope. "Rupert," she said, taking her hand from him. "When I was living here in the city I was with another man."

It seemed crazy that he should be shocked. They'd broken up months before she relocated, so it wasn't like he expected fidelity. Moving away had been a break from everything in her old life, including him.

"Jarvis Hagan?"

Repulsed, she stepped back. Her lip curled and even with a hand on her throat to settle it, she was sure she tasted bile. "No! God, no."

"So who?"

"It doesn't matter," she said. "It's over, but… what is important is that I owe him something. No, not him. That's not right. I owe something to what we had… Ever since I've been home, I've had this feeling I couldn't figure out. I was just sick all the time and now… I know what it is."

"You loved him," he said.

The way he deflated infused her with guilt and pity. Though subtle, it was an indication of the strength of Rupert's feelings for her. The optimism he'd had about their future was being taken away.

"I love him," she said, preferring the present tense.

Slowly, he nodded. "You're going to him."

If wishing made it so. Going to Floyd's, tracking Ryske down, it was a cruel dream she often woke from these days. The cold truth of reality was a harsh wakeup call.

"If I could, I would," she said, figuring something else out.

Even if Ryske had let her go back to Rupert, and even if he'd been able to stay away, she wouldn't have been capable of sliding into an unsatisfying, comfortable existence in suburbia while her real love was out there.

Playing house, pretending she was happy, it wouldn't

be fair to either her or Rupert. Ryske had said there was nothing in the city for her, but that wasn't true. The city wasn't done with her yet.

She didn't belong in suburbia. Whether or not she belonged in the city remained to be seen, but finding out would never happen if she didn't get out of her pit and make plans.

"I don't understand," Rupert said.

Pulling him down, she kissed his cheek. "I'm not the woman for you, Rupe," Harlow said. "I wish you every happiness." Squeezing his hand, she met his eye. "Go find her. Do whatever you can to find the love you deserve. Take risks. Don't hesitate. And once you find her, don't give her up for anything. Embrace every second. You never know when it will be over for good."

Making eye contact, she smiled one more time and for the first time in three months the curve of her lips was genuine. She had a purpose, a cause, and no one was going to divert her from it.

THREE

"I'VE FIGURED IT OUT," Harlow said, marching into Clyde's apartment before he even had the front door open all the way.

"I… Harlow? Oh my God. What are you doing here?"

Stopping in the middle of the living room, she tossed her purse onto the couch and bent down to yank off her heels. "I figured it out," she said again, throwing her shoes aside and pulling her earrings out to drop them on the coffee table.

Closing the door, dubious Clyde walked to her, raising and lowering a hand, gesturing at her body. "You look… great. Amazing, actually. Incredible."

That was probably why he was frowning and scratching the back of his head. The melancholy woman he'd been talking to on the phone for a month was barely able to feign an ounce of enthusiasm. In contrast, the woman in front of him now felt like she was glowing. Every one of her atoms was jumping and fizzing with anticipation.

"I saw him," Harlow exclaimed. "I saw him and it changed everything."

Pausing in front of her, Clyde didn't appear to get it. The grin on her face burned her cheeks. Adrenaline pumped through her heart; she wanted to jump up and down. Instead, she settled for grabbing Clyde's shirt in both fists to pull him down and kiss each of his cheeks.

Stroking her face, he stooped to her level. Examining her, concern was written all over his face. "Who did you see, Har?"

No wonder he was worried. Her former colleague had a look on his face like he thought she'd lost her mind. Her exuberance probably made it sound like she had.

Harlow just smiled. "You think I'm crazy, but I've never felt more sane and in control," she said, pushing his hand away to go past him into the kitchen. "You got any liquor in here?"

"There's wine in the fridge."

Just because she had purpose didn't mean she'd forgotten her triggers. In her nightmares, when she relived the night he'd died, she'd wake with the sweet taste of wine on her tongue. It didn't matter that the sensation was only in her mind, it still had the power to make her retch.

"Something harder," she said, opening and closing cabinets.

He came to set a hand on her waist, halting her. Leaning over to open the next cabinet, Clyde produced a bottle of Jack Daniels. Though he put it on the counter, he kept his hand around the neck and cupped her face again, directing her attention away from the booze.

"Do you think it's smart to drink? How much have you had tonight?"

"Not enough," she said, snatching the bottle, and two glasses from the same cabinet. Carrying all three things into the living room, she kneeled on the floor by the table to pour. "This is a celebration."

Clyde sat on the couch. "A celebration of what?"

Pushing one glass toward him, she held up her own and waited for him to respond in kind. "A celebration of my new purpose," she said, raising her drink higher and letting her eyes ascend to the ceiling. "Crash, you never were subtle, baby."

She tossed back her drink and winced at the strong

taste.

Even after she slammed her glass to the table, Clyde still hadn't drunk anything. "You think if he went anywhere, it was up there?"

She grinned, taking what he said as a joke more than a judgment; throwing drinks in two men's faces in the same night might be overkill.

"I think heaven would be more of a hell to him than hell itself," she said and laughed, pouring herself another measure. "I'd say the devil's been watching him a while and probably didn't want him taking over."

Clyde slid his glass onto the table. "Did he come to you before or after your first drink?"

"He?" she asked, sipping the liquor and licking its potency from her lips now that she was getting used to its flavor. "He, who?"

"You said you saw him," Clyde said. "Now you say you have purpose… You're talking about Ryske, right?"

With her lips around the edge of her glass, she scowled and finished her drink. "I only see Ryske after midnight," she said, leaning back to look at the wall-clock in the kitchen. "Not time yet."

Sliding the bottle away, he tilted his chin. "Yeah, that's enough alcohol for you."

At peace with his concern, her cause wasn't lost. In fact, it was just beginning. She slid her empty glass toward her friend, switching it out for his full one.

She bobbed her brows in triumph. "Hagan," she said after swallowing a mouthful.

Clyde's worry was replaced with surprise. "You mean… you saw Hagan? Jarvis Hagan? The man who ordered Ryske's murder?" She nodded. He dropped off the couch to sit on the floor, perpendicular to her. "Where? When?"

"Right before I came here. At my father's yearly company thing… It doesn't matter."

"Was Rupert there?"

"Yes, Rupert was there," she said, holding her glass by the rim, turning it in slow circles. "I told him it was over, completely, forever over."

"Rupert?" he asked. She blinked at him like he was an idiot. In her defense, it was a stupid question. "I'm sorry, but you jump from Ryske, to Hagan, to Rupert. I lose track. Last we talked, you told me never to contact you again and now you're here and happy and I'm—"

"I know, it's a head fuck. I'm sorry," she said and exhaled, trying to be calmer so she could explain. "I'm sorry for what I said to you. I was angry and you were right, maybe I was still in denial." Straightening up, she grinned again. "I'm not in denial anymore."

Clyde remained dubious. "I didn't know there was a crazy-eyed, manic stage in the cycle."

"Updated model," she said and finished her drink before shoving the glass away and bouncing onto her knees, flattening her hands on the table. "So I was sitting there at the SweSec thing, having a horrible, horrible time, feeling sorry for myself, mooning over Ryske, and who should pop out of nowhere?"

"Hagan."

Snapping her fingers, she pointed at him. "Exactly!"

"He was at your father's party? Why would your father invite him to—"

"Because he doesn't know who Hagan really is or what he did. No one does. And that got me thinking, why are we letting him get away with this?"

"Why are we…?" Clyde started. "Well, because if Hagan ordered one murder, what's to stop him ordering another?"

Simple for a person who saw the world in basic terms. She'd been one of those people once. Not anymore. Some risks were worth taking and fear was relative. Until someone had lost the thing most important to them, they could never understand fear. Anything less than that ultimate loss paled in comparison to regular distress.

"Do you think death scares me?" she asked, her chin dipping toward her chest. "The only thing I have left that can be taken from me is my life and if I lose that…"

She shrugged, what else was there to say?

Clyde blinked and reciprocated the movement. "If

you lose that... what?"

"I won't be around to care," she said, matter of fact about it. "Do you think Ryske is pining for me? Out there breaking his heart, missing me? No, he's not. He's dead. He can't care about anything anymore."

Clyde reached for the Jack Daniels and unscrewed the cap to drink straight from the bottle. "That's a beautiful sentiment, Harlow. Romantic. He's worm food, who cares if you end up worm food too?"

"They probably got him cremated," she said, holding up a hopeful glass.

Clyde slumped back, clutching the bottle to his chest, showing he planned to keep it to himself. "What makes you think that?"

"He wouldn't want a permanent erection," she said and laughed loud, running a finger around the inside of her glass. "Monument would probably have been a better word to use there."

One side of his mouth rose. "I think Ryske would prefer you trust your first instinct."

"Hmm, no doubt," she murmured.

Touching her fingertip to her lip, she sucked the digit into her mouth and thought about those mornings in the shower with him. How he'd press her against the tile and kiss her. Sometimes Ryske had all the patience in the world, he could kiss her for hours, even in spite of his need imprinting itself into her.

Even when he'd been hard during their make-out sessions in bed, he'd been generous enough to take her at least to the cusp of her own orgasm before he'd think about letting her touch him. Sometimes the torment of that tease was enough to heighten her arousal.

"You're thinking about his dick, aren't you?"

Snapping out of her daze, she noted Clyde's nausea and laughed. "Yes," she said, nodding and leaning across to take the bottle from his slack hand. "Yes, I am... He had a magnificent cock."

"Okay," Clyde said, snatching the bottle back after she'd poured more liquor into each of the two glasses. "The first time you think about opening up to me about him and that's what you start with?"

Picking up her drink, she shrugged. "You asked."

"I didn't! I asked if you were thinking about it, not for a description," he said. She opened her mouth wide while inhaling; Clyde was quick to raise a hand. "I really don't want to know about that." Enjoying another drink, she was happy to be selfish with her thoughts. "I do want to know where this enthusiasm for suicide came from. What did Hagan do?"

"It's not enthusiasm for suicide," she said. "It's enthusiasm for doing what I should've done months ago." He shook his head, showing he wasn't following. "Ever since I went home, ever since it happened, I've had this… I don't know, this feeling inside me I didn't know what to do with. I felt sick, and angry, and unfulfilled. Something was eating at me, and I didn't know what it was. I was indifferent to everything. The only thing I cared about was Ryske. He's the only thing I care about."

Clyde put a comforting hand over hers on the coffee table. "That's a normal thing to feel after losing someone."

"No," she said, sliding her hand out from under his. "Before Ryske I… I don't know what I believed about love. I don't know if I believed in soulmates or The One and all that BS… I don't know that it matters. What I do know is that just because he's not here anymore doesn't mean what I feel for him isn't here anymore either."

Bobbing his head, he took another drink. "Again, normal."

"Ryske is dead. I can't do anything about that… I *can* do something about the people who took him away from me."

Though Clyde hadn't exactly been light and breezy since she came in, he got even more serious fast.

"Revenge," he said. "That's what you're talking about, and it's incredibly dangerous."

"I don't care about the danger," she said. "I should never have left this city without doing something to punish the man who took down my love. Do you think Ryske would've let it go so easily if someone had taken me from him? Do you?"

Solemn, Clyde lowered the bottle to the floor. Although she could tell he didn't want to, he told the truth. "No."

"Hagan was a coward. Alleyman too," she said. "They think they won, that they did something clever. They didn't, but it's my fault they believe they're the victors. In truth, they're both weak… Hagan wouldn't even face Ryske himself and probably made sure he had a rock-solid alibi. Alleyman was in and out fast. He targeted a distracted man without giving him a chance."

Guilt niggled at her for being the one who'd distracted Ryske with her ridiculous sulk. That was just one item on a long list of things she wouldn't forgive herself for.

Her friend considered her words. "Alleyman was the one who shot him?" he asked. Harlow nodded. "What's his real name?"

"I don't know," she said. "That's just the nickname I gave him because I met him in an alley. It's possible he's known as Animal… Ryske never told me for sure."

"If you think Hagan has an alibi, and this Alleyman is valuable to him as a hitman if nothing else, what makes you think you'll be able to convince the police—"

"I'm not interested in the police," she said, tracing the rim of her glass again. "Ryske wouldn't have gone to the police."

This time Clyde was more forceful about taking her glass away and he didn't forget the second one either.

"Ryske had a lot more experience in this than you do," he said. "He had a team behind him, and he knew all the players."

"I know the players."

He shook his head. "Not enough to trust them. And whether you care about your life or not, getting yourself killed helps no one. I guarantee if there is a heaven and Ryske is up there, he'll kick your ass for giving up your life for nothing."

Though it was a ridiculous fantasy, she'd consumed enough liquor that the idea of seeing Ryske again, mad or not, curved her lips. "Then I'll have an eternity to show him how sorry I am, won't I?"

"You're really determined. Why the hell would you want to do this?"

Her smile flattened. "Because my purpose in life was to be with him and this is the only way I know how to hold onto that… I have to make him proud."

Taking her hand again, Clyde put the bottle down and pulled himself to his knees to rest both elbows on the table. "Listen to me, Harlow. I haven't been through anything close to the pain you must be feeling right now." Admitting the pain wasn't something she wanted to do. She tried to pull her hand away, but Clyde tightened his grip and wouldn't allow her to retreat. "I didn't know Ryske well, but I know he loved you, I know it."

Her lip trembled, which was exactly what she wanted to avoid. "I love him," she managed to whisper.

Get it together. Sucking her lip into her mouth, she willed herself not to get upset. The last thing she needed to do was regress to the beginning of her grief and run the full gauntlet again. Would she have it in her to survive that again? Doing that could kill her before she got to revenge. Her heart was heavy enough already. Surrendering it to the depth of her love for Ryske always meant a return to the pain.

Smiling, Clyde stroked the back of his fingers across her cheek. "I know… He wanted you to be happy, didn't he? Isn't that what he wanted?" She nodded, clinging to her lip with her teeth. "He wouldn't want you out there putting yourself in danger in his name."

Maybe. Maybe not. But she'd listened to Ryske once and had been ready to walk away from him when he'd claimed it was what he wanted. Except now she doubted that was true. The statements he'd made in the closet about sending her back to Rupert, about there being nothing left in the city for her, were canceled out by the three profound words he'd shared with her in the back of the ambulance. Ryske loved her. He had loved her.

Grief was an easy out. For three months, she'd used depression as an excuse for inaction. No more. No matter what, she would not let Clyde take her back there with soft words and tender sentiment. She had to toughen up, to harden herself for what lay ahead.

Pulling away, she pressed her hands into the table to rise. "Crash once told me to prove my dedication to him. This is how I'm choosing to honor the man I love."

Clyde grabbed her wrist. "Harlow, he wouldn't want—"

"He's not here to want anything, Clyde!" she said, yanking herself from his hold and opening her arms. "I'm here. I'm alone… I need to do this for me. For my sanity. For my love for him. I won't ever be able to move on without doing what has to be done."

Grabbing the glasses, she took them into the kitchen to pour their contents down the sink.

"And what is that? What has to be done?" he asked, surprising her with his proximity when he opened the cabinet to put the liquor away. "Just what is your great plan?"

She jumped when he slammed the cabinet. "I… I don't know the details yet."

"No?" he asked, one hand on the counter, the other on his hip. "So you thought you'd act on impulse? Just like you did when you left the city to go back to your parents after he died? Except now you're saying that was the wrong thing to do… How do you know in three months you won't feel that way about this?"

"I don't," she said, losing none of her determination even in the shadow of his skepticism. "How the hell can we be sure of anything when the world can change like that?"

She snapped her fingers.

"Then how can you be sure you love him?"

Stepping in, she pointed at him. "Say any damn thing you want about my sanity or my plan, but don't ever question the way I feel about Ryske."

"If he was here right now," Clyde said. "If he could say one thing to you, in this minute, knowing what you're thinking, what would he say?"

She didn't have to ponder the answer for long.

Curling her nails into her palm, she raised her hand to show him her star. "Highs and lows until we're dirt in the ground… He's dirt, and until I am…" She smiled. "I go with it."

Heading back into the living room, she wasn't surprised Clyde wasn't convinced.

"You think you've got it all worked out, but you don't even have a plan."

"I will," she said, sitting down on the couch and bending to tuck her shoes under it.

He appeared at the end of the couch. "You don't even have a change of clothes. What do you plan to do? Wage war in a cocktail dress?"

Glancing at her apparel, she hadn't considered logistics. "Clothes are the least of my problems. I'll buy some."

"From where? With what? If I'm not mistaken, you've been out of work for three months… What happened to your apartment?"

"Movers packed everything," she said, "it's all boxed up in my parents' basement."

After inhaling, he breathed out slowly, which she hoped meant he'd made his peace that this was happening whether he supported it or not.

"We'll take a trip there tomorrow, grab what you need. I have to be at work on Monday."

She shook her head. "I'm not going anywhere until this is done. If I go back to my parents, they'll try to counsel and cajole me. No. I'm staying right here in the city…" His brow rose. "You did say I could crash here, right?"

Another deep breath. Clyde swung around to head into another room and came back a minute later with a blanket and pillow.

"What about Floyd's?" he said, putting the bedding on the back of the couch.

The place Ryske had said she'd sleep for the rest of her life? He hadn't been right about that either. The idea of going to the bar was better than the reality of it. She'd been so nervous walking in there after not seeing Ryske for a month.

Given what had happened the last time she'd been there, she was in no rush to confront that particular demon.

Not only that, but the guys hadn't tried to contact her,

just as she hadn't reached out to them. Her relationship with Ryske's crew was going to be a complicated fix to say the least.

Confessing another shame was disheartening. "I… I don't know if the guys are ready to see me… I abandoned them. I didn't even call."

An odd kind of shock grabbed him. "You… you don't know?" he asked. "Oh my God, Harlow, I thought you knew." The way he rushed around the couch and sat beside her didn't fill her with confidence. "They're gone."

"Gone?" she asked, struggling to understand. "Who's gone? What do you mean gone?"

"I mean I went over there a couple of days after the shooting to ask if they'd heard from you or knew how to contact you since I had no way to do it…"

He trailed off. His look of trepidation filled her with dread. Was he worried she'd lose her temper? Wouldn't be the first time she'd snapped at him for being the messenger.

Her mind worked. Hagan said Ryske's crew had faded away. At the time, she'd taken that to mean none of the guys had pursued him. Except, how much did Hagan know about the men Ryske worked with?

"And?" she prompted, eager to the point of desperate to know more. "What? What is it?"

"The place was boarded up. Chains and padlocks on the doors, Floyd's has been abandoned."

What did that mean? Where would the crew be? Her gaze drifted around the room. Her unblinking eyes probably betrayed building panic. The guys had been so devastated by the loss of their comrade that they'd abandoned their home.

Something provoked them to flee. Were they together or had losing Ryske made them turn on each other? Could it be they'd had different ideas of what to do after he was gone? Without Ryske's guiding hand, she could believe that the rest of them couldn't agree on a plan.

Ryske didn't only excel at charming women, he could appease and mediate too. He knew how to handle each member of his crew, and they were used to his voice being in the mix.

"Oh, God," she said, grazing her fingertips across her

tattoo. "Everything fell apart... Everything he built is... gone."

"Yeah," Clyde said, putting an arm around her, guiding them into a slump against the back of the couch. "I figured they probably needed some time out."

Twisting, she peeked up at him. "Why didn't you tell me?"

"I wasn't sure if you knew," he said, rubbing her arm, comforting her. "I didn't want to be the one to break the news if you didn't... You split town fast. I guessed they did the same for the same reason... or that you all had some kind of strategy for what to do if something like this happened."

It was possible the crew had a contingency plan. They must have talked about what would happen if one of them was taken out. Bale told her the story he planned to feed the cops about Ryske's demise. But if law enforcement hadn't bought it, or even if they had, maybe it was the crew's contingency to go their separate ways and maintain a low profile for a set time until they were sure everything had blown over.

Bringing her tattoo to her mouth, her lips moved against it. "Oh, Crash."

Clyde didn't seem to hear her silent plea. "If they took off as fast as you did, they probably left your stuff there," he said. "Unless you think the place has been ransacked."

One thing the Floyd's crew wouldn't have to worry about was the building being broken into.

"Anyone who knows who the bar belongs to wouldn't touch it," she said, sitting up, out of his embrace. "And that's everyone."

Clyde got one thing right, she did need a plan, and tomorrow, she'd figure it out. Stifling a yawn, she was suddenly tired. Either liquor or adrenaline was catching up with her.

Her friend must have noticed. He put a hand around her head and pulled her close to kiss her hairline.

"Go through to the bedroom, get some sleep."

Shaking her head, she began to sink onto her side. "Here is fine."

"No," he said, catching her. "I insist."

Standing up, he pulled her onto her feet to lead her around the couch into the bedroom. He folded back the bedcovers and guided her feet under them after she lay on her side.

"Clyde," she murmured as he retreated.

"Yeah?"

"Thank you."

"What else are friends for?" he said and disappeared from the room.

Wearing a smile, she thought about Ryske and his crew. They were supposed to be friends and they did far more than offer each other a place to sleep.

She kissed the star on her wrist. "I'm going to fuck this up before I get it right," she whispered against the ink. "If you've got any hints, Crash. I'm open."

She didn't really believe in there being anything after this life, but she wasn't arrogant enough to think anyone knew it all. Maybe it was just blind optimism that drove her continued communication with a man without a life.

As sure as she was that this was the right path, she knew there would be no coming back after taking it. One way or another, getting payback was going to change her life… or end it.

FOUR

FORMING A PLAN didn't take long. Around noon, when she plodded out of Clyde's bedroom, he asked if she had a hangover. Despite her foggy head, she denied it; there wasn't time to let anything slow her down.

Her friend prepared food that she forced herself to eat while gazing out of the window, building a strategy. Information was key. What she knew was vital; figuring out *how* to use it was more important.

The ultimate conclusions? She needed more information, and she needed help. This wasn't going to be a half-assed op, she'd do it right.

Armed with her ideas about what she had to accomplish, she took a shower, put on last night's clothes, and left the apartment telling Clyde she'd be back.

Cash was first on the list. The only thing she valued anymore was Ryske's wristband, so she didn't flinch at the pawn shop when exchanging the remainder of last night's accessories for money. A pawn shop was a new experience for her. An odd sense of accomplishment accompanied her as she left there and continued onto the hardware store.

It didn't take long to grab what she needed and walk to Ryske's neighborhood. The crowbar raised a few eyebrows in the tattoo parlor, but no one questioned it. Charlie, the tattoo artist, listened to what she wanted and accepted her sketch. The buzz of the gun relaxed her, it represented space to zone out and think everything through.

It was evening by the time she got onto the street again. The back of her neck stung, but a good sting. One that revitalized her sense of purpose and renewed the determination in her step.

Entering a rundown apartment block, she considered it lucky she didn't encounter anyone on her ascent of the stairs. A dog barked in the alley and a couple on the first floor argued. The rumble of their voices accompanied her up to the third, where she went to knock on the door of an apartment she'd visited in the past.

While waiting for a response, a dog barked in the apartment at her back. The animal didn't scare her, though she did feel bad for him being trapped inside when he would probably prefer to be out the back with the other barker.

A click on the other side of the door brought her attention back around. The door opened to show a short Latina who took one look at her and started to close the door again.

"Mrs. Soto," she said, putting a hand on the door and stepping forward to stop it getting any closer to its frame. "My name is Harlow Sweeting. I don't know if you remember me?" Doubtful, Martina Soto stopped trying to close the door, but eyed what she held. Smiling, she tucked the crowbar behind her back. "Oh, I'm sorry, that's not for you… Do you, uh… do you mind if I talk to your son? Just for a second."

"My son is a good boy."

Martina's accent was thick but entrancing.

"I know," Harlow said and smiled. "He is a good boy."

"We no need the social people no more."

Harlow nodded. "I understand. I don't work for them anymore. I'm here as a friend… I just need some help… I'm Dover's friend."

Namedropping was probably out of line given the status of her friendship with Dover being questionable at that moment. But it worked. The mention of him loosened Martina enough to open the door a fraction more.

"He is a good man."

"He is…" Harlow said. "Can I talk to Felipe? Please?"

Martina stepped backward and called out to the boy. She tried to hide her wince at the shrill sound, and smiled when Martina opened the door further. The beauty had to be wondering why anyone would come to this neighborhood in a silk cocktail dress, carrying a crowbar.

Felipe appeared at the other end of the corridor inside the apartment, munching on some chips that he tossed aside as soon as he recognized her.

"Nightingale!" he hollered and bolted down the corridor to run into her embrace.

She hadn't expected such an exuberant welcome. Touched, her eyes warmed. Wrapping both arms around his head, she squeezed him tight. The youngster must've heard the other guys calling her Nightingale. The crew always corrected Felipe if they heard him calling her anything other than Miss Sweeting, but she wouldn't correct him. It sounded so good to hear someone using the moniker.

Felipe always looked up to Ryske, Dover, Noon, and Maze. He was young, and she understood their need to discourage him from identifying too closely with them. The idea was to stop the kid from getting involved in anything that could set him on the same path as his currently-in-prison father.

Letting her go, Felipe backed off with his head bowed. His hand went to his face, had he been overwhelmed too? As a young teen, vulnerability was mortifying, which would be why he swiped so aggressively at his cheeks.

Sniffing loudly, he straightened up, putting on an impervious front. "What's… what's up?"

His mom was no longer in the doorway, apparently trusting them alone.

She couldn't stop smiling at the teen and caressed his cheek. "I missed you, kid.".

He softened and shifted, shuffling his feet in a show of awkwardness. "I… I'm sorry 'bout what happened to Mr. Ryske."

Forcing a tight smile to her lips was difficult, but appropriate, necessary. Showing the youngster how difficult it was to hear condolences from someone who knew the man she loved wouldn't be right or fair. That was too big a burden for someone so young. No matter how he might deny it, Felipe was just a kid.

Few people treated her like the grieving widow. Not that she was Ryske's widow exactly. Having fled the neighborhood as soon as he'd passed, she'd left everyone who knew this part of her life behind.

Her family and Rupert were clueless. Hagan hadn't offered condolences and couldn't. Even if he'd tried, it wouldn't have been genuine. By his own admission, Clyde hadn't known Ryske. Although her friend's face had been closely acquainted with her love's fist.

Felipe was the closest thing to a member of the inner circle as she'd come across since that night.

"Me too," she said, sliding an arm around him to guide him down the hallway toward the cracked window at the end. Perching them on the windowsill, she propped the crowbar between her knees. "Tell me what happened, Felipe."

"Mr. Dover told me to run home," he said, eyeing the tool. "He was getting in a car with Mr. Noon and Mr. Maze, he told me to run home and not to come back until I heard from him."

That had to have been the night of the shooting, when the three of them were on their way to the hospital after Ryske had been taken away by ambulance.

"And…" she asked. "When did you next see him?"

Felipe shook his head. "I didn't… an envelope came to our mailbox. It had money in it, and a note, said the gravy train was gone and I should keep my head clear. I went to Floyd's; it was all boarded up, the very next night."

The boy had found himself a place to belong and lost it just as fast.

Putting an arm around him, she pulled the youngster tight against her side, and rested her head against his. "Have the gangs been after you?"

"Mr. Ryske told me a thing called consideration," he said, making her smile. "He said I shouldn't give anyone anything without getting something in return… And told me never take the first offer neither… He said, I should only run with a crew I'd die for… haven't found one yet."

A tear slipped from the corner of her eye. She swept it away before it could get lost in Felipe's hair.

Turning her mouth into his locks, Harlow pressed a long kiss into him. "Listen to me," she said, slipping off the windowsill to crouch in front of him, resting the crowbar across her thighs. "I want you to keep holding off, can you do that for me?" He blinked; his big, beautiful, brown eyes still radiated the innocence of a child, in spite of all they'd seen. "I might have a job for you soon."

"Mr. Ryske would want me to look after you," he said. "You could stay here with my momma and me. Auntie Camila is going to have her baby soon."

Poor kid was going to have a lifestyle shock when the baby arrived.

Cupping his face, she rose and kissed his forehead. "You are a good boy, Felipe Soto."

"Miss Sweeting?" he asked as she sank back to her haunches. Felipe nodded at the crowbar laying across her thighs. "What is that for?"

Harlow picked it up. "What? This?" she asked. "Just my house key, honey… Are you going to remember what I said? Keep holding off."

Linking their hands, she pulled him to his feet and led him to his mom's apartment. "Do you need me to help you?"

"No, honey," she said. "You've already helped."

Having a clearer picture of when the crew had fallen apart didn't make her feel better. From what Clyde said, she'd assumed the guys had at least had a chance to argue and maybe make decisions. Felipe's addition to the story suggested the idea of a pre-agreed contingency was more likely.

The Floyd's crew knew exactly what to do if one of them died. They hadn't wasted any time putting the plan into action.

Urging Felipe into his apartment, she ensured his mom saw he was back and gave the kid another hug before departing. There was only one thing left for her to do that day, and she'd been anxious about it since opening her eyes that morning.

FIVE

STRIDING DOWN THE SIDEWALK, Harlow waited for Floyd's to come into view. The closer she got, the more her apprehension rose.

"Yep," she whispered to herself, swinging the crowbar at her side. "This is me. Badass…" Peeking left and right, she checked there was no one around to see her talking to herself. "Bet you're getting a real kick out of this, Crash." Mumbling to herself was one way of not thinking about what she'd find on arrival. Playing the scenario through, she wondered just what she'd do if caught breaking into the abandoned building. "Yes, Officer, I do appear to be breaking and entering. This just happens to be my boyfriend's place… No, unfortunately, we can't call him… I'm not a crazy stalker… No, he didn't dump me… Well, actually, I guess he did… before he told me he loved me… No, I am not here to boil his bunny rabbit… Goddamn it." Ryske's smirk wouldn't leave her mind's eye; she imagined him laughing at her anxiety. "Fuck it. Confidence, right, baby? I'll just blow the guy. Bet cops like head too. Let's see how easy it is to laugh it up while you're watching that."

Reaching the corner, she immediately stopped and her mind blanked. There it was. Dark. Quiet. Deserted. Although she'd been a player in events the night Ryske died, she'd been too out of it to take in many details. For some reason, she got an out of body flash of what the scene would've looked like that night. Ambulance by the curb, lights flashing, patrons fleeing but lingering to rubberneck.

The vision was like a movie… A gurney pulled out and bundled into the back of the ambulance while the doctor called out orders laypeople wouldn't understand. Then just as he was about to close the doors, she would've dashed out, barefoot and covered in her love's blood. With pleading in her desperate gaze, at the back of the ambulance, she'd begged Bale for the admittance that he granted.

Funny thing was, she didn't remember getting in the ambulance. What she did remember was Ryske's eyes. The way he hadn't wanted to blink and couldn't take his attention from her. The memory of how they used to lock onto each other was still emblazoned in her mind.

Harlow didn't remember hearing sirens or the speed they must have used to get to the hospital. But she could remember the tug of elastic in her hair when Ryske pulled the oxygen mask from his mouth to whisper those final words to her.

Swiping tears from each of her cheeks, she sucked a breath in through her nose and hitched her chin higher.

"Carpe noctem," she whispered, thinking of the bracelet on her wrist.

In the darkness, she guessed this was a moment she was supposed to seize. There was still time to chicken out. Calling Clyde was an option. At a push, Bale would be too, but she wasn't sure she was ready for him yet.

Coming to Floyd's was difficult. Facing her loss wasn't meant to be easy, not when she'd lost someone who meant so much to her. Still, there was always something to be grateful for. At least if she went in there and lost her shit, no one would be around to see her in that horrific state.

Addressing Bale was going to be near impossible. He'd been there when Ryske slipped away. The doctor knew everything and would expect her to have questions, except she wasn't sure she wanted specifics or that she had the strength to even ask. Could she listen to him talk in technical terms about Ryske's heart, which had belonged to her, stopping? Was it her fault? Did she not love him enough? Not have enough faith in what was between them to force the organ to power through?

Swallowing hard, she forced the sickness down. Even though she desperately wanted to turn and flee, she could almost feel Ryske's hands on her back urging her on.

His words from the night they'd met echoed in her mind. *"You can handle Floyd's."*

Ryske had been right. Harlow was no coward. That was Hagan's specialty.

Gritting her teeth, she checked the intersection and strode across. No damn way was she backing out of this now. No fucking way.

Clyde was right. Boards were nailed across all the windows. The main door on the corner was boarded up too, though there was a cut out for a chain padlocked in place to keep the door closed.

Good thing she'd never intended to go in that way.

Walking up the street alongside the building, she went into the rear alley, noting a car parked parallel to the back of the structure, under the den window. Noon's car. Ignoring the increase of her pulse, she didn't slow down and went to the end, swinging a left into the dead-end alleyway where there was another entrance to Floyd's.

Her fingers shook. Planks and a wooden board covered the door. This was it. Breaking the law didn't bother her. This was liberation for her locked up heart. Until she could avenge her love, she could never hold her head high. Yeah, except the prospect of ripping her heart open again, exposing the raw wound to torture, bred apprehension.

Floyd's was ground zero. Everything Ryske had known growing up, his safety, his sanctuary, it was that building. She and Ryske first kissed in the den. First enjoyed each other in the apartment. They'd shared laughter here, she'd shed tears, screamed in anger and in ecstasy. As if that wasn't enough, her love, her Crash had received his fatal wound in this place.

Tackling it head on was going to test her resolve. But

she was ready for it. She had to be.

Not letting herself linger anymore, she raised the crowbar and began to work out the nails.

Four… no, three of the crew would've been responsible for putting up these boards. The guys would've made short work of it. She was a woman, alone, trapped in a space that had no escape if anyone found her there.

If the cops discovered her, she'd have some awkward explaining to do. There was some solace in the knowledge the cops didn't patrol this neighborhood much. Law enforcement would only find her if someone called, and people around there didn't call the cops.

At least, they wouldn't before they'd investigated what was going on themselves. Being she was the only person on the face of the Earth who'd ever offered table service to Floyd's patrons, anyone drinking in Floyd's during its final trading days would recognize her.

Another good thing about people in this neighborhood: they didn't ask questions. If she said she was good, they should accept that.

Still, any time she heard anyone on the street at the other side of the bricked off end of the alley, she'd pause until the sound faded. Floyd's was a long-standing, respected establishment in this community. The same family had owned it for decades. If any passersby heard her banging and swearing at the wood she was prizing from the frame, they'd probably guess Dover was returning to the place he'd inherited from his father.

By the time the nails were out of the board and the planks off the door, her fingers were blistered and bleeding. She didn't care about a few cuts or the mess of splintered wood and deformed metal strewn around her.

All that stood between her and victory was a padlock, looped through a metal strip. Sliding the crowbar beneath it, she inhaled. This meant something to her. It was more than symbolic. Getting inside was important. Why? She didn't know. She did know it had nothing to do with checking if her clothes were still there.

She wanted to be in the space again, she needed to be

there.

"Guess this is what it means to go all in," she said and threw her weight behind the crowbar.

It wasn't as easy as a simple split. It took a few shots. Hearing the splinter of wood and seeing the metal strip coming apart from the frame, she tried even harder until it popped free.

Fuck, her muscles hurt.

And she wasn't done yet.

The locked door set another challenge. Determined not to give up, she fought door and frame. Loosening the door, she kept the crowbar between the two pieces of wood and worked until she busted the lock right out.

"Oops," she said. Swinging the crowbar onto her shoulder like she was carrying a baseball bat from the field she'd just owned, she smiled at her triumph. "Some people are so careless with property security."

Teasing was easy while she was riding a high. That high plummeted fast when she sauntered into the dark stairway and was struck by the scent.

Her good mood evaporated.

Looking up the stairs in the direction of the private floor, she'd find the apartment up there. Downstairs led to the casino, where she'd never been. And straight ahead…

Fixating on the door in front of her, the reality of where she was and what she'd done seeped in.

Despite the apprehension, something drove her forward. Even in the midst of the fear and grief that circled her, she started to walk. Images from that night played in her mind's-eye. The way she'd drunk and laughed with Clyde, oblivious to how her night would end. Bale tried to stop her drinking. She'd refused to let him and had almost fallen during her attempt to free herself from the doctor. Someone had been there to catch her. Someone who would never be there again.

Proceeding into the dark bar, the only illumination came from the artificial light that broke through the cracks above and between the boards over the windows. The thick, short curtains were open over the high, shallow windows.

Most nights they were closed. This wasn't the kind of place that wanted to be accessible to prying eyes.

Furniture was strewn everywhere. Some dirty glasses and bottles on the tables remained upright while others were scattered on the floor. In a hurry, the crew wouldn't have cared about cleaning up. She'd guess they were trying to outrun the cops canvassing the area after word of a shooting had gotten out.

Bale would've had to say where he'd been drinking. The ambulance had been called to this location. A weapon was involved. The facts piled up. The cops would've known where to look. Chances were, law enforcement wasn't in a massive hurry to track down the truth, and might not have visited the bar until the following day, giving the guys a chance to clear out.

Her view opened up at the curve of the bar. Drawing in a quiet breath of horror, both hands clamped over her mouth at the sight that awaited her.

The dark stain on the floor could only be one thing… his blood.

This was the scene. Left exactly as it had been on that night. That was the spot where he'd fallen.

Someone must have done some clean up because there were no medical supplies strewn around. The clothes that had been cut from Ryske's body were gone too. Either the crew had cleaned up or the cops had come in to take the items away as evidence.

Her feet moved while her soul begged her to stop, to slow, not to go nearer. Yet, she couldn't stop. Before she knew it, she was sinking down to her knees, spreading her fingers across the stain.

Operating on instinct, she must've been breathing in and out, must have been existing. But she felt like a shadow, a glimmer of a memory existing out of time. Split from corporeal self, it felt like there were two of her. The one in the present was an observer, hovering, glitched out of the present moment to visit the past.

"You're going to be okay, Crash," she whispered, tracing her fingertips over the stain. "You're going to be okay, baby."

Guilt gushed through her. She'd told him he would be okay. She'd held his hand and told him that he was going to make it. Ryske would've believed her.

He'd once said that feeding her a deceitful line bothered him. That was nothing to how she felt knowing she'd given him false hope she wasn't qualified to give.

On the night they'd met, when he'd been bleeding out, she'd told him he was going to be okay. That time, she'd been correct. Ryske probably assumed she'd be right again.

Her assertion hadn't been educated. She hadn't thought about the wound or what Bale was doing. All she'd known was that she needed Crash to be with her.

Losing him had been unimaginable.

Yet, there she was.

Sliding down, she lay on the floor, pressing her hand against the stain. His heart had still been hers there. It had still been beating. He'd been with her.

Sorrow welled up. She couldn't handle the grief and the guilt at the same time. As seductive as the notion of falling apart was, she recalled the sneer of satisfaction on Hagan's face the previous night and forced herself to rise.

On her feet, she sucked up the sadness and reminded herself how good it would feel to wipe the floor with Hagan.

Casting just a brief eye over the remnants of her evening with Clyde and Bale still spread on the bar, she tried not to think about her proximity to the spot she'd pushed out of Ryske's arms for the last time. Maybe if she'd stayed, the bullet would've hit her instead of him. She could've saved him if…

No.

Shaking her head, she grabbed her wrist, closing her fist around her man's bracelet. "Crash," she whispered. "I'm going to do this. I am. I will not be a disappointment to you anymore."

With a quicker pace, she left the bar and passed the restrooms to go through the den and up the spiral stairs to the apartment. She'd come for her possessions, but now that she was there, part of the drive to be in Floyd's was because she wasn't done.

Though her stay here with Ryske had been short, this building felt like her home.

Stopping in the kitchen, by the open fridge, her gaze snagged on the curtain in the far corner. Behind that curtain was Ryske's bed. Just being in this space was bringing back memories; all of them provoked a sense of belonging.

She wanted to be there, where she'd been happy. Even in the midst of a fight, or when she wasn't sure what Ryske wanted, she'd been happy in this home.

Floyd's was her happy place.

Creeping across the room, she didn't think twice and slipped out of her dress and shoes. That wasn't enough. Stripping out of her underwear, she pulled the clip from her hair to let it cascade around her nude body down to her elbows. Her locks had grown a couple of inches since she'd last been there, but she liked the length and planned to keep it.

Crawling onto the unmade bed on her knees, she dropped her weight to her hands and closed her eyes when the smell of him hit. It was like he was there.

She needed more. Craved him.

Unlocking her elbows, she collapsed and landed face first in his pillows. She breathed in deep and out slow. Enveloped in the cocoon of their sanctuary, she could convince herself he was still with her, that they'd never been torn apart.

"Crash," she whispered.

Rolling to her side, her hand slithered up through her cleavage, a spot that Ryske loved to kiss.

He'd loved her breasts; there was no doubting he was a breast man. Cupping them, kissing them, spoiling them with his attention. Ryske was happiest with his face in her cleavage.

She didn't spend as much time spoiling her chest as he would've. Her hand skimmed higher, stopping at her throat to squeeze. It wasn't the same as his touch. Her fingers were stiff and sore from what she'd done downstairs, but her imagination was running with the moment.

Her fingers curled, trying their best to mimic his

strength. "Tighter, baby," she murmured.

The last time she'd orgasmed was under Ryske's mouth. She hadn't wanted to think about sex or anything connected to it at her parents' house. There, in his bed, it was instinct. Her free hand gravitated to her center and her legs parted as they would if he were with her.

Pleasuring herself while thinking of him was natural. Ryske was her indulgence and no man would ever be able to consume her body through her mind like he'd been able to. Somehow, he'd always had a way of doing that. It was in the way he touched her and talked to her. Hell, even the way he looked at her, or the way he breathed, turned her on.

She wanted him, wanted to be with him.

Surrounded by his scent in the bed they'd shared, it didn't take long to bring herself to climax with her deft fingers. Arching up, she screamed his name. With tears on her cheeks, love and regret in her heart, her eyes closed and she drifted off to sleep.

SIX

SHOWERING AT FLOYD'S without Ryske felt odd. Harlow had no choice but to get over it when icy water hit her skin. Damn, the water was cold. After that lesson, the goal became to get in and out fast. His soap was still there and his toothbrush too, so she could at least go through something that resembled a routine.

When she'd had lived there, the guys hadn't let her go into the basement. Once dressed, it was her first port of call. No one stopped her this time.

The basement casino was interesting and not nearly as nefarious as she'd imagined it would be. The rectangular space was about half the size of the footprint above. There were waist high tables lining the perimeter and fixed tables dotted around the center. On the opposite wall was a makeshift, but stocked, bar. Again, it wasn't as large as the bar upstairs and it was straight rather than L-shaped, but it would be sufficient to serve the number of tables.

Two doors flanked the bar. One led to the restrooms, the other to the kegs and storage area.

Despite being curious about the basement, a desire to snoop hadn't driven her down there. The fuse box was in the storage room and she needed power. Relief was sweet when she flipped the circuit breaker and the lights flickered on. Next time she showered, she'd have hot water. That in itself was enough to provoke a smile.

Without wasting too much time, she called a carpenter and a locksmith. While waiting for them, she cleaned out the fridge, turned on the hot water heater, and checked that the internet was still hooked up. Apparently, the crew left in such a hurry they hadn't turned off the utilities. With everything ticking over, there was no reason not to set this up as her base of operations.

The tradesmen were a little confused about why she needed the side door fixed. Rather than tell them the truth, she fed them a story about getting the place for a steal. They'd bought it and accepted her request to invoice the bar. So within the hour, she had triple locks and two fresh sets of keys.

The building was secure, which was a good first step. The next involved tracking down an address on the internet. Her plan was taking shape. After a little extra research, she was ready for the day.

Pressing a lipstick kiss to the top corner of the mirror, she grabbed Ryske's sunglasses to prop them on her head.

This was going to be a tough day, but she'd slept better last night than she had in months. With her new purpose came a renewed sense of optimism.

***

HARLOW COULDN'T GO anywhere linked to Ryske without memories nipping and tugging at her like they wanted to tempt her back into the abyss of grief. Since the night she and Ryske fled Bale's apartment together, she hadn't returned to the doctor's place. But there she was, going all the way back to the beginning.

Memories weren't the root of her nervousness this time. The prospect of talking to the man in the apartment did a fine job upping her anxiety. He'd accept her… right? Bale was a doctor and had to know grief did odd things to people. She couldn't imagine him being mad at her for leaving town… At least that was the hope.

Walking down the hallway, she was struck by how different this building was to Felipe's. Bale's hallway had fresh paint on the walls, a runner up the middle of the hardwood floor, and a tall potted plant in front of the window at the end.

Details could only distract her for so long. Eventually, she ended up at his door.

She smoothed her top and licked her lips. "Here we go," she murmured and knocked.

Being it was early evening, there was every chance Bale would be on shift. Whether he was in or not, whatever his work schedule, day or night shift, he'd be home, or due home, eventually.

She was prepared to wait.

The door opened.

Instead of the tall, dashing doctor she was expecting, there was a blonde woman, about her height, on the threshold. A very pregnant woman.

In the time she'd spent at Bale's, she'd never seen a girlfriend or any indication he had one, and she'd seen inside his closet.

"Can I help you?" the blonde asked, resting a hand on her belly.

Without any idea how long she'd been standing there gaping, she couldn't judge the blonde's impatience level, especially when she looked so uncomfortable just being on her feet.

Snapping to, she stuttered to life. "Oh, I'm sorry, I was… I am looking for someone. I thought he lived here… Do you live alone?"

The blonde's discomfort disappeared to make way for anger. "No," the woman said, copping an attitude. "I've been living here with my husband for two months. If you're one of George's desperate skanky hos who followed us here to—"

"No," she said, holding up both hands and backing away. "I've never met George. I… I'm sorry, it's a misunderstanding."

She fled without waiting to hear anything else. Dover, Noon, and Maze weren't the only ones who'd vanished. Bale was gone too… at least, he wasn't where she expected him to be.

It was possible the doctor had relocated after Hagan's men descended on them the night she and Ryske bolted. Not only would that have been a strategic shift, it would've been a smart one too. Ryske hadn't told her there was any plan for the doctor to move to a new apartment, but that didn't mean it hadn't happened.

Going to the hospital would be the only way to know for sure if Bale was still in town. The hospital where Ryske had died.

For that, she'd need reinforcements.

***

"HOWDY, STRANGER!" Harlow called, trying upbeat on for size when Clyde came around the corner onto his block.

Having known when her friend finished work, she'd killed some time getting food. Handing over the wrapped burger she'd bought for him, she looped an arm through his and turned him to walk away from his building.

"Howdy?" he asked, examining the burger like he was wondering what it was. "Where have you been? Where did you spend last night? You couldn't have called or—"

"I'm sorry, I fell asleep."

"Fell asleep where? You were gone all day."

His questions were justified. But if she gave him the truth, he'd make judgments and there wasn't time to debate the merits of sleeping in her dead boyfriend's bed.

Shrugging him off, she pulled herself closer. "I'll tell you all about it later. In the meantime, how do you feel about taking a little ride across town with me?"

"Across town where?" Clyde asked, peeling back the paper from his burger.

He'd just taken a bite when she responded. "I need to go to hospital."

Stopping, he turned, panic in his eyes. "Hospital?" he said, burger filling his cheek. "What's wrong? What happened? Damn it, you should've come to the office if you were sick or injured."

Widening her smile, she projected nothing but positivity. "I'm not sick or injured," she said, pulling him to the curb so she could hail a cab. "And I can't come into the office. I don't want Gina to know I'm around. She's connected to Hagan." They got into the cab and she gave the address. "You didn't tell Gina you saw me, did you?"

Though he was still eating the burger, she got the sense he wasn't enjoying it much. "Did I… No, I didn't," Clyde said. "You know how she is. Gina doesn't rub shoulders with the underlings unless we're screwing up or she's taking credit."

Looping her arm through his again, she settled against the seat. "It's sort of comforting that some things don't change."

He took another bite of his burger and swallowed before talking again. "If you're not sick or injured. Why are we going into a hospital?"

The poor guy had been pulled into something that had nothing to do with him. It wasn't fair, but she had no intention of endangering him.

"Oh, I'm not going in," she said, taking Ryske's money clip from her pocket to pull out the bills they'd need to pay for the ride.

"I don't get it," he said. "And where did you get that?"

Fingering the bills, she counted how much was left. "It's emergency money," she said, guessing that's why Ryske kept it in his underwear drawer.

"Where did you get it? And why aren't we going into the hospital if we're going there?"

Clyde had a great way of asking more than one question at once, which worked for her. It meant she could choose to answer whichever appealed to her and ignore the others. "*I* am not going in, *you* are… At least, I'd like you to… if you don't mind… please."

The frown on his face was more than confused; he was working hard to figure her out. "You want me to play sick?"

Being patient, she had to take a breath and be more explicit. "No, I want you to ask about a doctor," she said. "Do you remember the man who came to Floyd's the night…" She swallowed. "That last night?"

"He worked on Ryske. Yeah."

More than once. Bale had worked on Ryske before the night the bullet ended him. A stab wound had brought them together. During Ryske's recuperation their relationship had grown. Harlow would give anything to live those two weeks again. She'd give anything to have another minute with him. Another second.

Knowing how dangerous the path of 'what if' was, she diverted her thinking. "That doctor works at this hospital, or he used to. I went by his apartment today and he was gone. I just want to know if he's still in town."

"I don't understand, the doctor's gone too?" Clyde asked, folding his empty wrapper into his pocket. "Why would he—"

"I don't know," she said because at that moment, figuring it out was beyond her.

All she'd been told by Bale was that he was close to Ryske and wasn't on Ryske's crew. So why would he be included in any contingency plan that involved getting out of Dodge?

For three months, she'd kept her distance. For her sanity and because she hadn't been capable of holding herself upright. Facing any of the men who reminded her of the one she'd lost would've ended her. Except, now she was confronting the possibility she'd lost them all and it could be for good.

She'd meant to embark on a path that would avenge Ryske; she hadn't meant to stumble onto a new mystery.

Clyde seemed intrigued too, which worked in her favor. "You don't want to go in and ask for him yourself?" he asked.

The full truth was a little more than she was comfortable admitting. Harlow went with listing various other reasons why it wasn't a good idea for her to go back to the place where Ryske had taken his last breath.

"Someone from that night might remember me... I made a scene," she said. "There might be cops around too. I have a loose idea what Bale told them, but it would be helpful to talk to him before talking to them... just to make sure our stories match."

Those reasons were valid and true. None of them were the main reason for her hesitance to walk into that

ER again.

Accepting her rationale, Clyde nodded. "And if this Bale isn't there?"

Then either he'd vanished with the others, or the cops hadn't liked his story and he'd needed her. Had she let another man down? Jumping to conclusions would only freak her out.

She inhaled. "I'll figure that out once we find out what the hospital staff know."

"What's his name?"

"Doctor Bale Urban."

"What am I supposed to say about why I'm asking?"

From her time with Ryske and his crew, she'd learned a few things. She wasn't used to being a mentor; Ryske and the guys would've known on instinct how to play it. Clyde needed a softer, more thorough approach.

"Just tell them your mother is an ex-patient and you want to thank him for his care."

"Wow," he said. The sound he exhaled was enough to gain her attention. "You lie fast."

Not exactly a quality to be proud of, but one Ryske would've admired. Regardless, they didn't have time to deconstruct her personality and how it might have changed since she met the Floyd's crew.

"Will you do it?" Harlow asked.

His expression became very pointed. "If you tell me the truth about why you don't want to go in."

Damn, and she'd believed he hadn't noticed her discomfort. Now she sort of regretted that they were looking at each other. Still, given she was asking a lot of her friend, it was only right that she be honest.

The leather on her wrist gave her strength. "He died there," she said. "They took him away from me in that ambulance bay and I never saw him again… I just… I'm not sure I can."

With infinite patience, like he probably needed every day on the job, Clyde nodded. "I understand," he said, pulling her against his side to kiss her head. "I thought it was something like that. Saying it out loud helps the healing process."

One thing her friend hadn't gleaned from all her talk was her indifference toward moving on. Harlow didn't care about healing or the future. The plan was all that drove her. It gave her something to shoot for. After it was over, if she was still alive, what lay beyond was uncertain.

Paying the cab fare when they got to the hospital, she elected to stay around the corner out of sight. Or rather, away from the view. She didn't want to see the alley where her and the guys waited to hear confirmation of Ryske's demise, or the ambulance bay, or any of it. The previous few days had been tough enough; her sorrow needed no gravy.

Passersby gave the crazy, pacing woman some odd looks. What did she care? She didn't. Those native to the area must be used to stressed pacers given their proximity to the hospital.

An age later, Clyde came back around the corner. She didn't wait for him to get to her, she rushed forward and grabbed him, motivated by hope.

In less than a day, she'd gone from worrying about encountering the doctor to fearing she may never see him again.

Her heart pounded in her throat. "What happened?"

Clyde seemed bewildered, and his shrug genuine, yet something about his demeanor cooled her hope. Her hands dropped from his ribs, sensing what he was about to say.

"He quit."

Bereft, she staggered backward, coming up

against the railing behind her. "He quit," she whispered.

"Few months ago was all they said. No one wanted to say any more. I tried but... I guess there's confidentiality."

It couldn't have been a few months ago, unless he'd left the same night as the guys. That made no sense. Someone would've had to be around for Ryske, to take care of arrangements. Unless... was her love anonymous? Lying in some morgue? Labeled John Doe? Unclaimed?

Weight around her heart spread until taking a full breath became difficult. Pressing one hand to her chest, she clung to the railing with the other, struggling to keep herself upright.

"He quit."

"It's okay," Clyde said, putting a hand on her shoulder and moving in closer. "He's a doctor, he has to work somewhere. We'll find him."

Was Clyde being deliberately stupid or did he really think that would comfort her? Raising her chin to look him in the eye, it was wrong to focus her rage on her friend when really her rage was a combination of other emotions colliding and seeking an outlet.

Gritting her teeth and sucking in a series of breaths through her nose until she was almost panting, she fought to steady her blood pressure.

Clyde paled and his hand dropped from her shoulder. No doubt he could see her strained control.

"If Bale left when they left," she growled, "Ryske was left alone, abandoned."

Her friend wasn't quick to accept that conclusion. "You don't know that. You don't know that this doctor left the same day as the others... Even if he did, I... I don't know..." He ran a hand through his hair while searching the sky. "Maybe they took him with them."

That was at least shocking enough to shake her from her guilty stupor. "You… you think they stole a dead body from a hospital? Just bundled him up and, what? Dumped him in the trunk to drive cross-country with him? What the hell would be the point of that?" she asked and smacked his upper arm. "And why the hell would you think that would make me feel better?"

"I don't know," Clyde said, raising his arms in a wide shrug, then dropping them to rub the spot she'd hit. Releasing a frustrated growl, Harlow spun around to march away from him. "They're conmen, right?"

Something in the way her friend said that struck a chord.

She froze.

Turning slowly, Clyde was standing where she'd left him, still rubbing his arm.

"What did you say?"

"They're conmen," he said, coming to join her though his focus was more on his arm than on her. "You said that on the phone one time."

"Conmen," she whispered, disliking the direction of her thoughts.

"Yeah, they're used to playing people, and playing other people, like actors. I guess it wouldn't be that difficult to go into a hospital and play porters or something. If they had that doctor's help, it would be possible… I guess… I don't know… What do I know?"

Lifting her hand, she glanced at the star on her wrist.

Squeezing her eyes closed, she shook her head, and set her attention on Clyde. "Do you know this neighborhood? I need a burner phone."

"Uh, yeah," he said. "We have to come here for kids abandoned in the hospital, accidents, parental deaths, suspected abuse, that kind of thing. I've spent some time down here… What were you thinking a minute ago? You got all pale and distant."

"Nothing," she said, taking his arm to start them walking. "Show me."

"You can use my phone if you need to—"

"No, it has to be a burner."

"Why?"

He'd been such a help that she felt bad for not telling him everything, but he hadn't exactly been supportive of her goal. Anyway, for Clyde's own well-being, it was best he didn't know too much. If she let him get too involved, he'd be at risk, and she didn't have the skills to protect him.

"I can't tell you that," she said. "But I'll get a second one so you can contact me, how's that?"

For her that was a compromise to be celebrated.

Clyde didn't seem appeased. "I'd feel better if you told me what you were doing."

"I know," she said because he was one of the most genuine people she'd ever met.

She wasn't sure Clyde was capable of deception or misdirection. It was sweet. Clyde did just want to help people. She'd once thought she was like that. Her experience with Ryske taught her different.

Learning that not only was she capable of deception and misdirection, she was also more cynical than she'd thought, less tolerant, and definitely more bitter.

"I guess if you won't tell me that, you won't let me come with you to wherever you're going either." He sighed. "Will you come back to mine tonight? I'd feel better if I knew you were safe."

"I'll be safe," she said. "I'll text you before I go to sleep."

"Do you want to tell me where you're sleeping?" he asked, pausing by a convenience store.

Offering a furtive smile, she didn't answer and

just headed inside. Keeping her location a secret protected him too. After her meeting tonight, she'd firm up her plan, and decide how much more she wanted to share then.

Besides, Floyd's wasn't exactly the last place anyone would look for her if they really set their mind to it. For now, Clyde probably thought she was too fragile to go anywhere near the bar. That was part of the reason she hadn't wanted to tell him before she went. Until she actually walked in there, the possibility she'd chicken out had been real.

With that seal broken and the power back on, there was nowhere she'd rather sleep than in Ryske's bed.

SEVEN

HER NEXT MEETING was impromptu. After assuring Clyde she'd be fine, and watching him disappear in a cab, she'd gone back to Floyd's to change her clothes. The caliber of people she'd have to face next would be much higher than the others she'd visited over the last few days. That meant frivolous things she hadn't cared about since losing Ryske became relevant. Looking the part meant something to these people, and she didn't want to stick out. So she sucked it up and did her hair and makeup.

Noon had been kind enough to leave his car keys in his sock drawer. Next time she saw him—if she ever saw him again—she'd tell him not to be so obvious.

Driving wasn't her favorite thing and Noon's twitchy car didn't help. It didn't react like a regular vehicle; it was sensitive to every touch. He probably loved how responsive it was, but it felt like learning to drive all over again.

Still, at least the drive gave her a distraction. To keep herself on track, concentration was needed, which meant there hadn't been time to stress about what the hell she was going to say if she did actually get close to her target.

By the time she pulled into the rear service alley of the upmarket building, she'd just figured out how to shift the manual and corner without the ass drifting. That was one achievement to tick from her list.

Locking up the car, she tried to be discreet about leaving the alley and slipping into the flow of people on the sidewalk. It wasn't that busy, or that late. There were couples probably on their way to dinner, and singles most likely on a journey to meet others.

In her cocktail dress with her hair loose and her silk purse hanging on a delicate strap that lay across her body, she fit in with the other pedestrians who didn't notice she'd just walked out of an alley. Service alleyways weren't the sort of place classy people in this neighborhood hung out. They didn't even have hobos around here. God forbid.

Rounding the corner to head for the building entrance, no one was paying her any heed. The doorman even opened the door to allow her inside. Security was conversing, so with all the confidence in the world, she strode on past and went to the elevator.

The whole time she was waiting for the doors to open, her stress level grew. Her palms were beginning to sweat, and her heart pounded. It wasn't that she was doing anything wrong per se. But if she didn't get to her destination, she'd have to come up with a different plan. She'd rather just get this over with than have to connive new ways to achieve her goal.

The doors opened and she slipped inside to select her floor.

Closing her eyes, she sent silent thanks to Ryske for watching her ass. Security could have flat missed her. Though it was more likely that a single woman of her stature was such an unlikely crime suspect that they simply didn't care about where she was going.

Still, security could notice the lone figure and rush to intercept her at any moment. Getting to the right floor was a boost; she wasted no time going to the target's apartment and knocking. While waiting for a response, all she could do was hope this wouldn't be a replay of what had happened at Bale's place.

Despite her research, this could blow up in her face.

Plans often changed at the last minute and Harlow was out of the loop. Even if the setup was exactly right, a fight could be inevitable.

The apartment door opened. Her breath caught, amazed by the occupant's beauty, which hadn't lessened over time.

"Ophelia," she whispered.

Forgiving Ophelia for her moment of pure shock, Harlow clasped her hands in front of her, bracing for any potential reaction to her presence.

Still in shock, Ophelia's hand rose. It seemed to want to touch her hair but fell before it could.

"Harlow," she murmured.

At least Ophelia remembered her; that was a good start.

How did she broach this? Greeting over, there should be something, right? She should have a line or—Ophelia lunged forward and pulled her into a tight hug.

Rigid and stunned, the display of overt emotion was unexpected. "I…"

Leaning back, Ophelia clutched her upper arms, so she mirrored the move. "It's awful. Awful," Ophelia said. "I don't even know what to…"

Whether she'd felt it or sensed it, Ophelia's gaze shifted from Harlow's face to her wrist. Her breathing slowed when Ophelia took hold of her wrist to examine the bracelet and the tattooed star beneath it.

There was a new sense of determination on Ophelia's face when she looked up again. Whether or not it was set in Harlow's favor was a mystery.

"Ophelia, I—"

"We should get to work," Ophelia said, pulling her into the apartment.

Wow, that was… easy. She hadn't expected convincing the woman to join her cause would be so simple, so quick. She'd underestimated Ophelia's feelings. That had been a stupid miscalculation. She'd called it the night they'd met when each of them accused the other of being in love with Ryske.

Traversing a wide entry hallway, they rounded a central floral display and went into a living room at the head of the apartment. The large space had a focal fireplace with tall windows flanking it.

Ophelia took her to a pinstriped couch and sat her down before going to a decanter in the corner. "Sherry?"

Harlow nodded, pulling her purse closer to her stomach. Ophelia had sophisticated taste in décor, preferring muted shades. The air was perfumed by fresh flowers dotted throughout the room.

When Harlow's gaze settled on the mantelpiece an involuntary impulse put her on her feet. "Oh my God," she said, going to the central glass box that displayed a diamond ring, one she knew well, because it was the one Rupert had given her.

"It's my monument to the dead," Ophelia said, joining her and handing over a glass of sherry. After a sip, Ophelia nodded to an urn at the far end of the fireplace. "That's my mother. Jarvis has our father." Stepping backward, she revealed an urn at the other end of the mantel. "And that is half of the remains of my best friend."

"Anwen," Harlow said without really thinking about using the name.

Hearing it startled Ophelia, but she recovered quickly and moved closer, blocking Harlow's view of Anwen's urn and raising her glass to the display case in the center.

"Ryske gave me that the night he died."

Harlow knew that. Well, she didn't know that he'd used her ring to propose, though it made sense. Where else would he get such an expensive jewel at such short notice? She'd gifted it to the Floyd's crew, she couldn't be offended, even if the notion was a little disconcerting.

"It's beautiful," she said, sipping the alcohol.

Not telling Ophelia the truth of the ring's provenance was more an act of mercy than one of deception. Putting it in that case and in such a prominent position was proof positive Ophelia had been enraptured by Ryske.

"I'm not naïve," Ophelia said, touching the edge of the case. "I know the proposal was a move on his part... I don't know if he wanted to convince Jarvis we were going to be together or if he wanted me to think you were no longer a factor… maybe that was for Jarvis' benefit too."

Putting her sherry glass on the mantel, Ophelia lifted Harlow's wrist to touch the engraved metal strip. "You were there… at the end?"

Nodding, she put her glass next to Ophelia's. "Yes."

"Was it… quick?"

From the moment of the shot until his final words to her in the ambulance felt like a thousand years, yet it was over in the blink of an eye.

"He wasn't in pain," Harlow said, in another act of mercy.

The vision of Ryske's panic was imprinted on her. She'd never forget the sound of him fighting to pull breath into his failing lungs.

With a quiet nod, Ophelia seemed to accept the untruth. All of a sudden, she balled her fist and hit it against the front of the mantel.

"God, I hate him," she hissed. "This is all his fault."

"Jarvis'?" Harlow asked, stroking Ophelia's arm, hoping to soothe her.

She wanted to rip Hagan's head off as much as Ophelia did. Somehow both of them had refrained. That was a miracle in itself.

Cooler heads would prevail. They had to keep calm. Plotting Hagan's downfall would have a higher chance of success if they were deliberate rather than impulsive.

Turning away, Ophelia went to the couch and sank down to perch on the edge, worrying her hands on her knees. "Although, I have to admit… some of the blame is mine."

Guilt had been Harlow's companion too. "We could all point fingers at ourselves," she said, going over to join Ophelia. "What's important is what comes next."

They made eye contact. Harlow nodded while picking up Ophelia's hand.

"You want payback," the beauty said.

"I want payback."

Admitting that truth to Ophelia was a massive

exercise in trust. If she ran off to tell her brother, then Harlow's plan, and her life, could be all shot to shit before they began.

Instead, Ophelia straightened, taking on a serious air. "What do you need from me?"

"The deal," she said. "I want in."

"Oh, that all fell apart," Ophelia said. After a beat, she gasped, pulling Harlow's hand over to her own lap. "Of course, you won't know! You disappeared as quickly as he did… I admit I thought maybe…"

That Harlow had decided to join Ryske? Ophelia didn't finish the sentence, maybe because of Anwen, or perhaps because she didn't want to be accused of planting the idea.

"I thought about taking my own life," Harlow confessed, in a truth she'd never uttered to anyone. "I did."

"Why didn't you?"

There was genuine curiosity in the question. Did that go back to Anwen too? What had caused Harlow not to follow through when Anwen had? If Anwen and Ophelia had been such close friends, the former's suicide must have raised all kinds of questions for the latter. Should Ophelia have noticed something about Anwen's behavior? Was there something she might have done to stop her friend from committing such a final act?

"I don't know," she said, dropping her focus to their joined hands. "Ryske's voice in my head telling me I was stronger than that… No, that wasn't it…" If she was going to be honest then she had to go all the way. "Ever since it happened I've wanted to crawl inside myself… I was lost. Didn't know who I was or what to do without him… But something…" Narrowing her eyes, she tried to make sense of the senseless. "Something in me told me I wasn't done. That there was something left for me to do…" Lifting her gaze, she found Ophelia's. "It was this."

"You know if my brother finds out we even thought about this that he'll kill us both."

Harlow nodded. "I'm willing… for Ryske."

It took just a moment, but a smile crept to Ophelia's

lips.

Leaving the couch, she went to retrieve their sherry and waited by the mantel for Harlow to join her. "For Ryske."

Each raised their glass to the box on the mantel and then drank.

Harlow put her glass down by the display case again. "I need you to tell me everything about why the deal fell through."

"It was Ryske," Ophelia said, guiding them back to the couch. "As much as my brother wanted to cut him out, he was crucial to the operation. Without him there was just no way to follow through. Getting the drugs into the country was Yarker's responsibility; he has the connections to make that happen. Parratt was supposed to provide logistics for transport. Those two are thicker than thieves. I've never trusted either of them all the way, but with Ryske on top of them, I didn't have to worry."

Drugs. This was about drugs? The consortium had talked about a million apiece, that meant a four million dollar investment. In one shipment? Surely not, would men like Parratt and Yarker take such a risk?

"Ryske was distribution," she murmured.

It made sense. His connections had been referenced. The starched businessmen of the consortium probably didn't have a lot of call to associate with drug dealers beyond their own weekend dabbling.

"It was Ryske's job to bring in clients. More important was his duty to provide vendors..." Ophelia smiled. "He called them Hawking Hookers, I always thought that was funny." Hawking Hookers, what did that imply... She was still trying to figure it out when Ophelia's smile cracked. "You do understand that this is not just some common street drug. One hit costs upward of ten thousand dollars. This wasn't a flash in the pan operation either; it was a pilot. If it had been successful, we had satellite schemes ready to go across the country... We'd have made millions."

In illegal money, dealing in a dangerous and exclusive drug.

"Millions," Harlow muttered.

"Ryske had his own ideas for the future…"

Was Ophelia referencing his unexpected death or did Ryske have a scheme of his own outside the operation? Maybe it was both.

"Is it addictive?"

Ophelia went to the decanter to refill her drink. "I asked him that once," she said, watching the liquid stream into the petite glass. Replacing the stopper, she swung the sherry to her amused lips. "He said it depended on the woman." Ophelia laughed, just a short, private sound. "I suppose he was addicted with Anwen." Breathing out, Ophelia sounded both wistful and resigned. "The drug itself was developed by a European pharmaceutical company. Except they couldn't get approval. Something to do with funding and public perception… and the Europeans are supposed to be sexually liberated, right?"

"Seems their failure is our gain," Harlow said.

Another laugh joined Ophelia on her journey back to Harlow's side. "That was the idea," she said, sipping her drink. "Some contact or other got hold of the formula, I don't know how. They synthesized this initial batch and apparently the results have been impressive."

"Where are they testing it?"

"The Netherlands, of course, in their red light district," Ophelia said. "They are looking for global distributors. It hasn't been scaled yet and because of whatever's in it, it's expensive to produce. I wasn't involved in the consortium at first, though I suppose I became the glue. I found out what was going on when I overheard Jarvis talking about providing locations and geographical support. I asked him what was going on. I suppose I got him in a good mood, or maybe a desperate one, because he told me about the consortium… They didn't have anyone who could provide entertainment… It had been a while since I'd spoken to Ryske…"

"Jarvis couldn't have supported Ryske's involvement."

"No, he didn't. Parratt got Ryske involved. Jarvis would never have accepted it if he'd been aware in advance," she said. "Parratt has always had a soft spot for me and I may have whispered in his ear. I knew that he and Ryske had history… that there was an outstanding debt between them. A while before all of this, Parratt gave Ryske a shot to clear it by recruiting him to help Yarker out with his divorce."

By sleeping with Yarker's wife…. She'd heard the men discussing that the night she'd met them. Yarker needed evidence of infidelity and Ryske provided it.

The first time Ryske told her about Anwen, in the bathroom at Floyd's, he'd mentioned having a chance to square things with Parratt about six months after Anwen's death. He said he'd screwed it up. Could providing Yarker's evidence be the chance he'd been talking about? According to what she'd heard, he'd done that and hadn't screwed it up in any way.

"If Ryske cleared his debt to Parratt by giving Yarker evidence of his wife's infidelity… Why did you think the debt was still outstanding?"

Breathing in, Ophelia slid deeper into the couch. "Unfortunately, during the affair, Ryske made the mistake of having a threesome with Parratt's mistress… his favorite mistress, Lydia. Apparently, it had always been a fantasy of Yarker's wife. Parratt wasn't happy… to say the least. So I suppose that negated the repayment of the debt."

EIGHT

WOW, RYSKE had screwed it up. Big time. Her Crash didn't do anything by half. Sleeping with Yarker's wife wasn't a difficult instruction. Bringing a second woman into it, Parratt's woman, would've been a quick way to get back on his creditor's bad side.

"Did Ryske know the other woman, this Lydia, was Parratt's mistress?"

Circling her wrist in a flippant wave, Ophelia smiled. "This is Ryske we're talking about," she said. "Do we think for a moment that it would've mattered if he did?"

No. When it came to sex, little mattered to Ryske… except avoiding doing it with her. Maybe it wasn't her place to get involved with this. Ophelia knew the details and the players, and she had known Ryske for years before Harlow came on the scene. The beauty had more reason to want to hurt her brother; she'd lost her best friend, Anwen, by his actions too.

Yet, in the time since Ryske's death, Ophelia hadn't taken any action or planned her brother's demise.

Working things through, Harlow spelled out each stage. "Parratt was transporting the drug. Yarker was going to get it through customs. Your brother was providing premises where it could be peddled and used. Ryske was supposed to bring in clients… and Hawking Hookers."

"They'd have to be the high-class sort," Ophelia said, resting an elbow on the low back of the couch. "Ryske knew all kinds of people… The idea was to use my brother's club, Windsor's, to host exclusive parties. That was the whole reason for Jarvis buying the place. His task was to build up a customer base of people who may be interested in the drug, Pothos, that's what it's called. The other entertainment, the gambling and such, that was secondary, or it would be once we had Pothos. At the casino nights, they intended to make Pothos available… And because the drug's purpose is to enhance sexual experience, they needed available women to let the customers test the product."

Ryske had avoided giving out details about the consortium's operation. There was no time to ponder anything during this crash course. Harlow had to get as much information as she could.

"It's like Viagra?"

"Oh, no," Ophelia said, screwing up her face. "Pothos is far more sophisticated than that. I don't understand the specifics of how it works. Somehow it provides an endorphin boost. All those hormones and chemicals and whatever zaps around the body when people are having incredible sex, they'd be increased like a hundredfold… It wouldn't just be orgasms that would be stronger and longer, it increases the sensitivity of every nerve. Just a kiss or a touch can be as debilitating as a regular orgasm… Ryske did say it would increase blood flow, stamina, and prowess, so I guess it does the same thing as Viagra too. But that's more of a side effect than the purpose of it… It's the sex god drug. It basically makes everyone into a sex god or goddess. That's why they called it Pothos; he's some sort of Greek god or something."

The God of longing, which could imply the drug increased sexual appetite too.

"Oh, Crash," she whispered, grazing her thumb over her star tattoo.

"I suppose you were too busy having sex with him to

discuss any of this," Ophelia said. "Anwen always told me Ryske said business and love were incompatible bedfellows… I'm sure he didn't say it that way. Doesn't really sound like him, does it?"

No, it didn't. Had she known the man at all or was their whole relationship a con? Relationship? That was a loose interpretation. If they'd been together at all, it was for a week, and it hadn't been all the way.

Reeling from the gravity of these revelations, she wrung her wrist and licked her lips. "I… uh…"

"Oh," Ophelia said. "Oh, I'm sorry, this must be so difficult for you. Stay here. Just a minute."

Getting up to scurry off, Ophelia disappeared from the room.

Her mind was swimming. This was her chance to flee. She could get up, leave the apartment and never look back. A rush of adrenaline surged through her, just like the one she'd experienced on the night Ryske died.

"What the hell am I doing here?" she whispered to herself and stood up.

Going to the mantelpiece, she examined the showcased engagement ring. Ryske had proposed to Ophelia. He hadn't minded the whole world believing he was in love with the beauty. After his proposal, would he have been faithful to his fiancée?

Ophelia implied that she wasn't having sex with Ryske. The relationship wasn't real, so anything he did with other women was outside Ophelia's scope, or was it? The whole relationship was part of the con…

What was Harlow? What was her connection to him?

Of their own volition, the flats of her fingernails trailed up her body, over her breast and shoulder, beneath her hair until her fingertip touched the mark inked on the back of her neck.

The tattoo was meant to show she was a part of the crew. To prove she identified with what she'd become, that she was proud of it.

What had she really become? Ryske was gone. In his absence, she could make him anything she wanted him to be.

It was easier to remember the good parts; the lying in bed at Bale's, at her place or his, talking, bonding, enjoying each other.

Thinking of falling asleep in his arms or them pleasuring each other in the shower made her feel better. At what point had she conveniently forgotten that Ryske was a cocky prick who frequently undermined her free will with his own assertions?

In the end, she'd been right. Crash had vowed to bed her and technically, he never had. But that was only a technicality. He'd had her in every other way a man could have a woman, heart and soul.

No matter how hard she tried to tell herself nostalgia was tainting her memory of their connection, she couldn't shake it. Closing her eyes, she pictured his grin, and that look he'd give her after he'd said something that didn't impress her. She could still visualize his wink, his confidence… the way he'd spoken about her like she was his.

The idiot punched Clyde just for sitting beside her. He'd invited her to stay with him at Floyd's, in his home, somewhere he'd never taken a woman before. Crash had played it down like it was the only option. But she knew enough of him and his crew; if they hadn't wanted her in their home, they'd have found an alternative.

So many of Ryske's words and actions implied she was special to him, but he was a conman, he could sell anything. Although that was true, what did lying to her get him? Nothing she'd given him was lucrative, not even the information had monetary worth.

One truth was undeniable. Clutching the mantel on either side of the glass-encased engagement ring, she closed her eyes. Their whole relationship, and her reason for being there, boiled down to one thing: he'd told her he loved her. That's where her sense of ownership came from. Crash had said he loved her.

"Here, come and sit back down," Ophelia's voice rose behind her.

Turning just in time to see the hostess appear through a swing door carrying a glass of water, Harlow returned to the couch. Ophelia joined her, handing over the water.

She drank. "Thank you."

Ophelia took the glass and put it on a table behind the couch. "He said you were different."

"I was… oh."

She wasn't the only one obsessing about Ryske. Guessing what the guy had been thinking was impossible. To say that he wasn't always the most straightforward would be an understatement.

At one time, she'd believed he didn't lie to her. That was a lie in itself. Ryske could be whatever he had to be, for whoever he had to impress or charm. Nothing about him was certain.

Talking about him with Ophelia in professional terms was easier than broaching the personal.

"The slap was for show," the hostess said. "He told me you knew how to adapt and accept. I supposed if you were part of his crew that you would have to be good at that sort of thing."

Ryske had talked to Ophelia about her? He'd told her that, though had never shared specifics.

"What else did he say?"

Smiling, Ophelia seemed to understand her need to hear something new about the man gone from their lives.

"That you got him drunk."

What? When? She couldn't remember ever forcing Ryske to drink. "I never did! When?"

Ophelia laughed. "I think he meant figuratively." Oh. She relaxed her offense. "He said the moment your eyes first met, something in him changed."

The first time they'd looked at each other, he'd been suffering blood loss. She'd be surprised if he even remembered.

"He was full of shit," she whispered, smoothing her skirt.

Ophelia grabbed up her hand. "No, he meant it… He said he'd never met a person so fearless. He said you treated every day like you had nothing to lose. You stood up, no matter the personal cost. You were dedicated, and loyal, and determined… He said he was lost, that he didn't know what life was anymore, that everything since you had been autopilot because whatever he'd been before wasn't enough anymore… He was different, Harlow. I told you that the night we met. The Ryske who was with Anwen, the Ryske I knew before her and after… he wasn't the same man once you came into his life."

Fearing that if she opened her mouth, the burn in her sinus would become something uncontrollable, she steadied her breathing, using the reprieve to restrain tears. Ophelia cradled her hand and stroked the back of it.

"He couldn't breathe," Harlow sobbed when she dared open her mouth. "He was looking right into me and he knew… The pain of that minute, his pain…" She pressed her hand against her chest. "It won't leave me."

Ophelia's lip wobbled and when she blinked, a tear tracked down her cheek. "We're going to use that pain," she said, her own tone lost to grief though she tried to fight it. "The pain we both feel, we're going to use it."

Nodding, Harlow swiped away her tears and sniffed, exhaling a laugh. "God, you know the prick would love this," she said, picking up the water glass from behind the couch to drink some more.

"Two beautiful women blubbing over him?" Ophelia said and laughed too. "Yes, he would. And I doubt we're the only two women who've shed a tear for him." Probably not before or after his death. "Do you know what comforts me?"

"What?" Harlow asked, returning the glass to the table.

"Anwen has him now," Ophelia said. "Wherever they are, they're together."

Ophelia's understanding of that relationship wasn't the same as hers. But, as with the ring, Harlow wasn't going to take away the woman's illusions if they gave her comfort.

Losing themselves to grief wasn't productive. Harlow was determined to fight as hard as Ryske would for her.

"We need to get this deal back on track."

"How?"

Trying to figure it out, she was resolute in taking every

necessary risk. "We have to talk to Parratt. He was the initial mastermind, right? Do you think you could arrange a meeting with him without your brother knowing about it?"

"Yes," Ophelia said, drawing on Harlow's fortitude. "It will have to be soon. Gil's going to Europe next week."

Gil was Parratt's first name.

"Perfect," Harlow said. "The sooner the better."

"He'll meet with us," Ophelia said. "What are we going to tell him? Do you have a million dollars lying around? Because he won't let us in if we don't have the buy-in money… and without Ryske's connections—"

"I'll take care of that."

She'd surprised Ophelia. "You… you have his contacts?"

Neglecting to actually lie, Harlow resorted to smiling instead. She didn't have his contacts but had access to his possessions and didn't mind snooping. A certain conversation faded up in her mind. Harlow had a good memory for names. Ryske mentioned the twins Svetlana and Lyudmila. There were other names too, though those were the only two that Ryske had confirmed were hookers.

From that same conversation, she knew about Ryske's proverbial little black book, where it was, and how to access it. Without meaning to, the crew had secured her position and helped with her plan.

It was a place to start. The twins might know other women willing to take part. Svetlana was a madam, she had to have her own crew. Harlow would ensure the terms of the official agreement read that the woman not be required to take drugs and that they get to keep whatever money they made with the customers they chose to see. Because it was right, and because it was what Ryske would do.

Her mind was turning, thinking about how she'd come up with clients when Ophelia spoke again.

"We could split it down the middle?" Ophelia said. "I know it looks like I'm loaded, but I'm not. My brother controls everything. He pays my bills, but I don't have a lot of cash on hand. He'll notice if I start selling jewelry and furniture. He's here almost every day… I'll come up with half the money and the clients, something I was doing for Ryske anyway. If you can come up with half the money and the Hawkers."

Bobbing her head, that would be fair… if she had the first clue how to find that amount of money. That was a problem for later, no way was she giving up at the first hurdle.

"That's fair."

"The operation going ahead will benefit Jarvis. Parratt won't want him cut out, we need his operational support…" Harlow didn't want Jarvis Hagan cut out either. Having him involved was the point. "It will drive him insane to know we're doing this in Ryske's name and of course we should talk about him as much as possible. But is it enough to—"

"Let's worry about getting this off the ground, and then we'll take care of that."

She was glad Ophelia accepted that because she wasn't sure the woman was ready to hear her full plan yet. Cluing her in on a need to know basis seemed like the best idea, at least until their trust was more secure.

"Just having us around and involved will drive him nuts," Ophelia said, already confident, which Harlow liked. "He doesn't believe women should be involved in business. I tried to be a part of his corporation once and it was awful. It was a battle every day and I'm ashamed to say that I let him win… I won't let him win this time… I asked Ryske to help me take him down for Anwen, he refused… I have even more incentive now."

"We both do," Harlow said. "Meeting with Parratt in private will be the first goal. If we can meet Yarker after, that might help too. Having them on our side will be beneficial. We don't want to make it seem like we're only there to spite your brother… We have to come across as professionals."

"Definitely," Ophelia said. "Ryske's laid the groundwork for that. Jarvis always seemed so erratic whenever he was around or pushing his buttons. Parratt and Yarker are already wary of him… It wouldn't hurt to sleep with them."

Whiplash. She'd followed along with growing enthusiasm until that last part.

"Excuse me?"

"Ryske always said that to do what he did, he had to be willing to use every weapon in his arsenal… And, let's face it, we're hot."

Ophelia's words were effortless and unapologetic. To the heiress, it was just a plain, clean truth. If they had sex with Parratt and Yarker, they'd be able to manipulate them with ease.

Using sex hadn't occurred to her. "And you think that if we…"

Ophelia nodded. "They already think you're a hooker. So we tell them I came up with the money, you're coming up with the goods. If we want them to screw my brother along the way, it would make sense for us to screw them… You'd be willing to do that, right?"

Coming up with an answer didn't take as much as a second. Harlow nodded. If it came to getting naked with either of them, she would have to work hard to sell her interest when the notion made her sick to her stomach. But if it was the difference between this working and not, it didn't really matter what happened to her body. She couldn't say she was willing to die for this cause and then be precious about her virtue.

"Do you have a pen?" Harlow asked, happier to change the subject than to dwell on it. "I'll give you a number."

"Oh, sure," Ophelia said, retrieving a phone from the end table to hand it over.

Harlow called her burner from Ophelia's phone, ensuring they had each other's numbers. Once that was done, she got up, startling her hostess who obviously hadn't expected her to leave yet. Her task complete, there was no need to hang around.

"Let me know as soon as you have a meeting time with Parratt," Harlow said, walking toward the hallway and the front door with Ophelia in tow. "And don't tell your brother about any of this… it will be better to surprise him."

"I agree," Ophelia said, kissing each of her cheeks. "Work on pulling your half of the money together, I don't know how fast this will happen."

"Sure."

"And, Harlow," Ophelia said, stopping her just before she opened the front door. "Thank you for trusting me… We're going to make him proud."

With a smile and a nod, Harlow slipped out. It wasn't until she was in the elevator that she let herself breathe out. Staring straight ahead, so as not to draw attention to herself if there were cameras, she fought to maintain her composure even though her insides were soup.

This was on now. There was no going back.

She was going into the drugs business.

NINE

BEFORE THAT, she had to go into two other businesses: liquor and gambling.

After leaving Ophelia's, Harlow made a stop at the Sotos on her way back to Ryske's bed. She asked Felipe to come by Floyd's the next day.

Together, they cleaned up and got to work removing the boards from the windows. While they were doing that, a few guys who passed asked what was going on. They pitched in once she explained she was getting the bar running again.

Though most people who joined them knew her, Felipe was a great help in introducing her to those who didn't. The first time he introduced her as Ryske's wife, she'd been taken aback. But everyone accepted it, seeming to understand that the title was unofficial. Every person who stopped offered condolences as though she and Ryske really had said "*I do*" to each other.

Anyone with skill enough to help did. In the end, Floyd's looked better inside and out than it had on the night she'd first gone there.

Stocking the bar was easy. The liquor supplier didn't want to mess with anyone from Floyd's. So although the liquor license was still in Dover's name, they were happy for her to receive the delivery.

Contact details for everyone she needed were in the office. Word had traveled through the neighborhood, so Tom, Dick, and Larry weren't surprised to hear from her. The trio were happy to arrange dealers and customers for a Friday night event.

Lowan, Dover's bartender, was eager to come back to work. Though he was surprised by the change of management, he didn't ask questions. In this neighborhood, no one probed too deep. It was one of the things she loved about the people around Floyd's.

Plucking up the courage to call Svetlana took some time. Anxiety was unnecessary because it turned out the woman was patient and personable. After exchanging mutual regret about Ryske, the women agreed to work together. It transpired that Ryske had mentioned her to the madam. While she hadn't been expecting the call, Svetlana welcomed hearing from Harlow, who she'd been curious about.

They weren't on the line for long. By the end of the call, her confidence was high. Svetlana reassured her that she could come up with the goods and wasn't shy about being explicit in what her girls offered and their terms.

Getting that box checked meant a lot and gave her some piece of mind. Though it was only one problem solved. There were others she still had to get to grips with.

Caring for Floyd's came to be a substitute for caring for her crew. Harlow dedicated her free time to getting the place in shape, going so far as to move furniture around to clean underneath it. That led to a few interesting discoveries. She loved learning every nook of the home that meant so much to the man she missed.

It ended up being a tiring few days, but she wasn't going to let sore muscles and an exhausted mind slow her down. Nothing would slow her down.

Exiting the clean and tidy closet, she paused to scan the apartment. The whole building was cleaner and neater than she'd ever seen it. She grinned, would the guys recognize their home?

Just as she was about to go downstairs, her phone

rang on the kitchen counter.

Forgetting her amusement, she ran to pick it up. "Hello?"

"Saturday, my place," Ophelia said down the line. "Ten p.m."

This was it. The most important part of her plan had kicked up a gear.

"Okay," she said, sure, set, ready to make it happen.

"He's getting on a plane straight after, so we have to kill this, Har."

Ophelia could be as uncertain as she liked. She didn't have any doubt that she'd do whatever was necessary to get inside the consortium.

"We will," she said, locking her focus on the opposite wall. "We will… Will Jarvis be—"

"He has a date with a woman I know will put out on Saturday," Ophelia said. "We'll be fine. He won't drop by unannounced."

"Good."

There was a pause. "Harlow? Are we sure about this?"

Having Ophelia onside was crucial. So, as much as it frustrated her to hear Ophelia's nerves, Harlow chose to be calm and supportive.

"A hundred percent," she said, willing herself to encourage her ally. "As long as we have each other's backs, we'll be just fine… Don't be afraid of him."

Ophelia blew out a breath. "You're right." She laughed. "It's kind of exciting when you get over the terror, isn't it?"

Harlow exhaled her own laugh. "It is. Call me if you need anything. Otherwise, I'll see you on Saturday."

"Okay," Ophelia said. "Come late."

Pissing Parratt off wouldn't help their cause. "Late?"

"Ryske always came late… showed he had balls."

Her mouth opened in silent understanding. The advice was useful. Arriving late would give Parratt the impression she was confident and not so much of a rookie as was the reality. In her job as a social worker, she'd prided herself on being punctual, she never wanted to show disrespect.

Her alliance with Ophelia was paying off. Her newest friend just reminded her that her new life required a shift in her mindset.

The women said goodbye and hung up. Man, she'd gained a new respect for Ryske. Standing in the kitchen, she considered the man and his arrogance. His confidence and assuredness had pissed her off more than a few times. Now she learned that he wasn't just being a jerk for the sake of being a jerk. Ryske had to make himself larger than life, to make himself seem invincible.

Sure, there were probably times when he believed his own hype more than he should, but without that hype, he might not have made it as long as he did.

The second phone on the counter buzzed with a text message, stealing her from her reverie. Reading it, her smile warmed. Her friend had come to visit.

Harlow ran down the spiral stairs and through the den to the busy bar. The jukebox was playing an upbeat track, which increased her positive mood. As she ran up behind the bar and gave the serving Lowan a squeeze, those she passed raised their glasses to her.

Hurrying around the curve at the corner of the bar, her bewildered friend wasn't far from the spot where Ryske had decked him. Not that he'd appreciate her reminding him of that encounter. For her, it was better to recall that than focus on it being the same spot he'd been in when Ryske was shot.

"Clyde!" she said, slapping her hands onto the bar to boost over it and kiss each of his cheeks.

As soon as she was standing again, he opened his arms. "This is where you've been?"

She nodded and grinned. "What do you think?"

"I think this place is still owned by someone and when he comes back, he's going to be pissed," Clyde said, slipping onto a stool. She opened a beer for him. "Your customers are scary too, what are you going to do if something happens?"

"Everyone's behaving so far," she said, glancing around. "They knew Ryske and…"

"They're being nice to you."

"I guess you could say that," she said. "Most of them were here that night, so… yeah. But I'm not stupid." Pointing around the room, she indicated where Tom, Dick, and Larry were positioned. "I have security."

"They're working for you? How do you know you can trust them?"

"Two reasons," she said. "The owner of the bar you just referred to, who can be as pissed as he likes, it won't bother me, he's friends with them. That means he trusts them… at least to some degree."

He lifted his beer. "And the second reason?"

"I don't have a choice," she said, raising her shoulders in a pronounced shrug. "Anyway, stay here, have a drink. I'll be back."

Diving across the bar, Clyde grabbed her wrist. "What is that on the back of your neck?"

Tom noticed Clyde's sudden move and progressed a few steps closer. Harlow held up her free hand to halt him and smiled as she waved him back. The frown on Tom's face alone should be enough to reassure Clyde that her security could be trusted.

This was the first time her friend had seen her with her hair up.

Proud to show off her tattoo, she turned to give him a better look. "Do you like it?"

"What is it?" Clyde asked, touching it with a fingertip.

He could be forgiven for not knowing specifically what it was. Using miniature curved lines that ended in points, much like Ryske's tribal tattoos, Harlow had created her own, almost abstract, version of a small bird.

Spinning around, she didn't hide her satisfaction. "It's a nightingale," she said and winked. "Just like me."

Her friend only frowned. "Isn't that a symbol of love and death?"

That wasn't why she'd been given the moniker. To her knowledge, the crew used it because she'd been nursing

Ryske when they met. Except, given how her association with them had turned out, she decided to nod in agreement.

"I'd say so, wouldn't you? I lost my love to death, didn't I? Guess the next guy better watch out."

"Do you think you're ready for that?" he asked as she moved to leave again.

"For what?"

"Love."

It could only be that he was making a joke. To be polite, she laughed, though the sound may have come off as more than a little manic.

"Clyde, honey, I wasn't ready for love when Ryske found me… and I don't ever want to find it again." Raising one corner of her mouth in a way she hoped Ryske would be proud of, she winked. "But if you're asking about sex…"

His jaw dropping was a good indication he was too stunned to pull her back again. Harlow left him to absorb her tease and went to do a round of the room.

The best way to ensure no one would cause any trouble was to show them respect. When she gave it, they returned it. Sitting at each table, she got to know the patrons and let them teach her how to play pool.

Sometimes a hand would wander or one of the guys would move in close. That was when she'd talk about Ryske. Even though the man wasn't there, he was her safety net. If he'd been some faceless boyfriend, out at sea or something, they wouldn't have been put off. But these guys knew her ex and what happened to him.

If Ryske had been alive, they'd stay away in case they got a fist to the face or banned from the bar that was a hub for the neighborhood's underworld. But he wasn't alive. So, for all intents and purposes, she was single.

Reminding them of who she'd been with prompted the neighborhood guys to back off. Either in fear they'd have to deal with a weak—possibly emotional—woman, or because she managed to remind them of their own vulnerability in the dangerous life they chose. Over time, their reticence would change, but she'd deal with that then. There was no point in stressing about something that hadn't happened yet. Harlow had enough actual problems that she didn't need to be creating them in advance.

Costello had come in to show his support. Sitting with him gave her a reprieve from being hit on for a while. She'd met him on the street the day she and Felipe had been putting Floyd's back together. He owned a boxing gym a block over. Since then, she'd been squeezing in time to train with him twice a day and planned to keep on going as much as she could. Strength would help with her plan and the fighting moves he'd been teaching her could come in handy too.

After completing a circuit of Floyd's, saying hello to everyone who was there, she returned to find Clyde engaged in a debate with Tom.

"Aren't I paying you to do something?" she said but reached over the bar to touch Tom's beard.

"Thought this one looked like trouble," Tom said, accepting the soda she offered.

"Oh, he is," she said, raising her brows and nodding.

Clyde didn't seem to catch on that they were just playing with him. "Trouble? I'm not trouble, why would you think that?"

"I remember the first time I saw you," Tom said, pointing the top of his soda bottle at the floor between their stools. "I think you were underneath her boyfriend who was knocking seven shades of shit out of you."

Even though that was an exaggeration, she always got a ridiculous thrill to hear anyone talk about Ryske. While listening to Clyde argue with Tom that the fight hadn't been his fault, and had been kind of one-sided, she cursed herself for not coming back to Floyd's sooner.

At her parents' home, she'd locked herself up and wallowed in her grief. There, in this place that had become her home, she was among friends. There was a time that she'd feared this bar. Now she considered these people hers. Harlow was connected with them in a way she'd never felt connected to her parents' friends or the people she'd met in the suburbs.

The folks out there cared about mortgage rates and

soccer practice, things that didn't matter. In this neighborhood, people lived on the edge, making life and death decisions every time they left their apartments or talked to someone.

Coming back to the city led to many questions cropping up about her life and her future. Most of all, she wondered what Dover would say if he found out she'd been using company accounts and running the casino. She wasn't afraid of him, or of the other guys.

But she did worry.

In the nights when she lay awake, she still talked aloud to Ryske. These days, instead of voicing her grief and begging him to come back, she talked about the guys. About how worried she was for them, and how if he could, she wanted him to look out for them… wherever they were.

Ryske would be doing that anyway, if it was within his power, but teasing him was fun. Like they'd played in life, she told him to watch over the crew instead of spending so much time drooling over her taking a shower or lying naked in their sheets.

Tom said something that made Clyde squawk and she laughed. As long as her new bouncer was keeping Clyde occupied, her friend wasn't asking about her plans, and she was grateful for that.

She had to be ready for whatever happened on Friday when she opened the basement for the first time. The underground casino was the least of her concerns. More important was what would happen on Saturday. That was when she'd come face to face with Parratt, a man who believed she was a hooker and some sort of connected criminal too.

Hagan may disabuse Parratt of the notion she was a hooker once he found out about her and Ophelia's scheming. The second assumption Hagan couldn't deny. With every day that passed, she was meeting new people, many with dubious careers, most she'd consider friends.

When she came up with the goods, which she'd have to one way or another, none of the businessmen could doubt her role in the consortium.

Breathing in, she tried to project the confidence of a carefree hostess, but one other worry was looming over her and it wasn't one that would go away in a hurry.

Where the hell was she going to get half a million dollars?

TEN

FRIDAY NIGHT had been nerve-wracking. They'd agreed not to advertise that technically she was the highest point in the present management chain. Some of their patrons, who were all male, wouldn't be deterred from bad behavior if they thought they only had to answer to a feeble female. Didn't matter that she didn't consider herself feeble, or that Costello had been teaching her how to take care of herself. Anything she could do to keep the peace gave them an advantage.

So, instead of being the boss, she gave discreet orders as needed, and chose to serve behind the basement bar to watch what was going on. Tom stayed upstairs with Lowan, both of them provided security while Martina, Felipe's mom, poured the drinks.

Larry said the casino wasn't as busy as usual. People were nervous because the place had been closed for so long. Holding an event that went off without any hitches would encourage confidence in other customers who needed reassurance nothing sinister was going on. Business would pick up as word spread.

Ten grand was all the house cleared. Under other circumstances, that would be a lot of money, except there were costs to cover. Besides that, ten grand was nowhere near the half million that she needed to contribute to the Pothos operation.

Too soon, Friday was over. Saturday brought with it the time for the meeting at Ophelia's apartment with Parratt. Even though it went against her old nature, she bolstered herself with as much attitude as she could muster, channeling Ryske, and deliberately turning up after the designated time.

"Attitude," Harlow whispered to herself in the elevator on the way up to Ophelia's place. "Badass. Yeah, I've got attitude. Fuck. Fuck. Tits. Ass. Cock. Fuck."

She'd never been nervous like this. This was life and death nervous. Her life meant little to her, so losing it wasn't what she feared. She feared letting Ryske down.

Closing her eyes, she wrapped her fingers around her wrist, clinging to the leather and metal that always connected her to him.

"God, Crash, I need you to kiss me right now," she murmured, imagining his lips on hers.

Whenever Ryske kissed her, she could forget everything else. He had a way of erasing her worries and her fears. It wasn't that he made her feel safe; she felt anything but safe in his arms.

In the times she'd surrendered herself to his kiss, she didn't have to be mad or sad or anything other than his woman. She could just exist in the moment and be in the present with him. Ryske took care of her, not only her sexual needs, but every part of her. It was in the way he touched her. His caress and his kiss told her the lengths he'd go to in order to keep her safe.

She wanted to prove that she'd go to those lengths as well.

In the same moment her eyes opened, the elevator doors did too. Her resolve was back. Ryske was with her; she could feel him.

Glad that she'd been to Ophelia's before, she retraced her steps. Knowing the layout lessened some of her apprehension. Though a little anxiety was healthy when it was still possible Ophelia was in cahoots with Hagan. Until she went inside, she wouldn't know for sure. The end could be right on the other side of the wall.

Before her fist made contact with the door, she paused. If she was channeling Ryske and being badass—like the heavy makeup and slinky dress were supposed to suggest—she didn't have to be polite and follow the rules expected of society.

Reaching for the door handle, she swanned into the apartment like she had every right to be there. No one jumped out at her. There was no a-ha or gotcha moment. Hagan wasn't lying in wait, not that she could see. She kept on going past the centerpiece of fresh flowers and counted only two people on the couch.

Without acknowledging Ophelia and Parratt's presence, she sashayed into the living room and over to the decanter by the fireplace.

After pouring herself a measure of sherry, she took a sip while spinning around to face them. It was nice to see both of them taken aback.

Before lowering her glass, she winked. "What you guys talking about?"

"I... I—"

"Mr. Parratt," she said, going to him.

The way he leaped to his feet didn't remind her of the same intimidating, superior sonofabitch she'd met in the group meeting, though it was definitely him.

"You look... beautiful."

Seemed he liked women a little rough around the edges. She could work with that. Ophelia rose too, and took her time processing Harlow's confident, almost cocky, demeanor.

Harlow peeked at her ally for just a second before turning sultry eyes on Gilbert Parratt. "Are you flirting with me, Mr. Parratt?" she purred. If she thought about it for a minute, she'd realize her voice was deeper than normal. Instead, she focused on stretching her saucy smile. "Or is it the prospect of a million dollars and me sharing my wares with you that's getting you hard, honey?"

He blinked again, shocked, but not offended... at least she didn't think so. Pushing her shoulders back, her breasts distracted him from her moment of doubt. As soon as he looked at her chest, she ran the point of her full-finger knuckle-joint ring down his cheek.

The silver forefinger piece had been an addition she'd acquired at the tattoo parlor next door to the boxing gym. Her gym coach, Costello, told her it was a good idea to incorporate weapons into her wardrobe if she could. Accessories were a good start.

Sliding the point of her ring under Parratt's chin, she forced it up to make him meet her eye. "Not those wares, honey. They're still on hiatus."

Ophelia put a hand on each of his shoulders and moved in closer at his back. Her ally had the advantage of height and touched the back of their mark's ear with her lips. "She's still in mourning."

Tipping sherry into her mouth, the liquid courage was welcome. Drinking gave her a chance to regroup.

Whirling to face the mantelpiece, she left Ophelia simpering over Parratt to go and inspect the shine on the encased diamond.

"I was sorry to hear about Ryske," Parratt said.

Laying down the sherry glass, Harlow faced the couple again seated on the couch. Ophelia was stroking their mark's thigh. "Did you fill in our esteemed friend?"

"Yes," Ophelia said, opening her fingers to spread them over more of Parratt's leg. "He seems… uncertain."

Circling her shiny red lips, she wrinkled her nose. "Oh, I do not like a man who's uncertain. Confidence is sexy… isn't it, Ophe?"

She'd never shortened her new friend's name before, but she seemed to accept *"Oh-fee"* as a nickname.

"Sexy? Oh, God, yes. Confidence is sexy."

"You might not know this about us," Harlow hummed, pouting as she strutted toward him, pointing one foot in front of the other, never taking her eyes from his.

She imagined teasing Ryske. Thought about the way she'd looked into her Crash in the times he'd curled his fingers around her throat, which made it difficult to restrain the impulses driven by her hormones.

"Know…? Know what?" Parratt asked.

Keeping him off-kilter was key. Sinking down to her knees in front of him, Harlow opened her hands on his thighs, sliding them up, letting her fingers twine with Ophelia's in his lap. "Men who take risks turn us on… We like daring men… Men who are willing to go all the way."

Parratt didn't close his mouth for a full minute. Her head fell to the side, eyes still in seduction mode, she tried to think innocent with her pout. Ophelia took the baton and leaned in at his side, speaking to him with her lips just an inch from his cheek.

"We're not asking for you to show us special treatment, Gil. All we want is Ryske's part of the deal."

Pushing forward, Harlow rose enough to let her breasts plump against his knees. "And, believe me, Mr. Parratt, Ryske would want us to have it."

"Oh, he would," Ophelia said.

It was difficult to maintain her smolder when she caught Ophelia fighting to suppress a laugh. Yeah, they were playing this guy with cheap tricks. Unfair? Maybe. But it seemed to be working, so she was going with it.

"Ryske never left us unsatisfied," Harlow said.

"We were thorough for him," Ophelia said, getting even closer. "Just as we can be for you."

Noon's words pulsed through her mind. *Go with it. Go with it.* If this ended with anyone suggesting they move this through to the bedroom, she didn't have a clue what would happen. One thing was for sure, if she ended up naked with Parratt, she sure as shit wasn't giving the guy half a million bucks too. Living with herself after screwing him would require at least that amount in compensation.

Parratt didn't quite know which way to look or how to act. He only just managed to gather himself enough to ask her. "You have the connections?" Without blinking, Harlow nodded once. He turned to Ophelia and almost seemed startled by her close proximity. "You'll have the money?" Ophelia mimicked Harlow's nod. Parratt looked back and forth between them, probably trying to judge their veracity. "You know this isn't a done deal. When we had to pull out before, Arjan didn't take it well."

"Call it a blip," Ophelia said, tightening the weave of her fingers between Harlow's and drawing both their hands higher up Parratt's thigh. "All of us stand to make a huge amount of money from this endeavor… And once we're in, we're in. Yarker was the one who got cold feet and pulled the plug when we lost Ryske. We're not going to do that."

Licking her lips slowly, Harlow got Parratt's attention again. "We won't ask you to pull out."

Ophelia subdued her laugh even after a shiver went through Parratt. "You'll convince Arjan, won't you, Gil?" her ally appealed to their mark.

"I'll do my best," he said, looking at each of them again.

Parratt spent more time looking at Harlow's breasts than her face. The dress she'd chosen was proving its worth. His distraction let Harlow roll her eyes at Ophelia who smiled.

They couldn't sit here all day stroking and fawning. Ophelia seemed to be of the same mind because she pounced to her feet and pulled Parratt up too.

Playing her role as the assured seductress, Harlow stayed on her knees in front of him, like it was a place she was used to being every day of her life. Parratt actually had to shuffle sideways to get out from in front of her. Ophelia was ecstatic as she pushed him along.

"Ten days," Parratt said. "I'm back in town in ten days. If we're on, I'll need the money delivered two weeks today."

"Of course, Gil," Ophelia said, guiding him into the hallway.

Harlow stayed there on her knees on Ophelia's floor listening to the murmurs of the hostess showing Parratt out.

"How'd I do, Crash?" she whispered, straightening her bracelet.

It was Ophelia's scream that hailed the hostess' return. Harlow leaped up fearing something had happened. Only when she saw her new friend's grin did she know that Parratt was gone and they were in the clear… for that night anyway.

Ophelia dashed around the couch and pulled her into a hug. She pulled back to look into her face and then hugged her again.

"Oh my God!" Ophelia shrieked. "Now I understand why he fell in love with you!"

It took some amount of effort to squeeze out of her friend's embrace. Nice though it was to please Ophelia, the adrenaline hadn't subsided enough for her to relax and enjoy it.

"Do you think Parratt will do it?"

Strolling over to the drink Harlow had left on the mantelpiece, Ophelia finished it in one gulp. "He will. Parratt is all about sex and we basically just told him he could have it if he followed through. I know it didn't seem like it tonight, but he is articulate. He'll convince this Arjan that we're solid and we'll be back on…"

"And Arjan is…"

"His European contact," Ophelia said. "Our supplier… Gil will take care of him. All we have to do is get our money together. Are you on track?"

"I'm on track."

Pretending to be confident on the outside was easier than being confident on the inside. The truth? She wasn't close to having the money. Even with two more weeks of the casino, she doubted it would make half a million dollars. If Dover had been making a quarter of a million a week, he'd have been able to afford to fix the gutters at Floyd's.

Ophelia went to fill the sherry glass and picked up another like she planned to pour a second drink.

"None for me," Harlow said. "I have to go."

"What?" Ophelia asked with obvious disappointment. "I thought we could celebrate."

"I have somewhere to be," she said, backing toward the door. "Thank you for tonight. You are a pro…"

Ophelia rushed over and kissed each of her cheeks, then kept hold of her shoulders to examine her. "I can't work out if you're scared to get close to anyone because of Ryske or if you're just afraid to get close to me."

"Either way, it's about him, right?"

Blaming Ryske was meant to be a lighthearted quip, but it killed her high as she slipped out of the apartment. That man had carried her through the evening. He'd be the one to get her through this.

As for how else he'd changed her? She was still figuring that out.

ELEVEN

TEN DAYS WENT FASTER than expected. It was a bonus because time hadn't exactly been flying since she'd lost Ryske.

Floyd's gave her a distraction that made her less aware of what she'd lost and more aware of what had to be done. Running the bar and their casino nights kept her so busy that there wasn't much time left to dwell.

Ophelia had called her to say they were on. Parratt convinced Arjan that the deal was a sure thing. Now it was their turn to come up with the goods.

She couldn't bury her head in the sand any longer. The deadline was looming. Every day she'd been hoping something would turn up. It hadn't. Half a million dollars wasn't easy to pull together. If it was, everyone would be doing it all the time.

During her search of Floyd's, she'd found statements for a few bank accounts. Even if she emptied all of them, plus her own, and hocked what little jewelry she might be able to scare up at her parents—if she dared venture there and risk an inquisition—she'd still only have about twenty percent of what she needed, twenty-five percent at most.

The hard truth was, she couldn't pull the money together on her own.

Clyde wouldn't have that kind of money and probably wouldn't agree with her plan, so there was no point appealing to him for help. Her former colleague had visited Floyd's several times. Sometimes he tried to probe into what she had going on. Whenever he'd asked if she still had a plan for payback, Harlow went with vague and pivoted to whatever new thing she'd done at the bar.

Her plan for payback was all that mattered, which was why she'd swallowed her pride, and come to the threshold of her last hope.

Sweeting Securities, or SweSec as the family called it, had its offices on the corner of a beautiful Art Deco building in an area adjacent to the city's main financial district. The lobby was marble and the carpets beyond a deep red.

Though she'd only been there a handful of times since she and Rupert had broken up, the security men were the same and recognized her. They didn't hesitate to wave her through the bullpen where walk-ins were seen. To the right, deeper in the heart of the building was a vault used to house a bunch of safety deposit boxes and confidential files.

At the back of the bullpen was a set of double doors that led to the offices and boardrooms used by more senior members of the company.

Turning her head to the side, she hid her profile from Brysen Sweeting's office. Harlow didn't know if her father was in or occupied, but she didn't want to find out. If he caught her, he'd call her mother, and then she'd be peppered with questions she didn't have the answers for.

Without being too obvious about it, she hurried along the corridor and tapped on the familiar door with the fogged panel.

"Yeah," came the call from inside.

Peeking around the door, she couldn't help but smile at Rupert working behind his desk. For years, while they were together, any time they planned to spend time in the city, for dinner or maybe to see a play, she'd come to this office and seen him in exactly the same place, doing exactly the same thing.

When he looked up, she grinned at his surprise and

slipped in, closing the door behind herself. "I'm sorry to just show up."

"No," Rupert said, leaping to his feet and opening a hand to the chair on the other side of the desk. "No, sit down. You're always welcome."

Polite was the response she'd been counting on. Rupert may not be so accommodating after she explained what had brought her to him.

She went and sat down while he came around the desk to prop himself against her side of it. "Thank you."

"Are you okay?" he asked. "It's been weeks since I heard from you. You just walked out the hotel and your parents—"

"I know," she said. "I'm sorry. I didn't mean to worry any of you. I promise, I'm fine."

He smiled and leaned back, folding his arms across his chest that had been her pillow for so many nights.

If only it could've worked out with him, her life would've been so much easier. He was handsome and athletic, an amazing catch. Some woman would be lucky to have him, it just wouldn't be her.

"So to what do I owe the pleasure? If you need somewhere to stay, I—"

"No, it's not that," she said, bolstering her courage and wrinkling her nose figuring that all she could do was come out with it. "I need a half a million dollars."

His relaxed expression froze; his loose body grew rigid in increments. For a moment, he just looked at her, and she was happy to give him time to absorb what she'd said.

"Half a million dollars," he said, leaving the proximity of his familiar perch to saunter back around to his side of the desk.

Taking that as an indication he was switching on his professional mode, she didn't know if that was a good sign for her or not.

"I know it's a lot of money," she said. He blew out an incredulous breath in agreement. "I wouldn't be asking if it wasn't important."

He made eye contact. "Is it him? Does he need it for

something?" She shook her head. "Are you in trouble?"

"No, I'm not in trouble," she said, omitting that she would be if she didn't come up with the dough.

Clearing his throat, he seemed to have come to terms with her request. "There's fifty thousand in the wedding account."

"Oh my God, you still have that?"

He nodded. "Your parents and my mother did offer to match whatever we saved… I'm not sure they'd stand by that without a wedding though."

His smile made her laugh. It was her being polite. Seemed right to be kind to him. She was asking a lot and appreciated him not making her beg.

"Anything else? Can you get me a loan?"

Squirming, he scratched the back of his head. "Uh, you don't have collateral or anything for me to invest… do you?" She shook her head. "I'm sorry, Harlow, I can't authorize that amount without some sort of assurance."

Slumping back, she didn't know what else she'd be able to conjure up. Even if she took the full fifty thousand from him, and came up with a maximum of twenty-five percent elsewhere, she'd still be nowhere near the required total.

His next exhale sounded more like a sigh. "I'll get you the money."

Perking up, she sat straight and smiled at him. "You will? Oh, thank you! I'll pay it back, as fast as I can. I know the paperwork won't be easy with daddy asking questions, but—"

"I can't give you an official loan through SweSec," he said. "For one thing, you're family. In an audit that would flag us to the SEC given you're a questionable investment with indeterminate solvency."

The last thing she wanted to do was endanger her family's company in any way. "Then I don't understand. How—"

"You know I have savings and my grandfather left us that inheritance."

Shaking her head, she couldn't believe he was

suggesting a personal favor. "No, Rupe, I couldn't even think about—"

"You came here for money, I'll get you the money. When do you need it?"

"Rupert, I don't know if I'm comfortable with this," she said, taking a shot squirming.

He smiled and turned his hands up. "You wouldn't have come here with this request unless it was important… and I'm guessing this wasn't your first choice."

She couldn't deny that. If she walked out of there without taking him up on his offer, she may always regret it. Without the money, the plan was over. There was nowhere else to turn. After letting Ryske down and failing to get payback, she wouldn't be able to stay at Floyd's. The renewed connection would be severed for good. It was accept Rupert's offer or admit defeat.

"I will pay you back," she said, surrendering to the only option. "I don't know when or how, but I—"

"You don't have to pay me back, Harlow," he said, which surprised her. "If you come home."

She hadn't believed Rupert was the kind of man who'd ever suggest… what it sounded like he was suggesting.

"You'll give me five hundred thousand dollars in exchange for sex?"

Her incredulity amused him. "No," he said. "Home for good."

That stunned her more than when she'd thought he was asking for just sex. "What?"

He became serious. "In the hotel lobby on the night of the SweSec event, you told me to find the love I deserve. But, Harlow, the only woman I've ever loved is you. You're the woman I don't want to give up."

He meant it. Harlow knew this man better than anyone else. They'd been together for years, seen each other through the tough times and the easier ones. They'd been there for each other, celebrated and commiserated together. They'd planned to spend their lives together. At least, he'd envisioned his with her in it. Harlow wasn't so clear on what she'd seen.

She needed to give this half million to Parratt in just a couple of days. Time was up. This was it; she had no alternative.

Although combined the consortium was laying down a significant investment, no one offered any guarantee of when she'd see a return. Even when they did, she'd be at the bottom of the pile when they were handing out dividends.

Whatever they made back would go toward overhead costs first. As it stood, they'd have to wait after making the investment for the product to be produced and delivered. It could take months to build a customer base, and longer still before they started to see any return. Even then, she could be outvoted. Any equity could be invested back into the company rather than be returned as dividends... if criminal enterprises even worked that way.

Money wasn't her motivation. Reminding herself of that allowed her to nod. The chance of coming out of this with her life and liberty were slim. She was prepared to die or go to jail. Either was a possibility. In that event, she wouldn't hold Rupert to the deal.

"I need to do this," she said. "This thing with the money... give me some time, let me take care of this... thing I need to take care of... then we can talk about the future."

He smiled. "Our future."

It wasn't so easy for her to smile. Rupert didn't notice her discomfort because he was busy retrieving his wallet.

"Our future," she muttered.

Ryske was going to get his way after all. Even in death he was manipulating her.

Rupert stood up. "Come on, we'll go to the bank together."

Go to the bank and retrieve the money she'd need to avenge her deceased lover. The money that would tie her to the ex who wanted her back.

Life was getting more complicated by the day. Despite being tangled in a web of her own making, somehow, she felt relief. At least she wasn't letting Ryske down. She was going through with the plan and making progress. Every day was progress.

TWELVE

PARRATT ACCEPTED THEIR MONEY at the arranged Saturday meeting in Ophelia's apartment. His attitude disclosed that he expected a carnal celebration of their partnership. Ophelia saved them from the chore of getting horizontal by implying they wanted their return before he got his.

After that necessity was over with, she'd returned to her base. Going through the motions each day, in a tense wait for news of what would come next, Floyd's became her routine.

Clyde pestered her for information about her payback plan. To placate him, she'd let slip that Rupert helped her out, though her friend didn't know with what.

Implying that she had Rupert's blessing was an unintentional deception. The sentiment had gotten away from her because after discovering that her ex approved, Clyde backed off. That assumption seemed to give him the confidence to stop questioning her about what she was doing.

Compartmentalizing meant always remembering she couldn't trust any one person with everything.

Vengeance was emotionally exhausting.

Clyde wanted her to embrace the life she was building

now that he acknowledged she could handle herself at Floyd's. Costello was becoming a good friend too. They spent a lot of time training. Her fighting skills got better by the day… She was no pro but could defend herself in a pinch.

The next trick was going to be Jarvis Hagan finding out the identity of his new business partners. Ophelia asked Parratt not to reveal that they were involved. He confirmed that Hagan knew there was a new investor, but Parratt hadn't been drawn on their identity.

No doubt Hagan was dubious; he'd be an idiot not to be. She didn't care if he drove himself mad speculating, that was sort of half the fun.

Two weeks after they'd handed over their share of the investment to Parratt, Harlow and Ophelia had another meeting to attend. This time, it wasn't in Ophelia's apartment. The consortium was coming together at the same hotel Hagan had taken her to after keeping her prisoner in his apartment. The same hotel, and the same room.

In that room, Hagan would get the surprise of his life. He'd find out the truth of who he'd gotten into bed with… so to speak.

On the phone, before the day of the meeting, Harlow and Ophelia agreed to arrive together and not on time. Making a confident entrance would be crucial in letting the male members of the consortium know the women weren't intimidated.

Still, it was a risk. The others would have a chance to settle in, so she and Ophelia wouldn't know exactly what they were walking into.

But it was the decision they'd made, they had to own it.

Walking down the almost sterile gray corridor in the bowels of the hotel, she remembered the first time she'd been there, following Ryske's ass.

Grazing her fingertips under her bracelet, she touched the star tattooed on her wrist. "'Til we're dirt in the ground," she whispered.

Ophelia stopped at the last door, which had a security panel barring access without a code. "Did you say something?"

Widening her smile, Harlow tapped the vicious point of her full-finger ring on her chin and smiled. "Nope."

Ophelia returned the look. "You look like a badass, by the way."

It was difficult not to laugh. In her black leather mini-dress with her hair slicked back, she felt like one.

She leaned past Ophelia to type in the same code Ryske used to get them inside and replied, "I know."

The keypad flashed green and, in homage to her love, she winked at Ophelia. Her cohort laughed and threw open the door allowing them to stride in.

Of the two couches perpendicular to the grand fireplace, Parratt and Yarker were seated on the one facing the door. The pair had been in the same place the last time too. Though, this time, there was no extra woman.

Hagan was present as well, but he wasn't sitting down. The man paced back and forth in front of the fireplace, a few feet from Parratt and Yarker.

The moment he saw them, he stopped.

One corner of her mouth curled in satisfaction. Her hip copped a little attitude too. "Hello, Jarvis," she murmured and winked.

His mouth fell open. "What…" he stuttered, looking at his sister then at the men on the couch. Harlow's focus didn't waver from him; she wanted to absorb every second of this moment. "What the hell is this…? What the hell is she doing here…? What the hell happened to you?"

"Well…" Harlow said, swaying her hips as she went toward him. "Someone reminded me I have a duty to fulfill."

Incredulity and disbelief joined his shock. "That was… weeks ago."

"Five to be exact," she said, raising the point of her ring to the angle of his jaw.

The moment the silver made contact, Hagan snatched her wrist, clamping her bracelet beneath his grip. The pinch of the metal digging into her skin reminded her Ryske was with her.

"Cocky for a dead woman," Hagan hissed.

She tsked and shook her head, blinking innocent eyes from him to the couch and back. "Is that any way to talk to your business partner, Jarvis?"

Throwing her hand from his grip, he spun to face their associates. "You cannot let her be a part of this! I don't know how she conned you into it, but you don't know who she is, or why she's here."

Ophelia sank onto the couch opposite Parratt and Yarker's. In the center of the coffee table between the two couches was a miniature test tube stand. In it were three tiny glass vials with clear rubber stoppers. Each of the three tubes contained a foggy purple liquid.

"She's here because she's my partner," Ophelia said, smiling at her brother who stammered in response. "Harlow and I decided this deal was too good to pass up."

"I can't believe you would be this ridiculous, Ophelia," Hagan barked. "You stupid girl. This is a manipulation! She's using you! This is all revenge! This is about the fucking bastard who—"

"Do we have to listen to your tantrum?" Ophelia asked, feigning a yawn then turning her hand to check her manicure.

"She's right," Parratt said. "It's done, Hagan. You can bluster all you like. But the investment has been made."

Yarker opened his hand to the vials on the table. "We have samples."

Everyone's focus settled on the tubes.

"What are we supposed to do with them?" Ophelia asked.

Harlow had a sneaking suspicion what was expected.

"Test them," Yarker said.

Suspicion confirmed.

"Did you just proposition my sister?" Hagan barked. "Are you suggesting that you pigs fuck my sister?"

"No, no… I…"

Yarker was a wuss at the best of times, and having seen how easily Parratt could be reduced to a gullible hormone, she didn't expect him to put up much opposition.

His next suggestion chilled her.

"Ophelia may keep her virtue," Parratt said. "We have a professional on the team."

As though she was as inanimate as the vials on the table, everyone's attention swung around to her. The sheer smug satisfaction on Hagan's face was nausea-inducing. For a moment, he let his gaze trickle down her body and back up, proving how much he savored every second of her resentment.

Full of confidence, he side-stepped and plucked a vial from the stand. "Wonder if he'll turn in his grave when you climax with me inside you," Hagan said, holding the sample toward her.

She batted it out of his hand. "Never," she spat.

Yarker squawked and dropped to the floor on his hands and knees, scrambling to find the dose of Pothos she'd just let skitter away.

"You don't have a choice, Miss Sweeting," Hagan said, lunging down to grab another vial. "You'll open your legs on command."

"Hagan!" Parratt called.

Hagan wasn't listening. He was intent on his purpose. Grabbing her wrist, he wrestled her into his arms, attempting to kiss her. Try as he might, he couldn't land his mouth on hers. Harlow turned her head this way and that, fighting to get away.

Through Ophelia's screaming and Parratt's objections, Harlow fought, determined not to let Hagan have her. She couldn't let him do it. Before giving in or letting Jarvis Hagan have the pleasure of her body, she would let every other man in this building, this city, go first.

In the struggle, Hagan forced her behind the couch and down onto the table there. Getting between her thighs, he kept her pinned while trying to pull the stopper from the vial with his teeth.

"No!" she screamed, kicking at him.

His preoccupation with the Pothos sample gave her a window to free her arm. With as much force as she could muster, Harlow lashed out, stabbing the point of her ring into him. Ironically, the spot she hit wouldn't be that far from where Ryske was stabbed above his hip.

Hagan screamed and the vial dropped from his clutches. He staggered back, looking down at the blood spreading on his shirt. From point to her knuckle where the ring had stopped was only about two inches, so the wound wouldn't be fatal. But for a man who'd never been stabbed before, it had to be a shock.

Crunching up, she couldn't disguise her disgust and sneered at him. "Now your scars will match," she hissed.

Cupping his wound, Hagan looked at the blood on his hand and then up at her.

In a snap, rage quaked through him. "You bitch!"

He backhanded her with such force she tumbled off the table. Harlow was quick to pounce to her feet, but she couldn't get away. Hagan grabbed her hair and yanked her forward. The rattle of him loosening his belt verified this was no bluff.

Thrusting her hand up, she went for the throat, but he blocked and swept her hand away. "I'm gonna fucking kill you!" she screamed.

"Not before I fuck you," Hagan growled, pulling her to the ends of her toes to get right in her face. "And you're going to fucking love it."

"No!"

In her flailing, she managed to scratch the side of his neck with her ring. Hearing him hiss in pain gave her a shot of satisfaction. His hand left her hair to close over the slice on his neck.

Before she could get away, he hit her again, sending her down onto the table, which gave Hagan the opportunity to plant an arm on her chest, pinning her down.

Bending over her, he used his body to hold hers and stole her wrists to slam them down. This time when he got close to her face, she turned her head as far to the side as it would go and closed her eyes.

He kissed her cheekbone and trailed his lips to her ear. "To the victor go the spoils," he murmured.

Maybe it was his sinister laugh that brought home the reality of this instant. Whatever it was, the concept of him being victorious delivered a potent shot of adrenaline. She stopped panicking to focus.

Only a cool head, and Costello's training, would keep her alive. Judging Hagan's position, she waited for the optimum moment to utilize the greatest force. When he was there, she brought her head up fast, head-butting him hard.

The impact dazed Hagan enough that he loosened his grip.

Within seconds, she folded her legs against her body to plant her feet on his chest. Using every ounce of her lower body strength, she propelled him away. Still in a stupor, Hagan stumbled backwards and fell hard to the floor. He sat there blinking, probably trying to figure out how the tables had turned so fast.

She leaped off the table and grabbed a handful of his hair to tug his head back, exposing the soft vulnerability of his neck.

"Enjoy the spoils," she growled, preparing to strike.

The point of her ring was primed to meet the center of his throat in a hit that would kill him for sure. She planned to twist and drag, just like Costello taught her, and rip out Hagan's throat, then she'd dance on the bastard's corpse.

In the very second she intended to plunge the metal into him, the din behind was silenced by one voice. "Trinket, stop!"

THIRTEEN

NO… IT… NO…

The only way that voice made sense was if Hagan triumphed. He must've won and this was some in-the-midst-of-dying, out of body, something…

Numb. She was numb. Her fingers slipped from the victor's hair. Shuffling forward, Hagan fell against the back of the couch, using it to hold himself high on his knees.

In her peripheral vision, his position was revealed. Ryske. She hadn't moved. She wouldn't turn, couldn't.

Eerie silence hung in the air; its intensity kicked up her pulse. Harlow couldn't do it; she couldn't bring herself to believe that there was any chance…

"Oh my God," Ophelia whispered.

"But you're…" Hagan said, "you're dead."

Harlow's eyes closed slowly and a single tear fell. Not a tear of joy or even of sorrow. It was a tear of hope; one that wished she was dead and this was an afterlife experience. The alternative was too disgusting to contemplate.

"Well, I ain't been living."

That voice. It was his voice. She couldn't doubt it. Whether she'd joined him or he her, she existed again with him. Yet confronting it wasn't possible, she couldn't turn around and look into the face of betrayal.

"You're supposed to be dead," Hagan said, struggling to climb onto his feet.

"You can't always get what you want, Hagan," he said, part mocking, but also imparting wisdom.

"Oh my God," Ophelia said again, her voice a little stronger, and a lot happier. "Oh my God! Oh my God!"

"What the hell is going on?" Parratt asked.

Harlow knew the answer to that. She'd been duped. Damn, the lie had been a good one. She'd fallen for it like a naïve idiot.

Keeping her head dipped while turning, there was no way she wanted to seek him out, to see more than was absolutely necessary. Ophelia hung off him. Thrilled, her ally's exuberance at her fiancé's return saved Harlow from meeting anyone's eye.

The rabble escalated again as the consortium questioned what was going on and how this had happened.

Not her.

Harlow went straight to the door and strode out.

Without slowing down, she walked the length of the service corridor and round to the perpendicular one.

"Harlow!"

The sound of him calling out carried just a fraction of a second before the door closed behind her. All she wanted was to be out of there. If she could have erased herself from the world in that minute, she'd have done it.

But that wasn't possible. There was nothing to do, nowhere to go, she had to think fast.

"Trinket!" he called again.

For months, she'd wished to hear that pet name again. Now the moment was there, she wished it would go the hell away.

Bursting into the hotel ballroom, where the guests were enjoying a live music act while consuming late meals, she got her first break of the night. This room was familiar. There was liquor here.

Winding through the tables to reach the bar, she slapped down a hand, startling the bartender just a couple of feet away.

"I need two double Jack Daniels and a phone," she said, narrowing her eyes. "Do you have a phone?"

"Yes, ma'am," he said, probably wondering why she was dressed in a less refined way than the others in the room.

Black leather didn't scream sophistication. The live act was playing lounge music, this wasn't a rock concert. Silk and cashmere surrounded them and there wasn't a smoky eye in sight… other than hers.

People came up at her side. She felt their presence but wouldn't look at them. Why should she? How could she? Her eyes fixed straight ahead. Earlier, murder had been on her mind and the impulse hadn't been vented. The chance it would burst out of her was very real.

"Harlow," Ophelia squealed. "Look who it is!"

"I'd rather not," she grumbled.

The bartender returned with her drinks and the phone. After emptying one of the glasses into her throat, she dialed and used it to block out those loitering at her side.

It rang a few times.

"Floyd's," Tom answered.

"Hey, babe, everything good?" she asked, trying to keep her voice light.

"Yeah," Tom said. "No problems."

The bartender passed and Harlow snapped her fingers at him. "Another double," she said and threw her second drink into her mouth, swallowing it in one.

"You okay?" Tom asked.

"Yeah," she said and cleared her throat against the sting of liquor. "Anyone… unexpected there?"

If Ryske was here, the rest of his crew could be on their way home too.

"Uh…" Tom said like maybe she was nuts. "No." He laughed. "Who you expecting?"

"I don't expect unexpected people," she hissed for the benefit of those at her side. "I need you to shut it down."

"Shut… what?"

Tom might think he was shocked, but she'd only just learned the true definition of the word. Anything she'd experienced in the past didn't even come close.

"Shut it down. Clear the place out. Everything. Get rid of it all."

"You're not… you're not serious. Are you okay?"

"Yes," she said. "I'm peachy. Can you get it done?"

"Yeah. Nightingale—"

"Don't call me that," she snapped. "Don't ever call me that again… Just get it done."

Hanging up on Tom, she dialed again. The bartender brought her drink, and she took a mouthful. The numbers on the phone blurred; it was the alcohol, nothing else. Not emotion. She wouldn't let it be emotion.

"You're mad," Ryske said. His voice grated so much that she winced. "I get that, Trink. Will you let me explain?"

"He's here! He's alive."

Ophelia was ecstatic, that much was obvious. Just a shame she couldn't share the exuberance.

Giving up on dialing the phone, she finished her drink and tore the bracelet from her wrist to toss it at the bartender. "That should cover it."

At a loss, the bartender held it up. "This?"

"Yeah," she said. "It's worth more than it looks. I got it from a corpse. But I just found out that corpse was a lying, cheating asshole… Guess that's not fair, I already knew about the lying… and the cheating, so the asshole part wasn't a leap, right?"

"Funny," Ryske muttered.

She couldn't be less interested in anything he had to say. Spinning around, she put her back to them and stormed through the lobby, out onto the street. The frigid night hit hard. Not that she cared about the temperature. All she cared about was putting distance between her and whatever mindfuck she'd just endured.

"Harlow!" This time, Ophelia called after her. "Harlow! Hear him out!"

What the hell was Ryske going to say that she would buy? Go with it? Ha, that was a joke, and it was on her. Slowing at the corner, she waited for the intersection to clear.

That gave Ophelia a chance to catch up. "What is

wrong?" Ophelia asked, grabbing for her hand. Harlow snatched it out of reach. "Har, talk to me. Why aren't you over the moon?"

"Because I grieved the bastard," she said, catching the barest glimpse of him approaching.

Just the hint of him in her periphery diverted her attention back to the passing traffic.

"Trink, I was protecting you. You knew the plan, what was going to happen between us, what we talked about. I let you be free. I gave you the chance to—"

"Oh, you know what?" Rage compelled her to spin on him. "That's such a crock of…"

Her eyes cut to his and that was it, the words stopped. Ryske. Right there in front of her, tall and broad… healthy. A keen light in his eyes spoke of determination… and lust.

"Hello, Trinket," he murmured and smiled.

"Oh my God."

Harlow couldn't breathe. The whole city paused. No, the *world* was on standby and she was frozen within it.

Confident and slow, he moseyed closer. One hand slid out of his pocket and rose to skim her cheek with the softest of touches. The contact somehow relaxed her head and her eyes grew heavy.

The awareness of his lips meeting hers was a dream. A barest brush of mouths. It didn't take long for him to press harder, to build the moment until he could coax her lips apart to let his tongue stroke hers.

Ryske's kiss always had the power to intoxicate her and there on the street, she forgot herself. Harlow couldn't remember being mad or scared. All she could remember was being without him and the desperation she'd existed in for so long.

In the nights she'd wept for him, or spoken to him in the shadows, she'd promised to endure anything if it meant having the chance to taste him again. There he was, granting her wish.

"Crash," she breathed, her hands trailing up his body under his jacket to clutch at his tee-shirt.

"It's me. I've got you, baby."

Scooping his hand around to the back of her skull, he held her slicked hair in a tight fist, eased her head back and opened his mouth, begging more. She gave it, unable to deny him anything while caught up in satisfying their need.

He was here. The man she'd been fighting for was holding her, kissing her, loving her. It was over. She had him back. She didn't have to fight anymore, didn't have to cry and hurt.

Except, she wouldn't have gone through that trauma if he hadn't lied to her. And it wasn't a little lie. It was a lie that changed not only the course of her life, but the fiber of her being.

Pressing on his chest, she broke their kiss to search his eyes. Obvious in their need, his drowsy scrutiny burned with desire for her. Could she trust them? Could she trust anything of him ever again? What was his agenda this time? Why had he come back? Why was he here?

Slowly, her head moved side to side in a loose shake. "No," she whispered, retreating from his arms.

His smile faded as a frown creased his brow. "Trink—"

"You didn't do it for me at all," she said, unable to believe or to trust. "You don't do anything for anyone but you… This is a lie."

"A lie?" he said, grabbing her wrist to squash her palm against the prominent erection in his jeans. "Is that a lie, baby?"

Instinct drove her hand to his cheek in a slap that echoed down the block. "You think I gave a damn about that?" she hissed. "Do you think I did all of this for that?"

Teeth clenched, he brought his head around from where her slap sent it. "Harlow."

"Is that why you came back, baby?" she asked, spitting out the endearment. "Get lonely in the shower? Fuck you."

Turning, she intended to leave, but he snatched hold of her and hauled her back. Whirling around, she brought the point of her ring to the soft underside of his jaw, forcing his head back.

"Trinket," he growled.

"You saw what I did to the last man who tried to take from me, and I have no other dead lovers who'll swoop in to save you," she murmured. "Let me go or lose the life you weren't all that fond of anyway."

His fingers unfurled one at a time. "Carpe noctem, Trink."

It was then she noticed the bracelet on her wrist, he must have paid for the drinks, and put it back during a kiss. No surprise, she'd have missed an earthquake while caught up in his kiss.

Ryske was no longer the only one good at hiding his emotions; her poker face was in top form. She blinked her gaze away from the bracelet like it was nothing to her.

When he let her go, she backed off, opening her arms. "Don't you worry about that, Ryske…" Harlow winked at him. "These days, I'm a girl who knows how to have a good time."

With her fingers in her mouth, she whistled to stop a cab. Ryske took a step toward her as she slipped into the back. Thankfully, Ophelia got in his way, which provided a perfect opportunity for escape.

The couple on the sidewalk argued, distracting each other. Good. That disharmony gave Harlow a window to tell the driver her destination. Though where she went from there was anyone's guess.

FOURTEEN

"HE'S ALIVE!" Harlow exclaimed, striding into Clyde's apartment the minute he opened the door.

She went into the kitchen and retrieved whiskey from the cabinet to swig it straight from the bottle. More alcohol probably wasn't smart. Drunk, she wouldn't be capable of smart choices. Though events proved that even sober, smart choices weren't her forte. But if there was ever a good reason to make dumb choices, Ryske had given it to her.

"And you don't want him to be alive," Clyde said, appearing in her field of vision. "Wait… are you telling me your whole plan was to kill the guy? Are you nuts, Harlow? You can't murder someone."

Lowering the bottle, she squinted. "What? Who are you talking about?"

"This Hagan person. That's his name, isn't it? Or was it his guy? The one you call Alleyman. Is that who you were going for? I can't believe you would think about—"

"Murder?" she asked, slugging down more liquor. "I almost killed Hagan. I wouldn't have lost a second of sleep over it either. Do you know who stopped me?"

"Who?" he asked and shook his head. "No, I don't know who would have the power to—"

"Ryske."

"Ryske," he said and then paused as he realized what he'd said. "Wait… Ryske?"

Harlow could identify with the slow look of shock creeping across his face. It wasn't every day that someone came back from the dead.

With an outstretched arm, she offered him the bottle. He took it to gulp.

Going past Clyde, she went into the living room. "I'll admit, it did occur to me," she said like she was telling a story. "It did. For the briefest second, when we were outside the hospital and I was all grief-stricken that maybe his body had been abandoned…" Spinning on the spot, she dropped to let the couch catch her, and held up her thumb and forefinger an inch apart. "I thought about it for that long. I thought maybe, just maybe, those bastards had pulled something like this… I let it go. Stupid fucking bitch. I let it go."

Clyde paused in his descent to the end of the couch beside her. "You swear more these days than you used to."

Snatching the bottle, it felt better having it in her grip. "It's a new habit. I'm taking it up along with alcoholism and celibacy."

And because the liquid smelled like oblivion, she drank.

"Is that blood?" Clyde asked, eyeing her ring.

"Mm," she said, removing her lips from the bottle. "I did stab him."

"Ryske?"

"Hagan," she said and got a nod in return.

In silence, they both needed time to absorb the news. She'd had more time to process. So while Clyde languished in shock, her appreciation of the irony bloomed. Her lips twitched once, then again before they curved, and a laugh burst out.

The conversation was so normal. Compared to what else had happened that night, it was almost benign. Somewhere there had been a transition, but she'd missed it. Going about her life, taking each day as it came, she'd missed the moment when it had become normal for her to discuss murder like it was inevitable.

The laughter kept on coming. She couldn't get it together.

Clyde snatched the bottle and slammed it onto the table. Her laughter got louder and louder, increasing in its mania. Her friend grabbed hold of her, forcing her body around to face his.

"Harlow," he said, becoming stern. "Harlow, stop it. Har!" Giving her a shake, his worry was more tangible than rage. "Harlow!"

Sucking in a long breath, she released it in a groan. "Oh, what am I going to do now, Clyde? What the fuck did I do to my life for him?"

"You did what you had to do," he said, brushing her stiff hair from her temple. "You did what you thought was right."

"He's alive," she said, feeling the effects of the alcohol. "He never needed me to avenge him. Now I'm half a mill lighter, two tattoos up, and all I have to show for it is this lousy bracelet."

Raising her arm was easy. Bringing herself to look at the object that had given her comfort for more than four months was harder.

"He's an asshole," Clyde said. "But you've built a life here. You're not going to let him take it away from you… are you?"

"What choice do I have?" she asked. "I fell for it hook, line, and sinker… I'll bet the money is all he wanted anyway."

"This half a mill you just mentioned?" She nodded. "How did you give him half a million dollars if you thought he was dead?"

Too tired to explain, she wriggled out of Clyde's grip and slumped against the back of the couch. "It was supposed to be an investment."

"An investment goes into something," he said. "So the money's still there? Has it been spent?"

"Who knows?" she asked, pushing up a little to get more comfortable. "I stabbed one of my business partners tonight. I'd say my role in the operation is over."

His frown was set when he took her arms and pulled her upright. "I don't like seeing you this way."

"Drunk?" she asked and tried to reach over him for the booze, but he held her away from it. "I manage a bar, you know. If I want to get liquored up, I can…"

No, she couldn't. Floyd's wasn't her home anymore. It was over. It was all over.

"You're not going to let him get away with this," Clyde said. "We're not going to let him get away with it. You're going to get your money back."

"I don't give a damn about the money," she said, though that wasn't really fair. It wasn't her money not to care about. That said, having the investment returned was irrelevant to both her and Rupert. Repayment of the half mill wouldn't have anything to do with cash. Cold, and a little fazed, she was like a ragdoll, swinging and sagging. "I'll be paying that back for the rest of my life."

"I don't understand," Clyde said. "You haven't trusted me with your plan until now. I always thought it was about protecting Ryske. You don't have to do that anymore. So tell me, trust me."

There was no way out. Clyde didn't get it. She'd dug herself into a hole. And she'd been confident there until Ryske came along with his shovel to fill it in, burying her alive.

"I don't care," she whispered. "I don't care about anything."

At least when fighting for Ryske she could feel love for him and determination in her cause. Earlier in the grief process, the only emotions she'd been able to feel were connected to Ryske. Now, there was nothing to feel.

"There are things you care about," Clyde said, stroking her face. "You feel this way now because you're in shock. But you are not going to let him get away with making a fool of you. You're sure not going to roll over and let him keep doing it. You built Floyd's back up. You did that. You opened those doors. You got yourself invested in whatever this thing is. None of that goes away just because that jerk chose to show his face. This is better. It is. You're going to hold your head up. You have people who care about you, people who want to see you succeed."

"I don't care."

He shook her hard. "You do! You care, Harlow Sweeting. I know you do because I've seen your determination. I've seen how you can achieve anything when you put your mind to it, and that's exactly what you're going to do. You're going to get some sleep and wake up fresh. You're going to go over to Floyd's, get your stuff, and tell your friends exactly what kind of an asshole Ryske is."

Was she? Harlow didn't care about things, and she wasn't sure she cared what people thought about Ryske. He'd only convince them otherwise anyway. He was a pro who could convince anyone of anything, even the most resistant mind. He'd managed to convince her he was dead and she definitely hadn't wanted to believe that.

"I was full of fight," she said. "I thought I was capable of anything. You should've seen me tonight, Clyde. I was… I was on fire."

"And you're going to use that to see this through… get your money back and then have the life you want."

The life she wanted. That was a punchline in itself. Harlow hadn't been sure what she wanted before tonight other than to achieve her short-term goals for payback. Now her life was in the wringer and she couldn't unwring it. Why should she even try?

"I can't," she whispered, her head moving side to side. "I can't do it anymore. I'm done. I'm through… I can't go it alone anymore."

"Harlow," he whispered, his thumb tracing from her jaw to her cheekbone. His lips quirked a fraction and he shook his head. "You're not alone, sweetheart."

All she could do when he leaned in to kiss her was stay as still as possible. Clyde had been her friend through all of this. He hadn't lied to her. He'd told her the truth even when she hadn't wanted to hear it.

But this? She hadn't thought for a second he had any kind of attraction to her.

His kiss wasn't as consuming as Ryske's. In fact, it set

her mind into speed-think mode. Sleeping with Clyde would be a great way to show Ryske he was nothing to her, that he had no impact on her choices.

Horror pushed Clyde away.

Had she really just considered using her friend to get back at the man who'd destroyed her life?

Panicked, she leaped to her feet.

"Harlow, I'm sorry."

Talking was beyond her ability. She didn't know what would come out of her mouth if she tried. Getting up, getting going, getting out of there, those were automatic actions. Clyde called to her, but she didn't slow or so much as pause for breath at the door while walking out.

This night began full of optimism. Sure, there had been anxiety; there was no way to deny that when the stakes were so great. In spite of those nerves, she'd been certain the night would end on a high.

How wrong she'd been.

Wandering the streets without aim, it didn't matter that she would look a mess to gawkers walking by. Harlow felt too alone to notice anyone else. Minutes could have passed, or maybe it was hours of feeling ragged and numb. In a daze, detached from reality, making decisions and setting goals was impossible. Nothing made sense anymore. When her tears began to fall, they were a welcome progression.

Once sensation awakened again, she considered her options and came to the quick conclusion that three choices existed.

Clarity stopped her.

In seconds, she recognized her location. The spot where she'd met Ryske. Roaming without purpose brought her there, to the point where it all began. Something in her subconscious had steered her in the same direction she'd been walking that night.

Back then, she'd been innocent to what love was and how deep betrayal could cut. Her job, her life, her move to the city, they'd all been on her mind the night Ryske came barreling down that alleyway and crashed into her.

Life had never been the same since.

So there she was, at a proverbial cross roads. Harlow could give up and go home to Rupert, a good man waiting to welcome her back with open arms. She could do as Clyde had suggested and fight to get her money back. Or there was the third choice…

Turning her hands, she looked at the vulnerable, soft flesh of her forearms. Pressing the point of her ring to the inside of her wrist, she increased the pressure until the sting became pain.

It would serve him right. Hurting herself right there on that spot would send a clear message to him about what he'd done to her. That wouldn't be symbolic, it would be a harsh slap in the face. But for that to matter, she had to believe she meant something to him in the first place.

Dropping her hands to her sides, option three slithered off the table. Harlow had never been feeble like that. Not that desperate people were feeble, but she would not let herself be taken down by a man, any man, and certainly not Ryske, not for him.

Rupert would wait. He'd told her he would. Her ex wasn't pestering her to come home or asking about repayment yet. Yet.

That left door number two.

Ryske thought he could con her. It was only fair to tip her cap and admit that he had. Crying about it wouldn't change the fact he'd lied and broken her heart. It was her own fault. He'd been open and upfront about what he did from the night they met. His crew had anyway.

They were conmen. Criminals. Crooks. They lied and cheated and got what they wanted without worrying about anything like ridiculous morals or common decency. She was the one who'd ascribed benevolent qualities to them and imagined them as romantic heroes.

Ryske was not a romantic hero. He'd chosen to give her up rather than sacrifice anything about the life he loved. She'd *wanted* him to love her. That's why she believed him in the back of that ambulance when his oxygen starved brain prompted his utterance of those words. He didn't love her. Never had.

She should've known it was impossible for him to love her when he'd been so ready to send her off to Rupert. That was what he'd wanted to happen, even before he was shot.

Life was a bitch and she'd just have to get over it. No one cared if she was hurting or if she walked into a brick wall and bumped her head.

Had she believed losing him sowed her cynicism? Turned out that getting him back had transformed her into a full-blown misanthrope.

Well, if life wanted to fuck with her, she'd fuck with it right back.

FIFTEEN

COSTELLO HADN'T ASKED questions when Harlow woke him and requested to crash on his couch. His girlfriend, Isla, glared, but she hadn't cared if the woman wanted to come at her.

Felipe's had been her other option. She'd quickly dismissed that possibility. Lying to the kid, or putting him in the middle, wouldn't be fair. Soon she'd be leaving this life, and the neighborhood. Felipe would have to live here after she was gone. He may still see Ryske and his crew around. Not that she wanted Felipe to continue idolizing them. She vowed to speak to him about spending time at the bar. Martina Soto already had a lot on her plate, but Harlow would also talk to her about whether it was wise to let young Felipe hang out there. It was her fault the Soto family got involved with the Floyd's crew in the first place. She should have trusted her social work colleagues when they'd told her it wasn't a safe place to be. Even if it wasn't a physical danger to them, it could endanger the family in every other way.

Shaking off her thoughts about absurd emotion, she thrust her shoulders back and tried to remember the last time she'd been out so early in the morning. Being awake and being outside were different things.

While in mourning, insomnia plagued her. If she did drift off, it was usually closer to morning than bedtime. Time meant nothing to her then; nothing had meant anything.

Leaving Costello's place first thing seemed polite given the stink eye Isla kept throwing her way. Harlow needed the fresh air anyway and enjoyed the walk back to the hotel to retrieve Noon's car. She parked it around the back of Floyd's, leaving it where she'd found it, and retrieved the new Floyd's keys from the glovebox. If Ryske had busted his way in, the locks would need to be changed again. Though, with the bar open the previous night, he'd probably just strolled through the front door.

The side door was locked when she got there, which suggested her assumption was right on. If Ryske was alone, it was unlikely he'd bothered to clean up in the bar. Although she had a fleeting thought about checking, she accepted it wasn't her responsibility to deal with the business anymore. Besides, she'd cleared up the mess they'd abandoned when they fled, turnabout was fair play.

Running up the stairs into the apartment, she kicked off her shoes without caring about the noise. Ryske was there. As she crossed to go into the kitchen, she could hear him snoring in the corner bed. His bed. The place she'd been sleeping for over a month.

Part of her had hoped he wouldn't be there. A juvenile corner of her psyche didn't want to give up her role as landlady. Idiot. That was nuts. Floyd's was never hers in the first place, she had no claim to it.

Putting the car keys and a set of Floyd's keys on the counter, she prepared to relinquish the reins… in part anyway. The spare keys to Floyd's may still be in her possession, but why confess that?

It was too early in the day to start drinking, unfortunately, so she settled for switching on the coffee machine. All the time, a voice in her head reminded her to keep it together; she was strong, she could do this.

Ryske snorted and turned over.

Her eyes closed.

Now being there, listening to him breathe, relief crept

in. He was alive. It was sickening she could actually be happy about that. What was wrong with her?

Shoving away from the counter, Harlow went into the closet and tied her hair on her head. She'd showered at Costello's but needed a change of clothes. So she threw on a clean outfit and tossed a few other things into the sports bag she'd brought from her old apartment way back when.

Ignoring her criminology books, the bag went with her to the living room, and ended on the dining table. The coffee was almost ready. Standing there listening to it drip through, one sound was conspicuously absent. Ryske wasn't snoring anymore.

It had never been a loud sound, just definite. Why wasn't he snoring? Was he still breathing?

Pissed off that she cared enough to want to check, she gave in to the inevitable and went across the room to throw open the curtain.

Ryske was there in the bed, lying face down with the sheet over him, his hair the only thing visible. Longer than it had been before, it was the same hundred shades of brown that had been soft and thick between her fingers in the times he'd skimmed his mouth down the center of her body—

Closing her eyes, she shook her head. Thinking of him like that wasn't healthy or smart. Their relationship had been a lie, a con. Nothing between them was special; Ryske had been in it for the money. That was the only realistic explanation.

"Who's been sleeping in my bed?" he grumbled, his face buried in the bunched pillow.

So he knew she was there, but thought it was okay to play with her?

Folding her arms, Harlow widened her stance. "Maybe the Big, Bad Wolf," she said. "You tell me… Huntley."

A second passed before he rolled onto his back. His arm stayed hooked around the pillow, his hair a mess and his eyes scrunched. "Been a while since I heard that name."

She arched a brow. "Found your birth certificate. All of your birth certificates actually. You need a better hiding place."

With a grunt of acknowledgement, he raised his arms in a stretch that quaked through his whole body. "I don't even know where they are, none of us do. Floyd hid all that shit. None of us ever found his hidey hole."

Interesting to know. So everything under the loose board in the closet had been hidden there since Dover's dad had stashed it?

No way she'd reveal that juicy secret. "Your middle name is Casanova?"

"Used to tell girls that in high school," he muttered on a semi-laugh and relaxed his stretch. "Got me lots of action."

"Even if I believed you actually showed up to class in high school, I still wouldn't believe that."

Ryske didn't need a name to get girls; he could charm the panties right off them. His ability wasn't learned, it was innate and must've been present since birth.

He opened his mouth wide in a loud yawn and at the same time, pushed the covers away from his torso.

Wherever he'd been for the last four months, it hadn't been far from a gym. He'd always been cut, but not like this. If anything, he was a little bulkier than before. Her gaze wandered over the tattoos she'd once been so fond of, the tattoos she'd last touched in the ambulance when he…

The new scar on his chest snagged her attention. Once there, she couldn't tear it away. The mark was still healing. The color hadn't completely faded. The jagged edges betrayed the way the metal ripped through his body.

Hypnotized by the sight, a shiver racked her. Without thinking, she walked until she sank down on the edge of the bed. That blemish was a symbol of what had been taken from her, and it wasn't the man, it was the last shred of her innocence.

Slipping his hand under hers, Ryske lifted it off the bed to guide it toward his chest. "Chipped a rib," he said. "You want to feel?"

She tensed. "I don't," she said, attempting to take her hand away. "I really don't, Ryske. Let me go."

"Little fucking splinter ripped a blood vessel," he said. "Bale said it was worse than the bullet."

Despite trying to stand up, she didn't get far. Ryske pressed his thumb into the center of her hand and his fingers tightened, pulling her back to him.

"Don't."

"I'm here, baby. It's over. I'm here."

Lingering grief threatened to clog her throat. Instead of sharing the overwhelming emotion as upset, she shared it in anger.

"Over?" she said. "Damn right it is… I ought to beat the shit out of you."

Easing her hand closer, he meant to be subtle about straightening her arm. "I'm ready to take my punishment… Whatever you want to give I'll take." She wasn't wearing her ring, it was nestled somewhere in the sports bag. That worked out for him. If she'd been wearing it, she might be tempted to use it. "Just let me tell you three things first."

"Three things," she whispered, watching him lower her hand until the nails on her crooked fingers grazed his tattoo.

"Yeah," he said and licked his lips before guiding her hand from his tattoo to press his mouth to her wrist star. "This I love."

Loose, with her mind adrift, her arm stayed limp, which made it easy for him to direct her nails to his ab tattoo. "It was misguided."

"Still love it. That's number one."

"What's number two?"

"I love you," he said.

Startled by the declaration, she blinked out of her daze and pulled away. He didn't let her go though and chose that moment to sit up.

"Stop it, Ryske."

He ignored her discomfort and her efforts to free her hand from his grip. "And number three," he said, scooping a hand around the side of her head until it was curved beneath her ear. "I will never leave you again… that's my promise to you. I'll never leave you, Trinket."

Panting, she wasn't sure what to do first: scream or hurl. Instead, door number three won out. Lashing out at the inside of his elbow, she twisted her hand to liberate it from his grip. As soon as she was free, she leaped to her feet and paced across the living room.

"I don't know what con you're running now or what you hope to gain from this, but it won't work," she said, pointing to the keys on the breakfast bar. "Those will get Dover in the side door, and Noon's car is out back."

Ryske leaped out of bed and barreled toward her, completely naked. "Walk out if you want, babydoll. Turn around and every day I'll be there. I'm not going nowhere."

He had no shame about standing there in front of her without a scrap on. "Why the hell are you hard?" she asked and spun away to head for the closet.

"Because you're hot… and I haven't had sex since the day I met you," he said. She shrieked when he snatched her high-ponytail and pulled her backwards. "What the hell is that?" Tossing her hair over her shoulder, he smoothed his fingers across the inked curves on the back of her neck. "Is that a nightingale tattoo? Oh, baby, you're fucking teasing me now."

Stealing it again, he coiled her long ponytail around his hand until her back hit his chest. He crouched to touch his lips to the back of her neck. Harlow kicked back at his shin and dipped to turn so that even though he had her hair, she faced him.

"Someone's been taking lessons," he muttered his approval and tried to bow lower. "Mm."

"Need I remind you that you're naked and I have no qualms about grabbing your penis?"

Approval contorted his lips. Her proper language seemed to amuse him. It was nuts, since she'd lost him, the last thing she'd cared about was elocution. Yet, there she was, letting him bring it out in her.

"I have no qualms about you grabbing it either, Trink."

His misinterpretation didn't discourage her. "You might have qualms when I rip it from your body."

That cocky amusement didn't fade. "If I have no dick, how will we have kids? You want babies, right?"

Something he'd said caught up with her. "Wait," she said and held up a finger. "We met more than six months ago."

"Yep."

Did he honestly expect her to buy another lie?

She sneered. "You're unbelievable. Unbelievable! You expect me to believe you've been celibate for six months?"

Swagger bled into his satisfaction. "Well… we did some stuff, baby… need a reminder?" While at first he seemed smug, his enjoyment quickly faded to a frown, and he leaned back to peer down at her. "How many guys you had?"

"Too many to count," she said, backing away.

Though some strands pulled, her hair did untangle from his grip as she went to throw open the closet door.

Ryske stayed near the threshold while she progressed. "You're kidding with me, right? Who've you fucked?"

Retrieving a pair of boxer-briefs from his underwear drawer, she tossed them at him, but he didn't even attempt to catch them.

"Why would I tell you?" she asked. "It's absolutely none of your business." She pointed at the underwear on the floor. "Would you put those on, please?"

Ryske set his hands on his hips, unashamed of his body, and damn she hated that it was so mouthwateringly attractive. "You've had it in your mouth, babe, between your tits, covered in my——"

"Yes, I know where it's been, Ryske." Damn, she was giving him exactly what he wanted by pretending it offended her when in truth his tempting cock distracted her from her purpose. "Look, I don't want to play games with you. I came here this morning to return your keys and to tell you one thing."

"What's that, Trink?"

Her one thing came with an explanation. "You needed your buy-in. Ophelia and I paid it. You got your money, we fell for it, clever you." His scowl grew more puzzled than it had been earlier. "All I want is the money back, that's it. As soon as what I paid in is returned to me, I will be happy for you to take my place in the consortium. It's all yours, and if Ophelia wants to partner with you, that's fine with me too."

"You gave Parratt money," he muttered, figuring it out.

This guy was good. If she wasn't the subject of his deception, she'd be impressed. "Yes, Ryske, I gave him money. Are you going to pretend you don't know what happened?"

"When?" Her glare loosened him. "Humor me, baby. When and how much?"

"I'll humor you if you stop calling me baby," she said. "Two weeks ago. Ophelia and I came up with the money fifty-fifty."

A prickle crossed his shoulders and he swallowed. She couldn't fall for his act, she refused to fall for it. Except… he did look uncomfortable.

After a slow lick of his lips, he ran a hand through his hair and scratched the back of his head. "The million."

"We took your place," she said and folded her arms to lay some triumphant disapproval on him. "And, yes, I know all about Pothos, and your threesome with Yarker's wife, and what's expected of your role… and you can have it all. Nothing's different. Just get me my money and we'll call it even."

His eyes narrowed. Had he heard a word she'd said?

"Where did you get half a million dollars?" he asked, muttering to himself, so she doubted he expected an answer. "Daddy? No… he'd never hand over company money and doesn't have enough personal faith in you… The engagement ring wouldn't be enough…"

Until he brought it up, it hadn't occurred to her to tell him she'd covered for him on that front.

"I didn't tell Ophelia where the engagement ring came from. It was all she had of you and it meant something to her. I didn't want to be the one to break her heart. Now that you're back, you can take care of that all on your own."

He stepped toward her, ignoring what she'd just said. "So where did—" He snapped his fingers. "Marlowe… You got the half mill from your ex?"

"He doesn't know what it was used for."

Ryske folded his arms in a grump rather than making a point of being proud or cocky. "Not much of a drug kingpin?"

"Neither are you," she said. "You were never in it for the drugs or the sex."

Intrigued, his head tilted. "No?" She shook her head. "Why was I in it?"

"You owed Parratt."

A sound from the other room raised her hand to silence him. Her curious frown diverted him from whatever he'd been going to say.

"What?"

SIXTEEN

HARLOW HURRIED PAST Ryske, out of the closet, and across to the dining table.

Unzipping her sports bag, she dug around to find her ringing cellphone and answered it. "Hello?"

"Harlow," Clyde's said down the line.

Closing her eyes, she adjusted her thinking. She couldn't deal with Clyde while Ryske was nearby.

"I can't do this right now," she murmured.

"I'm sorry," he said with a desperation that made her feel for him. "We were drinking and I was… I don't know what I was… There's no excuse, I'm sorry."

Keeping her head down, she tried to be as quiet as possible without raising Clyde's suspicion… either of the men's suspicions. Though she didn't know exactly where Ryske was, she'd guess he wasn't far away.

"You don't have to apologize," she said, keeping it light. "It's no big deal."

Clyde wasn't appeased, his contrition was strong. "It's a big deal. I'm your friend and you came here for advice and comfort and I—"

"Don't worry about it," she said, smiling. "Forget about it, okay? Really, it's fine."

He took a deep breath. "You ran out of here so fast and I felt like shit. I didn't know where you were… Did you go to Floyd's?"

"No, not last night," she said, becoming aware someone was lurking behind her.

Subtle. Ryske's stealth confirmed his attempt to eavesdrop.

"Where did you stay?" Clyde asked.

Either Ryske knew she was aware of him or he'd figured out there was another man on the end of the line because he stopped sneaking. Full of pride and entitlement, he stomped into the kitchen to pour coffee, making as much noise as he could in the process.

"I can't talk now," she muttered into the phone.

"Where are you? I can come to you, I—"

"Not now."

"Lunch," he said. "Or dinner, whatever you want, Harlow… please."

Inhaling through her nose, she didn't want to sigh or show Ryske she was harried. "I'll come by later, okay? I have things to do today. I'll come to you when I'm done."

There was a pause. "Are you sure? I mean, you will come over? I don't want you to—"

"I will. Just… I can't do this now… You have to trust me."

"I do," Clyde said. "I do trust you and… I am sorry, Harlow."

"I know," she said and smiled again. "Didn't you once tell me there was no apology necessary? It's really fine. We'll talk about it later." It didn't feel right to leave it that way. "You have a good heart, you know? You're a good man."

Clyde still seemed unsure when she hung up, but what else could she give him? Turning the phone over, she opened it up to take the SIM out and snapped the card in two.

"Looking to get rid of someone?" Ryske asked. Although pleased to see he was wearing jeans, his bared torso didn't look any less inviting. Ignoring her hormones, she got the other phone from her bag and did the same thing with the second SIM. "Two phones… both burners?"

Ryske came over with two coffees. She stuffed the phones and the remnants of the SIMs in her bag again, planning to get rid of them later. Because it was there, she took the coffee and gulped some down, then put the mug on the table and picked up her bag to sling the strap across her body.

"I have to get going," she said. "Let me know on that money, okay?"

When she tried to go around him, he got in her way. "Don't you have questions?"

"What kind of questions?"

"About… everything? I'll tell you anything you want to know, everything. I'll never lie to you… never."

Oh, it was like slipping back in time. It didn't take long for her smile to curve. She breathed out something of a cleansing breath.

"Ryske," she said, trying to be as plain and calm as she could. "I wouldn't believe a word that came out of your damn mouth even if you read me the dictionary cover to cover."

"What about mine?"

That voice didn't belong to Ryske. It had come from the kitchen. Leaning to the side, a whole new kind of reaction struck when she saw the doctor at the top of the spiral stairs. Visceral rage swamped her. Somehow, his betrayal cut deeper.

Without thinking, she swept Ryske aside and strode into the kitchen to bring her hand across Bale's cheek in a swift slap.

"You are one sick sonofabitch," she hissed. "I don't know how you can look at yourself in the mirror."

"It was a split second decision," he said. "Harlow—"

"Don't say a thing. Not a goddamn word," she said and started past him, but came to a quick stop at the top of the stairs.

The spiral column was blocked, filled with the bodies of three other men ascending.

The whole damn gang was closing in.

"No," she whispered. "No way."

Turning on her heels, she crossed the kitchen past

Bale and even got by Ryske on her dash across the living room.

"Trinket," he called.

Nothing he could say would slow her down. In the stairwell, she descended in a run.

The door upstairs slapped off the wall and echoed behind her in time with the thunder of his footsteps. Even though he was barefoot, she could hear him hurrying after her. And, like an idiot, right up until the moment he captured her wrist to jerk her around, she kidded herself that freedom was possible.

Her fingertips had been just an inch from the external door handle, so close.

"No," was the first thing she gasped. Judging by his horror, he'd noticed the tears on her cheeks. Resenting every one of them, she swiped them away. "No, Ryske, I will not do it. I will not stand in a room with the man who pretended to love me and his posse of lying friends and listen to any of you belittle and dismiss what you did to me. Do I have questions? You fucking bastard, how dare you say that to me. How dare you!"

"Trinket," he soothed, reaching for her face.

With venom in her blood, she batted his hand away. "No! You do not get to touch me! I will never believe another word you say to me! Not ever! None of you!"

Ryske wasn't contrite, the potency of his anger matched hers. "You think I didn't want to be with you? That I didn't ache for you every damn minute of the day? I killed myself with thoughts of what that bastard Marlowe was doing with you! My woman! Guess it's easy for you to love a man when he's dead; harder when he's alive and you have to accept his flaws."

"Flaws? Ryske, we're not talking about your snoring, or your arrogance. We're not even talking about you reserving the right to screw any pussy that crosses your path! I was willing to accept that, all of that! I knew what you were, what you did, and I told you I didn't need any promises..." Swallowing some emotion, she hated showing him how he'd hurt her. "I won't let you hide behind the excuse you were trying to protect me. What you did to me these past four months is inexcusable. I won't accept it. I can't. You have no idea what I've been through and I had to do it alone. You left me. All of you left me. Abandoned me. When I thought you had no choice and your crew were going through the same grief as me, it made sense. I understood it. But this…" She shook her head. "I won't ever understand this."

"Let me explain it to you," he murmured, softening to tenderness. "Harlow, I meant it when I told you I loved you, in the ambulance and right now. I loved you then and I love you here. I love you."

Much as he sold it, honesty was all she could give. "I don't believe you."

"I know. But I'll make you believe it. You're my crew now," he said and nodded upward. "You before them. Now and always. I've told them that, they understand. All that matters to me is our future. Your happiness."

It was unfathomable that he couldn't grasp it was too little too late. He'd dug his own grave, and now he had to lie in it, dead or not.

"Where were you all the nights I was begging you to come back to me?" she asked, jerking her hand from his reach when he tried to touch her again. "You hurt me, more than anyone ever has, and it was my fault. I gave you the power to do that to me… I won't do it again."

Backing away, she twisted her arm behind her back to open the door and walk away. The goal? To put as much distance between her and Ryske as she could in the least amount of time, and to keep it that way for as long as possible.

SEVENTEEN

HOW COULD SHE deal with him? Adjusting her dial was difficult, from grieving widow to… what? Figuring that out would take time. Just looking into Ryske's face, into his eyes, tempted her to believe him. What a fool. Though it was the rush his proximity provoked in her hormones that she resented the most. How could she still want him?

For so long, she'd craved him, been willing to do anything, tolerate anything, to have him back. And now that he was available, she felt only pain and betrayal. He didn't love her. He couldn't. Even if she let herself believe that he did, she'd never be able to accept what he said as truth.

Now what? She had a limited amount of time to plan her next move.

First problem, okay. Without a base, she had nowhere to dump her bag. Her usual morning session with Costello was out too. If Isla saw her rocking up with possessions in tow, she'd have a fit. Putting Costello through the aggravation wouldn't be fair.

Be logical, linear, every step was progress. She couldn't be defeated, couldn't give in to whatever grief threatened to consume her. It may be a different melody, but the song was the same. Now she didn't grieve what he wasn't, she grieved her own sanity.

Going over to Felipe's was the first port of call. She explained to the kid that the crew were back and that she wouldn't be around Floyd's anymore. The youngster didn't understand; he assumed she'd be sympathetic with Dover and the others. Oh, the simplicity of youth.

Explaining Ryske's return was more difficult. She couldn't answer the kid's questions about where Ryske had been and what happened.

At that point, probably sensing her desperation, Martina interjected and sent Felipe off to do chores, giving them a chance to talk. It was nice to bond with a woman whose man let her down over and again. Felipe's father, Pablo, was in prison and wasn't a first timer. Martina said she wasn't going to take Pablo back this time and seemed to be sticking by that, for now at least.

She did her best to empathize but couldn't exactly compare the situations. If Ryske had gone to jail, she would've stuck by him. No hesitation. From their early days, he'd been clear about what he was. The law catching up to him had always been a possibility.

At least in prison, she'd have known where he was and that he was alive.

His death destroyed her. Her ideals, her emotions, all of her obliterated. Who was she now? What was left? He'd made a fool of her. It was that thought which stuck out after leaving the Soto's house. Everything she'd done since losing him, right up until he came back, made complete sense. She could justify all of her actions… if he'd really been gone.

Thinking of how she'd romanticized him mortified her. Her flaws were no secret and she hadn't forgotten them even in her anguish. But, for some reason, in her imagination, she'd molded their relationship into some kind of tortured love forbidden by fate… Even that was romanticizing it.

She'd wanted to believe the bullet had woken him up to the truth of their love the same way it had done for her. That if he'd survived, he'd have known she was his purpose, and they would become an invincible force capable of anything, with nothing powerful enough to tear them apart.

Boy, talk about wrong.

He was a guy, like any other. He'd seen an out and taken it. Just because he'd chosen to show up out of the blue didn't mean instant forgiveness.

And that was another thing. Ryske had come back for a reason. Though a part of her wanted to know what it was, she'd never be sure he was telling her the truth even if she asked.

Harlow had one thing clear in her mind. Just one. She had to go it alone. No one else was reliable. She could count on herself; that was it.

Only one other person had been hit with this as hard as her. Harlow couldn't ignore her sympathy for the woman who'd been a kindred friend. Hence why that person's door was her next stop.

Knocking, Harlow waited for the door to open. "Ophelia," she said as soon as she saw her friend.

With a sigh, Ophelia pulled Harlow into her arms. The women hugged there on the doorstep for a good minute before going inside.

"I don't even know what to say," Ophelia said, leading her to the couch. "Would you like a sherry?"

It wasn't yet lunchtime, but given the day she'd had, saying yes was tempting.

Resisting that temptation, she shook her head. "I wanted to come and check how you were doing."

"I'm…" Ophelia opened her mouth and shook her head, appearing bewildered. "I don't even know what I am, Harlow."

"I understand that," she said, linking their hands, noting the engagement ring was back in place on Ophelia's finger. Subduing her surprise was near impossible, but Ophelia was gazing at the fireplace and didn't notice. "Are you taking him back?"

"I can't… not," Ophelia said, twisting toward her. "I don't know, seeing him again… Oh, Harlow it was all I wanted for so long. Yes, I'm confused and probably hurt, but that's nothing to how grateful I am just to have him with us again."

He hadn't not been with them, but Ophelia's wonder kept her from pointing that out. That need was understandable, and it wasn't her place to judge Ophelia's gratitude.

"We did know what he was," she said.

Ophelia nodded.

Harlow had faced that truth herself. She'd known he was a con man. Part of her suspected this outcome for a glimmer of a second, as she'd explained to Clyde. Dismissing it had been her failing, not Ryske's. With him, anything was possible. Nothing was as it seemed. Her naivety, her gullibility, failed to predict someone would go as far as Ryske had.

"We did," Ophelia said. "I am surprised that he didn't confide in either of us… I'm sure he had his reasons. But he didn't lie to us about what he was capable of." She grinned. "And I suppose we can make him apologize to us in any way we want for as long as we want."

Try as she might, her smile didn't reach much more than feeble. "I guess we can." Though it poisoned her throat, she forced herself to ask. "How is your brother?"

Ophelia's shoulders rose when she inhaled. "Incensed. Just as you'd expect him to be."

"Because Ryske is back or because I stabbed him?"

Wariness crept over Ophelia. Harlow couldn't blame her friend for being dubious. An evil corner of her soul did heat with pleasure whenever she thought about causing that bastard harm.

"I'm sorry for the way he acted," Ophelia said. "He isn't happy. I think he… he wants your blood."

"Better my blood than my body."

Her friend disagreed. "Oh, Harlow, if you'd just—"

"I agreed to share my body with Parratt or Yarker if we had to go that far," she said. "I did not promise it to your brother… You have no idea what that man did to me."

The statement offended Ophelia. "He took Ryske from both of us and he was responsible for my best friend's death. I know what he's capable of and I understand it would sicken you to be intimate with him. But it's sex, Harlow… When it's revenge you want, there can't be any line you won't cross."

Half the battle would already be lost if she gave herself to Hagan like that. Ophelia didn't get it.

Not that it mattered anymore. Walking away from Ryske meant walking away from Hagan, the consortium, and her revenge.

"I told Ryske he could have my stake," she said. "He'll return my investment and then you two can partner."

For a moment, Ophelia examined her. "You want… out?" Harlow nodded. "You're giving me and Ryske your blessing?" Again, she nodded. "You… don't want to be with him anymore?"

"No," she said, failing to restrain an ironic laugh. "No, I want to be as far away from him as I possibly can be."

Her friend's head tilted. "I thought you were in love with him."

"So did I, Ophe," she said, watching their fingers thread together. "But I can't forgive this. I'm not built to… be made a fool of."

"You're embarrassed?"

"Yes," she snapped, louder than intended, which startled Ophelia. "I'm sorry, I… I'm angry at myself more than at him. Like you said, we knew what he was. What he was capable of… what they were all capable of, but…"

"You were deeper than I ever was," Ophelia said, shifting closer to comfort her. "You knew everyone in his life."

"Not everyone," she said. Although she couldn't think of anyone specific, assumptions could be dangerous. "But, yes, I…thought I was important, that…" Forcing another smile, she patted the back of Ophelia's hand. "It doesn't matter what I thought. What's important is the reality we're in."

"You're leaving?" Ophelia asked. "Where will you go?"

"Home," she said, just coming to the decision in that minute.

The truth was, she had no choice. She couldn't stay at Floyd's, Costello wasn't that close a friend, and her friendship with Clyde had been tossed on its ass. Going to her former colleague's apartment would be awkward now that there was… that between them.

"Will I see you again?"

"Maybe," she said, "there's a guy I… I'll invite you to the wedding."

Ophelia grinned. "I would love that."

"Just don't bring your brother as your plus one," Harlow said and pointed to the engagement ring. "Or your fiancé."

Both of them stood.

Ophelia laughed. "God, can you just imagine?"

She didn't want to. Harlow couldn't think of anything worse than seeing Hagan again, much less having him in a room with Rupert and Ryske too. It would be awful.

They went to the door. Harlow opened it, less concerned with security now that she'd been there a few times.

"Thank you, Ophelia," she said. "You were there… when I needed someone. You were there."

Smiling, Ophelia cupped her jaw and bowed to kiss each of her cheeks. "Take care, Harlow."

She didn't expect leaving Ophelia's to be so emotional, but in the elevator, there were tears. That was it. The new life was over; time to return to the old one… which was exactly as she'd left it.

EIGHTEEN

RUPERT HAD BEEN understanding about her need for time.

After returning to her parents, moving back into her childhood bedroom, again, she spent some time trying to remember who she'd been before deciding a challenging life of adventure might be fun.

There wasn't much opportunity for conclusions. On her fifth night home, while running down the stairs, the sound of her sister's laugh in the dining room halted her with a hand on the banister. That was her sister's flirtatious laugh.

Lena loved male attention; but she was coy about it in public, especially at her parents' dinner table. At least, she usually was.

Her mom, Jean, was the next person heard. "Her birth name was Harlean," Jean explained. "So when we were trying to pick a name for our second daughter, Lena seemed to fit."

Her mom loved to tell people how all of them, mother and both daughters, were named after Jean Harlow.

Leaving the bottom stair, she tried to figure out who could be at dinner and ignorant to the fact the three women were named after the same starlet. It was usually the first thing her mom brought up with new people. Since she'd been home, Rupert had come to dinner every night, but he'd heard the story probably as many times as she had.

On entering the dining room, the question of whether she should've dressed for dinner was on her lips. It got no further when she spied their guest. Ryske. Sitting there right next to her place at the table like he had some right to be there.

Rupert always sat to her left, and there was Ryske to her right. Being stuck in between them would be some version of hell. Harlow didn't want him there at all; but if she had to tolerate him, she'd rather do it from a distance, not from between him and Rupert.

Though instinct wanted to demand an explanation for his presence, or how he'd bagged himself a seat at the family table, she did some quick math. Ryske was a con man. Somehow, he'd conned her family. That was the only explanation.

The last thing Harlow wanted to do was draw attention to the fact she'd brought a criminal into their midst. Ryske wouldn't have known the Sweetings existed if it wasn't for her. So whatever story he'd fed to whomever, he only wanted to be there because of her. To hurt or to help… though she'd assume it was the first.

Her deduction led to one conclusion: she had to play it straight and figure out what Ryske wanted as soon as she could get him alone.

"Fuck," Harlow murmured.

The word wasn't meant to come out. In fact, she wasn't sure it had until her sister gasped.

"Harlow!" her mother exclaimed, pausing in her pouring of the wine. "What has gotten into you? I am sorry, Mr. Ryske…" Ryske was shaking his head, his expression blank and forgiving. "I assure you we are not usually so uncouth."

"It's fine, really," he said, holding up a hand to the wine. "That's plenty for me, Jean. I wouldn't want to end up being uncouth myself."

A series of polite titters went around the table. Her mother's smile fell when Harlow wandered deeper into the room. The two of them made eye contact, and Jean made sure to convey her disapproval with a stare. Yeah, okay, she got that her mother was unhappy; she didn't have to punctuate that fact with the stink eye.

"I believe my eldest daughter has already broken that barrier," Jean said.

Harlow didn't switch her glare on until her mother looked away. Hers was reserved for their guest, rather than her family. Fixated on him, she wished for the power to cause him pain. Whatever game Ryske was playing, she couldn't let him get away with it.

She touched her hair. "I haven't done my hair," Harlow said. "I worried I would embarrass the family."

The glint in Ryske's eye betrayed his teasing mood. "You look beautiful," he said, like he was just being polite.

"Yes, you do," Rupert said, playing catch up.

Given their new captive audience, Harlow dispensed with the usual cheek kiss and instead bowed to press her mouth to Rupert's, pushing deeper to kiss him like she hadn't since before their break-up.

"Harlow!" Jean scolded, forcing her to break the kiss.

Slightly flabbergasted, Rupert had to clear his throat more than once to recover. Rather than checking on the man she'd taken by surprise, Harlow's eyes went to Ryske's. Sliding her hand across Rupert's shoulders, maintaining contact as long as she could, she descended into her chair between the men.

"This is a passionate family," Ryske said, sharing a smile with her parents, who attempted to return it despite their mortification. "Are you dishing those out to all the guests, Miss Sweeting?"

Startled that he'd look her in the eye and ask that here, she did her best to stay proud. "Ask again and I'll give you something really special," she hissed.

His lips just curled. "I'll take anything you're offering."

Opening her mouth with intentions of retorting, she was cut off by her mother.

"Harlow Abigail Sweeting, your attitude is atrocious. Keep yourself in check."

Spreading a tight smile to her lips, she calmed herself. "I will, Mom. I apologize... I just didn't know we were having guests for dinner."

Lena leaned toward the middle of the table. "Mr. Ryske is a millionaire."

Wasn't that just hilarious. Restraining her hilarity, she instead raised her brows. "Is he?" Harlow asked and turned to him nodding, selling a humility she wasn't buying. "Isn't that nice, Mr. Ryske? A real life millionaire, wow... not a billionaire? That was just, what? A stretch too far for you?"

"Harlow!"

Ryske's lips quirked. "You're a feisty one."

"Oh, Mr. Ryske, you have no idea," she said, stealing a baby carrot from his plate.

"What has gotten into you?" Jean chastised. "Leave the man's plate alone."

"He's a millionaire, Mom. He can afford his own carrots," she said, linking her fingers over her plate with her elbows on the table. "Which I suppose brings me to the question of just what he's doing at our dinner table... Times rough, Mr. Ryske? No rooms at the Hilton?"

"I believe the hotel in your town is called the Meadowbank," he said. "It's a cozy place... quaint."

"Quaint," she said, bobbing her head in a nod. "In this context, isn't that some sort of condescending synonym for small?" Letting her eyes roll upward, she pretended to ponder. "It's a word that's not used enough. We should bring it back, shouldn't we? How would we do that?" She wrinkled her nose. "Hmm... Given tonight, I'd say it's a quaint world..."

The game provided the opportunity to get in a discreet jab against her former love.

But, of course, it didn't dent his monumental confidence. "I'd tell you not to sweat the quaint stuff," Ryske said, understanding she'd replaced the word small with the word quaint.

"It's just a quaint wonder, isn't it?"

That her ex just happened to saunter into her family dining room and snag a seat beside her was no coincidence.

Letting him know she was onto him was less important than conveying her displeasure with his tactics.

Still, no contrition from Ryske. "Be grateful for quaint blessings, Miss Sweeting," he said, spearing a carrot. "I am."

"Or quaint mercies," she said, plucking the carrot from his fork before it could reach his lips.

"Mine or yours? I can't say I'm fond of quaint talk."

"Mm," she said, exaggerating her agreement as she chewed. "Nor am I of quaint packages."

His brows rose as he struggled to quell a smile. "Not those you find in the quaint hours."

This time he speared a carrot from her plate with his fork.

"You know it's a wonder you ever found our quaint town," Harlow said. "Such a big frog in this quaint pond."

He shook his head. "I'm just a quaint cog," he said and winked as he slid the carrot from the fork with his teeth.

Damn her, but she smiled too. In her anger, it was easy to forget how smart and quick he was.

"I… I don't understand," Lena said.

When reading her sister's confusion, it seemed her parents were just as taken aback. She didn't even dare turn to Rupert.

"So you're working together," Harlow said to her father. "Mr. Ryske is dangling the prospect of his business in front of you, and inviting him home to your family is your way of soliciting it?" No one got a chance to respond. "Tell me, have you seen evidence of his great fortune? I'd be fascinated to know where someone such as him stashes his vast means."

"Harlow," her father said and tried to smile at Ryske. "We shouldn't talk business at the dinner table."

"No," she said. "Business and love are incompatible bedfellows…" More confusion. "Something a dear friend said to me once… And there's just so much love at our table, don't you think?"

Lena laughed. "Harlow, you are in such a weird mood."

"You are," Rupert said, putting a hand over hers.

"Are you feeling ill?"

"I am sorry about my daughter, Mr. Ryske," Jean said.

"I like a woman who speaks her mind," Ryske said. "Don't apologize for her on my account."

Rupert drew her face around to explore her expression with concern. His tender caress provoked her smile. Her ex-fiancé was sweet, far different from the other ex at the table.

Ryske's mocking irritated her, so she gave him a swift, hard kick under the table. Though it was probably heard by others, Ryske didn't react, so no one else did either.

"I don't see a wedding ring," Lena said. "Do you have a girlfriend, Mr. Ryske?"

"Yes…" Harlow said, picking up her water glass from next to the wine she habitually ignored. Turning to him, she acted enraptured. "Please, Mr. Ryske, do tell." She pointed her glass across the table to Lena seated opposite Ryske. "My sister, Lena, has aspirations to be married before she's twenty-five and she just turned twenty-two. She's looking for candidates… and you're rich, so she doesn't have to care whether or not you treat her right."

Lena laughed, but her mom hissed at her again. "Harlow."

Ryske carried on, without acknowledging Jean's displeasure. "Flattering as that is," he said. "I am spoken for."

In a faux pout, Lena appeared disappointed, but just for a second. It never took her little sister long to bounce back.

"Yes," her father said. "That is how Mr. Ryske finds himself in our midst."

"It is," Ryske said. "I'm looking for property in the area."

Just what Jean wanted to hear. "Oh, your girlfriend, or, uh…. partner would like to move?"

Always so concerned with being modern and not offending anyone, her mom often made an idiot of herself when she tried to be PC.

This time, Harlow fought the impulse not to roll her eyes. "He's not gay, mom," she said around the food in her mouth.

Jean blushed and Lena laughed.

"How do you know?" Ryske asked.

Breaking more rules, she kept eating and talking. "Because gay men tend to be polite and well-presented. You're rude and haven't had that mop cut for months."

"Harlow," her mother hissed.

It was a wonder that Jean kept drawing attention to her rudeness with the hissing, especially given it didn't work as a deterrent.

"My barber is out of town," Ryske said.

"I'll bet," Harlow said, cutting into her chicken. "Wait…" Putting down her flatware, she picked up her napkin to dab at the corners of her mouth before addressing him. "I do know who you are."

His brow arched. "You do?"

"Yes, I do," she said. "I know your fiancée."

Ryske grew dubious. His doubt wouldn't be obvious to anyone else at the table, but she could see he was intrigued about where she was going with this.

"My fiancée?"

She nodded. "Ophelia Hagan."

"Oh," Rupert said as soon as she'd spoken. Harlow got little chance to read Ryske's reaction because instinct turned her to the man at her other side. "You introduced me to her brother."

Thorns of disgust pricked at her, linking to the sickness churning in her belly. "I did."

Harlow couldn't even focus enough to do anything about Ryske's hand when it curled over her knee. She wanted to think it was an attempt to comfort her but knew better than to assume anything positive about him.

"You never did tell me what went on between you two," Rupert said. "There seemed to be an… energy between you."

"That's one way to put it," she said, reaching for the wine.

The moment the liquid met her tongue, a torrent of emotion deluged her. Terror and revulsion clashed with grief and anger. She had no choice except to swallow and surge to her feet. Without looking at anyone or acknowledging the calls that followed her, she dashed from the table and out of the room.

NINETEEN

RUNNING INTO THE DOWNSTAIRS powder room, Harlow flung the door out of her way and heaved over the toilet. Nothing came out, her body was just overwhelmed with the urge to dispel the assault. Trouble was, it wasn't so easy to purge emotion.

Standing up, she leaned against the wall, fighting to calm herself. Sweat beaded on her brow. She was shaking like after an adrenaline shot. Having had a lot of experience with that recently, she recognized the sensation.

"Harlow?"

Opening her eyes, she saw Rupert coming into the room, pushing the door over behind him without closing it.

"I'm okay," she said, going to the sink to splash water on her face.

"You don't seem okay," he said, stopping beside her. "You're erratic, have mood swings, and now this... You would tell me, wouldn't you?"

Standing up, she snagged the towel that hung on the wall by the sink. "Tell you what?"

"I'm saying," he said, making eye contact with her reflection. "It would be okay... I'd accept it."

"Accept what?" she asked, hanging up the towel

again. "Rupert, I don't—"

"You said you'd been with someone… in the city. You said you were with another man."

Yeah, and that man was sitting in the dining room, setting her on edge. "Why are you…?"

His gaze dropped to her stomach. "We can raise him or her together… We can be a family. I don't want you to think you have to hide anything from me."

Shocked, she was too dumbfounded to react with anything other than incredulity. "You can't be serious," she said, turning to face him, holding up both palms. "Let's just forget we had this conversation."

Leaving him in the bathroom, she chose to go into the kitchen instead of the dining room. Filling a glass from the faucet, she sipped and then crouched to retrieve a small washcloth from beneath the sink where the medical supplies were kept.

When she closed the cabinet door, a pair of legs stood on the other side. "Something you want to tell me, Trinket?"

"God, you're like a creeper," she said, standing up to run the cold water over the washcloth. "What are you even doing in here?"

"Told them I was going for a smoke."

"You don't smoke," she said, wringing the water out of the fabric.

His fingers crept onto her belly. "They don't know that."

She slapped at his hand. "Stop touching me."

"You know I wouldn't let him have you," he said. "You do get that, right? Both of you are mine."

Rolling her eyes to the ceiling, she released a breath to the count of five. "I don't even want to know how you overheard us in there," she grumbled, then pinned a side glare on him. "And you seem to have missed a few sex ed classes. You can't actually get a woman pregnant with oral. And you have never ejaculated anywhere near my cervix."

Taking the washcloth from her, he squeezed out the excess liquid and leaned in while folding it in to a long rectangle. "Something I'm happy to change this very minute."

Piling her hair onto the top of her head, she held it there with both hands and faced him when he pressed the cool, damp cloth to the back of her neck. "Because that's what my parents want to find in their kitchen? Their millionaire, engaged, prospective client, screwing the daughter they're a day away from committing to an insane asylum."

"They're not a day away from committing you," he said, picking a piece of her hair and slipping it under her thumb before adjusting his hold. His hands were curled around either side of her neck with his fingers supporting the washcloth at the nape. "Your parents have a beautiful home."

"What are you doing here, Ryske?" she asked, tired and stiff. Rocking her head side to side, she didn't fight against her eyes closing. "You want something and I won't let you dupe my family. I won't."

"You didn't tell them the truth as soon as you saw me."

"No," she said, opening her eyes to him. "Because I didn't want my father to feel foolish and because Rupert was sitting there… Do you want him to know what…?"

Something about his mouth distracted her. Harlow didn't realize she'd trailed off until he finished her sentence for her.

"I've done to you? That's why I'm here."

"You are not going to tell him," she said, suddenly very awake. "You are not to tell any of them what we… were."

"Are," he corrected her. "And I don't care what they know about our past. I'm here about the future."

That piqued her intrigue. "What does that mean? We don't have a lot of money, Ryske. Anything my father makes, he puts back into the business. The house is probably worth something, but it's all assets, we have no cash on hand, if you think I'll—"

"What I want from your father is not his money."

Ignoring the shameless implication in his eye, she changed the subject. "What does Ophelia think about you coming out here?"

"I haven't seen much of her this week," he said. "The thing with Ophelia is bullshit. You know that better than anyone. Did you have to bring her up at the table?"

"Yes," she said, proud of her proclamation. "You're the one who told everyone you were involved."

"I was talking about you."

"No, you weren't," she said, snagging the washcloth to run it under the water again. "Now you've had dinner, don't keep Noon waiting. Say your goodnights and—"

"Noon isn't here," he said. "I'm just me."

Pausing, she peered around at him. "Just you?"

He nodded. "You before them."

They were still looking into each other when someone else spoke.

"Mr. Ryske," Jean said. "Would you like a brandy?"

"A brandy," Harlow muttered, rinsing out the cloth. "Geez, it's one of those nights… He probably has to drive, Mom. He can't get drunk."

Her father and Rupert appeared in the doorway behind Jean.

"One won't hurt," Rupert said.

If anyone was going to be on her side, she'd expect it to be Rupert. Maybe if she accused Ryske of groping her, Rupert would be more eager to get rid of him. She was still thinking about this, folding and unfolding the washcloth when a sudden cheer brought her attention back to the conversation.

"Of course! We have a guest bedroom," Jean said. "It makes perfect sense. You should stay for the weekend while you visit the properties you're interested in."

Harlow spun around to gape at them. "Uh, what?"

"I wouldn't want to impose," Ryske said, feigning reluctance.

"Yes, he wouldn't want to impose," she said, straightening up. "Mom, you can't invite random men to sleep in the house when Lena is home."

Lena still lived with their parents, so she was always home.

"Oh, Harlow!" Her mother dismissed her and her father practically laughed. "Mr. Ryske isn't a stranger, he's our friend. There's no need for him to be in a hotel when we are here to show him around. He'll see plenty of properties and we can introduce him to people."

"That would be helpful," Ryske said, nodding. "There's nothing more valuable than local knowledge when choosing a place to live."

She scowled at his profile, he'd moved from next to her and was now half a step in front of her.

"Your fiancée, will she be joining you?" Jean asked. "We have plenty of space."

"No," he said. "I'm just scoping out the area."

"Casing the joint," she mumbled, though she didn't know if anyone heard her because they all ignored the comment. "Ophelia likes the city, she wouldn't be happy here."

"It's a wonderful district to raise children," Jean said. "Do you plan to have a family?"

Ryske's laugh was self-deprecating. "I leave all that to my girl," he said. "I just do what I'm told."

Everyone, except her, laughed.

"That's what you've got to do," her father said, putting a hand on Jean's shoulder.

"If she chooses the city, that's fine too," Ryske said. "But I know the city, I can advise her on that. I don't know this town, I'd like to get to know it."

"That way you can weigh the pros and cons together," Jean said.

"The decision will be hers," Ryske said and glanced at her. "Her happiness is all that matters to me."

She scowled at him, not believing him though her mother swooned.

"I prefer a man with a more take charge attitude," Harlow said. "A man with balls."

"My girl knows I can take charge too," he said. "She gets the best of both worlds."

"Oh," Jean said. "And there's a charity gala at the club tomorrow night. You could come as our guest, get to know some people."

"Yes," Ryske said.

Harlow yelped. "No," she said, snatching his hand.

It didn't feel unusual to be holding Ryske's hand. He couldn't have thought so either because he didn't pull away. For her parents and Rupert, it was startling. When they looked down, Ryske's gaze followed, and then hers did too.

"Harlow?" Rupert asked. "Why shouldn't Mr. Ryske join your father and me?"

She cleared her throat, failing to be discreet in removing her hand from Ryske to wipe it on her hip. "It's just… those things can be… overwhelming."

"Nonsense," Jean said. "He's probably used to those sorts of events. Aren't you, Mr. Ryske?"

"Yes," he said. "But if you're worried about me, Miss Sweeting, why don't you join us? We can all go together… look after each other."

"Lena loves these types of events," Jean said. "Harlow's always reluctant to take part."

"Oh? Why's that?" Ryske asked and looked to her, which made everyone else do the same.

"Rich men bore her," Rupert said. "That's what she always told me."

He said it like it was funny, but Harlow didn't find it funny at all. "I think it's ridiculous that they all stand around talking about how smart and wealthy they are," she said, rolling her eyes. "Tell a joke for God sakes, you know?"

"Funny men are overrated," Lena said, squeezing between their father and Rupert to come into the room. "I like rich men."

"And rich men like you," Harlow said. "You're going to be fine out there, little sister. You'll get your millionaire, he'll knock you up, and you'll both live happily ever after."

"You're supposed to have babies first," Lena said, heading for the wine rack.

Rupert shifted. "Uh, maybe Mr. Ryske has a friend he could introduce you to, Lena."

That put a grin on her face. "Yes, Mr. Ryske. Do you have any friends or are you friendless? We only want to know about the millionaires in your life… Any business owners? Maybe someone into computers or a car fanatic perhaps?"

Wearing a polite smile that he turned into a laugh

when he looked to her parents, Ryske took everything in stride. "I'm not sure my friends would be able to handle a Sweeting woman."

"Oh, I'm nothing like Harlow, they don't have to worry about that," Lena said, pouring herself a large glass of wine. "Harlow's been insane these last few months... She used to just lock herself in her room for days and days. We wouldn't hear anything until she started screaming her head off in the middle of the night. Terrified us all."

"Lena," Jean said, though there was more warning than scolding in her voice. "Mr. Ryske doesn't want to hear about that."

Mr. Ryske was the reason for that, though she didn't admit it.

"I do," he said. "I do want to hear about it."

"You can drink brandy with my father, you can rub shoulders with smallminded society," Harlow said, tossing the washcloth into the sink. "But my screaming in the middle of the night is none of your business, Mr. Ryske." Her mother probably intended to chastise her again. No need, she was done. "I'm going upstairs. I don't feel well. Goodnight, everyone."

Her bedroom had been her sanctuary when she didn't have him and now that he was back, she was using it as a barrier. Her father and Rupert wanted to impress the man they thought would bring them big business. Her mother loved to entertain and enjoyed showing off new acquaintances to her friends.

Harlow would go to the event, to keep an eye on Ryske, and to make sure no one signed anything at his request. One way or another, she was going to have to get him out of their lives and ask about the money he owed her.

The sooner he repaid her, the better, because then they would have no need to see each other again. Though, she'd thought that before he appeared at her family's dinner table. Ryske loved to surprise her; she wasn't sure how many more surprises she could take.

TWENTY

ANY HOPES THAT Harlow's bouts of insomnia were a thing of the past were dashed that night. She'd read for a while, trying to forget that the laughter and conversation downstairs involved a man who may wish her family harm.

In truth, his potentially wicked motives weren't why her ears piqued at every sound. She liked it. It tore her up, but she liked knowing that he was near. God, it was insane. She couldn't trust the man. She *shouldn't* trust him.

Except now the shock was subsiding, she was coming to terms with the fact that the love she'd thought was dead was actually alive.

Ryske, who she'd cried and ached for, was alive.

She'd been in bed with her lights off by the time she heard Jean showing Ryske to the larger of the guest rooms, which happened to be the one adjacent to hers.

There had been the mumbles of quiet goodnights, movement in the guest room for a minute or so, and then silence. For hours, she lay awake, trying to forget Ryske was sleeping just through the wall. Sometimes she caught herself craning to hear if he was snoring, but it had been hours since she'd last heard any sound. Her parents had gone to bed, Lena too, and the house was quiet.

But Harlow was still awake.

Accepting that laying in bed watching the minutes dwindle away was pointless, she tossed back her covers and got out of bed to go over to the window seat. Admiring the foliage that lined the perimeter of the Sweeting property, she thought about playing out there as a child.

While being so young and innocent, it would've been impossible to foresee the kind of woman she'd become or the kind of man she'd fall for. It hadn't even been on her radar that this kind of existence existed when she was a kid leaping through the sprinklers and playing with her friends.

The sound of her bedroom door opening rolled her head on the wall to shift her focus from the outside to the person creeping into her room. Though she hadn't predicted it, Harlow wasn't surprised to see Ryske closing the door carefully, silently.

"You're too early," she said, startling him when he turned to the room. Given the time, he must have expected her to be in the bed, not at the window. "If you were looking to take liberties while I was passed out, I don't go to sleep until at least five thirty."

"I don't mind taking them while you're awake."

Despite the darkness, there was enough light coming from outside her window to allow them to see each other.

"We both know you didn't come here to have sex with me," she said, sighing and returning to the view of the backyard. "I offered it to you once, you didn't want it."

"I did want it, Trink," he said. "I've always wanted it. Fuck, I wanted it, and you know that."

The sincerity of his tone was surprising enough to switch her inspection to him as he crossed the room. He chose to sit on the edge of the bed parallel to her position on the window seat with her legs stretched out in front of her. Still, he was a good four feet away and it wasn't like Ryske to respect her personal space.

"You didn't that day."

"I did," he said. "I wanted it from the minute we met. I'd have taken it if you'd given it up early… But by the time you called me out… Trink, I was so fucking in love with you… I knew I had to let you go. It ripped me up, but I knew it was best for you and if I'd had you… Damnit, baby, being inside you once was never going to be enough… I'd never have been strong enough to give you up if I knew what you felt like."

Letting her legs slide from the seat, she twisted to face him. "Why are you talking like this?"

"I'm re-learning a few things," he said. The smile he aimed at the floor seemed almost embarrassed. "My way with women has always worked. It's always worked… I've never cared about it working with anyone, so I never thought that much about it… not until you. You… you don't want it. It doesn't work for you. You call me out on everything. Every damn little thing."

"Faking your own death isn't a little thing."

That brought his head up fast. "I didn't fake my death, and what Bale said was true. Everything that night was real. Everything. Hagan sent Animal to kill me. That shot was real, Bale working on me, the ambulance, everything I said… it was all real… I did die in that ambulance. I… I don't remember much after telling you I loved you… Bale filled in a lot of the blanks. They worked on me in the ER, got my heart going again, and pulled me back."

"So he just took it upon himself to—"

"No," he said. "Bale told me you were a wreck, that you'd lost it in the ER… he told me after. That's why he decided to wait before telling you I was alive. He waited for me to wake up so he could check for brain injury or something… He said he didn't want to give you false hope, and wanted to have answers to the questions he knew you'd have. So after bringing me back and stabilizing me, he sat with me, and waited until I woke up."

"And the first thing you said was 'let's play a cruel joke on Harlow'?"

Shaking his head, he didn't seem to be enjoying this. She couldn't say it was in her top ten best life moments either.

"I made a kneejerk decision in a moment… Bale did a bunch of tests, asked me a bunch of questions. The last question he asked was if I had a girl… I said your name, he made a joke about how you'd make me pay for scaring you."

"You decided to be a coward."

"Maybe," he said. "Maybe that's what it was… As soon as I said your name, I thought about what we'd said, about how unsafe you were with me… Getting shot in the safest place I know, almost dying in my home, in your arms… The risk felt real. I didn't want you anywhere near that kind of danger."

Harlow didn't want to cut him any slack, but his words rang true. It had never occurred to her to be afraid in Floyd's after she'd gotten to know the crew.

"Hagan said that to hurt you, he'd have to hurt me," she murmured, recalling what had happened the night Hagan returned her to Ryske in the hotel.

"Yeah, and don't think I forgot that for a second," he said. "You knew it was over between us. Me getting shot didn't make the situation any better or safer. You were always going to be better off without me, just like we talked about. You were going to be with Marlowe. That was the plan; that was what we'd decided."

"What you decided," she muttered.

"I told Bale to tell you I didn't make it… He didn't get it. I know he didn't, and he argued with me. I told him to trust me; that it was for the best… This wasn't his fault… Setting it up wasn't hard, he just had to turn off the machines and give me a shot of something. He didn't want to… he kept going on about how dangerous it was, how important it was to monitor me… I didn't care. I wanted you safe… safe and free… without us in the back of your mind. I didn't want you sticking around just because I'd been injured."

Talk about playing down the drama.

"You were shot, Ryske. You died," she said. Although he'd been brought back, his heart *had* stopped. Technically, he had been dead. "It wasn't just a boo-boo."

"Exactly," he said. "You'd have stuck around, just like you did after the stabbing. Only this time, you'd have to answer questions from cops and doctors, maybe even feds. I didn't know what state I'd be in or if I'd be capable of looking after you. Our plan before the shooting was for you to go back to Marlowe. My injury didn't change that. Telling you I was gone was supposed to make it easier. I figured I'd just be some secret part of your past you could move on from. I thought you'd come back here and be happy with him. I was trying to make it easier on you. I didn't want to drag you down… I couldn't give you the security you deserved. You'd never be safe with me."

"That's bullshit," she said, subduing an urge to raise her voice given everyone else was asleep. "It wasn't your place to take my choice away. I make my decisions about what I want and who I want to be with."

"It made sense in the moment," he said, rubbing a hand across his brow. "The logic made sense."

"And your doctor, the man who's supposed to be level-headed and act in the best interest of his patient just went with it?"

He snickered a contradictory sound. "No. No fucking way. He argued with me… which was something… He likes you, fought for you… I told him we were protecting you. That you deserved better than the life I could give you… and he understood that. He understood."

She shook her head. "I don't believe it. I don't believe a man who values his career, a kind, sensitive, careful man, would just go with it. Bale is smart. He might owe you something, and I don't know what that is, but it can't be that was enough to have him lie to me for the sake of it. Why would he do that? Why would he risk everything for—"

"He's my brother," Ryske said, dropping his head to meet her eye. Shocked, she didn't know what to say. "My mom had him before I was born, she put him up for adoption… He found me when he was looking for her. I was sixteen, he was twenty-one. Green little fucker, all wide-eyed and innocent, a gullible angel… he found me in Floyd's. I was already smarter than him, though he was deep in the books by then. His adoptive parents died and he was using their insurance money to get through school, but it wasn't enough for the medical school after… We made a deal. It was a game, I guess, a bet… I told him I'd pay for his medical school. He laughed. Me, a dumb, stupid sixteen-year-old kid from the street telling this college boy I'd finance him… He said if I could do it, he'd give me and my crew free medical care for the rest of our lives…"

"And you did."

He nodded once. "And I did. That's when the cons started to get bigger. Me and the guys practiced our trade to finance Bale. It was fun, gave us a reason to do what we'd been doing for kicks before. We didn't see much of him, he kept his head in the books, and we didn't want to risk him being connected with us in case things went wrong. But I never let him down."

Putting the pieces together, things were sliding into place. "That's why he left with you," she whispered.

"Yeah, I wasn't in good shape and you know how he goes on about being in charge of the medical stuff. He told the cops I was unconscious, fobbed them off while the guys got what we needed. Soon as the sun came up, we were out of there. I gave him an out, told him he could stay, to give the guys instructions, but he didn't take it. He packed supplies, swiped what we needed from the hospital, and left his life to look after me."

It took a minute to absorb the story. One question stuck out above the others.

"Why come back?" she asked. "Why now? Why not stay gone?"

His smile ascended. "Because one person didn't stick to the plan. One person couldn't do what she'd been told."

She?

"I don't understand."

"You, Trinket," he said, leaving the bed to join her on the window seat. "You were supposed to stay safe in your sheltered existence with Marlowe who was going to provide for you and, I hoped, eventually make you happy… I really thought you'd forget about me and move on."

He tried to take her hand, resisting, she slid down the bench away from him. "If you thought that, you didn't have a clue what I felt for you."

"I don't think I did," he said, his chin rising, drawing her focus. The discerning expression on his face intrigued her.

"I don't think I knew… maybe if I did, I… I don't know, Trink. I told myself you didn't feel for me like I felt for you. Maybe it was a cop out—no, I know, it was a cop out. It was easier for me to believe you were attracted to me, but that was as far as it went."

Twisting toward him, she drew a folded knee up to the seat between them. "How could you think that, Ryske? I'd been obsessed with you since the moment we met."

"Obsessed, maybe, yeah, I would've believed that. I figured it was a crush. With all your criminology stuff and the way you talked about what we did, in my head, I was a temporary distraction. We never talked about… feelings. You said you didn't want promises, and then we were fooling around, but you kept your virtue to yourself. I was happy to have fun, stoked to play with that incredible body…" When he attempted to snake a hand under her nightshirt, she pushed it back to his thigh, and he grinned. "We were having fun, Trink… and I fell for you. That never happened to me before. I'd never felt… love."

"You felt it for me," she said, and he nodded. "And you thought you were my academic exercise." Which was what he'd called himself when they were talking in her apartment. "You didn't think much of me, did you?"

Standing up, ready to ask him to leave, she didn't get the chance. He grabbed her hand and yanked her back. Standing between his open legs, gazing down at him, the wonder in his focus was mesmerizing.

"Seems stupid now," he murmured. "You were as in love with me as I was with you… if I'd let myself believe that, I wouldn't have let us be apart for a minute… I won't let us be apart."

Shaking her head while his fingers slid up her jaw and over her cheek, he had no trouble reaching despite him sitting to her standing. "You don't get to decide that. We're through."

"If that's true," he said. "I was right to do what I did because you can't love me as much as I love you… There's nothing I wouldn't forgive you, Trinket… These last four months without you have been hell… Every second has been you and we haven't even been together. I couldn't not belong to you if I wanted to. Har, I don't see other women anymore, except to compare them to you, and you win every time."

"Ryske," she said, trying to push his hand away, but he just used her resistance as a way to twine their fingers.

"The woman who did this," he said, picking up her other hand to present the star tattoo. "She loved me." He turned her hand to show the glint of her bracelet in the moonlight. "The woman who wore this every minute, she loves me."

"She thought you were someone else," Harlow said. "And this… it's all some elaborate seduction, I know it is."

"Keep your pussy if that's what you need to do," he said, sliding his fingers deeper between hers on both hands, pulling her body closer to hold her steady while he rubbed his face against her abdomen. "I'll go through every trial, endure every punishment, I will do whatever you need me to do for however long you need me to do it… but I will not let this go. I will not lose you again."

Quite a turnaround from the man who'd said he'd have her. When they'd met, he'd been arrogant enough to tell her they were going to have sex. But as he sat there telling her they were going to be together, she didn't get the same sense of that arrogance. This was more like resolve. Yet, he was tender, like just being here was a gift.

In that regard, he was right. Them being together again was a gift. She'd vowed never to take him for granted, even after he was gone. Except she kept pushing him away, just like before, when they'd had the chance to be together.

TWENTY-ONE

EVERYTHING HE SAID made sense. Still, she'd be naïve to forget again that Ryske was a con man.

Even if she wanted to, Harlow didn't know if she could believe his explanations. "Did you wait for me to pay your buy-in?" she asked. His drowsy eyes rose to hers. "Is that why you came back? Because I did what you needed me to do? You know what the sad thing is? If you'd asked me, I'd have found a way to get you anything you needed."

"Baby, I didn't know. The shit I've learned this week…" One of his hands loosened from hers and he swatted her ass hard; her mouth opened in shock. "I should lock you up for your own damn safety. My girl should never go out there and put herself in fucking danger, especially not without backup."

"I thought you were dead," she said, watching her fingers move through his hair. "I didn't give a damn about my life."

"I know, baby," he said. "I'd have felt the same way… and I'd have gone after the people who hurt you too."

She smiled. "I knew you would've."

"Bale said you left the hospital. We assumed you were here, moving on with your life. I thought the plan had worked like it was supposed to… I was too cut up to check on you. Guess I was worried I'd find a wedding announcement or something… I focused on the physio, on Bale's routine, on working out… that was it. My head was in that, nothing else. I barely spoke to the guys."

"How did you find out that I was—"

"I walked in on them talking."

"The guys?" she asked.

He nodded. "Something about bills for Floyd's. Dover had everything setup to come out direct deposit for the utilities, and he got some email with the amount of the electric… Suddenly it was higher than it had been the last three months… He checked online. There were liquor orders, utilities being used… That's when we knew someone had opened the doors again. Floyd's was trading."

Much as she hadn't known the bills would be taken from the Floyd's bank account, it was an obvious assumption. Maybe some part of her hoped the guys would find out she was there, waiting for them. Though, she'd never have known Ryske was with them.

"How long did it take to figure out it was me?"

"About three seconds," he said. "They were all standing around speculating. I said one word… Nightingale. After that, they got it… We'd never left a man behind before."

Never until her. The first one of the crew to be ditched. That wasn't a title to be proud of.

"You were just going to abandon it?" she asked. "Was Dover mad at me?"

"Proud, I think," he said. "We didn't plan to stay gone forever. A few months, a year maybe, just until the dust settled…" Until Hagan lost the notion to send shooters after them. "You changed all that, Trinket… You couldn't just live a boring, normal life, could you?"

"You changed me," she said, sinking down to sit at his side, the length of her thigh resting on his. "Everything about what I went through in the city changed me…"

"We thought you'd come back to the city and got Floyd's going again as some sort of tribute," he said. "We had no idea you had this whole plan for revenge… Ophelia told me everything."

Her attention leaped to him. "That's why you came to the hotel?"

"No, she told me this week. I didn't know what the meeting was at the hotel until I got there. Soon as we figured out you were at Floyd's, I needed to get to you. The guys wanted to wait, to figure out a plan, to find out what was going on… I wouldn't wait…You'd come back for me, I just knew it. You'd turned your back on the life you were supposed to have, for me… I had to be with you… Since probably the day after I told Bale to lie to you, I regretted the choice. Sure, it made sense. Yes, it was smart… But, damn, baby, I missed you… I only got through it by reminding myself it was best for you… 'til you proved otherwise… You wouldn't stay put. You put yourself in danger; proved the life you wanted wasn't out here in Nowhereland. You chose what you wanted… You took what you wanted… I left the guys determined to get to you as fast as I could."

All his information suggested she was at Floyd's, but that wasn't where he'd found her. "How did you find out about the meeting in the hotel?"

"Maze told me. Soon as I got to the city, I called them to tell them I was back… To be honest, I thought I'd find you in Floyd's and we'd spend the night arguing or fucking. I wanted to get the call out of the way before I tracked you down… The guys were worried about me."

"Obviously," she said, not disguising her judgment. "Because Hagan already tried to kill you twice."

Ryske wasn't as focused on that. "Maze said he'd hacked Hagan's schedule and found an entry marked 'social', which was the term he always used for consortium meetings… All the consortium meetings were at the same hotel, in the same room. I was only a couple of blocks away and had no plan to hide from the fucker. Made sense to check it out."

"You wanted payback of your own?" she asked. Had he gone there to take his revenge? "Were you even armed?"

"I didn't go there to kill him. I thought if he found out Floyd's was up and running again, he'd send his people to check it out. My coming back wouldn't have been a secret for long. What was the point in ducking and hiding? I didn't know you would be there, baby... When I walked in that room and saw him with you, Trink... You... and... Fuck, baby... The man killed me and I didn't want him dead... but seeing him hurt you... Shit, I wanted to bleed the fucker dry."

"Then why did you stop me?" she said and nudged his thigh with a fist. "He put his hands on me, Crash. No man gets to do that."

Sliding his fingers onto her cheek, he brought her attention around to his. "You are fucking badass, Trinket. When I saw the way you handled him... Shit, baby, no woman's ever got me hard that fast."

"You want me to do it to you?" she asked, wrapping her fingers around his wrist.

Before she could remove his hand from her face, he tightened his hold and pulled their mouths together.

Ryske might be a lying asshole, but he was still the best kisser she'd ever known. Her stomach flipped, like going through a teenage experience for the first time. The bottom dropped out her gut and a flurry of excited bubbles ascended in a rush to her heart.

The sheer volume of endorphins that surged through her brain gave her a head rush, making her giddy and drunk at the same time. Still recovering from the maelstrom of sensation, she was static when he pulled back.

"You called me Crash," he murmured, running his thumb back and forth along the underside of her lower lip. "Tell me you can forgive me, Trinket. Tell me there's a chance... That's all I need... Just give me a chance."

Trying to moisten her mouth, she eased the weight of her head from his hand and focused on the bed. "I used to argue with you," she whispered. "I used to scream into pillows about how selfish you were and how I'd pummel you for leaving me alone if I ever got the chance." Standing slowly, she left him to go to the bed. "I didn't tell you I loved you. The guilt of that ate me up... We were in a fight when it happened... I don't know if you remember."

"I remember everything about being with you," he

said, rising and moving in close, sliding his hands onto her shoulders from behind. "I remember the smell of your hair when we were falling to the ground the minute we met. I remember the defiance in your voice when you told Animal to go fuck himself."

Angling her head in his direction, her lips came to rest against his fingers on her shoulder. "I didn't say that."

He lowered his mouth to her hair. "No, but I can quote what you did say word for word if you want." She smiled, believing he probably could. "I remember telling you to run and you said, 'Like hell.'"

A laugh slipped from her lips onto his hand. "I did."

"You told me Floyd's was dangerous and refused me a last request... I remember it all, baby... Right up to you telling Bale I didn't need my eyes. That as long as my dick worked, I'd be just fine."

"That's still true," she said, tilting her head to rub her cheek against the back of his hand.

"The very last thing you said to me before the bullet was, 'Don't Trink me.' And the only thing I cared about when that bullet was ripping through me was telling you I love you."

A tear slipped free. She didn't even try to stop it from slithering down to the warmth of his knuckle. "It was the last thing you said to me," she whispered, turning around to face him. He brushed the moisture from her cheeks, but she didn't care about her tears, all she wanted was to see into him. "You told me you loved me and you said you were sorry... Why were you sorry?"

"For not being selfish. For not telling you I didn't give a damn about what was safe... For not listening to you when you told me to hold you tighter... You told me to take what I wanted, to take it from you; that was what you wanted..."

"Yes," she said, the word barely a whisper.

"You never wanted me to treat you soft or shelter you... You wanted it all. You wanted it raw, and dirty, and all the things I am... I didn't see it. Don't think I understood how far you were willing to go, what you were capable of, not until I saw you ready to rip out Hagan's throat... You were gonna end him for hurting you."

Sheer admiration and pride shone out of him.

She raised her palms to his cheeks and smiled. "No," she said with the slightest shake of her head. "I was going to end him for touching what was yours… He'd already taken you from me. I wasn't going to let him take me from you…"

"Trink," he growled, snatching her waist and hauling her close. "I fucking love you."

His vehemence freed her from whatever weighed on her. She laughed, unable to pass up this gift of a chance.

"I fucking love you too."

The clash of their mouths turned their next kiss into a battle. Harlow didn't know what the prize would be at the end; she didn't care. Bending her knees, she jumped up and coiled both legs around his torso, grabbing his hair in her fists, forcing him to kiss her harder. Yes. This. Them.

She didn't know he was moving until they fell back and landed on her bed. Fighting to restrain her laugh, aware they couldn't make any noise, she struggled to contain herself while her lover quarreled with the buttons on her nightshirt. Giving up the fight of fumbling with them, he grabbed the edges and ripped them apart, baring her naked body.

There was something feral about the grin he flashed at her. It was only a glimpse because he was quick to dive down and taste each of her breasts, kissing and nibbling on them, reminding her just how much he adored her figure.

"Crash," she whispered like a schoolgirl striving to control her eager, hormonal boyfriend. "Crash, we can't go all the way. Someone will hear us."

"I don't care," he grumbled in her cleavage.

"I care," she said, her cheeks burning against the stretch of her grin. "Crash…"

His middle finger slid into her and she groaned, forgetting to smile and to object in the same breath.

"Mm," he purred at her reaction.

"Oh, that's not fair," she panted and bit her lip when he massaged her clit. "Oh, you're a bastard…" Her hips wouldn't stop moving against his hand, enjoying the skills she'd forgotten he had. "Where the hell is Noon when a girl needs him?"

His fingers didn't withdraw, but they did stop moving. She opened her eyes to his frown. He tilted his head and brows in question. She laughed and grabbed a pillow from the head of the bed to swing it at him.

"For the interruption," she said.

Ryske stole the pillow and tossed it away. He dropped down to kiss her neck, her jaw, her throat, until his lips found their way to her ear. "You want me just to eat you, that's all I'll do."

Grabbing his head, she forced it around to bite his earlobe, hard. "I want you to come inside me," she whispered and pushed him back to confirm her need with a certain gaze. "I don't care if I climax… Fuck yourself inside me until your balls are empty… I want every drop, Crash… All of it is mine."

His nostrils flared. Was he still breathing? He hadn't opened his mouth for a few seconds. "Goddamn… I've never met a woman so good at teasing me."

With both hands, she reached between her thighs to take his hand. Folding his other fingers down, she sucked his middle finger into her mouth all the way, loving how his panting came hard and fast.

Soon as she was done with his hand, she grabbed his hair to pull him into a kiss. Sliding her tongue across his, sharing her taste with him, this was what he'd been missing.

Before he could sink into it, she hauled him back. "If you loved me, you'd be inside me already."

Like that was challenge enough, he pushed her shoulders, throwing her down and grabbing her thighs to force them far apart. The sting of his strength manipulating her body aroused her so much that she deliberately battled to push her hips up against his will, fighting him, provoking him into being more forceful.

Pinning her down, he wouldn't even let her go long enough to take his underwear off. One hand gripped her hip, and with the other, he pulled his cock from his boxer-briefs to thrust himself into her.

Oh, shit. She hadn't had sex since Rupert. Both her

and Ryske looked a little surprised when he stopped just a couple of inches inside her. Relax, Harlow. Relax. Was she too tight for him or was he worried he was close to going off already?

She didn't mind the latter. Sacrificing her climax didn't reflect her expectation of sex or any sort of self-esteem issue. There was just something alluring about the idea of triggering a man as powerful as Ryske into losing control.

Remaining over her, he drove in a little deeper then slid his hand up the center of her body to coil his fingers around her throat.

Oh… Oh, God.

So much for him losing control. Her own need built and time ticked fast. Oh, that felt good. Amazing. Her body loosened around his, granting him access to plunge himself in deep.

His groin hit her hard and she whimpered.

He tightened his fingers. "Shh," he said, not because he was afraid of them being discovered, that was a command. "Don't make a fucking sound."

Pulling back, he shoved into her again, anchoring himself with his hold on her neck. If she thought about making a noise, he gripped tighter, narrowing her airway, not enough to cause alarm, but plenty to arouse her.

Hormones danced and effervesced within her, warming her blood and softening her core. Ryske skimmed his fingertips from her hip to her clit to rub in slow circles while hammering his cock into her.

"You are gonna come," he grumbled. "You're gonna come with me right here." He pushed in hard, forcing the head of his cock against her g-spot. Her yelp only tightened his fingers. "You're gonna do what you're fucking told, Trink. You want my spunk in you, for only you, you're gonna come when I say and only when I say."

"Crash," she hissed, the pressure of need increasing. "Oh, God, Crash."

"Shh," he said again and pulled out to slam into her, giving her the final shunt she needed to tumble into the chasm of orgasm.

It kept going in waves of mounting pleasure. Over and over. Drowning her. Saving her. Consuming her.

Desperation to call out almost overwhelmed her. With her eyes closed and her head back, she feared losing control of herself until he fell over her and sank his tongue into her mouth, stealing her scream into his own throat. In time with the rhythm of his tongue, his body granted her wish. He came inside her, but kept moving his hips, working his groin against her clit until her next orgasm subsided to the shivers and quakes of enduring aftershocks.

When he moved away, he didn't look at her. Whatever his reasons for putting space between them, she couldn't focus… or think… at all. One of her hands fell to her upper chest and the other spread on her belly.

After sex with Rupert she'd always accepted his polite goodnight kiss and gone to the bathroom to wash up before settling down to sleep.

Somehow, she knew that routine wasn't going to work tonight.

TWENTY-TWO

HARLOW WAS STILL lying on her back, trying to come to terms with what they'd done, when Ryske shifted to sit on the edge of the bed.

"Oh, I'm in fucking trouble," he said, scrubbing a hand through his hair.

Her head flopped to the side. Working any of her muscles took effort she barely had. Keeping her elbow on the mattress to steady her forearm, she let it drop until her fingertips came to rest against his spine.

"That's not something a woman wants to hear right after sex."

Reaching around to catch her hand, he wound her arm around his head as he dropped onto his side next to her. "I love you. How's that?"

The sensation of him nuzzling his face in her hair curled her lips. "Better."

Shifting onto her side made it easier to draw her fingernails around his shoulder tattoo. As long as he could cup and caress her breasts, he seemed fine with letting her.

"Mm, Trinket."

"I think I like sex more than I thought I did."

There was a purr in his voice. "You're good at it,

baby."

"I feel better we're not treading the line of deception now. It always bothered me that people assumed we'd had sex."

"Should've told me," he said and stole a kiss. "I'd have cleared up that guilt for you."

She didn't mind his teasing. It hadn't taken him long to get back to being his usual cocky self. Inwardly, it aroused her that she was one of the few people, maybe the only person, to have seen his softer, more tender, side.

Opening her hand on his arm, she stroked him. "You should go back to your room."

"Prefer this room," he said, forcing his arms around her waist to pull her body against his. "You Sweetings are mighty hospitable."

"Yeah, and if you stay, I'll end up hosting you again. We're playing with fire doing it here when no one can know."

He groaned. "Okay, okay… I guess I have to break up with my fake fiancé before I tell your dad you enchanted me," he said, kissing her head, then springing off the bed.

"Oh, he'd love that."

"He'll get used to me," he said, offering her his hand. "Not like I'm going anywhere."

She sat up to take his hand, yet that was a concerning statement. "You're still going to stay the weekend?"

Ryske pulled her onto her feet. "Why not? I'll tell them my fiancée dumped me on the phone or something. Doubt they'll ever talk to Ophelia about it."

"I wouldn't bet on that," she said, resting her forearms against him when he wrapped his arms around her. "My father and Rupert were courting Hagan. They might meet Ophelia… I think Rupe understands I'm not a fan, but I'll check they're not planning to pursue his business. I would never trust that man to employ my father or fiancé."

His brows rose. "Excuse me? Your what? Hagan doesn't employ me."

Smiling, her arms slunk around his neck to pull herself up for a kiss. "You're not my fiancé, and I don't think anyone could employ you. You're an in charge kind of guy."

"That's right, I am," he said, taking her elbows to pull her arms from around him.

His frown took her aback. "What's wrong?"

"You meant Marlowe. He's your fiancé."

"Well, I suppose that's premature, we haven't talked about marriage, but—"

"I thought that damn kiss at dinner was a sham to piss me off."

Glancing at the door and then back at him, she rushed to grab her robe from the head of the bed. "Will you keep your voice down?"

Typical that they could get away with having sex without rousing the house, but he'd lose his temper and blow their cover two minutes after.

"You think I'm gonna let you marry that fucking guy?" he snapped and pointed at nothing like Rupert was right there with them. "Are you fucking him?"

"Ryske," she hissed, trying to quiet him.

"I know something went on with that sap you used to work with. He came into Floyd's this week," he said, his anger apparent when he glanced to the side. "That fucker. I should've put him in the ground when I had the chance."

Storming over, she got in front of him. "You have no right to hurt him, or any other man who's ever touched me."

Ryske bowed to get in her face. "It's my right to do what I damn well please when it comes to my woman."

"I don't belong to anyone," she said and started to turn, but he grabbed her arm to haul her back.

"You belong to me and we're going to make this work."

"My future is with Rupert," she said, losing some of her anger when it seeped in there was one thing she hadn't made clear. "Baby—" Now it was Ryske's turn to back off when she tried to touch his face. "I'm sorry, Crash. I'm so sorry. I thought you… I thought you knew."

"Knew what?"

The truth was, thinking about it, he couldn't have known something only she and Rupert knew.

"That was the deal," she said. "The money."

For a second, he examined her, then he exhaled in relief. "Is that all? Shit, baby," he said and grabbed her wrist to tug her to him. "I'm getting the money together. We'll have it soon. Just keep holding him off."

"No," she said, shaking her head. "It's not about the money. He doesn't care about the money. I wanted it back from you as a show of self-respect. Rupert never wanted it back."

The way he scrutinized her grew more intense. "He only wanted you," he said. "And you agreed?"

Harlow shrugged. "It didn't matter, did it?" she asked. "It was what you wanted… and I knew I wasn't going to find love like I felt for you, so what did it matter who I was with?"

He let her go but didn't push her away, he just set a disapproving eye on her. "Do you want to be with him? Is this the life you've decided you want?"

This life had always been available to her, even since she shunned it the first time. "You know the answer to that," she said. "But what choice do I have?"

"Do you want to be with me?"

That shouldn't be a difficult question to answer. Usually, when she was asked a direct question, she knew her heart and head enough to know what she wanted. A fog of possibilities could be overwhelming and disorienting, but if it was boiled down to a simple yes or no, usually it was easy to come up with an answer.

"Wow," he said and took a step back. "Guess I've still got work to do."

"Ryske…"

Though she'd just hurt him, he didn't pout. Her Ryske was too persistent to pout. He bowed to kiss the top of her head.

"I prefer Crash from those lips," he said, his mouth in her locks. "You're gonna be a Ryske soon, baby. I guarantee it."

He smacked her ass, hard, and ignored the shock in her loose jaw to saunter out of her bedroom.

Having sex with Ryske when so many things were up in the air probably hadn't been smart. Yet, she couldn't say she was sorry they'd done it.

After slipping into bed, she lay staring at her ceiling but wasn't awake for long. Her body relaxed and she drifted off into a sleep more satisfying than any she'd had in her childhood room for a long time.

TWENTY-THREE

HARLOW CAME DOWN the stairs the following night to find everyone already waiting in the lower hallway. Their polite conversation faded when they noticed her.

Their inspection stalled her a few steps from the bottom. "What?" she asked.

"Do you think that's appropriate?" Jean asked.

Looking at her outfit, she opened her arms to present herself. "What's wrong with it?"

"It's…" Rupert cleared his throat, "short."

"And tight," her mother followed.

Spinning on the step to give them the complete picture, she peeked over her shoulder. "And backless."

"I love it," Ryske said.

On reflex, she smiled.

The rest of the room remained on pause, which didn't matter because she was focused on Ryske's exuberant grin. The way he checked her out wasn't the same way her family and Rupert did. Which probably wasn't a great idea given that they weren't supposed to know each other. Yet, she was enraptured.

They hadn't seen each other since he'd left her bedroom last night. By the time she got up, Ryske had returned to the city with her father and Rupert. What they talked about all day, she had no idea, but he was making an impression anyway.

"My breasts are covered," she said, descending one stair and then another. "I haven't gone all out."

"Only thing I don't like about it," Ryske said.

His appreciation was risky… and flattering. In her attempt to be subtle about nudging Ryske with her hip when she reached the bottom of the stairs, she caught Rupert's eye. Her ex was watching her, a frown set on his face.

Aiming her wide smile at Rupert, she left Ryske's side to go and take his arm. "Are we ready to leave?"

"Yes," Rupert said, tucking her hand inside his elbow. The group walked outside. "I didn't mean to imply you don't look beautiful… you do."

Sweet of him to apologize, but when she turned to offer a grateful smile, she couldn't help but notice Ryske right at their backs.

"Thank you, Rupe," she said, ignoring Ryske. "You look very handsome too."

Raising his arm, he showed her his cufflinks. "I wore your favorite."

"That's very sweet."

They came to a stop in the driveway and the group fanned out. Her father's car was there, Rupert's too, but the third car broke her smile. Pointing at the gleaming BMW, she intended to ask where it appeared from when Ryske spoke up.

"Beautiful, isn't it?" Ryske asked, sliding his hands into his pockets as he sauntered up at her side.

Rupert was discussing travel arrangements with Brysen, giving her some cover to grumble at Ryske. "You did not."

"No, I didn't," he said, a tease in his smile.

Leaning in closer, she glared at him. "You know damn well that when I say you, I mean Noon… Did he do this for you?"

Picking up his hand, he showed her a key. "For us."

Her growl of aggravation only heightened his amusement. "And if you're pulled over in a stolen car… what happens to your elaborate cover?"

"Not that elaborate," he said. "I'm a rich fuck here to take what's actually mine."

"Mr. Ryske," Jean said, interrupting their stare. "Would you like to drive? Brysen and Rupert are both happy to, if you'd prefer not to—"

"I'm driving," Harlow said, snatching the key from Ryske's hand and striding toward the BMW.

Getting it out of her parent's driveway was preferable to leaving it there or having the cops bust into the country club to take them down. If she got pulled over, she'd act drunk, and let the cops take her in for that before they ran the license plate.

The car opened, impressive, that meant the key was genuine... or that Maze knew how to program them. Adjusting the seat and the mirror, she got the engine going and was checking her lip gloss when Ryske slid into the passenger seat next to her.

"Want to tell me how he did it?"

"He's a magician," Ryske said. "Doesn't reveal his secrets."

"He showed me how to pop a lock once."

"I'll tell the cops that if they stop us." His obvious attempt to rile her didn't last long. "What you doing letting him show you shit like that?"

Rolling her eyes toward the mirror, she touched her lashes. "You should see some of the things his buddy shows me."

Her eyes trailed to his. Their eye contact only lasted a second before his gaze descended to her covered chest. "Next time, I want you to show 'em to me."

Pushing her shoulders back to accentuate what he couldn't see, she was proud of her wardrobe choice. Tormenting Ryske was fun.

"What makes you think there will be a next time? I picked this one because I know they're your favorite part of me."

"Tease," he muttered a moment before the two back doors opened.

People were joining them? The decision was made without her input. Her mother got in one side and her sister the other. Typical that all the women were drawn to Ryske.

"Ready to go?" Jean asked with an edge of apprehension.

"When was the last time you drove a car?" Lena asked, putting on her seatbelt.

Harlow put on hers too. "I borrowed a friend's in the city. You're good, Lena. I need to keep you around long enough for you to marry your millionaire." Rupert's car pulled out of the driveway, she followed behind him. "You do know I plan to exploit him for all he's worth."

"Oh, Harlow," her mother chastised.

Lena laughed. "We can go on shopping trips together."

"Shopping trips?" she said, glancing at her sister in the mirror. "I want a house, and a Mercedes, and a safety deposit box filled with jewels."

"Why would you want that? You don't even wear jewelry," Lena said. "Except that bracelet… where did you get that anyway?"

Glancing from her bracelet to the man at her side, the energy of the air between them changed.

"Off a dead man."

"Ew," Lena said. "Is that true? Why would you want to steal something from a dead person?"

"Because he stole from me," she answered, keeping her eyes on Rupert's lights in front of them.

Lena gasped. "What did he steal?"

"My naiveté."

Silence settled over the car. Confusion reigned in the back, while tension crackled in the front.

On cue, Ryske switched the mood by inhaling and twisting to look into the back seat. "I know I said it already, but you ladies really are stunning tonight."

Lena was happy to giggle and launch into a full dissection of her outfit and her mother's too. Ryske did a good job of sounding interested. It was a testament to his professional skills that he managed to remain attentive long after Harlow had given up listening.

After four or five minutes, she interrupted. "You know, Mr. Ryske," she said, sliding her hands to the top of the wheel. "It occurs to me that a man of your means should have a driver."

"I do," he said. "And she's beautiful."

Flashing his grin at her glare, he proved his arrogance survived his death.

Harlow drew her focus back to the road. "I meant a permanent driver."

"I do," he said. "Gave him the weekend off. Told him I was spending it with three gorgeous ladies."

"Something you do often I imagine," Harlow said.

"Do you have a limo?" Lena asked. "I love limousines… We've never had our own personal permanent driver though. That must be amazing… Does he drive you to dinner and the theater and all those lovely places?"

"He drives me anywhere I have to go."

Struggling against her urge to groan, she did a double take when Lena shifted to stick her head between the front seats. "Do you think you could take us out in it?"

"Lena," Jean said, chastising her other daughter with the same vehemence Harlow got. Finally! "Really? Give the man a chance to extend an invitation."

"I'd be delighted to take you out," Ryske said.

Lena whooped and started chattering with their mother.

Knowing it was unlikely to ever happen, Harlow grinned at Ryske. "Does your driver wear a uniform?" she asked. Ryske smiled. "Does he have a little hat?"

She could tell from his expression that he was enjoying the idea of Noon dressing up as the dutiful employee as much as she did.

"I'm sure that can be arranged," he said and she laughed.

The country club gates were open and flanked with twinkly white lights. Rupert stopped to check in at the security box. He must have spoken for her too because the guy waved her through without speaking to her.

"Wow, free pass, and that was without my breasts on show," she said, winking at the guy as she drove by him.

Up ahead, Rupert pulled over to the right and got out to give the valet his car key.

Harlow slowed to a crawl. "Do you want me to park it?" she asked, glancing at Ryske, figuring they shouldn't let too many people into this stolen vehicle.

"Do you want to park it?" Ryske asked.

She stopped, ten feet away from the valet lane. "Will you be mad at me if I scratch it?"

"Do you want me to be mad at you?"

The tone of his question got her attention. It didn't take long to identify the mischievous glint in his eye. Making him mad might be fun. She liked him to be rough… wanted to be punished.

Rupert's car had gone, one of the valet's had driven it to the parking lot. The next valet was probably wondering why she hadn't pulled forward.

Ryske brought out the daring in her. Intention raised the corner of her mouth. She changed gear and shoved her foot down flat on the accelerator sending a skid of gravel out from beneath the wheels as the car flew forward.

Her mother and Lena called out, their volume matching that of the valet outside, but Ryske's encouraging snicker fired her up. The gate to the parking area was on a sweeping turn, so she kept her speed for a few yards, then used the brake to drift around the curve. The shocked valets coming through the gate scrambled out of her way.

Doing a circuit of the parking lot, adrenaline heated her blood.

"There," Ryske said, pointing to a spot that would let her drive straight through and come out the other side, lined up with the exit gate.

Aiming for the spot, she swung the car around, gunned it across the spaces and slammed on the brakes to bring them to a lurching halt. Turning off the engine, she breathed out, still zipping with the thrill of being crazy.

"That was uncalled for," her mother said, getting out with Lena not far behind.

The pair of them went tramping across the parking lot, away from the car, probably regretting ever getting in it.

Panting, Harlow shimmered, feeling alive for the first time that day.

"Come here," Ryske said, taking her by surprise when he drove his hand around the side of her head to pull her across the center console and plant a kiss on her mouth.

Though she mumbled a semi-objection, she relaxed after one weak push against his ribs. The urgent need of his tongue driving deeper into her mouth compelled her to force them apart.

"Anyone could see," she whispered, catching a glance out the windshield.

Didn't seem he cared because he increased his grip on her head, pressing the length of his thumb against the front of her ear. "I'm gonna fuck you good tonight."

Searing arousal and heated excitement rebelled against the need to contain herself. "Crash," she whispered, touching a finger to his lips. He yanked it away and forced another kiss to her mouth. "Stop it… You can't do this here."

Keeping his hold on her head, he shoved his other hand up her skirt between her thighs. "I can do whatever I goddamn like to you, any time I want."

Yanking her thigh toward him, he forced her legs apart and discovered her secret. His shock dropped and then flew up to her eyes.

She grinned. "Oops," she purred, like neglecting to put on panties was an oversight.

It couldn't have been more deliberate.

Using his surprise, she slithered out of his grip and the car. She'd straightened her skirt and went a few steps toward the club building before he leaped out of the car to rush up at her side.

"No," he said, grabbing her arm in an attempt to pull her back, but she swung out of his grip and kept going. "No, baby, you can't tease me with that and then take it away."

Sly in her smile, she kept her shoulders back and her stride as long as she could to make up some time. "I can do whatever I goddamn like to you, any time I want," she said, spouting his words back at him.

He stopped moving and disappeared from her side, his groan vibrated through the air. Although pleased with herself, she was also worried about their delay being conspicuous. Still, Harlow didn't dare turn around to check if Ryske was coming. He could watch her ass sashay away from him and make his own excuses for being last to catch up… if he ever did.

Rupert, her parents, and Lena were standing in a group a dozen feet from the external club stairs. They were chatting amongst themselves and didn't question what had kept her or where Ryske was.

Rupert rested a hand on her lower back, accepting her into their circle. Her parents were talking about something Rupert was only half-listening to because he bowed to murmur to her.

"Edgar Charnock is here."

She groaned. "I hate that guy."

"I know," Rupert said, stroking her bare back. "That's why I wanted to warn you."

"He's so pompous," she said. "Are any of his children still in his will? Last I heard he was ousting people left and right for not living up to his righteous standard."

Rupert shook his head. "He cut Nigel out after his heart scare."

She blinked at him. "Edgar had a heart scare?"

"No," Rupert said. "Nigel. He was supposed to take a meeting and didn't get there because he had a heart attack."

That was so appalling, she almost couldn't believe it. If anyone else had said it to her, Harlow would've called them a liar.

It was… astounding. "Edgar cut his son out of his will because his son had a heart attack?"

Rupert nodded. "Double bypass. Edgar didn't even send a card let alone visit him."

"Wow," she mouthed, shocked, yet not surprised. Edgar always had been an asshole. "Didn't he just get married again?"

"Edgar? Yeah. She's twenty-five."

"You know he should be the commercial for anti-Viagra," she said. "There should be something his kids can slip him that will cut off blood supply to that part of his anatomy… It's disgusting, the guy's a slime."

Rupert laughed. "You told me he propositioned you."

"More than once," she said, nodding, then shivering at the memory. "It's not even a compliment. He literally expects every woman to fall to their knees for him." She shook her head and suppressed a gag. "I would slit my throat before I'd let his dick touch it."

The air behind her changed. Somehow, without even registering Rupert's side glance, she became aware of Ryske at her back.

"Suicide's a little extreme," Rupert said, hooking her hand into his elbow when her parents started to move.

Presumably now all their party was present, they were ready to go inside.

"You'd be surprised," she said. "It doesn't take much for a person to be pushed into considering it. And that, my friend, would definitely push me beyond considering it."

Rupert's fingers tightened around hers. "You've considered suicide?"

That hadn't really been the point of what she was saying. After reading his concern, she tried to play it casual and indifferent.

"Once."

Stopping on the top landing, Rupert didn't seem to see anyone except her even though there were plenty of people around. "When? Harlow, I—"

"It's not a big deal," she said, feeling awkward with Ryske right there beside them.

Her one-time lover was in no hurry to get past as others were.

"Not a big deal? I—"

"You know," she said, putting a hand to both Rupert and Ryske's chests. Each were happy to focus on her and didn't seem interested in acknowledging the other. "I'm a lady. You're both keeping me outside in the cold… and I'm not wearing much. Wouldn't it be more fun to take me inside and get me liquored up?"

Spinning around, she marched away, leaving them to watch her ass. She'd forgotten how Rupert could zoom in on details like that. Anyone else would have laughed off her comment, but he knew her too well and read into the statement.

She'd have to be more careful… with both the men courting her.

TWENTY-FOUR

THE SWEETING TABLE was at the opposite side of the room, right on the perimeter. Lena was over there already, putting her purse by her place and removing her pashmina. Didn't take long for her little sister to be whisked away by one of her cronies. Their little posse thought they were tight, though they wouldn't know the meaning of keeping a secret.

Harlow chose to seat herself on the far side, back to the wall. The Sweeting parents were off schmoozing too, which meant she was alone at the table when Ryske and Rupert joined her.

With full entitlement, Ryske swung into the seat next to her.

Rupert approached her other side. "Would you like a drink?" he asked.

"Yes," she said. "Yes, I would like a drink, Mr. Marlowe… Scotch. Neat."

Rupert cleared his throat, drawing her attention up. "Do you think that's a… a good idea?"

"Why wouldn't it be?" she asked. "In fact, let's make it a double."

Sinking down into the chair by hers, he took her hand. "That's not good for you," he said, lowering his voice to a whisper. "In your condition."

Though Rupert glanced at Ryske like he was nervous they might be overheard, she was less discreet.

"We agreed to forget that conversation," she said. "I am not pregnant." Harlow emphasized the negative in hopes she'd never have to correct him again. "Now, I would like a double Scotch and if that's a problem for you, I'll get it myself."

Maintaining certainty, she conveyed how she didn't like his assumptions or that he'd brought them up in public.

Rupert rose on a nod. "No problem," he said and headed for the bar.

Her peace only lasted a second before Ryske broke it. "You could be, you know."

"I could be what?" she asked, observing the dozens of social darlings fawning over each other.

No one was close to their table. The main hub of activity was more central. Good. She was happy to be detached from it all, watching events unfold from a safe distance.

"Pregnant," he said, slithering a hand onto her stomach. "We weren't careful and I gave you what you asked for."

"I'm not a rookie teenager," she said. "I'm on birth control."

"Why would you be using birth control? I've been dead for four months."

"I haven't," she said and twisted to face him. "Stop rubbing me."

Except her shift in position slid his hand from her stomach around to her hip.

Ryske's fingers were happy to creep farther and rest on the small of her back. "Tell me it wasn't the sap… anyone but him."

"Clyde is not a sap," she said, pulling his hand away from her body to push it back to him. "He's a better kisser than you might think."

The words came out before her mind caught up to their implication. Both of them froze for a few seconds.

Panic quickened her pulse, but Ryske was nurturing a rage. "I'll cut out his fucking tongue," he grumbled.

"No, you won't," she said, sliding her hand up his thigh. On instinct, he relaxed to give her access when she pressed her hand over his fly to begin rubbing. "It didn't mean anything. I was vulnerable and drunk and—"

"You think it makes me feel better that he was taking advantage of you? Just means I'll make it hurt more."

"Crash," she whispered, her hand stroking the length growing and hardening beneath her palm. "I plan to get drunk tonight… I'll be vulnerable… won't you take advantage of me?"

Becoming the target of his vehement rage, she parted her lips in a pout, teasing him into adjusting the flavor of his emotion to something more carnal.

"It's not taking advantage if you're begging for it, babydoll."

"What if I say no?"

One side of his mouth rose. "I'll try harder."

It was insane. All she wanted to do was nestle closer, to put her head on his shoulder and kiss his jaw. Being this close to him, touching him in this way, felt so natural, so normal. Yet, they didn't belong to each other. Couldn't belong to each other.

"Never defeated, are you?"

"Turn around and every day I'll be there, Trink."

She sighed. "You know we can't be together."

"I know you think that's true," he said, nodding downward. "You're slacking."

Her wandering mind slowed her hand. With his reminder, she pushed harder and sped her strokes, which wasn't easy when she had to conceal the movement of her arm from the room.

"I like that you let me touch you like this… that you react to me this way."

His heavy eyes hardly moved when he blinked. "If you wanna drop your napkin and open those lips…"

Excitement fizzed through her, pooling and gathering between her thighs. "What if we got caught?"

Didn't bother Ryske. He raised one shoulder in an apathetic shrug. "Tell them I paid for the privilege."

"Wouldn't be the first time I've played hooker," she said. "Though, if I was supposed to charge you for every blowjob, you'd owe me a fortune."

"I'll pay it back in barter," he said, reaching over to slide a hand up the outside of her thigh and beneath her skirt to grip her ass. "Come sit in my lap."

Her heart was pounding so hard she could see it beating through her dress. "Thank fuck we're not together," she panted, opening her lips, fixating on his, desperate to kiss him while fighting to restrain herself.

"Why's that, Trink?"

"Because if I was allowed to have you, I'd be riding you right here."

Curling his fingers, they dug deeper into her ass cheek. "You're allowed, Trinket," he murmured. "I'll clean up the mess."

"They'll call the cops," she said, knowing she should look beyond his shoulder to check no one was watching them, but damn it, she couldn't tear her eyes from his.

"I won't leave you hanging," he said. "I'll make sure you come before they cuff me."

Desperation lodged a yelp in her throat. Harlow didn't need his hand on her ass, she wanted to be in his grip. Grabbing his wrist out from under her skirt, she thrust his hand to her neck and didn't have to tell him what she needed. He squeezed hard, forcing her mouth to open wide to fight for a breath.

"I need to fuck you," he hissed, clenching his teeth. "Now."

In urgent agreement, she tried to nod. Running out of there together may prove difficult given how fraught and frantic they were. Neither of them could be discreet with their shallow breathing. Before they could come up with a solution, they were interrupted.

"Excuse me?"

The sound of another male drove Ryske to whip around so fast he almost pulled her out of her chair. Her instinct to grab his arm was the only thing that prevented him from shooting to his feet and setting upon the intruder.

Still, she needed a few seconds to gather her own wits. As her mind cleared, she noticed a man beside them, glancing from her to Ryske, wearing confusion and maybe a tad of fear.

She coughed and covered how she'd grabbed for Ryske by coiling her fingers around his upper arm. Perfectly normal. Nothing to see. This was allowed in polite society.

"Yes?" she asked.

"I'm sorry, I… didn't mean to interrupt… I…" His gaze rested on her. "I felt like I should know you… that we've met, but I can't quite place you…"

"You think she's never heard that line before?" Ryske spat.

Soothing Ryske, she stroked his arm while their guest blinked in surprise. "I'm sorry. I didn't mean to suggest anything im—"

"We've never met," she said, managing a practiced smile. "But I do know who you are." That surprised both men. Offering the hand of friendship seemed like the least she could do. "I'm Harlow Sweeting, and you are the brilliant Christian Hyslop."

Her knowledge took him aback, which made her laugh because he'd been the one to recognize her first.

"I am, but… I'm sorry, I still don't—"

"I'm a friend of Ophelia Hagan."

The absent beauty's connection to her and to the man at her side was the reason Harlow chose not to introduce Ryske. Withholding information was smart and could prove valuable in future. Though, at a basic level, she just didn't want the lies to overlap.

If, through the grapevine, Hyslop knew Ophelia was engaged to Ryske, it could prove difficult to explain why they'd been panting all over each other a moment before.

"Of course! Ophelia," Hyslop said. Harlow gestured to the chair next to Ryske, indicating that Hyslop should sit, so he did. "How is she?"

"Wonderful the last time I saw her," Harlow said, though it had been almost a week since she'd visited her friend. "Tell me, did you get the investment Jarvis was helping you with?"

If the fates were fair, she should get bonus points for saying his name like it wasn't poison. Ryske's acknowledgement of a fingertip on her knee suggested he thought the same thing.

"No," Hyslop said, shifting in a display of disappointment. "That fell through. We didn't get the chance to go to the meeting."

"That is a shame," she said. "Ophelia says such wonderful things about your brilliant mind."

"Ophelia is too kind," Hyslop said, noticing Rupert approach with a tray-carrying server in his wake. "Well, it was nice to see you again." Hyslop stood up, opening his hand to request hers, so he could offer a polite kiss to her knuckle. "Tell Ophelia I say hello."

Hyslop left the table and Rupert sat. "Friend of yours?" he asked, looking beyond her to Ryske.

He'd probably assumed Hyslop was a friend of Ryske's, which was just fine, it saved her coming up with an explanation.

"Something like that," Ryske said.

Rupert touched her shoulder and nodded to the corner. "Charnock is holding court over there."

Selecting her drink from the tray the server left on their table, she enjoyed its scent and its taste. "You have fun with that, honey. Let me know how it works out."

He laughed. "Okay, I'll be back."

Rupert kissed her cheek and departed the table to go wait his turn to kiss Edgar Charnock's ring, as it were.

Watching him go made her shiver. "I hate that guy."

"Can't say I'm fond of him either," Ryske muttered, picking a drink from the tray.

She switched her glare over her shoulder to him. "I was talking about Edgar Charnock."

"Oh," he said. "Yeah, I don't know that guy."

"You don't really hate Rupert," she said, relaxing in her chair. "He's not a bad person. He never beat me or anything like that."

"Fucked you though," he said, finishing his drink in two mouthfuls. "I don't hate him… Feel sorry for him, to be honest."

That piqued her curiosity. "Why?"

"Because he's at the end of his time with you," Ryske said, being discreet about curving an arm around her to lay it on the back of her chair so he could draw slow circles on her spine. "I'm at the start of mine." Harlow didn't get a chance to respond because he leaned back and carried on talking. "You ever think about a tramp stamp?"

"No," she said, putting down her glass to twist farther toward him. Cupping her breast, she drew a line under the curve of it. "I want a tattoo here… Well, it will start here, curve under my boob and go down to my hip. Charlie has this great design; we've been working on it together. It's tribal lines kind of like yours, but they're thinner, more delicate. It would be a sort of hourglass shape, wider under my breast and on my hip, but narrower in the middle."

"Who's Charlie?"

"My tattoo guy," she said. Fixated on her body where she'd drawn the shape of the tattoo against the side of her torso, he shook his head. "No? Why not?"

Ryske's eyes narrowed. "He gay?"

"Is he… No, he's not gay. Why? Do you have a fantasy about doing it with a tattoo artist?"

Picking up her glass, he managed to sample some of her drink before she could snatch it away.

"I've done it with a tattoo artist…" he said, "few of them actually."

Scanning the room, she sought a distraction from that visual. "Course you have," she muttered, pleased to have liquor in her hand.

Ryske wasn't a gentleman about it and leaned in to murmur in her ear. "Jealous?"

"You're in enough trouble, so why you would think playing with me is a good idea…" she said, examining the various groups congregated in the glittering space.

His fingertip trailed up her spine. "I always want to play with you." His finger traced up and down, sending little skitters of tickling awareness through her. "I agree, no tramp stamp… But you should get my initials tattooed somewhere… Huntley Ryske's Harlow."

She tipped her chin toward her shoulder. "That would be HRH."

Laughing, he straightened from his slouch until his chin almost met her shoulder too. "Exactly. You are my queen."

"I don't want to be your queen," she said, happy to hitch her chin in defiance. Though, her next thought made it difficult to keep a straight face. "I want to be your whore."

"You're that too," he said, sinking against the back of his seat to let his fingers return to their delicate stroking of her spine.

Lifting her hand, she presented her star tattoo. "That's for you."

"I know," he said. "It won't be as significant after you get the other four."

"Other four?"

Ryske sat up to take off his jacket and presented his shirt sleeve to her. "Take that out."

Undoing his cufflink, she watched him fold back his cuff to reveal a new solid black star on his wrist. Though it was in line with the originals, the new star was smaller and had a second concentric star around it in a thin line of black ink, highlighting it as significant.

"Oh my God," she said, touching the edge. "When did you get that?"

"When I was dead," he said. "Had to wait for Bale to finish with the antibiotic shit. Dover did it… he's the steadiest hand of us all."

She hadn't noticed it in Floyd's, maybe because she'd been too focused on his cock. Last night, in her dark bedroom, her interest had been elsewhere. Overwhelmed and flattered, Harlow outlined the shape with her nail.

His request rang in her ears. "Where?" she asked, her attention springing to his.

Ryske's brows rose in question. "Where?"

"You can pick anywhere on my body."

"Uh, your pussy," he said.

Laughing, she should have known he'd pick there. "Okay. We will have to disguise it as something else so Rupert won't know it's another man's name."

His brows snapped to an instant scowl. "What are we talking about?"

"Your initials."

He grabbed her arm. "I thought we were playing pin my tail on the Trinket… I'll get my whole fucking name tattooed in block capital letters down there if I want; that prick won't ever set eyes on it."

"You're being illogical, we just talked about this," she said, peeling his fingers from her arm so she could fold his sleeve down and return his cufflink to its rightful place. "We're not going to be together."

Flipping his hand over, he snatched her wrist so hard she gasped. "We *are* together."

"No," she said, struggling to get her hand out of his grip, finding it impossible at this proximity without making a scene. "We're not and you don't pout, so stop pretending you do."

"Damn right, I don't pout, I take action," he said. "Haven't met a challenge I can't conquer yet."

"Well, it's nice to meet you, Mr. Ryske, because you just did," she said, twisting and pulling. "Let me go, Crash."

Gripping her tighter, he gave her another yank. "What happened to 'Tighter, baby'? Huh?"

Something about those words propelled her into a flashback. Suddenly, she was back in Floyd's on her knees next to him, his blood spilling on the floor. The country club vanished. The people, the music, the light, all of it, and it became dark.

Cold, scared, and desperate, she existed only in that black moment. "Please, baby," she murmured.

"Harlow." She heard his voice. Somewhere. Immersed in the memory, she couldn't respond. Ryske shook her hard. "Trinket!" The force of his stern tone coupled with the vigor of his shake snapped her into the present. She blinked into his gaze, fighting to focus. "Where'd you go, baby?"

His fingertips grazed her cheek and kept going around to her hair until he was gripping the side of her head.

"Everything okay?"

Harlow had to forget whatever she'd been about to say when Rupert's voice joined them. Turning out of Ryske's hold, she found Rupert lowering into the seat at her side. Her parents and sister joined them too.

"Everything's great," she said, and made herself smile. "I'm just going to use the restroom."

Leaving the table was her way of seeking a reprieve. Just when life was supposed to be making sense again, she was more confused than ever. Being pulled in so many directions, there were moments even breathing was a chore.

This wasn't the life she wanted. Country clubs and polite conversation were supposed to be her past, not her future.

What choice did she have? The deal with Rupert still stood. She couldn't go back on it just because Ryske's lie set them on this course. Whether she wanted it or not, this was going to be her life. She would hold onto whatever fun she could while it lasted, but there was no way it could last forever.

TWENTY-FIVE

FUNNY THAT HER thought on the way to the restroom had been savoring the fun while it lasted.

On her return to the party, Harlow's ponderings ran more along the vein of how torturous the rest of the night would be. Ditching Ryske at the table would be fun, if that didn't mean leaving him with full, unfettered access to her family. No way he'd let it slide if she snuck out on him. God only knew what he'd tell her folks if she left him unsupervised.

Using both hands to twist a length of her hair, she wound through the partygoers, absorbing a lay of the land. Her apathy ran in stark contrast to the smiling faces of everyone else in the room. They exuded nothing but enthusiasm for the event... It was probably fake... Turned out she hadn't been raised that far from people with Ryske's skillset after all.

Someone stepped into her path.

Assuming the obstruction was unintentional, she stepped to the other side, intending to past him, except the guy got in her way.

When he did it again, their eyes met.

She grinned while exhaling a forced laugh. "And what are we doing?" she asked.

He had the deepest blue eyes she'd ever seen in her life. They were clear and keen and only emphasized by the contrast of his jet-black hair.

When his lips widened in a curve, he looked incredibly pleased with himself. "Hi," he said, his voice a languorous purr.

"Hi," she replied, tilting her head. "I don't know you."

Taking her hand, he traced his fingertips from her wrist to her knuckles. "Not yet."

He raised her hand toward his mouth as though he intended to kiss it.

Harlow tensed to prevent the contact. "Listen, buddy, if you're hitting on me, you've really got to take a number, 'cause my dance card is full."

The curl in his lips tightened like he was restraining a laugh. "Damn, man," he muttered. "How does he always get the best ones?"

As if the question conjured him, Ryske materialized. Swerving around the stranger, he swept an arm around her waist to pull her against his side.

"Ha, Penzance," he said, then lowered his voice and spoke through a static smile. "What the fuck are you doing here?"

"I'm talking to this beautiful woman," he said. "You see her? She's beautiful."

Ryske pulled this Penzance person's hand away from hers, which she was fine with. Though he seemed to have forgotten they had a cover of their own to consider. Reminding him, Harlow pushed Ryske's hand from her hip and sidestepped out of his embrace.

"This beautiful woman is spoken for," Ryske said, glancing at her hand when she wiped the back of it down his shirt a few times, ridding herself of the remnants of Penzance's touch.

It wasn't that Penzance had actually kissed her, but she was perturbed he'd taken the liberty of caressing her.

Ryske picked up her other hand to reveal her tattoo.

Penzance clicked his fingers. "I thought I recognized

that," he said. Like it was loose on his shoulders, his head flopped down and to the side, so he could take a closer look. "You got this one to mark herself for you… that's deep cover."

"If it was, you just blew it," Ryske said. "Want to tell me who you're working?"

"Nothing as beautiful as you've got," Penzance said and clucked his tongue in appreciation. "How close you been to her panties?"

Harlow freed her tongue from where it rested in the corner of her mouth. "I'm not wearing panties."

Penzance's brows rose fast. Ryske took another shot at curving a hand around her hip, but she swatted it away.

"Oh my God, I think I'm in love," Penzance muttered.

The guy was attractive, no doubt about that. Probably around the same age as Ryske and his crew, it was obvious from the energy in the air that these men had history.

"I'm not that easily swayed," she said.

Penzance grinned. "My dick's bigger than his."

"Is that any way to talk to a lady?" she asked, swiping Ryske's possessive, snaking hand away again.

"Gotta do something to get your attention," he said.

Harlow propped a fist on her cocked hip. "Why do you need my attention? Am I your mark?" She distracted him by licking her lips and plumping them. "Tell you what, Mr. Penzance, you prove you're not a liar and I'll let you frisk me for anything I've got on me."

That drew him closer. "Can I keep what I find?"

Without stepping away, she leaned back. "I'd say yes, except you already lost," she whispered, intriguing him. "You can't prove you're not a liar because you are one."

"Am I?" he asked. "How do you figure that?"

"Because it's not my attention you want to get, it's his…"

Nodding sideways, she assessed Penzance's reaction as he checked out the crowded table at the other side of the room headed by Edgar Charnock.

There was admiration in his gaze when it trailed back

to her. "How do you figure that, Precious?"

Her confidence level was high. "Because he's the richest man in the room. He's pompous, arrogant, full of himself, and has complete faith in his own ability to notice anyone who wants to slide behind his defenses. He has a daughter who despises him and a gullible favorite granddaughter with her eyes on the prize… If you want to make a fortune, you'd be a fool not to aim high and commit yourself to the long game."

"And that's why you figure I want his attention?"

"No," she said, resting her shoulder on Ryske's arm. "I figure that because you were eyeing up Charnock's granddaughter when I walked in here."

Her powers of observation seemed to knock him down a peg. "You, I—"

"Emma is not the prettiest or the smartest in the room. You're a man who likes a challenge and she wouldn't pose one if sex was your goal… She's young and gobbles up male attention. You have the skills and the looks to get into the panties of the pinnacle of the room, the real prize, the most obstinate and alluring woman present. A man like you doesn't go for a girl like Emma without an ulterior motive… I trust you have the skills to pursue this without making that obvious?"

"I…" Penzance looked to Ryske and then to her. "I do."

"Good. I assume Penzance is a nickname. How do you like to be introduced?"

His mouth fell open. "Vane… my name is Samuel Vane."

Harlow switched her focus to Ryske and straightened his tie. "Excellent. You'll have more of a chance to gain favor in the family if you make it seem you want to impress Edgar for the sake of winning his granddaughter. He believes in his own importance. Get to her through him, thus you get to him, etc…" Turning her head, she made brief eye contact with Vane to ensure he understood. After Vane absorbed what she said, she slapped her hands onto Ryske's chest. "Crash, you're going to flirt with his wife."

That startled him. "Excuse me? I'm going to what?"

"Kylie is young, and beautiful. She's a swimsuit model."

"I don't need her measurements."

"Vane will have an easier job if Charnock dislikes you. He won't miss another man spoiling his wife with attention."

"I thought I was supposed to be engaged."

"You are," she said. "But my family have had their minute with Charnock. They won't be over there again. You're good."

Ryske shook his head. "I'm not in on this. There's a code that says we don't blow each other's cover, but that's it… Why should I help this schmuck out? I won't be getting a cut."

Licking her lips, she rose on her tiptoes. "Your cut comes later, Crash, because I want to play." Pushing away from him, she spun on the spot. "Follow me, gentlemen."

***

HARLOW WAS STILL riding the high of being involved in something naughty. Edgar Charnock was a fool who treated his staff and his family horribly. Whatever Penzance was up to, it wouldn't hurt for Charnock to be taken down a notch.

The old slimeball had been thrilled to see her approach and only paid marginal attention to the two men with her during introductions. Harlow underestimated her own ability to help. Edgar had done his best to put the moves on her. So while he had noticed, and disliked, Ryske getting close to Kylie, he'd been on his own mission.

Seeing Ryske flirt with another woman was an odd experience. If someone had asked her, Harlow would've said she'd hate it. Yet, to her surprise, there was something powerful about watching her man at work. Something alluring about knowing he was acting and that he was only doing it because she'd asked him to.

It might be different if she thought things were going to get physical, but Kylie would be going home with Edgar. Harlow didn't have to worry about Ryske's virtue.

After an hour of playing, she made her excuses and

returned to the family table. Ten minutes later, while half-listening to her mother and Lena discussing their dislike for women in high-powered jobs, Ryske appeared behind her father.

"I'm sorry," he said, rounding the table. "I met an old friend."

"Oh, I love it when that happens," Jean said. "Serendipitous meetings."

Ryske took his seat next to her again and leaned in to murmur, "Vane's got this," he said, picking up his drink as cover for the lean.

Under the table, she gave his knee a discreet pat.

"Mr. Ryske, does your fiancée have a job?" Lena asked.

Ryske's mouth was on his glass, so Harlow answered. "Ophelia tried her hand at business when she was younger. But she never acquired a taste for it."

That garnered understanding all around the table. "Some women just aren't built for it," Jean said. "She sounds like a very astute woman."

"Very," Ryske said.

"Probably not your type, Rupert," Lena said and the table laughed.

Rupert put an arm around her. "I prefer my women headstrong."

"Can't deny I'm that," Harlow said.

Something snagged her attention. A man who'd just walked in at the other side of the room. Why did she notice him? A familiar face… though it didn't appear particularly happy. Turning to Ryske, she side-nodded, attempting to draw his attention to his friend.

Ryske noticed her heightened awareness. "You okay?" he mouthed.

"Maze," she whispered.

Concern crept to his expression, and he turned to seek what she'd seen.

As soon as he did, he stood up. "Excuse me," Ryske said and without another word, started across the room.

How much was Ryske keeping the guys in the loop

about his movements? Maze may just be there to track down the errant crew member. Except, she'd assume if the Floyd's crew discovered Ryske stalking her, they'd have waited at her parents.' The fact that any of them had come to the country club couldn't be a good sign.

The way the men interacted increased her worry. Matching their trajectories to meet, purpose in the gait of both men put her on alert. Ryske laid a hand on Maze's arm while the latter explained something in a quick series of words. Ryske nodded and patted his friend's arm.

"Harlow?" Rupert said at her side. She couldn't tear her attention from the serious pair. "Is something wrong?"

"I don't know," she murmured, assuming he could see what she was seeing. "I'm worried it might be Ophelia, excuse me."

That wasn't the truth at all. Short of Ophelia dying at the hands of someone they knew, why would the crew rush to tell Ryske her fate? But using her friend and Ryske's fake fiancée gave her cover to hurry across the room to find out what was going on.

Ryske didn't see her coming, but Maze did. He stopped talking before she reached Ryske's side.

"Crash?" she said when it seemed like Maze wasn't going to keep talking with her in earshot.

Ryske didn't fill her in either. "Baby, I've gotta go," he said, sliding a hand onto her back, taking way too long to tear his attention away from Maze. Something was going on. Something serious. "I'm gonna come back for you when—"

"Crash," she said, "tell me." There was no way she could let him walk out without an explanation, except he hesitated. "You said you wouldn't lie to me."

"I know, baby," he said, combing his finger through her hair at the side of her neck. "That's not why I…" Glancing at Maze, he gathered himself. "It's the kid… he's in bad shape."

Searching his expression, it took a second to catch up. "Felipe?" she whispered.

Ryske nodded. Just when she needed his support the most, his hand dropped and he stepped back.

The reason for his retreat became apparent when Rupert stopped with them. "Everything okay?" he asked, putting a hand on her shoulder.

"Marlowe, something's come up," Ryske said. "I have to leave."

"I'm sorry to hear that. Is there a problem?"

"Yes, actually, a friend—"

"Of Ophelia's," Harlow heard herself interrupt Ryske. The moment she did, she turned to Rupert. "I have to go and make sure she's okay."

"You…" Rupert was taken aback. "You're leaving too?"

"I have to go," she said, reaching behind herself to push at Ryske. "I'm sorry, I'll call you."

Bouncing up, she kissed Rupert's cheek, then spun around to hurry out with Ryske and Maze who were already on their way to the door. Both men stepped aside to let her exit first; she didn't miss a step or slow for a second.

Running down the external stairs, fraught with thoughts of Felipe in pain, Harlow only started to feel grounded when Ryske's fingers threaded between hers.

"I don't have a ride," Maze said. "My parents' guy dropped me here."

She had no idea Maze even still saw his parents. Why had he been with them that night? It worked out for them that he'd been close by.

"We're good," Ryske said, taking the BMW key from his pocket to hold it up. "Noon's got our back."

The three of them understood the urgency and kept up the pace on the rush to the parking lot. All three got into the car in sync. In the driver's seat, Ryske screeched out of the parking lot, controlling the drift in the back end to take them from the country club and out to the street.

Harlow felt cold.

Overwhelmed by her worry for Felipe, she couldn't dampen the disgust churning inside her over what she'd just done. She'd lied to Rupert. Straight up lied. In the past, she may have been guilty of omitting information, which was bad enough, but she had never told him blatant lies.

They weren't technically together. They hadn't been on a date or slept together since she'd returned. The only real kiss they'd shared was the one she planted on him to spite Ryske. Still, it felt wrong to lie.

Conversation between the men in the front broke through her reverie. "You got an ID?" Ryske asked.

"Dover's on it," Maze said. "Whoever did this… they screwed with the wrong crew."

"I'll fucking say," Ryske growled.

Tension was palpable. All of them were frustrated at being so far away.

Shifting to the middle of the backseat, she slid forward to hook her elbows on the shoulders of the two front seats. "What happened?"

"He was jumped," Maze said. "Noon called. Said he was beat pretty bad. He's in the hospital."

At least someone had been smart enough to get him there instead of avoiding 9-1-1. "How bad is it?"

"I don't know."

Sliding deep into the backseat, her stomach bottomed out and her mouth parched. "This is my fault. They were pressuring him, and I… I did nothing."

"Hey, this is not your fault," Ryske said, seeking her in the rearview mirror. She could see his head moving but kept staring out her side window. "Trink, look at me. This is not your fault. At least you were there… we weren't even fucking there."

"Which was my fault too," she said, her gaze dropping to her knees.

If it wasn't for his need to protect her, Ryske would have been at Floyd's instead of faking his own demise. He'd left, him and his crew, because they wanted her to have a life separate from theirs.

"We only met the kid 'cause of you," Ryske said. "And he'd have been in the shit months ago if it wasn't for you. Trinket, look at me, baby… I'll pull this fucking car over now and make you look at me if you don't gimme those goddamn eyes this minute."

She didn't want him to read her fear and guilt. Still,

she blinked her eyes up to his in the mirror because she knew better than to test him. Delays would increase her guilt. They had to get to Felipe as fast as possible.

"Good girl," he said. "Now give me your hand."

Dragging herself to the edge of the seat, she let her body sag against the shoulder of the driver's and flopped her arm across him as best she could. Picking it up, Ryske kissed her knuckles, her palm, and her star.

"He's just a baby, Crash," she whispered.

"I know, Trink," he said, laying her arm across his collarbone, holding it there, stroking back and forth. "And he's gonna be just fine."

Frustrated and angry at both Felipe's situation and her own, a familiar burn in her throat signaled the prospect of descending into either a panic attack or a crying jag. She didn't want to do either.

Heading them off, she was boosted by the urgent need to keep her shit together. Seeking anything that might anchor her, anything that would give her a distraction, she needed a focal point that wasn't the abyss of emotion.

Rising in a crouch, she pulled her arm away from Ryske's control to yank his tie knot. "I hate you in a suit," she said, pulling and tugging. To achieve her goal, she wrapped her other arm around his headrest to reach him from behind. "I hate it."

Dragging the tie off, she tossed it away and yanked at the buttons on his shirt until the top few were loose. Sliding her hand inside the fabric, she immediately felt better after flattening her palm on his pec. She relaxed against the corner of his chair, her head on the shoulder.

The roughness of his scar rasped her palm. Closing her eyes, she stroked the beat of his pulse and the warmth of him. This man was alive. Ryske. The man she'd feared was lost. The man she'd cried for. The man who'd been torn away from her, leaving her bereft and empty, was here.

"Guess you two made up," Maze said. "Nightingale—"

"I don't want to talk about it," she murmured. Would the specter of grief ever leave? "I want to see Felipe. That's it."

Another emotional discussion about everything they'd been through wouldn't help. Beyond that, it was impossible to explain what was going on between her and Ryske when she couldn't figure it out herself.

Getting to the hospital to see their young friend was all that mattered. Harlow just hoped that rallying around would help because it was about all they could do.

TWENTY-SIX

IN THE HASTE to get to Felipe, Harlow hadn't thought about what seeing him would involve.

Ryske parked the car on a quiet street. She got out, while the guys stayed behind to wipe prints and erase evidence they'd been present. They wouldn't be returning to the vehicle.

Wandering to the corner alone, drawn by the glow of the hospital lights, she stared down the perpendicular block to a gap between the buildings.

The ambulance bay.

This was the first time she'd seen that entrance since the night of fleeing. Even when Clyde went inside to ask about Bale, she hadn't come this close.

Ryske and Maze strode past her.

"Come on, Trink," Ryske said and kept on going.

Except she couldn't.

He was halfway across the street by the time he glanced back to find she wasn't moving. Shooting a whistle over his shoulder, Ryske got Maze's attention as he flipped around to head back to her.

"What's going on?" Maze called from the other side of the street.

Transfixed on the building, she shook her head. "I can't."

"Can't what?" Ryske asked, stopping three or four paces from her. "Baby, we've got to—"

"I can't."

Turning her back on the hospital, she squeezed her eyes closed. There was a boy in there who needed her support. A friend who would be there for her if she needed him. Yet, she couldn't even get close to the building.

Ryske came around to take hold of her upper arms. "Trink?"

This time when she shook her head, she let it fall back. "It's so stupid, you're right here."

His grip loosened. "You're thinking about that night."

"After I came back to the city, I went to see Bale. Except, of course, he wasn't in his apartment," she said. "I couldn't bring myself to go into the hospital to ask if he was there. Clyde went for me. I stood around the block, I couldn't..." Swallowing, she moistened her lips, taking a moment to herself before carrying on. "I can't go in there, Ryske." Her gnawing, irrational anxiety inspired illogical fear. "What if I have to walk out without you again?"

"Baby," he said, scooping both hands into her hair at either side of her head, clutching her tight. "I'm not going anywhere. Every day I'll be there."

Her hands drifted to his chest. "But you won't be," she whispered. "I'll have to go back to him and..." Dread narrowed her throat. "God, we were so stupid. You were right... You were right all along. You were right in the closet. You were right about everything... It's so much harder now... Why did we sleep together? Why did we...?"

Talk. Admit their feelings. Give into their desire. The tiniest glimpse into what life could've been with him was too much to ignore.

Going back to Rupert would be so much more difficult post-sex with Ryske. Speculating about why Ryske had come back was easier when she could peg him as a selfish, conniving bastard with despicable motives. Forgiving him for lying about his death might take a while. But her attraction to him, her feelings for him, they'd been too strong to cast aside.

Before his death she'd believed herself infatuated with Ryske; she'd been woman enough to admit her desire. After losing him, love was all she could feel. It tortured her.

Hating him for the lie gave her an excuse to shut herself off from the prospect of being hurt again. Dwelling on her anger when she found out the truth was easier.

Last night, she'd been stupid enough to get swept up in just having him there. His presence and his words had seduced her into believing their love was real and potent and inescapable.

On this cold, dark street, reality was tangible. Even with his hands on her, it didn't feel like she'd found him. Harlow felt lost, bereft, like her grief was crashing over her again.

Before they'd arrived her fear for Felipe and guilt about Rupert pushed her into a vulnerable corner. The terror brought on by this location was the cherry on her cake.

Except, wasn't it the truth that she'd have to get used to lying to Rupert? He could never know what she'd been through or where her heart truly lay.

"How can I spend the rest of my life with a man I have to lie to?"

"You can't," Ryske said, pulling them closer and crouching to her level. "You can't spend your life with him. You're going to spend your life with me. And you never have to lie to me."

Moisture trickled from her lashes down into the grooves of his thumbs. "I made a deal," she said. "I broke his heart once, I don't want to do it again… but I'm terrified that he doesn't know who I am. How can he be with a woman he doesn't know? It's just like before. He wants me to be what he thinks I am… but I'm not that woman, Ryske. I was never that woman. I'm even farther from her now than I was then."

Ryske drew her into his arms, holding her body and her head tight against him. "We're gonna work it out, baby," he said, his fingers catching in her hair as he caressed her. "I'm here. I won't ever leave you again."

These warring thoughts couldn't have come at a worse time. Leaning on Ryske was a tempting idea. Leaning on him came with strings and, at their core, her feelings for him terrified her. The dilemma wouldn't be solved there on the street.

The boy in that hospital needed them and she wanted to see him, to support him. Except going inside could mean reliving her nightmare.

"Felipe needs us," she whispered.

They were no closer to finding answers. Their relationship would never be what it was and her future was far from her past. None of that mattered while that kid was lying in a hospital bed. If she'd been able to put aside her anxiety and grief to do what was right for Ryske, she'd have to find a way to do it for Felipe. There were no truths out here. Nothing that could be done in this minute for anyone except the kid in there.

"I don't want you to feel this way," he murmured, hauling her higher to kiss her head.

Visiting the kid would boost his morale. She also had to let him know that Floyd's was a safe place. Maybe Felipe wouldn't have found himself in this predicament if she'd left the neighborhood without telling him to avoid the Floyd's crew.

"Stay with me, Crash," she whispered. "Promise me you'll stay with me."

Sliding his hands up her back, he brought them around her neck until he was cradling her face as he had been before. "I am not going anywhere," he said, enunciating each word. "We're gonna talk more about this, baby. But I am telling you right now, even if you go back to Marlowe... I'm gonna be with you. I didn't come visit your parents because I wanted to get to know them. I'm insinuating myself into your life, so that no matter what... I'm gonna be there."

Asking him to stay during their time in the hospital visiting Felipe was a far cry from what Ryske had taken her question to mean. He was talking forever. A forever that they could never have. When he was so genuine, it was difficult to keep her guard up.

"Come here," she whispered, curving her hands around the sides of his neck to pull him down for a kiss.

Tomorrow would bring more drama and hard decisions. For now, she was going to kiss the man who'd chosen to be with her… even if he could never have her.

***

THEY CHOSE TO go through a side entrance rather than the ambulance bay. Ryske did a good job of steering her away from any part of the hospital related to the night he'd died.

Finding Felipe in a room at the other end of the ER was a reprieve. And as long as Ryske kept hold of her hand, she managed to block out apprehension.

The kid had been beaten up bad. It broke her heart to see his bruises and the swelling of his eye and head.

His mom, Martina, was there and torn up about the whole thing. The matriarch swung back and forth between snapping at her son for being near the gangs at all and fawning over her baby.

Though Felipe tried to be tough and assert how hard he fought back, his exhaustion was obvious. Seeing her and Ryske together surprised everyone. Dover, Noon, and Maze were already in Felipe's room by the time she and Ryske arrived. Regardless of the ambiguity of their relationship, it was best for Felipe to know he could trust the guys, so Harlow explained they were all friends again.

There was no need to bore the kid with the details and he didn't ask questions. Felipe was immediately thrilled to have his gang of big brothers in his life again. Martina's nerves were so taut, she'd have accepted any lifeline. Anyone who might protect her son was a support she needed.

Martina took her aside to say Felipe wasn't telling her, or the cops, anything about the people who'd done this to him. Harlow tried to draw out details, but he was reluctant to discuss it in the group. Something about the way Felipe kept glancing at Ryske prompted her to offer up a chance for the two to be alone. The youngster jumped on the suggestion. The rest of them loitered in the hall while Ryske talked with the kid on his own, and she kept him in her eyeline.

Half an hour went by and then Ryske came out to say Felipe was asleep. Martina hugged and kissed everyone goodbye before returning to Felipe's side, leaving Harlow and Ryske's crew to find their way to the sidewalk alone.

On the corner, Noon pointed to a parking lot across the street. "We're in there."

The guys moved toward the curb while she took a step backwards.

Noticing her retreat, Ryske did a double take, which drew the others' attention to her as well.

"Trink," he said. "Come on, we're going home."

She shook her head. "I can't."

He snickered in an awkward way that didn't suggest humor. "Sure you can. Floyd's is your home."

"No," she said, scanning the crew. "Thanks, I'll pass."

"Nightingale," Dover said. "We should talk. All of us should talk."

"Not tonight," she said, creeping backwards. "Soon… I have something I have to do."

"I'll come with you," Ryske said, starting toward her.

Harlow raised a flat hand to halt him. "No. This is a solo mission. Go home."

His frown edged from concern to anger. "I don't want you on the street this late by yourself."

"I can take care of me," she said, then appealed to the guys behind Ryske. "Take care of him… like I know you will. Goodnight."

Striding away, she hoped Ryske would respect her and not make a big deal of this. Distance might give her perspective, but she also had to right a wrong. There were so many of those in her life that she couldn't fix, it made sense to remedy those she could.

TWENTY-SEVEN

THIS TIME, there was no barreling inside without invitation. Harlow knocked on the apartment door and waited until it opened.

When it did and he registered her identity, the occupant opened his mouth. Without forming words, he closed it again.

Harlow couldn't blame him for not knowing what to say. "I'm sorry, Clyde," she said. "I'm a coward."

Breathing in, he stepped back to open the door wider and presented the apartment to her. Moving beyond the threshold, it felt wrong to be too familiar, so she waited for him to offer her a seat in the living room before sitting down.

Joining her, Clyde sat at her side. "I'm the one who should apologize, Harlow," he said, taking her hand. He didn't hold it for long. Second guessing himself, he quickly let her go. "I got caught up in a moment and I wanted to make you feel good… though why that would make you feel good, I don't know, but…"

Shading his eyes with a contrite hand, his elbow dropped to his knee in a display of shame. Her friend had been a support when she needed someone. It was awful that she'd abandoned him to his guilt. Since the night he'd kissed her,

Clyde had been dealing with these negative emotions and she'd been too caught up in her own bullshit to do right by him.

"It did make me feel good," she said, guiding his hand down from his head to show him a smile. "It was a good kiss, and maybe under other circumstances—"

"Don't," he said, sitting up and this time he kept her hand when he took it. "Don't give me the polite brush off. I get it, okay?" He smiled. "You have enough men complicating your life."

It was beyond sweet that he was being so kind.

"You're right about that… But you should at least let me apologize for standing you up. I said I would come over and then I didn't and I… that was spineless."

"I was disappointed not to see you; I wasn't mad. The more I thought about it, the more it made sense. What were we going to say to each other? You needed to get the Ryske stuff straightened out in your head. Coming here to appease me… it would've been too much."

Resting a hand on his cheek, she was grateful and contrite at the same time. "You are too sweet for your own good, you know?"

He smiled. "Yeah, probably… What do they say about nice guys finishing last?" If she could feel that way about Clyde, he'd be a better bet than Ryske. Shame her hormones didn't care about safe and sensible. "Enough about that, get me updated. I'm guessing you didn't come here for my sparkling wit."

No, she hadn't. "You're right. I didn't just want to apologize. I came here because I… I did want to apologize, don't get me wrong, but I… I guess I needed to be with a friend… I don't need to off-load on you. I don't want to. That's not why I came. It's unfair that every time I show up, I use you as a sounding board… I just needed some space and to walk for a while… Felipe's in the hospital… he was beaten up."

Clyde straightened. "Oh my God, is he going to be okay?"

Clyde knew Felipe the same way she did, through

their work with family services. If the two were at Floyd's at the same time they would talk or joke around together. They weren't exactly close, but neither would wish the other harm.

"Looks that way. They're keeping him overnight, just to be sure. He got knocked around the head pretty bad. Martina doesn't have any insurance, but Ryske said he'd take care of it, so…"

How he would do that, she wasn't sure. Ryske had said he was putting money together to repay Rupert. She should've told him to use that for whatever Felipe needed. Repayment could wait; Martina didn't need the extra stress of financial worries hanging over her.

"You've seen him?" Clyde asked. "You've seen Ryske?"

Seen him and then some. Averting her eyes, she bobbed in nodding confirmation. She'd seen him, felt him, tasted him… done just about everything one person could do with another.

Scooping a hand under her jaw, he drew her gaze up. "Harlow, what kind of friend would I be if I didn't offer you all the support I can? You don't have to hide anything. Don't worry about using me as a sounding board. If there's anyone who needs one, it's you…" His thumb caressed her. "And, you know, the day my lost love comes back from the dead, I'll be knocking down your door, you better answer."

She laughed and took his hand from her face to link their fingers. "Deal."

"So tell me everything you want to tell me."

Harlow told him everything. Absolutely everything. Maybe it was a moment of weakness, but the words just tumbled out of her. The chaos made it difficult to put the pieces together. Nothing made sense anymore.

Clyde asked questions and the conversation kept on going. They talked for so long that food was ordered to sustain them.

Harlow hadn't had good Chinese food for a long time. What they ate that night probably wasn't the best in the city, it only tasted like it because she'd been denied her guilty pleasure for so long.

Their discussion covered everything that happened that week with Rupert and with Ryske, right through to Maze appearing at the country club and them rushing off to see Felipe… Which reminded her she hadn't called Rupert, but she didn't need a clock to tell her it would be too late to do that.

Tossing her food box to the table, Harlow sank into the corner of the couch. "And that's it," she said. "The guys wanted me to go back to Floyd's with them, but… It was just too normal, you know? What would've happened? Either they would've wanted to talk…"

At the hospital, talking seemed like the last thing she wanted to do. Both mentally and physically exhausted, Harlow had thought it was beyond her. Obviously, Clyde brought it out in her. This had been like a productive therapy session. Sure, she was tired, but sharing the burden did lighten her.

"Or go to bed," Clyde said.

With Ryske, that's what he meant. If she had any kind of integrity, she'd assert with confidence that getting into Ryske's bed would never be a part of her future. Except, after accepting him into her body in her childhood bedroom, her integrity wasn't exactly a sound leaning post.

"Am I supposed to slide in next to Ryske like nothing happened?" Sitting up again, she drove her fingers through her hair, knowing it wouldn't have been outside the realm of possibility. "I lost my head the night we had sex. I know it was stupid to let him into my bed… and into my body."

Rubbing her thigh, he soothed her. "Don't beat yourself up. It's easy to get caught up in the moment… it's happened to all of us at some point in our lives."

They shared a smile.

"I'm not saying I blame him. Or that I regret it. I just… It was fast, you know? There's still so much we haven't said, and…"

"I get it," he said. "You were caught up in having him back. The guy was dead for God sakes. Just having him there probably felt like a gift."

"It did… I didn't think I'd ever have the chance to… We got to say everything we never said, got the chance to be together. It *was* a gift… it was special."

"For you, it was goodbye. You're trying to honor your deal with Rupert; sleeping with Ryske complicated that. Now he thinks you're back together and everything is good. You know it's not that simple."

"It isn't that simple."

Being intimate with Ryske had been instinct. At the time, it hadn't been about goodbye or getting back together. Her thoughts hadn't been that ordered. All she'd wanted was to feel him. Losing him proved how fragile life was. Passing up the opportunity to be with him, when he could be taken from her again at any moment, would've been foolish.

"For you," Clyde said. "It isn't that simple for you."

"After what Ryske said tonight…"

"About insinuating himself into your life?" Clyde asked and frowned. "Yeah, that is worrying."

She wasn't sure if he meant worrying as in "crazy stalker" worrying or "complicated" worrying. Ryske wasn't a crazy stalker. Not that she could be sure he wouldn't turn into one. Whichever way he chose to go about it, his presence would complicate her life. Letting go of her city life would be impossible if Ryske kept popping up to remind her of it.

But it was more than that. How could she ever be faithful and true to Rupert if the man she loved was always loitering in the background? Given the way she and Ryske had been together at the country club, it would only be a matter of time before Rupert started to figure out there was something going on between them… if he hadn't already.

Running from the club with Ryske probably raised suspicions. Although she didn't think anyone noticed their antics at the table, it was possible they'd been spotted. Some people liked gossip so much that even smiling at the wrong man could lead to marriages being destroyed after the rumor mill went into overdrive.

Harlow didn't care about rumors or gossip, but Rupert would, her parents too. She wouldn't even be able to deny the accusations because whether or not they acted on them, the feelings were there. They were real.

Telling Rupert there was nothing between her and

Ryske would mean lying to him again. Even if she didn't like it, denying that she was in love with Ryske would be lying to herself. She'd been ready to lay down life and liberty for the man. Feelings linked to convictions like that didn't go away overnight.

"I can't see a way out of this," she whispered, admitting the futility of her overthinking. "I can't."

Clyde's tone was both optimistic and realistic. "You have to explore each of the three options… Play them out as best you can."

Already he'd proved to have more clarity than she did. "Three?"

"Yeah," he said, hooking a finger around his thumb. "First option is you say screw them both and go it alone… You don't need to be with either of them."

That was an option. But where would she go? What would she do? Staying with her parents wouldn't be a possibility. As long as she was around and single, Rupert would believe there was a chance for them to be together.

Ryske had vowed to be around no matter what. If she felt nothing for him, it would be easy to spurn his advances. But what had happened in her bedroom proved she didn't have much resolve when it came to rejecting him.

"Second option is Rupert. Whatever happens, you have to give him back his money; that's just decent."

"I agree," she said, having intended to do that anyway. "Except if I don't have Ryske's help and I don't have the Pothos deal, how will I repay him? I don't even have a job."

He frowned. "Do you think Ryske would cut you out of what's owed to you? Do you think he's capable of being that unscrupulous?"

Ryske was capable of doing all sorts of despicable things. Even to her, as faking his death demonstrated. Withholding would keep them connected for longer, so it wasn't beyond him. Apparently, he'd decided he wanted to be in her life. Shaking him wasn't going to be easy.

"I think he's capable of anything," she said. "Though you've got to remember, he hasn't actually done anything with

Pothos…" That led her to another line of thinking. "I haven't even talked to him about it… I don't know if he's planning to take my place or not… Maybe they won't make any money on it."

Which would mean she'd bought into something worthless. The men of the consortium were willing to get involved with an illegal venture. There was no reason they wouldn't be willing to screw her over. It could be that she'd handed over a vast amount of money to a group who'd take it without compunction and never return her investment. What threat did she pose?

At some point, she'd have to touch base with Ophelia and find out the state of the operation.

Sensing his discomfort when he cleared his throat, Harlow peered at Clyde. "Would you…?"

"Would I what?"

"Consider going back to Ryske… at least until Rupert had his money back."

"String him along?" she asked. "Ryske?"

Sleeping with him had deepened their connection. Deceiving Rupert made her feel ill because he was such a good man. Lying to Ryske might be easier given the knowledge he'd lie to her. But, as parents told their children the world over, two wrongs didn't make a right.

Aside from the fact that it was vile to treat someone that way, her secret desire was to be with him. She would only fall more into her infatuation with Ryske if she committed herself to a relationship, whether dishonestly or temporarily.

"It's horrible, I know, I'm sorry, I shouldn't have—"

"It's okay."

Soothing him with a shared smile, she didn't want to admit aloud that she'd considered doing much worse in recent weeks. Agreeing with Ophelia that they would both sleep with Yarker or Parratt was up there on that list. Using Clyde to get back at Ryske was probably the worst. Of course, she couldn't forget that, just for her amusement, she'd introduced Penzance to a man he planned to rip off.

Harlow wasn't the same benign, harmless person she'd been on moving to the city.

"Ryske is the last option," he said, touching his middle finger. "If you're together and you tell him you want to get Rupert his money, I'd guess that he'd help you... But if you're with Ryske for real, you'd have to back out of your deal with Rupert."

What would her family think about that? As far as she knew, they weren't aware of the deal. But they were close to Rupert and her return to the family home came with expectations. Would they accept her and Ryske together or would they see the relationship as a betrayal of Rupert?

If they did, what could she do? Avoid her family home out of respect for what she'd done to Rupert, or push to spend more time there in the hopes they would eventually accept her choice?

Going back to Rupert would mean marriage and kids. The life she'd shunned the first time it was offered. That was what Rupert expected of their future. She couldn't call foul when his wishes had been made so explicit in the past.

"You know what I keep coming back to?" she asked.

"What?"

She blinked her eyes to his. "None of this would've happened if he hadn't lied to me."

Clyde nodded. "It wasn't a little lie."

"No," she said, picking at the engraved metal on her bracelet with a fingernail. "It wasn't a little lie. And none of this is Rupert's fault. I'm not in love with him. I don't want the life I'll have with him... But I was willing to give up everything to do what I thought was right for Ryske. I made decisions, made deals, did things I'd never have done before... And I made those decisions fully committed to seeing them through."

Blaming Ryske was easy, but she had no way to know how things would've played out if he hadn't lied. The plan had been for her to go back to Rupert. If she'd done that and either she or Ryske changed their minds later, Rupert would've been hurt through no fault of his own.

"Now Ryske's come back from the ether and is asking you to go back on your word."

Whoever's fault it was, the only blameless person was

Rupert. "Exactly," she said. "Last night, I… I lied to Rupert. I told him a straight-up lie, and it didn't feel good. I've known him for a decade and we used to be so close… We were great friends at the start of our relationship. It was difficult for him to balance us and his bond with my dad. The pressure he was under only got worse as he took on more responsibility. I mean, he's basically being groomed to take over everything. I don't want it. Lena sure doesn't."

"So being with Rupert would make sense and would be the right thing for your family… And if you're going to have children with anyone, he'd provide a safer life for them, and they could take over the firm if they're inclined to."

"Yes," she said.

It was all logical. Rupert did make the most sense and she had made a deal with him. He'd never treat her badly or hurt her. He'd never lie to her like Ryske had and she would never be put in jeopardy with him.

On the flipside, she would never feel like she fit with him. Would never feel the carnal thrill of being near him or be overwhelmed by his proximity. In her heart and libido, there was no comparison between the men. But it was her heart that had got her to this point and her life was a damn mess.

With Ryske she could be open and tell him everything, any detail, he'd never judge her. He would support her through almost everything. Everything, except her choice to be with Rupert.

Rupert wouldn't understand half the things she'd done. Being with him would mean concealing a part of herself. It would mean keeping secrets in order to protect him… just like Ryske had done to her.

"You don't love Rupert," Clyde said.

The acknowledgement of her conflict was comforting but didn't resolve it.

"I do love him," she said, unsure if she was trying to convince Clyde or herself. "It's just not… it's not the same kind of powerful, overwhelming love…"

"You said you've known Rupert for a decade," Clyde said. "Ryske is new… maybe you'll feel that way about him in ten years."

"Maybe," she muttered.

It could go that way, but she doubted it. Maybe they wouldn't make ten years or maybe they'd hate each other after that amount of time. She couldn't imagine ever feeling for Ryske the way she did for Rupert.

For one thing, she hadn't experienced the same powerful, overwhelming love for Rupert in their early days together. Ryske was the kind of man a woman could lose herself in and he'd always keep her head above water even if she felt like going under.

Rupert was more stable. He was a pay the bills and take camping trips with the family type of guy. As a couple, they'd raise a family. In their life together, the most terrifying issue they'd have to deal with would be the phone bill one of their teenagers racked up.

Harlow's biological drive to have kids hadn't reared its head. Maybe it never would. She loved kids but birthing them had never been a life goal. She'd always assumed that if it was going to happen, it would happen, and whatever the setup, she'd make it work.

In her time with family services, she'd learned that children needed love and security. If they had both of those things, most would be just fine. Parents with money and stability could be abusers or raise criminals just the same as parents without money and a busier lifestyle.

One thing she didn't doubt was Ryske's ability to love their children... if they had them... if he was around to love them. But Rupert would be an excellent provider and a stable influence on youngsters. He'd bestow a strong moral compass on his children while Ryske's kids would be charming swindlers... just like their father.

The future was uncertain. Predicting it was going to be impossible, just as she'd never have predicted meeting Ryske, much less losing him and then getting him back again.

Those kinds of things wouldn't happen with Rupert. He was the epitome of predictable, always where he was supposed to be. Always there when she needed him.

Her heart knew who it wanted to dedicate itself to, but she'd made a deal. That was what it boiled down to. Was

Harlow a woman of her word… or wasn't she?

TWENTY-EIGHT

SLEEPING AT CLYDE'S had been fitful at first. Once she got over her agitation and drifted off, Harlow had been out for the rest of the night. Obviously, she'd needed her sleep. By the time she woke up, it was almost noon. Though she couldn't say she felt particularly rested. Too many thoughts danced in her subconscious to really give her a break. It sounded insane, but Harlow felt the weight of them in there, throbbing and swelling, taking up space.

Buckling down to her purpose, she took a shower, and put on the previous night's clothes. The notion of food made her nauseous though morning coffee gave her a boost. Something about sitting in silence, breathing in the steam, was refreshing. The peace was welcome. Clyde was at work, so it was just her… and her coffee. The peace couldn't last, there was too much to be getting on with. So she finished fast and left the apartment.

Checking in with Costello was first on her to-do list. The intention was to make it a flying visit to let her friend know she was still alive. But he'd noticed her high stress level and talked her into a session. Sweating with him gave her the excuse to pound out some of her frustration. After, she changed into his gym-branded apparel.

Sportswear felt more appropriate than a cocktail dress for going around the grocery store. The supplies were for the Sotos. Stocking the kitchen of the family who were enduring so much seemed like the least she could do. Dropping the groceries off provided the chance to talk to Camila about Felipe. In that conversation, she discovered the youngster was going to be released that afternoon, which was something of a relief.

Camila still hadn't given birth and spoke of how desperate she was to get the child out of her. Labor had to be a terrifying prospect, but her overriding thought during the discussion was how much safer the child was inside its mother than it would be out in the dangerous world.

She considered a second cup of coffee with Camila, a sure sign of procrastination. Harlow forced herself to refuse. Sitting in the Sotos kitchen was safe, but she couldn't put off going to Floyd's forever. Time was trickling away. It was evening already. The bar would be open. There would be people drinking and getting rowdy. It was time to bite the bullet.

One reprieve with the bar open, she didn't have to knock to be granted entry. It wasn't busy, and while every face there was familiar, no one quizzed her about where she'd been or what was going on.

Hugs and kisses greeted her, and she loitered at a couple of tables to shoot the breeze. Socializing wasn't her purpose and the last thing she wanted was to be blindsided by a member of the crew.

Deciding to rip the Band-Aid off, she went to the back, getting the nod from Lowan who probably knew more about what was going on than anyone else present.

Heading through the den, the jovial exchange of the guys in the apartment above faded up as she ascended the spiral stairs. Slowing to get her bearings, Harlow was putting off the inevitable more than attempting to eavesdrop, though that was a side-effect of her delay.

"Six, at a push," Maze said.

Three guys laughed.

Noon objected. "Nah, at least an eight."

"My ass," Dover said. "A five."

"You're a weird fucker," Noon said.

"What the fuck does that mean?" Dover said to the laughter of the others.

"He's right," Ryske said. "You've got some weird-ass standards."

"Coming from the guy who has no standard at all," Dover said. "I'll take it."

"Uh, have you seen my girl?" Ryske asked. "She's a fucking eleven."

She stopped on the spiral stairs about three quarters of the way up, just out of view. Closing her eyes, she let herself be a part of the moment, a part of the happiness.

"Nightingale is," Maze said. "Can't deny that." Murmurs of agreement went around the room. "Probably why she's guaranteed to be dumping his ass soon as she figures out she's worth ten of this jerkoff."

More jeering.

"I don't get in if you fuckers don't show," Noon said. "I said three friends and she guaranteed we'd all get laid."

"I don't need you making deals to get me laid," Dover said.

"Me either," Maze said and then laughed. "Won't stop me from going though... You said models, right?"

"Models? Yeah," Noon said. "Plenty to go around she said."

"You guys can divide up my share of the spoils," Ryske said only to be greeted by a mixed response of groans and objections.

"It's a party," Noon said. "You have to come. I said three... she needs guys."

"I might've come if you'd said four," Ryske said. "But, I gotta say, I'm not sorry we'll have this place to ourselves for the night. Rules on women stand. You go to their places."

Dover laughed. "Says the guy who wants the apartment to himself so he can have a woman stay over."

"Difference is, this is my woman's place too."

No, she didn't have anywhere to call home. It seemed

like she'd been a nomad forever. From Rupert's place, to her parents, into the city, here, Clyde's, she hadn't set roots, and just bounced around without anywhere to call her own.

"Think Nightingale would want to come?" Noon asked.

"Yeah, it's basically a sex party," Maze said. "An orgy is a far cry from where I found you guys in her parents' fancy country club."

"It's your parents' fancy country club too," Ryske said. "And you didn't see what we were doing before you got there."

Inhaling to bolster her courage, she pulled on the banister to finish her ascension to the top. "A hand job under the table gets low points at a sex party," she said, garnering the attention of them all.

Dover was in the kitchen, propped against the counter, coffee in a curved hand. Noon was at the dining table, though she couldn't see what he was doing. Maze and Ryske were in the living room beyond.

The jovial mood evaporated. Tension crackled.

As was his job, Ryske attempted to break it. "We'll go for as many points as you want, Trink," he said, like it wasn't odd she'd just intruded in their space. "You know me, anything that doesn't involve you with another guy is a go from me."

The trio she hadn't conversed with were more solemn than their buddy.

"Nightingale," Dover said as though Ryske hadn't spoken at all. "You did good here. You looked after the place for us and did it well… I was impressed."

Broadening her smile, she went over to take his coffee. "I'm an impressive woman," she said and enjoyed a sip.

Pointing to her cheek, she indicated it was okay for him to kiss her as he'd always done in the past. Dover bowed to give her that kiss as she returned his coffee.

Leaving the kitchen, she noticed Noon had a bunch of objects laid out on newspaper on the dining table. They looked like car parts, but what did she know about that kind of thing?

Going over to kiss Noon's cheek, she then dipped to kiss Maze too. His kiss was closer to her mouth and more mutual. Before she could leave his side, Maze took his hand from the laptop on his knees and curled his fingers around hers to give her a squeeze.

Ryske was on the couch. She didn't go near him, though she did offer a smile. He nodded at her sweater. "You spent the night at the gym?"

Wearing Costello's brand might give that impression. "No," she said. "Costello's girlfriend would blow something if I spent another night with her man."

No laughter. Their lack of humor was probably related to their uncertainty about the state of her relationships with the various men in her life. Hmm, she couldn't say she was all that clear herself.

"Where did you sleep?" Maze asked.

In some ways, being with Ryske would be like being with four men. She wouldn't have only one checking up on her. They'd all be vigilant and that could work for or against her.

That truth only gave her another pro for the Rupert column.

"Guys, I don't want this to be weird," she said, twisting to make sure they were all included. "I know you probably think there's a lot to talk about. But the truth is, there's nothing to say."

"Nothing?" Maze asked. "You don't want to know where we've been or why we did what we did?"

"Ryske told me why," she said, her hand drifting out of Maze's. "I've spent a lot of time thinking about it and I've decided talking is pointless. What's been done has been done. There's no going back."

Asserting she wouldn't go back even if she could was a step too far. She probably would. Granted, if Ryske hadn't lied, the plan had been for her to go back to Rupert. But if Ryske had been recuperating after the shooting, in the hospital or out, she'd have visited him, spent time with him. No one could know what decisions they may have made during that time.

"No going back," Noon said, turning away from his car parts. All the men's expressions became stern with concern. "What does that mean?"

Licking her lips, she prepared herself to say the words. "I'm here to pack the rest of my stuff," she said. "I'm leaving."

All four men were on their feet and crowding around her before she could finish her sigh. Their disapproving objections overlapped. Raised voices made it difficult to pick one from the other.

Ryske's whistle silenced the room. "Guys, give us the space," he said.

The other three began to withdraw.

"No," she said, swerving out from between their bodies. "You don't have to do that."

Heading into the closet, she retrieved her empty suitcase. Pack. Leave. That was it.

Ryske came in and slammed the door. "Where are we going?"

Crouched on the floor, unzipping her case, she paused when he went to a trunk in the corner to produce another sports bag. "What are you doing?"

"Guess it doesn't matter," he said, taking the bag to his dresser to begin filling it with clothes. "I know you don't like the suits, but they can be useful."

Leaning to the side, he pulled a packed suit bag from the end of one of the racks and tossed it onto the couch.

"Ryske," she said, straightening her legs to stand at full height. "You're not coming with me."

Slamming the drawer, he spun to face her. Rage tensed his body when he threw the bag aside. "I told you I wasn't going anywhere. Any time you turn around, I'll be there."

Shaking her head, she stepped over the suitcase to get a few feet closer. "Life isn't as simple as that," she said, reminding herself she wasn't allowed to cry. His wrath was a cover for his hurt. Harlow knew how deep it cut him because she felt it too. "Life isn't as simple as saying I love you... We might not have used the words, but we both acknowledged feeling that way in this room before… We acknowledged our emotions when we faced why we hadn't had sex, when we agreed I should go back to Rupert."

"Things have changed since then," he said, thrusting a certain finger toward the floor. "It's different now."

"Yes," she said, trying to keep herself calm even when he came closer. "Things are different, but not in our favor."

Grabbing her throat, he thrust her head back. "You love me."

"Yes," she said. A telltale streak of moist heat on her cheekbone betrayed she'd lost the battle to conceal her grief. "I do love you, Ryske."

TWENTY-NINE

FORCING HIS MOUTH over hers, Ryske kissed her hard, giving no option of retreat. Turning them around, he rushed her back against the dressers, pinning her under his mercy.

Wrong as it was, she wanted to kiss him. That was why she fought his tongue so hard because goddamn him, he'd made her want him. Goading and tasting his mouth, she flattened both palms on the wood pressing into her back, absorbing the man she'd so often craved.

But when Ryske plunged his hand down the front of her sweatpants, she had to push him away.

"It's not as simple as that," she whispered, her fingers fumbling their way up to his stubble. "It's not as simple as words and sex, baby."

"You're going back to him," he said, appearing as confused as he sounded. He didn't need to hear her answer. "You're leaving me for him."

It wasn't easy to say it, but she had to. "Yes."

The next backwards step he took was his own choice. His body ebbed from hers, kicking up her heart rate. Panic squeezed at her lungs. Losing him was a nightmare come to life. But this was the decision she'd made, so she did her best to disguise her terror with confidence.

"You expect me to let you go without a fight?"

"Like you were planning to," she said. "Before you died… This isn't anything we haven't talked about before."

Striving to be as calm and matter-of-fact as possible, she tried to make it seem like this wasn't tearing up her insides. Like her whole world wasn't collapsing into a tsunami of regret and longing. Her fingers shook so bad, she wouldn't hold up under his scrutiny for long.

Going to the dresser she'd shared with him, she built piles of her things, extracting them from their places mingled with his.

"Are you gonna marry him?" he asked. Focusing on the task at hand, she blocked Ryske out. Oh, how could she believe he'd make it that easy? A moment later, he grabbed her arm and forced her around to look at him. "I asked you a fucking question, are you gonna marry him?"

"I don't know," she said. "He hasn't asked me."

Though she attempted to return to her task, he wouldn't relent and renewed his grip on her arm to hold her in place. His low brow darkened his eyes, bringing uncertainty to whether or not rage was a strong enough word for what he was experiencing.

"And if he does," he growled. "What are you gonna say?"

It was difficult to pretend she was strong enough to handle this. The only support she could muster was to curl her fingers into her palms in an attempt to regulate her breathing. But that pacing was shattered when Ryske shook her in demand of an answer.

"I'm going to say yes, Ryske," she said. "I'm going to say yes. I will marry him and I will bear his children."

Stunned like she'd just sucker punched him, Ryske's hand slid away a fraction of a second before he staggered back. What else was there to say? She'd slammed the proverbial door in his face. That was the truth. She'd said it. He knew. It was done. Over.

Harlow couldn't bear to look at the expression of pain and disappointment creeping onto his face, so she spun around to gather her things. Taking them to her suitcase, she dumped them inside and did another trip to the dresser to grab more things.

Her vision blurred, a sure signal her courage was running on empty. There was only so much of this devastation she could handle, and his looming intensified her suffering.

This was her doing. Her choice. It wouldn't be fair to ask him not to feel what he was feeling. But she couldn't stand to be there, knowing she was doing this to him and that she had the power to change course.

Zipping up the case without even knowing exactly what she'd packed, she was determined to get out of there. Fast. Standing up the case, she extended the handle and got a few steps closer to the door before he spoke.

"You don't love him," Ryske said, his tone deep. "He won't make you happy."

With a weight on her shoulders and a pain in her chest, she glanced back over her shoulder. "You knew that when you ordered me to go to him before."

"I didn't know the lengths I'd go to for you then," he said, growling in his vehemence. "If you think this is over, you don't know me at all, Trinket." Stalking toward her, one slow step at a time, his words sounded more like threats than promises. "I will be everywhere you are. Everywhere he is. I won't give up. I'll be there to exploit every moment of weakness you have. I'll be in your head when you kiss him, in your heart when you're lying under him… I'll be the only man you'll ever crave and I will take you from him." He stopped in front of her. "You belong to me."

A shiver went through her, forcing her to swallow away a curl of apprehension. "I don't belong to anyone."

The corner of his mouth curled in a display of swagger. "You told me to take what I want and that's exactly what I'll fucking do… even if I have to gut the motherfucker to do it."

A different kind of fear seized her. "Ryske, you can't—"

"I can do whatever the fuck I want if he puts his hands on my girl."

Slamming down the handle of the case, she turned

her body to his. "You can't hurt him. Do you think I would ever be with you again if you hurt him? He's done nothing wrong. I made this deal. Be mad at me, not at him."

"If he was any kind of man, he wouldn't have to blackmail you into being with him," Ryske said. "The fucker will get his money back. He doesn't get to have you too."

"The money isn't your responsibility either," she said. "I'm going to handle that."

Frustration and rage collided to make him growl out a loud groan of infuriation. "What the fuck is this hard-on you've got for going it alone?" he asked, holding up his arm to show the line of stars that now included hers. "Highs and lows until we're dirt in the ground. You're one of us, Trinket. We fight our battles together."

"And me before them?" she asked. "What was that? You would cast your crew aside so easily and without—"

"No," he said, every second, the tension in her muscles increased. "I didn't say fuck them. I didn't say we were through with them. They just know you're my priority, as you should be… and you're a priority for them too. You are one of us. They know what's going on."

"Good," she said. "I'm glad to know you told them my private business."

"Your business is crew business. We're a unit, and you are not abandoning us."

She folded her arms. "Like you all abandoned me?"

"Is that what we're talking about here? Because if it is, the guys and me, we're willing to apologize, to grovel, whatever it takes. They want to make it up to you, to talk about it. You're the one shutting them down. And, whatever we did, whatever they did, it was under my direction. Take it out on me, don't punish them for it."

"No one's being punished," she said. "This is not a reaction to anything. This is me, looking at where all the pieces are on the board and making the smartest, most honorable, decision for all of us."

"Most honorable?" he sneered. "What the fuck is that? Most honorable?"

With a disdainful laugh, she leaned back. "It doesn't

surprise me you don't understand the meaning of that word given that your way of getting out of a relationship is to play dead."

Ryske didn't accept that. "I was out of our relationship," he said. "We were through. That's why you were so fucking pissed at me the night I died. I played dead to protect you, to stop you feeling any obligation to come back."

"And, yet, now you're telling me I am obliged to stay," she said. Their anger was a deflection, couldn't he see that? Groaning, she grabbed for her hair. "God, Ryske, can't you see why this is insane?"

"Insane that you would want to leave? Yes! You fucking love me!"

"It doesn't matter!" she screamed so loud she startled him. "It doesn't fucking matter!" Hitting the center of her chest, she pressed her hand to her body. "Don't you think this isn't ripping me apart? Don't you think I want to tell you I'm staying and that everything will be okay? I want to lean on you, to ask for help, to be part of your crew."

"Then stay."

"No," she said, shaking her head. "I made a deal. Just because we don't like that deal doesn't mean I can renege on it. And the fact that I even made that deal is both our faults. Not his. It's yours and it's mine. I wouldn't have made it if I thought you were alive, but I wouldn't have had to make it if I hadn't chosen to take on my vendetta… I should have listened to you. You said vendettas ruin people and you were right, Crash." She opened her arms wide. "I'm ruined."

Swooping closer, he yanked her so hard their bodies collided. "I want you anyway," he said, holding her tight. "If you're ruined, so am I, so are the guys, and we don't give a damn, baby. You're allowed to be ruined here. You're allowed to be anyone you want to be, so long as it's who you really are." Weird thing for a con man to say. Like he'd read the thought, he smiled. "In these four walls, with your crew, you be who you are. Have as much baggage as you like, be as screwed up as you like, we'll still welcome you. You'll still be one of us… You'll always be one of us. This is your home… I'm your home… I love you, Trinket. But even if we fuck this up and hate each other tomorrow, you'll still be on the crew. You proved that to us when you took charge of this place."

Proved it. He'd demanded that she prove this was the life she wanted once before. At the time, she hadn't thought he actually meant she should go out and do something to prove her dedication.

Creeping suspicion brought doubt. She didn't like it, didn't like wondering if the guys had only come back because she'd grabbed the reins of Floyd's and gone out to avenge Ryske. A foolish plan in the end.

Even if that was the case, should she be offended? Ryske had said he set her free by faking his death. His plan was for her to go off to her life with Rupert, guilt and conflict free.

That she hadn't been able to do that showed them, and her, that she was destined for this life whether any of them wanted her to be or not. If she hadn't had that epiphany about her purpose in life, she wouldn't have known she was capable of all she'd achieved. Even if it was misguided, she was proud of the resolve she'd shown and her dogged determination to fulfill her mission.

"Crash," she whispered, snaking her fingers up the front of his tee-shirt to scratch his tattoo. "Is there anything you wouldn't do for me?"

"No," he said, splaying his fingers on her back to squeeze her closer.

One of his hands ascended to cradle her head. Before he could exert any force, she tipped it back to look at him.

"Let me go, baby," she whispered. "You have to let me go."

His grip didn't relax. His own determination was sure when he shook his head. "I let you go once and it tortured me every day. I won't do it again."

Nothing she could say would change his mind.

Purpose was her only hope. "I spoke to Svetlana when you were dead," she said. They'd only go in loops if one of them didn't just face the truth. "She has some girls interested when the time for Pothos comes. I know you'll look after them."

"Trinket…"

Reaching around to her back, she found each of his wrists and dragged them away from her body so she could step out of his embrace. "I love you, Crash," she said, maintaining eye contact while slipping the bracelet from her wrist. "Don't ever doubt that I do. No matter what happens."

"I can't let you walk out of here."

Harlow tucked the bracelet into his jeans pocket. "Yes, you can." She smiled and curved a hand around the back of his neck to pull him down for a kiss. "You can handle anything, Crash. Anything at all. Go with it."

His forehead came to rest on hers. They stood like that for a minute before her tears escaped. Hoping he hadn't seen them, Harlow spun on her heels and left, dragging her case along with her.

She had to leave and this time, she knew she may never come back.

THIRTY

AFTER ANOTHER NIGHT at Clyde's that involved ice-cream and alcohol, Harlow got a cab to Costello's to work out and say her goodbyes. Everyone was surprised to learn she was moving back to the suburbs for good, but they were all too polite to ask about her and Ryske.

Harlow got the impression that most of them thought she'd return eventually anyway. Given the amount of ping-ponging back and forth she'd done, it was impossible to argue with that assumption.

Avoiding Floyd's was in the forefront of her mind on her walk to Felipe's. Any of the crew could be out and about and she didn't want to run into them. The kid was doing okay, though he refused again to talk about what had happened or who had beaten him up. That left Harlow with few options. All she could do was advise him to trust in Ryske and the rest of the Floyd's crew. He'd promised he would.

Just in case, she gave Felipe her parents' phone number and told him he'd always have a safe place with her. More than once, she reiterated that he shouldn't hesitate to call if he needed anything. It was tough. She wanted to be there for him, to be a friend to him. But being so far away, she'd be little help in emergencies. If it came to it, she'd call

Floyd's and send one of the frequent flyers to his aid.

Once the serious stuff was out of the way, the two of them watched some TV. Harlow laughed at his jokes, and ate potato chips, but eventually had to say goodbye.

It was nice to have the time to let everyone know how she appreciated them. Leaving the city wasn't happening in a mad dash. This time, she was doing it properly.

There were only two more places left for her to visit. Once those were checked off her list, she'd head over to Sweeting Security to tell Rupert that it was time for her to make good on their deal.

Showing up to give herself to him would be a surprise. Finding out they were together again would shock her parents more than it would Rupert. They'd be stunned to discover she was living with her ex-fiancé again, but it was her plan to move back in with him. There was no point putting off the inevitable.

Even though she'd already said goodbye to Ophelia, the women had business to discuss. The visit wouldn't be a chore though, she was looking forward to seeing her friend again.

Ascending in the elegant elevator, the building was perfect for the sophisticated Ophelia. This would probably be the last visit she'd ever make to the building. So many lasts before a cascade of firsts.

Her first home. Her first wedding. Her first child.

She shivered.

Leaving the elevator to walk across the hallway to Ophelia's door, the track of her life should be the last thing in her mind. Once Rupert had the green light, she didn't have to be clairvoyant to know how events would unfold. Her future would take off like an express train on a clear line. It wasn't like she hadn't lived through the whirlwind before. Slamming on the brakes hadn't been easy the first time, it would be impossible to do again.

Knocking on Ophelia's door felt final. She held her head up and waited for her friend to answer.

When she did, Ophelia seemed taken aback. "Harlow," she said. "What are you doing here?"

She couldn't remember a fight or a falling out. Ryske hadn't said anything about Ophelia having a problem with her. Yet, the woman she'd considered a friend definitely had a standoffish air suggesting she wasn't pleased to see her. It wasn't anger that emanated from Ophelia, no, it was something else, like impatience and discomfort.

"I needed to talk to you for a minute," Harlow said. "If this is a bad time…"

"No," Ophelia said, as if reminding herself of her manners. "No, sorry, I… I just wasn't expecting you…" Stepping back, she gestured her inside like she was herding children. "Come in, come in. What do you need?"

Perceiving a need for urgency, Harlow went into the living room with Ophelia hot on her heels. "I wanted to talk to you about the money."

With a sound of frustration, Ophelia dropped onto the couch. "You have to give these things time, Harlow. I can't produce money from thin air. If I'd known you'd be at me—"

"No," she said, noticing her friend's patience was frayed. "I'm sorry. I didn't mean to imply that I expected payment today."

Pushing past her awareness of being unwelcome, she stopped taking Ophelia's attitude personally and sat down at her side.

"What's going on?" she asked, trying to read her friend. "You're not yourself."

With a sigh, Ophelia touched her pendant. "I'm sorry. I'm being rude. I just… I haven't been sleeping well and Jarvis is on his way over."

That changed Harlow's mood too. The last thing she wanted to do was see that asshole. But she didn't want anyone to think she was afraid of him, and abandoning her friend wouldn't be right.

"Is he harassing you?"

Ophelia's smile was tight. "He's my brother; he's been harassing me my whole life." Her brows moved. "Something's been different since Ryske came back." Letting her gaze drift down, Ophelia fidgeted with the engagement ring. "I can't get in touch with him."

They weren't talking about Hagan anymore.

"Ryske?" Harlow asked, putting a hand over Ophelia's to bring the woman back to the moment. "You've been trying to reach Ryske?"

Ophelia nodded and clung to her hand, burning with a desperate hope. "You know how to contact him, don't you? Where to find him?"

Yes, Harlow knew where to find him. It didn't surprise her that Ophelia wasn't aware of Floyd's location. Anwen wouldn't have known it either. Before her, women weren't allowed to be in the apartment. That's what the crew said.

Hagan knew about the bar, and may have assumed his sister did too. The couple were engaged after all. That the siblings hadn't discussed it spoke of how little Hagan wanted to acknowledge his sister's feelings for Ryske.

"What do you need from him?" Harlow asked, aware that when Ryske came into contact with Hagan, he often found himself at the edge of life. "From Ryske?"

"I need him to call me. I need direction. I need—"

"What does Hagan want?"

The noise Ophelia made wasn't encouraging.

Hagan wanted Ryske dead. The hatred that blazed from him was rooted in what had happened with Anwen. Harlow didn't know if Hagan even knew about the original robbery at the auction, probably not. He'd have been too focused on Anwen's betrayal.

While telling her the story of his history with Anwen, Ryske had explained they'd met when the crew were running a con on Parratt. Hagan probably assumed that con had brought Ryske to the auction and into Anwen's path.

As for the truth of what went on between Ryske and Anwen, Harlow doubted anyone knew that. Ophelia didn't. Ryske let them all continue to believe he was the bad guy to honor Anwen's memory.

"My brother is eager to get Pothos underway. Parratt is working hard to get the shipment expedited. I told Jarvis that Ryske would be working with me, as my direct partner…

that you were backing away… Was I wrong?"

Harlow shook her head. "No… Ryske can take my place if that's what you want. All I need is my money back."

"I understand," Ophelia said, peering into her. "Have you seen him? I know you wanted nothing to do with him the last time you were here, but… he seemed so determined."

Last time she'd been there, anger stirred her blood. A lot had happened since then, though, fundamentally, nothing had changed. During that visit, Harlow had told Ophelia that she could have Ryske. That was the same. If she was going to leave his life and merge hers with Rupert's, Ryske would have the freedom to explore relationships with other women.

Ophelia was a strong woman; her resilience was impressive. The only time there was a crack in Ophelia's façade was with Ryske. The woman was besotted and had been probably since the two met.

Harlow didn't think that Ryske courted Ophelia's interest. Until she'd spelled it out, he hadn't been aware of the depth of Ophelia's affection for him. At that time, he'd dismissed her observations, maybe he still didn't believe that Ophelia was as infatuated as she was.

Ryske knew he had the ability to charm and impress women. For him, all he saw was the ease of drawing their attention and flirting with their attraction. The grifter was less aware of how deeply a woman could fall for a man who paid her the kind of attention Ryske bestowed. He had a way of making a woman feel like he could shrink the world and put it in her pocket to keep forever. Whether alone or in public, being tender or cocky, he gave a woman his absolute focus and could make her forget every insecurity.

Pulling herself from the daydream, Harlow sat up straight. "We've talked, and we've made our peace, but…" Turning Ophelia's hand, she held the ring up between them. "He's yours now, Ophe."

"I don't know about that," she murmured.

Trying to cheer her friend's spirits, Harlow gave her hand a shake. "I know that your relationship with him wasn't as real as you wanted it to be. But everything's about to change and he's going to need your support."

"Change?"

"Yes," Harlow said. "He'll need an ally in Pothos, you will too. You'll be able to look out for each other. I won't be around to help; I'll need you to rely on each other."

Ophelia was dubious. "You said you were leaving before…"

"And I did leave," Harlow said. "A friend of mine was injured. I had to come back to check that he was okay. I am just stopping in here on my way back out of town."

A wave of relief swept across Ophelia. "Ryske… will you tell him to contact me?"

Ophelia's focus never strayed far from the one thing that mattered most to her. Although she might not like that Harlow had been deep in Ryske's world, Ophelia was so eager to hear from the man that she didn't mind lowering herself to ask.

There was no shame in the question, but there was a thread of desperation in it. Desperation. Man, she'd been lucky to gain Ryske's attention. Poor Ophelia. Harlow couldn't imagine how devastating it must be to want Ryske only to be greeted by indifference.

Her friend was asking her to contact Ryske, except, she hadn't planned to be in touch with anyone from Floyd's again. At least not for a while. Letting things settle down into a rhythm was a better bet.

But Ophelia had been there for her, so she smiled and nodded. "I'll make sure he gets the message."

In no rush to call, Harlow figured maybe tonight or tomorrow, she could phone the bar directly and have one of the guys pass on the message.

The pledge was enough to prompt Ophelia to squeal and lean over to kiss her cheek. Even that show of gratitude wasn't enough for her friend who yanked her off the couch to hug her tighter.

The embrace was short-lived.

"You better go," Ophelia said, taking her hand. "Jarvis will be here any minute."

Ophelia didn't mention which of them would be avoiding the other. But, given she was in no rush to come face to face with the man who'd attacked her, the same man she'd stabbed, she let herself be led to the door.

"Take care, Ophelia," Harlow said, hugging her again. "And look after Ryske for me."

"I will."

The women said their final goodbyes, and she wasted no time in crossing the hallway to press the call button for the elevator. If she could get out the building and across the street, she'd be home free.

Unfortunately, the universe had other ideas. The elevator doors opened to reveal someone inside: Jarvis Hagan.

For a moment, they stared like outlaws sizing each other up. Alone in the hallway, they were a shout away from Ophelia, yet neither of them called out.

"Miss Sweeting," Hagan said. "Why do we continue to come across each other?"

"I always say that trials are sent to test our mettle. Facing you is a real test. Every time."

He smiled like she hadn't just insulted him. "How is your ghost?"

With venom in the back of her throat, she stepped aside, giving him space to exit. "Why don't you ask your sister?"

He made no move to leave the elevator. "His time will come to an end, and I'll be there when it does."

Proud of twisting the knife, Hagan traversed a few steps toward his sister's apartment like he'd actually caused her harm.

Impervious to the jibe, she strolled into the elevator. "Or perhaps we'll be there for yours," she said, pressing the lobby button.

Hagan stopped and turned. She winked at his outrage, believing she'd been triumphant.

The sense of victory was premature.

His anger loosened. "How is that kid?" he asked. "The one from your neighborhood... heard he almost didn't make it..." It took a few seconds to figure out he was talking about... Felipe. The doors began to close; her hand shot out to stop them. Her horror was heightened when Hagan smiled.

"Incompetence seems to surround me. I think I need a better hatchet man… don't you?"

The elevator doors slid shut, leaving her alone in a stupor, which lingered until they opened again in the lobby.

Hagan would only know about Felipe if he'd been responsible for the beating. Who would claim responsibility for hurting a child?

The truth was plain to see. Hagan was a disgusting, despicable man who wouldn't think twice about dismissing a child as collateral damage in this war he was waging with them.

They'd fought back. She and Ryske were responsible for their actions. But Felipe? He was an innocent child.

Stumbling her way out onto the sidewalk, a new determination fueled her when the breeze from the street whipped at her hair. The resolve flowing through her veins drove her to head for a specific place, ready to return to the purpose she'd lost.

THIRTY-ONE

HARLOW PAID THE CAB driver and leaped out before the car had come to a complete stop.

In hopes of bypassing as many witnesses as possible, she entered through the side door as opposed to the main entrance.

Hurrying up the stairs into the apartment, she was a woman on a mission. Looking left to right, she found who she was looking for on the weight bench, sitting up and wiping a white towel across his damp, bare chest.

"Trink?" he asked, raising the towel to his upper lip. "You're back."

Infused with adrenaline, she stormed toward him. "No, I've just been… delayed… temporarily. Do you remember back at Bale's after you were stabbed, you offered to get me a weapon," she said without waiting for him to respond. "Can you do it? Can you get me a gun?"

"Why do you need a gun?" he asked, tossing the towel aside and sliding his ass to the end of the bench.

Stopping between his parted thighs, her legs almost touched the bench between his thighs. "That doesn't matter. Can you get one for me?"

Loose and relaxed, as he always was after a workout, he raised his shoulders in a slack shrug. "No."

Much as she hadn't expected that answer, it didn't discourage her. "Okay," she said, inhaling through her nose as she began to turn away.

"Hey," he said, catching her hips to twist her back to him. "Where are you going?"

"I know other people who can help me. You're not the only capable man I know. Not anymore."

Staying calm, Ryske tried to impart some of his composure though she wasn't sure she wanted it. Being clear-headed might be smart, but she was angry and didn't want to lose that drive.

"I'm not handing you a weapon while you're amped like this. Sit here," he said, sliding back a little and pulling her down to sit side-saddle on the bench between his legs, perpendicular to him. Tucking her hair back from her neck, he bowed to kiss the ball of her shoulder, resting one hand on her stomach and the other on the small of her back to support her. "Deep breath." She complied. "Now, who are we planning to kill?"

"I don't want to tell you," she said. "You'll take it away from me." His sticky body made her recoil a fraction. "You're sweaty."

"I am," he said, pulling her back to him and lowering his voice to a hum. "Let's see what we can do about that energy of yours."

Kissing her cheekbone, he nuzzled closer to kiss her ear, and down to kiss her neck, her jaw, her chin. She didn't remember deciding to turn her head toward his coaxing mouth, but she must have because their tongues met.

His kiss gave her energy a different outlet and it sure wasn't an unwelcome one. Whimpering, she pushed her mouth harder against his and lifted her palm to his cheek. Her hand slid higher until her fingers got lost in his hair.

The knot that held the edges of her top together across her breasts loosened. His fingertips skimmed across one mound and then the other, easing the edges of the fabric aside to allow him to unfasten the front clasp of her bra.

Cool air met the sensitive flesh of her breasts, a tell-tale sign they were exposed to the room.

Tearing her kiss from his, she panted. "Kiss me."

Okay, so he had been, except her mouth wasn't where she meant. This wasn't why she'd come to Floyd's, yet she didn't hesitate to push his head down, forcing his mouth to her breasts. Accepting this kind of comfort could threaten the potency of her determined energy. Why did Ryske have to be so difficult to resist?

She hadn't promised herself to Rupert yet. These stolen moments with Ryske would be her last. With him, it was so easy to justify being naughty. As she'd said, this delay was temporary, a gift, time allowing her to avenge her young friend and experience Ryske's mouth one last time.

Suckling one breast, Ryske caught her between his teeth, holding her nipple as he dragged his mouth free. That was what she needed. Who she needed. Ryske made her feel alive, feel wanted, feel capable.

Moaning, her head relaxed and her fingers slid through his hair. Her whole body arched toward his pampering mouth that had switched to her other breast while his hand fondled the one already aroused.

"Mm, Crash," she mewed.

Something about the sound of his name on her lips reminded her where she was and how wrong this was. Shit, what was she doing? Her mouth was not supposed to be uttering his name in such ecstasy. This was supposed to be part of their past.

Horrified by her own weakness, she stood up, stealing her breasts away from him, leaving him fondling midair. Ryske reached for her, but she took a backwards step, grabbing the edges of her blouse to cover herself.

"Where'd you go?" he asked, standing up in her personal space. "Bed?"

He bent over like he intended to scoop her up, but a noise in the kitchen interrupted and he looked over her shoulder.

"You better be out of the shower, fucker," Noon called, appearing around the corner from the kitchen.

Whirling away from the sight of their friend, Harlow faced Ryske in a hunch, attempting to make herself as small as possible. The dream would be to turn invisible, though she hadn't managed it yet.

"Is that Nightingale?" Noon asked.

Fumbling with the clasp of her bra, she tried to fasten it again.

"Yes, Fuckwit," Ryske said, scooping both hands over her breasts to stroke them, preventing her from closing her bra. "Who else would I be getting fresh with in the middle of the afternoon? Go away, we're going to bed."

That assumption stunned her into forgetting the bra. "No, we're not," she said, spinning around to get away from Ryske's obstructing hands and to assert the truth to Noon.

Except she never got that far.

Noon's eyes widened at the sight of her exposed chest.

"Okay, less of the show, Trink," Ryske said, grabbing her arm to yank her around behind him.

Ryske would be setting a glare on Noon like it was somehow his fault she'd been careless. That was just fine with her; his annoyance gave her the opportunity to fasten her bra.

"What's going on?" Maze's voice came from the kitchen.

"Nightingale has amazing tits," Noon said.

A burst of laughter came from Maze. "Don't doubt it. Why'd you say that?"

"Just saw 'em in the flesh."

"She's here?"

Harlow finished tying her top and tossed her hair out the way to peek around Ryske. "Hey," she said. "I'm just leaving."

"Seems that's all you do these days, show up to leave," Maze said from next to Noon. "What's going on?"

If Ryske wouldn't help her, the guys wouldn't either.

There was no point in piquing all their curiosities. "Ryske's good at oral," she said, trying to creep away.

Without even looking, Ryske snagged her wrist and held her in place, precluding her from going.

"That's not why she came here," Ryske said to his guys, then switched his focus to her. "Babe, your crew are here. Let us help."

Shaking her head, she got in close to kiss his cheek, hoping that would give her cover to peel his fingers from her wrist. "I won't make you accountable for my actions."

Freed, she took just one backwards step before he grazed a finger down her cheek. "Wait there."

"Cra—"

"Humor me," he said, retreating toward the closet. "Sixty seconds. I did just…"

With a finger, he gestured between her breasts, which made her scowl. Yes, his mouth was good, but he loved playing with her boobs as much as she loved to feel him doing it. Getting intimate with her chest wasn't any hardship for him.

Still, she opened her hands, signaling acceptance and he turned to disappear into the closet, leaving her alone with Maze and Noon.

"I know you don't want to acknowledge this, but I just want to say I was right," Maze said. "Just so we're all clear."

"Right about what?" Noon asked.

Maze leaned against the corner of the kitchen wall. "I told her Ryske loved her first."

"Was there a time we didn't know that?" Noon asked.

Maze nodded at her. "There was a time she didn't."

The closet door opened. Ryske came out holding a pistol up as he checked the clip.

"Whoa, what the fuck is that for?" Noon exclaimed.

Ryske ignored him and presented the weapon to her. "Do you know what you're doing with this?"

Though her nod was meant to be confident, it didn't appease Ryske who turned her around and put the weapon in her hands, showing her how to hold it. "Safety's here. It's loaded. Just point and shoot." After giving her a quick lesson on how to keep the weapon safe and how to load it, he left it in her hands. "If you use it, bring it back to me, okay? You bring yourself and the weapon here. The minute after you shoot, just haul ass to the apartment, you hear me? If you get stopped or intercepted or arrested before you can get back, you tell whoever asks that you were here with me."

"What if I wasn't?" she asked, testing the weight in her hand.

When he didn't immediately respond, she looked up to see his smile stretch. He stroked the side of her head. "Baby, you *were* here with me."

Appreciative of his trust and his willingness to accommodate her without pushing for answers, she fell a little more in love with him.

God, she wished she could give him all he needed. "My Crash," she sighed.

He winked. "That's me."

Delaying her exit was only making this worse for all of them, so she backed away, gun in hand.

"Thank you," Harlow mouthed before turning around and running down the stairs and out.

Equipped and ready, she had to arrange the next part of her plan.

***

THIS TIME WHEN she arrived on Ophelia's floor, she wasn't interested in knocking or going inside the apartment. This visit had a different purpose. Jarvis Hagan had come to visit his sister, and the hope was that he was still enjoying his sibling's company.

In the short hallway outside Ophelia's apartment, Harlow opened the blind to flood the space with light. It silhouetted her when she propped herself against the wide windowsill.

In that position, she'd be out of sight of the security camera above her head. If security were paying attention at all, they'd have seen her come upstairs without actually entering any apartment. But she'd learned on the first visit that security in this building didn't pay much attention to anything.

About twenty minutes after occupying her perch, Ophelia's door opened. Harlow was out of view of the door itself and stayed still.

A smiling Ophelia stepped into the hall with her

brother, offering him two air kisses. Whatever she'd been nervous about before her brother arrived seemed to have been dispelled during the visit.

"Harlow," Ophelia said, noticing her before Hagan did.

Spinning around, his look of surprise was enough to make her smile. "Didn't want to interrupt."

"Do you… Are you okay?" Ophelia asked. "Is it Ryske? Does he need me? Is there something wrong with him?"

"No, he's just peachy," Harlow said, maintaining her focus on the male Hagan. "Do you mind giving us a minute, Ophe? Your brother and I have something to discuss."

Giving his sister's lower back a pat, Hagan nodded, urging Ophelia back into the apartment.

With his sister out of sight, Hagan swaggered toward her. "You can't stay away from me."

"Seems that way, doesn't it?" Harlow asked, standing tall. "We need to talk."

His brow arched. "Do we? About what?"

"Oh, so many things," she said, not shrinking when he came into her personal space.

"Where? When? If this is a setup—"

"Why do you think I'm here alone?" she asked, opening both hands at her sides. "I came wielding nothing." Except the gun in the purse on her hip, but she wasn't going to say that. "I want to talk, alone. Get rid of your goons, the security, everything from your place."

Without hesitation, he agreed with a nod. "Tonight," he said. "One a.m."

"So late?"

With a fingertip, he touched a strand of hair that hung across her brow. "There's something romantic about the dead of night… wouldn't you agree?"

He didn't give her the opportunity to reply and instead crossed the hallway to call the elevator. Not that it mattered, there was nothing else to say, not now anyway.

Sliding her hand over her purse the gun weighed heavy, it would be easy to dip her hand inside and pull out the weapon. Hagan was there, with his back to her, oblivious to just how far she'd go.

The moment of temptation passed when the elevator doors opened and Hagan went inside. So instead of acting without getting answers, she watched him select the lobby without moving an inch. They made eye contact, and she winked just as the doors slid shut.

Blowing out a breath, each step was progress. Now one final item was needed. Would she ever stop living like this? Adjusting the plan and the course of her life with every new revelation? It was an erratic way to exist, but an enlivening one too.

She wasn't tired or fed up, she was bolstered. For a minute, she'd been ready to slip into a quiet life with Rupert without holding Hagan accountable. If nothing else, tonight's meeting would mean answers. After all she'd been through, that wasn't too much to ask.

THIRTY-TWO

ONE A.M. CAME faster than it ever had before. In the time since setting the appointment, Harlow had done her best to stay calm. More than once she'd pushed aside stray thoughts of how much easier it would be to relax with Ryske's mouth distracting her.

Though this setup was a first, she'd been one on one with Hagan in the past. That experience didn't calm her anxiety. This time was different. This time she'd made a plan, which gave her time to anticipate and overthink.

Going into a meeting armed with more than her ring was another first. Carrying the gun was necessary, of that she was certain.

Creeping out of Clyde's apartment while he was asleep, she avoided rousing his suspicions. The why was self-explanatory. At a basic level, if she'd told him, her friend would've tried to talk her out of it. Not this time. She was dedicated to her goal and wouldn't be dissuaded.

Not telling her friend that she intended to meet with Hagan also protected him. Sure, she didn't want to answer a hundred questions about her purpose, but she also didn't want Clyde facing jail time for her actions, if it came to that.

The items inside the purse slung across her body gave

security. Her gun and keys provided protection and access to her sanctuary respectively. The third object on her person was the voice recorder she'd purchased that day.

Around the corner from Hagan's building, she stopped in the shadow of an alley to turn the device on and tuck it into her cleavage. It would provide the Floyd's crew with everything they needed if she didn't make it out.

Those three objects were all she needed.

Knowing that Hagan wasn't trustworthy, it was a possibility he'd go back on his agreement to dismiss security. If she had to fight her way out, she would. Even if she went down, she wouldn't make it easy for them.

An odd sort of peace came with the knowledge that even if she failed, Ryske would take over the cause. If she died, Ryske would avenge her, just like she'd wanted to avenge him. In an ideal world, he'd be nowhere near danger. She would be able to protect him and he'd always be safe. But just telling him not to take over the fight, to forget her, that there was no obligation, wouldn't make a difference even in spite of his previous assertions about vendettas.

Once upon a time, Ophelia had asked Ryske to ruin Hagan and he'd refused to do it. Keeping a clear head, and not taking things personally, were two of Ryske's specialties. She and Ophelia had proved that they found it harder to keep emotions out of it. Somehow, she knew Ryske would find losing her harder to ignore.

The first time Harlow had come to Hagan's apartment, she'd been oblivious to the businessman's identity and how cruel the world could be. So much had changed since then.

Just after one a.m., she strolled up to Hagan's building. The external doorman did his job granting her access. There was no security in the lobby and she ascended in the elevator without any impediment.

Either Hagan had stood true to his word or she was being lured into a trap.

There was no time to second guess herself. Hesitation could get her killed. It certainly wouldn't get her what she wanted.

Inhaling some confidence, she didn't bother to knock on Hagan's front door. Shaking her hair down her back, she strode into his apartment with full entitlement just like Ryske would.

Finding Hagan alone at the bar, lit by intimate candlelight pouring two glasses of wine, was unexpected. This was more like a date than a showdown.

"You're late," he said, without so much as reacting to her intrusion.

"And you're insane if you think I'm going to drink that," she said, ascending the marble stairs to join him by the bar where he propped himself on a stool.

"I have to admit, I'm intrigued," he said, checking out her legs beneath her short leather skirt that had a slit up each side. "You request to meet me alone and your guard-dog hasn't broken his leash to chase you?"

"Just me," she said, sliding onto a stool, ignoring the wine. "What about you? Did you renege on our agreement?"

"We are alone, Miss Sweeting," he said. "And given how our last meeting went, I'm surprised you were brave enough."

That put a smile on her lips. "Our last meeting?" she asked, bending her index finger to trail the point of her full-finger ring along the edge of the bar. "You mean when I put you on your ass?"

Picking up his wine, he took a mouthful. "I assure you that won't happen again."

Leaving his stool, he went around to the other side of the bar. Waiting to see what he was doing, she didn't flinch. There were drinks already poured, they didn't need more.

When he ducked down and stood up again, there was something about the way he looked at her that increased her trepidation.

Palm down, he put his hand on the bar. It slid away slowly to reveal something beneath.

Pothos.

One of the sample vials she'd first seen on the night Ryske came back from the dead.

Without revealing that it unsettled her, she turned her

discomfort into a smile. "Do you think that's why I came here? For sex?"

"It has to be tested."

"Tell Parratt to spike his wife," she said, and picked up the wine glass to smell the liquid it contained. The last time wine passed her lips, she'd ended up almost throwing up. That wasn't an experience she wanted to repeat. "Or let Ophelia take it with Ryske."

"Would you like that?" he asked, beginning his stroll back around the bar. "To know my sister is being intimate with the man you love?"

"They're engaged," she said, returning her glass to the bar. "Haven't you heard?"

Hagan came up behind her, whispering in her ear as he curled around her to return to his seat. "Over my dead body," he murmured and sank back onto his stool.

Harlow didn't have any problem with that. She didn't want Ryske married to anyone, but Hagan's corpse, she'd be okay with seeing that.

"You should be more supportive of your sister's choices."

"My sister is a fool," he said. "Enraptured by a man who uses her, a man who treats her like she's invisible… He doesn't want to be with her, he wants to hurt me… It's pathetic."

"On his part or hers?" she asked, scrutinizing his disgust as he sipped his wine. "It seems he wouldn't have proposed if he didn't feel something for her."

"Even if there was a marriage, it would be a sham," he said, putting his glass down. "Ryske wouldn't be faithful to her. He wouldn't love her. He isn't capable."

Touching the rim of her glass with a fingertip, she wasn't doing a good job of hiding her secret smile. "I think you'd be surprised by what he's capable of."

"Oh, I think it's obvious he's had you believing his crap since you met." Hagan shook his head. "I don't understand how women can be so naïve. He's a man incapable of feeling anything for any of you. Taking you for everything he can is all he's interested in. Sex, Harlow. The man is driven by sex."

On a breath, she draped her forearm on the bar. "Maybe that's why he's so good at it," she said, amused by his aversion. "Anwen certainly thought so."

Slamming the side of his fist on the bar, he clenched his jaw. "Do not talk to me about that woman."

"You talk about the man I love being intimate with other women and take pleasure from my reaction," she said. "Why shouldn't I return the favor?" Sliding off her stool, she relished how he tensed when she got closer. "You have no idea what it is to be taken by a man like him. He possesses a woman in a way most men can only dream of… When he's inside you…" Breathing out a whimper of pleasure, she let her eyes close. "The world ceases to be and we would do anything… anything to exist with him inside us forever. The way he touches us, the pleasure of his mouth on our bodies, the brush of his fingertips…" She shivered. "Idol is too weak a word to describe the man who teases and tortures us with arousal and climax. He's our drug, Mr. Hagan. Ryske has the power to intoxicate our souls. In the moment he touches us, we dedicate ourselves and all we are to him… No other man can ever measure up."

The movement of Hagan's hand was so quick that she didn't have time to react before it came across her face. Her head snapped to the side, jolting her neck. A sting of pain raised her middle finger to the corner of her mouth where she found a spot of blood.

Her tooth had cut the inside of her lip. It wasn't a deep wound, but it was enough. Dragging her revulsion up to him, she showed just how unimpressed she was with his feeble attempt to hurt her.

Picking up her wine, she tossed the liquid in his face and dropped the glass from apathetic fingers.

After the satisfying sound of glass shattering silenced, Harlow retreated to slide back onto her stool. "I suppose I should feel special," she said, touching the blood again. "You usually have your men beat women who aggravate you, don't you? Anwen didn't have the pleasure of your anger, did she?"

Still sneering, he spat out a noise of contradiction. "I

never laid my hands on her… I should've. Maybe if I'd taken a stronger stance, she wouldn't have gone to that fucker."

Twisting toward the bar, he picked up his glass and threw the last of his alcohol into his throat. After scowling at the glass, he slammed it down and got up to stalk around the bar again, his shoes crunching over the smashed glass on the floor.

Anwen told Ryske Hagan had his men beat on her. "But you… she used to have bruises."

"Yes, she did," he said, opening a new bottle of Scotch to pour some into a heavy crystal tumbler. "That Ophelia put there."

Ryske had been so sure of what Anwen told him.

She hadn't expected to learn that information wasn't accurate. "What? But I thought—"

"Is that what he told you?" he asked and laughed with the Scotch nearing his lips. "I suppose that would be the best way to garner sympathy for an affair." He took a mouthful of his liquor, then put both hands on the bar, one still curled around the base of his glass. "I did not beat her. Never. Believe it or not, I was a different man when I was with Anwen. Much less cynical than I am now." He took another drink. "Your lover took that from me."

Her lover couldn't have taken that from Hagan, not on purpose, unless he'd flat lied to her. In Ryske's story, Anwen had bruises when she came to him. The woman claimed the injuries were put there at Hagan's behest. Anwen had told Ryske that Hagan ordered his men to hit her when she stepped out of line.

Had Anwen been lying? But why? To get sympathy from Ryske? To protect the true perpetrator? By all accounts, Ophelia and Anwen had been friends. Had Anwen cared more about protecting Ophelia than telling Ryske the truth?

The possibility that Ryske lied to her still existed. She'd accused him of taking her naivety, so there was a chance he'd done the same thing to Hagan. Except, everything Ryske did had a purpose. He wasn't malicious for the sake of it, especially to someone who, at that point, had done nothing negative to him.

The truth had to lie somewhere in between Anwen's account and this new one.

"You made Ophelia hit her," she whispered. "It wasn't Brash. It was Ophelia you manipulated to—"

"Manipulated?" he asked. "I can tell you don't know much about my sister either. She's far more manipulative than I ever was, and her temper is far shorter. Ophelia has had impulse control issues since she was a child. It was a serious problem. So serious that our parents had to have her home schooled. They seemed to have it under control... or I thought they did until they died, and I was left to deal with her alone... She's not an easy woman."

"Ophelia is a sweetheart," she said, wary of being swayed.

"She is," he said. "Until you take something away from her or refuse her something she wants. It was that way with her and Annie. They would be best of friends, closer than any two people could be. But if An dared disagree with her, that's when the hit would come... Ophelia was always apologetic after the fact. An would forgive her... I was less understanding... It became so much more intense just before Annie died. I don't know what went on between them... Looking back, I assume the affair caused a rift between them, perhaps deeper than the one between An and I."

"You wouldn't have accepted Anwen sleeping with Ryske, don't try to feed me that bullshit."

"I wouldn't have, no," he said. "But as a couple we could've chosen to work through her betrayal or go our separate ways. It was an affair and it hurt me, I did take it personally... But I never hit her."

Ryske had implied Hagan was an unreasonable man. Yet, wasn't it a given that any man whose fiancée was having an affair was entitled to be unreasonable to a degree?

Dismissing Anwen's tales of domestic abuse was impossible knowing how the situation ended.

Anwen killed herself.

The woman had to be at a desperate level of despair to take her own life. Except, Ryske worded the revelation in a way that implicated Hagan in her death. Harlow remembered having that thought at the time.

Could it be that Ophelia was involved in some way? Did Ryske know? Had he hidden the truth of Ophelia's violent tendencies or was he as in the dark as she'd been?

Hagan's glass lowered from his lips to reveal a more discerning expression. "You thought I was involved somehow… in her death… didn't you?" Harlow was speechless. "I was devastated when Anwen died. She hurt me, but I never wished her dead. Losing her, it changed me. It changed a lot… I haven't been the same since… I wouldn't want to be. No one should be the same after losing the love of their life."

She could identify.

Over the past year, she'd moved her life, fallen in love, lost that love to death, got him back, and seen enough to make her head spin. She wasn't the same person. Although most of what she'd been through was difficult, she wouldn't take it back for anything. Harlow wouldn't change who she'd become.

These admissions altered her opinion of the man in front of her. Not that she could get so far as to feel sorry for him. She'd be an idiot to forget what he was capable of.

"You ordered Ryske stabbed," she said, recalling the first time she'd learned Hagan's name.

"After he left my club owing ten thousand dollars and disrespecting Anwen's memory with his disgusting mouth."

Something she'd sort of done tonight too… maybe she deserved that slap. "You had him shot."

"After his proposal to my sister. I couldn't let that wedding go ahead. Ophelia was losing her mind making plans, getting giddy, it was insane. She wouldn't see the truth of who he was. I had to protect her."

"That doesn't justify killing someone."

"No?" he asked and raised his brows in acquiesce. "Perhaps. But, as I said, I've changed. When you lose the person you love, as I did Anwen, your perspective skews. Since losing her, I've cared little about what happens to me. For a time, I tried to let it go, but it's not an easy thing to do, to know that the person who stole your love from you is out there in the world, living without repercussions."

Clarity wrought her gasp. "That's why you said that to me," she said. "At the SweSec event, you told me it was your duty to take him down, and mine to avenge him... You've been avenging Anwen, all this time, all of this is..."

"You and I have a bond that few do. We understand the unique sensation that comes with the clash of love and hatred. We know what it is to completely love a person incapable of loving us back... While at the same time we deal with the burning acid of hatred. Hatred of the person who took them from us. Our bond gives us an affinity, but we have no loyalty to each other."

Why had Hagan encouraged her to take revenge? Did he consider death may be a release, as she once had? How did someone feel at the end of the journey to destroy another?

THIRTY-THREE

IN ALL RESPECTS, Hagan had achieved his goal for revenge when Ryske died. What came after that? Was there relief? Release? Comfort? Contentment? She doubted it.

Harlow was lucky she'd gotten Ryske back. If she hadn't, and she'd followed through with her plan to destroy Hagan, what would have happened after, even if she'd succeeded? What would've been left?

As a person, Hagan adopted a new hue. It seemed that after achieving his goal he'd needed another opponent and seen her as a worthy one. Losing Anwen and eliminating the man he believed to be responsible for her death would've left Hagan lost and aimless. Perhaps he'd been looking for a way to end his own hollow suffering and didn't have the courage to end it himself.

Even in the face of her new understanding of his motivations, she couldn't forgive him his actions. "*I* didn't take Anwen from you," she said. "I wasn't a part of whatever happened to her. But you attacked me... You would have raped me if I hadn't fought back."

There was understanding in his expression. "At our last meeting with Parratt... Yes, you're right... I won't apologize. I would have followed through. You're a desirable woman and I am untethered. I have nothing to lose. At least I don't care enough about anything to worry about losing it… The only explanation I can give you is that my behavior wasn't driven by animal desire… though you could say its motivation was baser," he said. "My hatred for him shouldn't be underestimated… You were his Anwen… or as close as any woman could be. I saw an opportunity to do to him what he did to me… to take some of his pride, his dignity… You suffered for that. You did nothing but ally yourself with him, and that was enough. Hatred can spread more rapidly than love… Rage can consume us all."

The angles and opinions changed so fast that she couldn't begin to figure out the truth.

"You thought attacking me would give you back some of the dignity you felt he took from you when he slept with Anwen," she murmured.

"I'm no saint," he said. "I've witnessed how others in the world act in a way to maximize their own pleasure. It seems those who pursue their own agenda and live without compunction are those who get furthest in life. Living right, living righteous, it got me nowhere and got my fiancée dead. After that, I got to a nihilistic point where I thought 'fuck it.' What was the worst thing that could happen if I chose to be as selfish and vile as others in the world? My rage had been festering since her death. My hatred for him growing and fermenting. So when Ophelia brought Pothos to me—"

"Ophelia?" she said, her head snapping up. "She brought it to you?"

He nodded and his expression twitched. "How else would I have known of such a thing?"

In Ophelia's version, she'd overheard the men talking and that's how she'd gotten involved. Ryske once made an off-hand comment about Ophelia being the trigger. Stupid, she'd dismissed it. Now it came to light she'd been deliberately misled by Ophelia, though she couldn't figure out why.

Ryske met Anwen at an event hosted by Jarvis Hagan. He'd only been there to get close to Parratt who must have been invited by Hagan. That implied the two men were affiliated. Unless Ophelia had been the driving force there too.

Harlow couldn't remember Ryske mentioning Parratt and Hagan having any direct dealings before or during that original con. Were Parratt and Hagan acquainted enough that one would feel comfortable going to the other about Pothos? Such a sensitive, and illegal, deal?

She'd never asked Ryske where he'd met Ophelia. She'd just assumed it was in the same time bracket as the con on Parratt. Ingratiating himself would've meant going to social and corporate events, which were probably frequented by the Hagans and by Parratt. Ryske met plenty of beautiful women, but Ophelia had taken a shine to him.

Ryske had no reason to complicate the situation by engaging in a relationship with the female Hagan. Ophelia must have wanted to pursue it, even way back then. Except, before Ophelia could make her move, Ryske met Anwen and the rest was history.

Or was it?

Not everything was as she'd thought. Perhaps it wasn't as Ryske thought either. Hagan couldn't have killed Anwen because he'd been chasing Ryske all this time believing him to be responsible for her suicide.

Her game face was getting more difficult to sustain with each revelation. "Felipe…" she said, remembering what had driven her presence there. "You said—"

"I heard about that from my man on the ground," he said and shrugged. "Taking credit was opportunistic, a chance to provoke the man… Did you even tell him?"

Ryske… everything had regressed for Hagan. Just like her, he'd thought Ryske was dead. Learning that he wasn't put Hagan back on his original path. He wanted Ryske dead.

"No," she murmured without looking at him. Her gaze snagged on the couch she'd sat on the first time she was there. "Why does everyone assume I go running to him all the time?"

She had gone running to him for a weapon, but she hadn't ever expected him, or any man, to clean up her messes or fight her battles.

"It's what most women would do," Hagan said. "He's a jerk, but he has skills that can be useful." The thread of admiration in his tone drew her eye, and he smiled. "I'll deny ever having said that."

"Skills with women?" she asked and angled her chin. "What about your skills with women? You convinced my former boss to do your bidding."

"Gina?" he asked, wearing a smirk. "That was simple. There was nothing sinister about it. I simply told her that I needed you to help with some of my charity work. I donate significant amounts of money to the city and to departments I may find useful to have in my pocket. One never knows who he'll need a favor from. In this case, it worked out for me. I'll admit, she was confused, but I implied I'd had dealings with your father's company... and maybe that you weren't suited for such an... urban role."

Such a simple line, a basic con, and it exonerated Gina from the reprehensible role she'd been cast in. Turned out that the boss she'd once considered so strong and street savvy was as fallible as the rest of them.

"Why are you telling me this now? Why did you—"

"Because I thought damaging you was a good way to damage him," he said, putting down his glass to lean over the bar and touch her jaw. "You are exquisite, Harlow Sweeting, and formidable. But you will never succeed."

"In taking you down?"

Shaking his head, he peered closer like he was trying to beseech her. "You have nothing left to fight for... your cause is gone. Your war is over... But you must be warned."

"Warned about what?"

"Despite your questionable alliances, I believe that you are, at your core, a good person. In light of that, there are things you have to know. It's important that you put aside your prejudices about me and listen with an open mind, Harlow. I have put together a gift for you. One that will protect us both. This is important, Harlow, what I have to tell you is—"

The sunken door at the foot of the stairs by the bar opened, startling them both.

"I thought you said we were alone," Harlow said, leaping from her stool and backing up a few paces, bracing for who may come in and what they might do.

The last person she expected to appear at the top of the stairs was Ophelia. "Ophe—"

One pop followed another. In the low lighting, it took a minute to see the weapon in Ophelia's outstretched hand. Hagan turned to face her, his fingers on his chest. The stunned fear in his eyes was an expression she recognized… she'd seen that look before.

Their eyes stayed locked until he collapsed behind the bar.

Mouth open and body braced for what might happen in the silence that followed, all she could do was switch her attention from where Hagan had been to Ophelia. The woman still had her arm out in front of her, weapon shaking in her grip.

For a minute, Ophelia just looked at the floor. She was at the end of the bar by the opening, and had to be fixated on her brother.

Shots. The popping had been gunshots. Oh, God. She'd heard that sound the same night she'd seen the look of surprise on Ryske's face; the same one Hagan had just been wearing.

Checking her own body with a quick hand, she was intact. There was no blood on her, but Hagan…

If Harlow was going to use her gun, this was the moment to do it. Except, that could escalate the situation fast. Ophelia had come in and taken her target down without hesitation. If she intended to take Harlow down too, surely she would've done it by now.

Erring on the side of optimism, she didn't want to go on the offensive, especially given she wouldn't be quick enough to draw and shoot before Ophelia who already had a weapon in hand.

"Ophelia," she murmured.

The sound of her name startled Ophelia. That motion forced her gaze away from behind the bar.

"I… I couldn't stand it, Harlow," she said, a glaze in her eyes, dampness on her cheeks.

"It's… it's okay," Harlow said. "Just put the gun

down, honey."

Blinking at the weapon like she'd forgotten it existed, Ophelia dropped the gun onto the end of the bar. Only when it was out of her hand did she move.

As soon as she got to Ophelia, the woman collapsed into her arms. There were no sobs of despair, they just stood there, holding each other, looking down at Hagan's motionless form.

Blood stained his shirt around the two wounds on his chest.

"Is he… dead?" Ophelia asked, peeking at him from Harlow's arms.

Much as she didn't want to, Harlow was careful about not disturbing anything, and put a foot between Hagan's legs to crouch and feel his wrist for a pulse. There was nothing. Not a twitch.

"He's dead, honey," she said, twisting around to look up over her shoulder. "You killed him."

It seemed Ophelia needed to hear the confirmation.

Wasn't it obvious? The woman had shot him twice in the chest. What other outcome did she expect? Was Ophelia in touch with reality? It had to be shock.

And she dealt her own with a grin. "Good," Ophelia said and whooped. "Oh, don't you feel so much better?"

What in the hell…? She couldn't fathom it. Even coming here with a gun in her possession, a gun she'd thought she was willing to use, she couldn't understand the jubilation over another human being's death.

Ophelia had just shot her own brother. Without any warning or reason, no one had been in peril, they'd been having a conversation, and Ophelia just gunned him down.

Rising, she grabbed the scarf from Ophelia's neck and wiped down the bar for prints.

"How did you get in here?" Harlow asked, cleaning anything she might have touched.

"There's a service stairway behind the kitchen," Ophelia said, poking a thumb over her shoulder. "Why do you seem so stressed out? This is a good thing… Ryske is going to be thrilled."

She couldn't help but feel a little sick. Maybe it was the similarity to Ryske's shooting that churned her stomach. Ryske had been standing unprepared and unarmed when he was shot. Maybe if Animal had shot twice instead of once like Ophelia had, he'd have been gone as quickly.

"You have to get out of here."

"Me?" Ophelia asked. "Why? No one will be here until the morning." Reaching over her brother's dead body for the Scotch he'd opened, Ophelia slugged straight from the bottle. Very unrefined for such a sophisticated woman. "This is a celebration. The bastard is gone from our lives! We're free now." She sloshed some alcohol on his legs. Harlow intercepted the bottle and righted it before Ophelia could pour any more. "I knew this was the perfect opportunity when I heard your conversation in my hallway this afternoon. My brother's never alone, not like this, not here. This is perfect! It could've happened any time, anyone could've done it. He has so many enemies. You have no idea."

If Hagan had so many enemies, it would've made more sense to wait until one of them did the job than to do it themselves. Adrenaline pumping through her, Harlow picked up the gun with the scarf and wrapped it up, tucking it into her purse and pushing Ophelia toward the sunken door.

"Show me the service stairs," she said. "Show me them now."

Ophelia led her through the apartment, singing as she went, drinking more of the Scotch. On the other side of the vast kitchen was an open doorway. Ophelia went through it first. Harlow followed and together they ran down the concrete stairway.

When they got out into the alleyway, the best option might be—Ophelia was already dancing her way up the alley, giving her no choice except to follow. They crossed out the back of another alley and ended up going through a chain link fence into a parking lot.

On the other side of it, Ophelia offered her the bottle. "Would you like to drink with me?"

"No," Harlow said, trying to crowd her toward the quiet street ahead. "You need to get home. You need to stay there until morning and if anyone asks, you tell them you didn't leave your apartment all night."

Ophelia winked. "I left through my fire escape," she said and touched her temple with the rim of the bottle. "I'm a smart cookie."

Not smart enough not to kill someone.

"Good," Harlow said, pushing her in the direction of her apartment building. "Then go. Go home. Be safe."

Ophelia came back and planted a kiss on her cheek. "Oh, I feel so light and free," she said, twirling down the street, singing and swaying until disappearing around the corner.

If only she could be so confident. Turning, she could just see the edge of Hagan's apartment building. He was in there. Dead.

What was she supposed to do now?

Licking her lips, she breathed. Be calm. She hadn't shot anyone. She'd only seen it happen.

Too many people were being hurt. Too many people had been lost already. And, for sure, Hagan was another one who wouldn't be coming back.

Taking the recorder from her cleavage, she switched it off and tucked it into her purse beside the two guns.

She didn't know what to think of what Ophelia had done or of what Hagan had told her.

For now, there was only one place she'd feel safe.

Sticking to dark alleys and quiet streets, Harlow moved through the city knowing it would take an hour to get to Floyd's given her indirect route. Having the night air around her and in her lungs should help her feel human again.

By the time she got to the bar, it was dark and locked up tight, as she'd expected. Using her keys, she was quick and quiet about slipping in.

All the guys were sleeping. None of the curtains were pulled around the beds, so she could see a lump in each and none moved when she entered. Tiptoeing across the living room, she slipped into the closet.

Stripping off her short skirt and light top, she folded them into a plastic grocery bag that she got from the desk.

Thank goodness there wasn't much material in her apparel and that the couch was on wheels. Moving the couch as quietly as she could, she flipped over the corner of the rug to uncover the loose nail.

This was the hidey hole she'd discovered when her jean snagged on the nail during one of her cleaning sessions while she'd lived here alone. Retrieving a letter-opener from the desk, she popped the nail out, and lifted the floorboard just enough to slip her purse and clothes underneath. After pushing the nail back in, she did her best to use the handle of the letter-opener to force the nail in deep.

Sliding a hand across it, she checked the floor wasn't marked, and was pleased the nail was in tight. Perfect.

Putting the rug back down, she wheeled the couch to its previous position, checking and double checking that the wheels were in the same grooves.

Standing nude in the middle of the closet, she didn't want to think about what she'd just done, or why she'd done it. The best thing to do was forget what she'd seen. To forget what had happened. Forget, move on, and never think about it again.

Leaving the closet, she figured that all four men were sleeping and wouldn't care that she was nude. She snuck into Ryske's bed beside him. Although he stirred when her cold toes touched his shin, he didn't wake.

Nestling as close to him as she could without waking him, she stared into his sleeping face. How would he react if he ever found out she was an accomplice to first degree murder?

That was the last thing she remembered thinking before exhaustion pulled her under.

THIRTY-FOUR

THE SMELL OF COFFEE woke Harlow the next morning. She hadn't heard the beans grinding; it was the scent of the alluring java that opened her eyes.

Stretching out, it took a minute to remember where she was. When she felt his solid body under her head, she smiled. There was no mistaking the man when he was as ripped as Ryske. Not that she would ever mistake the texture of his skin, the smell of him, the comfort she got from his embrace.

When she recalled what brought her there, her smile didn't linger.

Pushing away from Ryske, she ran a hand over her hair while sitting up, clutching the sheet to her breasts. Noon was asleep in the bed to her right. With his face half buried in a pillow, he looked so peaceful, so innocent.

"Coffee?" Dover asked from the other side of the apartment.

He was pouring sweetener into one of the two mugs in front of him. Maze was in an armchair, his back to the dining table and to Dover. At the same time Dover gave her his attention, Maze lifted his chin to look at her over the lid of his laptop.

Clearing her throat, she drew up her knees. "I… I didn't violate him."

"I don't think he'd have cared if you did," Dover said, going to the coffee machine to pour another cup.

Ryske rolled toward her onto his side, still ensconced in slumber, oblivious to the conversation.

"I think we'd have heard if she did," Maze said. "You weren't here when we went to sleep, right?"

"No," she said, tucking her hand under the covers to stroke Ryske when his knuckles bumped her.

His hand wasn't the only thing trying to make itself known. His erection was being kind of rude about prodding her.

"How'd you get in?" Dover asked.

If she didn't have so much to feel guilty about, the answer might have made her squirm. "Key," she said. Both men looked at her again. She shrugged. "I locked up."

"I told you they never give just one copy," Maze said to Dover who brought her cup across to her.

Careful about the handover of the hot liquid, she was grateful for the comforting smell and the welcome taste of the delicious drink.

"So you moving back in?" Dover asked. "You need to be put on the schedule for shifts downstairs?"

"I…" Harlow sipped her coffee. "That might be premature."

Lying back, she put her cup on the nightstand, intending to sit up again. Except Ryske's hands snaked onto her hips. He pulled her ass backwards, bringing her into more intimate contact with his cock.

Smiling, she tipped her chin toward her shoulder. "I'm naked, Crash," she said. The grifter was not as asleep as she'd thought. "Be careful. You pull me any harder and that thing's going to slide home."

The purr that came from behind her made her laugh.

"Yeah, and we're sitting right here, so keep it away from home," Maze called out and shivered like the idea of witnessing that creeped him out, as it should.

Rolling over, Harlow tucked herself close to Ryske,

curling one leg up over his hip and picking his hair from his brow.

Ryske's eyes opened to slits.

"Hey, Gorgeous," she whispered.

"Come here often?" he grumbled, his eyes closing again.

He hadn't been awake for three minutes and already he was spouting pick-up lines.

Harlow laughed. "Only as often as the host eats my pussy."

"My favorite breakfast," he said, his fingertips gliding up the inside of her thigh. "Was I good?"

Wriggling closer, she brushed her lips over his. "Good?"

"We had an agreement you'd take advantage whenever I was passed out."

That he could remember a conversation they'd had so long ago touched her sentiment. Taking his hand from her thigh, she set it on her breast, encouraging him to fondle her.

"I didn't want to disturb you…" she murmured. "You looked so peaceful."

"That's 'cause you were with me," he said, touching the underside of her chin to draw her mouth to his.

Mornings like this were supposed to be a thing of the past. In spite of that, she decided not to pass up the gift of another. Responding to his kiss, she was moaning into his mouth, tangling her tongue with his when he scooped her body under his.

"Shit, man, at least pull the curtain," Maze said.

Elevating his mouth, Ryske was grinning, even though his eyes still seemed to be asleep.

Brushing his nose across hers, he kissed her again. "Shower?" he murmured.

Assuming the question was for her seemed premature when the guys answered. "Sounds like an excellent plan," Maze said.

"Perfect," Dover said like they were making this decision by committee.

Groaning, Ryske rolled off her and rubbed both

hands up and down his face. "What the fuck, guys?"

"We don't want to watch you having sex with Nightingale," Maze said. "Let the woman keep a little mystery."

"Oh, he's so sweet," she said, shifting onto her side, pressing her breasts against Ryske's ribs and drawing her nails around his shoulder tattoo. "I missed waking up with you, Crash."

She kissed his chest without paying much attention to where she'd been aiming for. Her lips grazed his scar. The sensation of touching the spot where the bullet entered him brought her back. Gazing at it, her fingertips retreated to test the sensation.

Bullets. Gunshots. Blood. It reminded her of what happened last night. It wasn't until Ryske flattened a hand on top of hers that she snapped from her trance and blinked up at him.

"You okay, Trink?" he asked, displaying sincere concern. "It doesn't hurt."

"I know," she said, assuming it couldn't being it was healing so clean.

"You can touch me anywhere you want, but if it upsets you, we'll find something else to tattoo right there… your pick."

Aroused and eager to forget where her mind had been going, she slithered up on top of him, pulling the blanket over both of their heads, affording them some privacy.

Ryske was more interested in curving his hands around her ass than who was watching them.

"I think I want to try shower sex after all," she whispered, wrapping both arms around the top of his head to hold him in place while they kissed.

"I think I want to try Trinket on top sex," he said, squeezing her ass in both hands then taking her hips. "Slide down a bit, baby."

She laughed. "Here?"

"No! Not here," Maze called out and they both laughed.

"He's not that much of a prude," Ryske said, and

cradled her head to call over her shoulder. "He's just busting my balls."

"That's all your balls are gonna get today, buddy," Maze replied.

He didn't get a response because she and Ryske returned to their kissing. Mm, the best way to spend a morning.

A noise outside their cocoon broke the air.

"What the… Is he alone in there?"

That was Noon's voice.

They stopped kissing for long enough to smile on each other's lips.

"God, I wanna fuck you," Ryske murmured, grabbing her lower lip in his teeth.

The sting of his bite provoked her arousal until she tasted blood. Catching the top edge of the sheet, she wrapped it around her breasts and sat up, straddling Ryske's bare abdomen. The sheet kept her and his lower body covered.

Touching the corner of her mouth, he'd opened the cut Hagan caused last night. Damnit.

Ryske sat up against her. "Are you bleeding?" he asked, holding her in place with his drawn up knees at her back and his torso in front.

He hadn't bit her there. The cut was on the inside corner. He pushed her hand aside to inspect it for himself. Dragging his hands away from her mouth, she eased him away enough to reach for a pillow.

Tucking the sheet around her naked body, she climbed off the bed, tossing the pillow onto Ryske's lap to conceal his erection, not that he was modest.

She nodded at Noon while retrieving her coffee from the nightstand. "Morning."

The newly-awakened guy was perplexed, but there was nothing she could say to alleviate his confusion. Holding the sheet in one hand and drinking her coffee with the other, she headed across the room.

"Why are you bleeding?" Ryske asked. "I didn't bite you that hard."

"It's nothing," she said, going into the kitchen.

Finishing her coffee, she put the cup in the sink and turned to Dover. "Do you know if any of my stuff was left here? I seem to be sans clothes."

"Why can't you put on what you were wearing last night?" Maze asked, setting aside his laptop to leave the armchair.

Valid question. One she couldn't come up with an answer for.

"Those clothes are… unavailable."

Though that wasn't exactly true, it wasn't far from wrong.

"Where are they?" Maze asked, joining them in the kitchen. "In a meeting?"

Dover put a hand on her shoulder. "Check Ryske's dresser. Whatever was in the laundry will have been put back there."

Thankful for being distracted when packing up her things, there would be something left behind. Especially given how many of Ryske's clothes she'd found tangled in hers.

"Thanks."

"When did Nightingale get here?" Noon asked.

The poor guy was still half-asleep. This was too much activity and talking for him to take in so early.

She intended to offer him a smile of sympathy but didn't get that far. Her attention snagged on Ryske seated in the middle of his bed, pillow on his lap, like she'd left him. The scowl on his face was magnetic.

Trying her best to appear innocent, she shrugged. "What?"

Her love wasn't moved. "Where's the gun?"

As much as she didn't want to squirm, the impact of his stern suspicion was difficult to conceal. "Want to have that shower now?"

"Fuck, Trink," he said, rolling to the side to pull a pair of boxer-briefs from his nightstand.

He only had one pair in that drawer, and this was apparently emergency enough to use them. While he put them on, she tried to think of a good excuse to run out of the apartment but came up blank.

Her focus on Ryske had been so absolute, she hadn't noticed everyone else was staring until the two men in the kitchen closed in around her.

"What happened?" Dover asked.

Ryske fell into formation with them, blocking her in. The only route out was down the spiral stairs, and given she was naked that didn't seem like a smart option.

"I can't…" Swallowing, she looked at each of their faces. "I don't know what to tell you."

"Tell us the truth," Maze said. "Whatever happened, we've got you, but we need to know what you did."

"I did nothing."

Noon appeared between Maze and Ryske, wrapped in his own sheet. He was wearing sweatpants, so the sheet had to be for warmth. Maybe he just wasn't ready to let go of his bed yet. She didn't know how anyone could be cold, the temperature was off the charts. Standing there under the crew's scrutiny provoked her sweat glands.

"Ryske told you to come here if you used the gun," Maze said because he'd been in the room when Ryske gave her that instruction the previous day. "Now you're here without clothes, without the weapon, and without a good story… So what happened?"

"I…" Ryske wasn't going to extend any reprieve. His frown was more intense than all the others, which was an achievement when every looming face was stern. "I was scared," she said, looking only at Ryske though aware of the others. "I was tired, and I was scared, and I wanted to feel safe. That's why I came here."

"No one has a problem with that," Ryske said. "All of us consider this your home." No one contradicted him. "We need to know where that gun is and what happened."

"I can't—"

"If the weapon was used in a crime…"

"It wasn't," she said, shaking her head. "I promise you, it wasn't."

The guys didn't seem convinced.

Ryske broke away from his friends to come close. With a hand on either side of her face, he crouched to her level. "Baby, you need to tell me every single detail."

"I—"

"Whatever it was," he said and smiled. "It's okay, we've got you. You are safe here. Every one of us will stand behind you." Loosening his smile, he gripped her tighter. "I'm going to be the one who has to answer for it, so you need to tell me everything. I can't get any detail wrong with the cops or in front of the judge."

That was… anxiety became instant foreboding. "You…" That implication flooded her with outraged horror. Throwing her arms up, she thrust his hands away. "What the hell, Ryske? You think if I went out there and killed someone that I'd let you walk up to the cops and confess? That I'd let you take the rap for my crime?"

Ryske smiled, his expression full of swagger. "I think you wouldn't have a choice," he said. "These three are way bigger than you and as long as they're holding you down, I can do whatever the hell I like."

"You asshole," she whispered and smacked her chest. "I take responsibility for what I did. I make my choices and they are mine to make. I do not need you to take ownership of anything I do."

Stepping back, he circled a finger to indicate them all. "We are owners of everything we all do," he said. "And we do what is best for the whole… You in prison is not what's best for the whole."

"But you in prison is?"

"We make decisions *as* a group and *for* the group," Ryske said, raising his arm to show his line of stars. "Highs and lows until we're dirt in the ground."

Before she could retort, Noon raised his arm, Maze did next, and Dover was last. Her eyes moved from one line of stars to the next. Every single one of them had the same new star like Ryske's. Close to their wrist, smaller than the others, it had the line of a concentric star around it. That more delicate star symbolized her.

"You…" she whispered, her fingers moving toward Dover's tattoo.

Grazing the ink on his skin, she was so moved that

tears pricked her eyes.

"You ready to take yours?" Dover asked.

Her lips twitched into a smile that fell and jumped to her lips wider than the others. Nodding, she had never felt so sure or excited about anything since accepting her love for Ryske.

"Good," Ryske said and turned to Dover. "Get setup for her." He landed a pointed look on her. "This conversation isn't over. Get your tats and tonight, we're gonna hear every detail."

"Ryske," she said, catching his attention before it could leave her. "I love you." Her gaze flitted between them all. "I mean, I love all of you."

"Yeah," Ryske said, grabbing her hand. "But I'm the only one you shower with."

Pulling her through the other guys, he led her into the bathroom. As they crossed the threshold, she dropped the sheet, letting it catch in the door that didn't close anyway. Ryske dragged her into the shower and turned on the water.

Making love against the bathroom wall, she decided that not only had he been right about shower sex, but he'd been right about the crew too. Whatever happened to her, they all took it upon themselves to be responsible for it.

She wasn't going to push them away anymore. It may not change the future, but once their ink was on her arm, she'd be a part of them forever, and they a part of her.

THIRTY-FIVE

GETTING HER TATTOOS had taken a while. Doing them in the apartment meant they could take breaks whenever she or Dover needed them. It ended up taking the better part of the day to complete the work.

The other guys went out and came back several times, going about their business while she got a star tattooed for each of them. Dover added a line around the one she'd had done for Ryske, so that her stars matched the rest of the crew's.

When Dover was done, the guys congregated in the kitchen to admire his handiwork. Floyd's was already open, but each man took the time to place a short kiss on the star meant for themselves. Harlow laughed and asked if they did the same for theirs. Judging by their reactions, they hadn't.

Ryske followed up his kiss on her arm with one on the lips. He'd coiled an arm around her waist after, and she'd stayed pinned to his side until he said he had to go out with Maze. For a minute, it seemed like the guys were braced for her to object. She hadn't. This was his life, she'd never expect special treatment.

It was just a shame she wasn't so sure of what her own life was.

She hadn't spoken to or of Ophelia and decided it was best to keep her distance from that part of town for a few days. In fact, she'd decided to stick close to Floyd's until the news got out. After that, she didn't know what would happen.

Someone would have found Hagan that morning, meaning the cops had to be investigating already. Word would seep out onto the street. As soon as the news got back to Floyd's, the guys would know what had happened, or at least, that there was a connection between Hagan and her appearing there. These guys didn't believe in coincidence; it made them suspicious, something she learned firsthand the night Ryske crashed into her.

"I won't be long," Ryske said, bowing to kiss her.

She accepted his kiss but curled her fingers around the side of his neck to hold him there. "Can I… borrow you for a minute?"

"No," Maze said, catching Ryske's arm to tug him away from her. "You don't have time for sex."

"No, hey, now wait a minute," Ryske said, unhooking his arm from his friend's grip. "We might have time for quick sex."

The guys seemed to think this was cause to joke. Spirits were high. She'd just had her tattoos finalized and they looked great. The guys considered this her initiation into the team. But, to her, she couldn't be one of them until she told Ryske the truth.

Taking both of his hands, she didn't want to give the others cause for alarm, figuring that might prevent them from giving her and Ryske privacy. Telling all of them together would lead to a flurry of questions and be too much for her to handle.

She needed to tell Ryske. Alone.

Giving him the chance to absorb and respond was the least she could do. It also wouldn't hurt to forewarn him. Once he'd processed the news, he could help the others come to terms with what had happened.

Walking backwards, she led Ryske out of the kitchen. "Just five minutes, guys," she said.

Ryske winked at her, then cast a look of smug

contrition over his shoulder. "Twelve minutes."

"Going to treat her twice?" Dover asked. Their cohorts laughed. With one hand on Maze's shoulder, and the other on Noon's, Dover directed both of them to the spiral stairs. "Send him down when you're done."

Harlow rolled her eyes at Maze, who exhaled as he started down the stairs. She mouthed her thanks to Dover who slapped the wall to kill the apartment lights. When the guys were gone, she dropped one of Ryske's hands to lead him toward the closet.

"Bed's over there, babe," Ryske said when they went into what had once been the master bedroom. He wandered deeper into the room. She flicked on the light. Strolling in an arc, he came back to her and slid his hands around her hips. "You want to christen every room?"

He bowed lower, coming in for a kiss.

At the same time his hands settled on her ass, just before his lips found hers, she spoke, "Jarvis Hagan is dead."

He froze. For a second, nothing happened. He retreated a few inches, his hands reversing their journey. Their eyes met. Time to process, that's what this was, so she said nothing. Except he didn't either. She nodded to confirm she had said what he thought he heard. It was true.

Comprehension changed his mood. It literally crept across him, tensing each inch of his muscles until it reached his emerging scowl.

Once his body was rigid, he seemed to stop breathing.

All she could do was brace for his reaction.

It burst out of him.

Spinning around, he leaped a stride away. "Fuck!"

Inhaling, a dozen emotions hit her at once. "I'm sorry!" she said because it seemed like the right thing to say. "I'm sorry, baby."

Whirling to face her, he threw his arms up. "Why the fuck didn't you come to me? Why the fuck did you let yourself—"

"It wasn't like that," she said. "It wasn't like I—"

"What? Like you planned a murder?" he asked, holding up his hand to touch a finger. "That's premeditation, babydoll. That's murder one!"

"I know! I know!" she said, gasping in a breath. "I didn't—"

"That's twenty years to life! You get that? Twenty years minimum…"

The idea narrowed her throat. For a second, she couldn't catch her breath. When venturing onto the path of revenge for Ryske, prison was a likely end. It was that or death. But it was different now. So different.

The gun she'd taken from Ryske wasn't meant to be used in a crime, except in a desperate situation. After almost being raped by Hagan once before, it seemed like a sensible precaution to have protection. But going in there with a weapon, Ryske was right, that suggested premeditation.

"Okay," Ryske said, inhaling a deep breath and blowing it out. "Okay. It's okay, baby."

Coming back to her, he gathered both of her hands and guided her across to the couch to sit them both down. Cupping her face, he pulled their mouths together to kiss her.

"I'm sorry," she whispered.

"No," he said, grazing his thumb along her jaw. "I'm sorry. I didn't mean to shout."

When he brushed his fingers across her cheek, moisture smudged beneath them. She was crying and hadn't even noticed.

Clinging to his shirt, she pulled herself closer and blinked into his smiling eyes. "Do you still love me?"

"Baby, I'd still love you even if you put a bullet in me."

"That's not funny," she whispered, letting her fingers move over his shirt where his scar would be. "I would never hurt you."

"Ditto," he said, combing his fingers through the length of her hair. "You did the right thing telling me."

"I didn't want you to go out and hear it somewhere out there… I guess he was found this morning."

"This happened last night?"

She nodded. Her mouth was dry and her fingers shaking. "I… I want to tell you everything, can you… Do you have time to listen?"

"For you," he said, cradling her face. "Always."

She smiled and kissed him. "I'm going to splash some water on my face… and I'll get you some hard liquor. Wait here for me?"

His eyes rose to their top corners. "I'm trying to imagine where I wouldn't wait for you."

Keeping his hand, she got up, smiling. "If there's time, we'll have sex after. If you still want to."

He kissed her knuckles and let her hand drift away from his as she retreated toward the door.

Sinking into the corner of the couch, he lifted one ankle to the opposite knee and locked his fingers together behind his head. That was the laidback Ryske she knew, smug and accepting…and sexy as hell.

"Oh, there's always plenty of time for that, Trinket," he said and winked at her. "And I always want to."

Saying the words out loud was a weight off. At least she'd told him. That was the hard part over. After she'd relayed the whole story, he'd figure out the best course of action.

Finishing in the restroom, she dried her hands and face and stepped into the dark living room. Before she could even turn around, flashes of blue and red filled the dark space. That could only mean one thing. Frozen on the spot, she couldn't focus. Those lights, the engine sounds, the distant sirens…

Ryske.

Protect Ryske.

The overhead light in the closet might be concealing the brilliance of the primary hues sweeping and flashing around the vast room. It also helped that the only window in the closet was to the front of Floyd's. So if the colored lights were only coming from the rear, Ryske might not see what she was seeing.

Unlikely.

There was no time to decide what to do. The light and noise got more intense, suggesting the number of vehicles was increasing. Floyd's was in a high-risk neighborhood and the cops weren't fond of visiting it. Coming here to bring someone down would mean bringing as much firepower as was available. Definitely more than was required.

Firepower.

She didn't want anyone getting hurt because of her. Was that an overreaction or a valid fear? Maybe they weren't there for her. Oh, yeah, how many other people in the building were party to murder last night? No, there was a chance—

What sounded like a bullhorn whistled to life. A second of static sounded before a strong male voice echoed through the walls.

"Harlow Sweeting!"

Well, there went that theory.

Beyond the chaos, movement in the closet focused her. No. No, no, no. Instinct drove her across the room fast to turn the key in the lock, imprisoning her love.

"Oh, God," she whispered, and jumped when Ryske tried the door only to find it wouldn't budge.

Rattling it, he pounded a fist on the wood. "Harlow! Open the goddamn door!"

"Harlow Sweeting," the voice came through the bullhorn again. "If you are in there, come out with your hands up!"

Time seemed to slow. This was unexpected. Why were they there? How had they found her? What the hell was the purpose of such dramatics? Cops weren't welcome in this part of town. It was doubtful they'd come into Floyd's and ask for her politely. Law enforcement would expect the patrons to employ a strategy of shoot first, cover each other's asses later.

Downstairs was a room full of crooks, some of them part of her crew.

Raising her arm, she looked at her stars. "Until we're dirt in the ground," she whispered when the bullhorn went again demanding she come out.

Noise on the spiral stairs revealed someone coming up. On reflex, she went the other way. Sprinting for the stairwell, she descended, taking the stairs two at a time until she burst out into the alley at the side of the building.

On three sides she was surrounded by walls. Blue and red light flashed at the opening to her far right and above the wall to the left. She really was surrounded. There was no avoiding the inevitable. Not that she'd ever run. No way. Ryske had threatened to confess to her crime. If she went on the run, he could do just that to save her ass, and she wouldn't let him do that.

This was it. There was no time. If Ryske got down there before the cops got hold of her, he'd drag her inside, or one of the guys would, and her love would take the fall for Hagan's death.

Kissing her fingertips, she touched the Floyd's door one last time and then went down the alley toward the lights and the ruckus.

Swallowing her terror, adrenaline drove her forward, one step at a time. One more step, then another, until the alley opened out and the flash of glaring lights blinded her.

"Put your hands up!" a voice called out. Opening her arms, she let them rise slowly, showing that she had no intention of resisting. "Harlow Sweeting?"

"Yes!" she called over the noise of the cars. "I'm the one you're looking for."

Cops rushed to her, pulling her forward, yanking her arms around to her back. "You are being arrested on suspicion of the premeditated murder of Jarvis Hagan," someone said and proceeded to read her rights.

The one talking stayed somewhere nearby. Another pulled her around to the back of the cop car and pushed her against it to frisk her.

The last words were repeated to her more than once. "Do you understand your rights as I've read them to you?"

A strong grip on her shoulder pulled her into a standing position. It was then that she saw him, all of them, lit up in the apartment window above.

Ryske was in front, with Dover at his back, holding his shoulders while Maze pressed one of his hands to the window frame. Noon had hold of Ryske's other arm. They were restraining him. Just as she'd thought, he'd wanted to chase her. Maybe he had started to come after her, but the guys dragged him back. Thank God for them.

Ryske's prophecy had come true. The guys *were* holding someone back while the cops took another of their crew in. Only Ryske was the one being restrained and she was being arrested. Tears trickled from her eyes. They didn't overwhelm her until Maze shifted to show his row of stars. Dover did the same and Noon too. Ryske was the last; the others were reluctant to let him go.

Like he was made of lead, Ryske's arm slid from where it had been pinned by Maze and landed on the window.

She couldn't reciprocate because of the cuffs restraining her hands at her back. Curling her lips, she winked instead.

Someone gave her a shake. "Do you understand?"

"Oh," she said, being manhandled into the back of the car. "I understand perfectly."

In the backseat, she couldn't see the guys in the upstairs window anymore. As far as she could tell, none of the cops noticed them up there. Not that it mattered if they had; solidarity wasn't a crime.

The sirens whooped and the car moved. Her head fell against the side window. Twenty years was what Ryske said. If she was convicted of murder one, her life would be over. Ryske would move on. Rupert too. She'd have no future outside of prison walls.

Harlow might not have committed the crime, but she knew every detail. Once again, she had a decision to make. Only this choice was new. To deal or not to deal?

TO BE CONTINUED...

Thank you for reading this tale!
If you can, please take the time to review.

~

**Ask your local library for more Scarlett Finn
novels!**

~

**For all things Scarlett Finn
check out:**

www.scarlettfinn.com

BOOK THREE

GO ALL OUT

SCARLETT FINN

OUT NOW!